THE WHITE DOOR

PIERCE TAYLOR HIBBS

TRUTH ABLAZE

NONFICTION

In Divine Company
Theological English
The Trinity, Language, and Human Behavior
The Speaking Trinity & His Worded World
Finding God in the Ordinary
Struck Down but Not Destroyed
Still, Silent, and Strong
Finding Hope in Hard Things
The Book of Giving
I Am a Human
God of Words
The Great Lie
Christmas Glory
One with God
Wielding Words
Insider-Outsider
The Christ-Light

POETRY
Borrowed Images
word by Word

For Christina, who lets me dream and stands beside me wherever we go.

And for Grace Smith. I hope you are doing some wonderful world-building with God.

CONTENTS

Present-Day Map of Dingmans Ferry

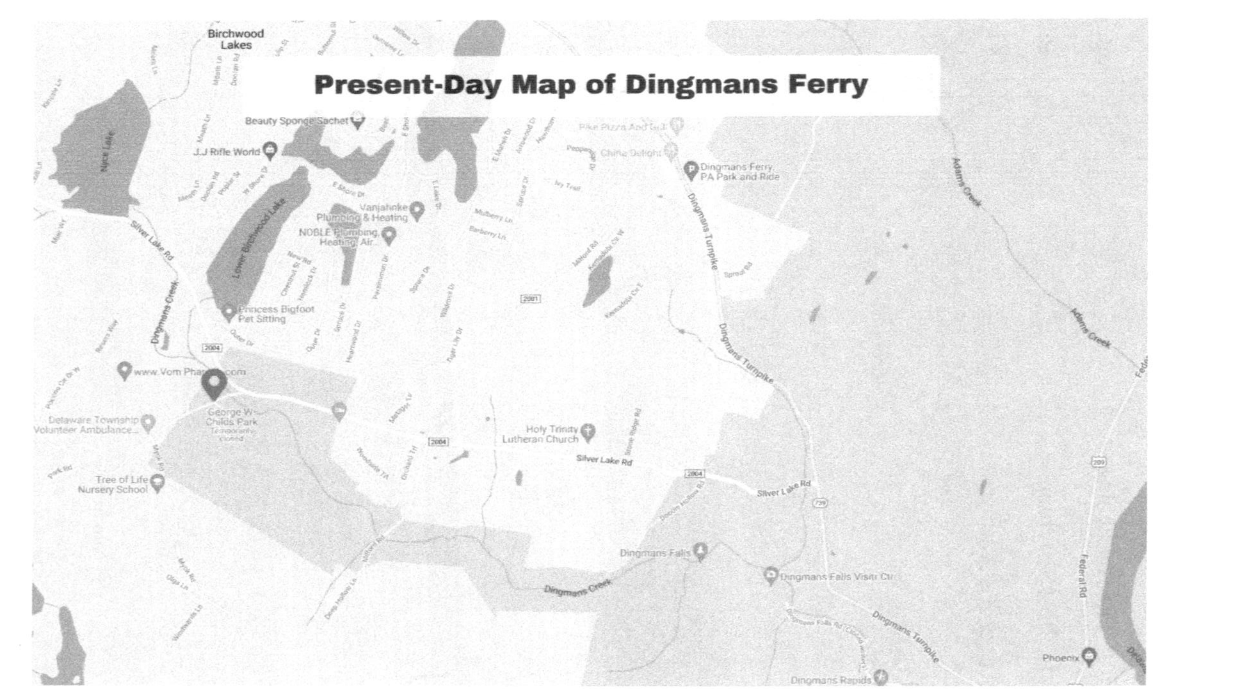

1

THE LOSS AND THE LIGHTS

DINGMANS FERRY, PENNSYLVANIA, 1985

BEFORE SETH LOGAN DIED, he knew he would have to choose between the two marbles he carried in his right pocket: one of transparent blue glass and the other woven throughout with smoke-curl wisps of orange and red—a fire in a teardrop. One was a world you could see through; the other, a world you must see around.

Our part in Seth's story begins with a man named Cleft Warrington.

***

Cleft didn't hear the tires crushing gravel in the driveway, or the whining steps outside the bedroom door, or the padding of feet on the hallway carpet. He hadn't heard anything. It was the *lights*—the pulsing red lights punching the walls in the hallway next to his bedroom, splashing the eggshell white with mocking red.

A boy stood in front of him asking for his name, but Cleft could utter only one word. And so he said it over and over again, muttering like a madman: "You, you, you, you."

"What's he doing?" the boy asked. A woman in the corner crouched over a body. She let the boy's question hang in the room like the stone-still pull cords of the overhead fan. A moth pinged itself against the tired gold dome of the light, trying to get inside something beautiful that only had the power to kill it.

The boy's Adam's apple rose and fell with labored swallows. He bunched his pale fingers into a fist and then released them. Cleft stared at the boy's hand, watching it expand and contract, expand and contract, like a heart. He knew the boy was anxious. And on any other occasion, he would have been the first to console and reassure, following his pastoral instincts. But not now. This was *his* time. And so he sat like a sculpture in the corner of the room, white-knuckled, clutching his knees and sputtering his almost voiceless "you."

"He's just saying 'you.' Should I ask him anything else?"

"No," said the woman. Another paramedic peeked into the doorway and met eyes with her.

"Anything, Janet?"

She shook her head. "Bring the gurney up. Let's get her downstairs. I'm going to stay up here with Ben for a minute." Janet was focused and calculating. But weariness weighed down the corners of her eyes as she pieced together the next steps. The last thing she felt like doing was making this a training session for Ben. But she stood and turned her body towards him, her nostrils flaring as she settled into the situation.

"Ben, ask him for his name again. If he can't say it, then find a piece of paper and a pen, and see if he can write it down."

Ben knelt a few feet from Cleft and listened again. With his right hand, he was still bunching up his fingers and releasing them—a nervous reaction that began in pre-school whenever he did something wrong in the presence of strangers. Cleft's eyes only left Ben's hand when the medics went to lift the body.

"One, two, three"—then a chorus of grunts as they heaved the woman up onto the gurney. Her frame was limp but heavy, as if her bones were full of lead. The metal gurney squeaked at the joints as she settled into place, leathery and lifeless, her lips sealed like an envelope.

Cleft stared at her motionless chest—that still and steady horizon of her sternum no longer rising and falling with the tides of moments. Time was gone with her. But Cleft still stared, wishing beyond hope to see her heart chamber expand and contract once more, to move like the boy's hand, to pump with vitality, lifting and settling with the gift of life. But there was only stillness. Halt. Absence. The woman he had loved for forty-five years was not there. She was somewhere else—in another place. *Where?* That was all he wanted to know in the moment—not in his head (he had an answer for that) but in his heart. *Where did she go?* He asked the question despite all he knew and believed. This was the deepest test of his resolute faith, staring up at him like a black abyss, daring him to jump. It would be so easy. A baby's breath could push him over the edge.

The moth rested on the face of the ceiling light now, its thread-thin arms and legs praying for entrance but sentenced by the hot glass to remain an outsider. At best, it could only find a way in and then die in the presence of a false sun, a dead god. There its papery frame would lie with the others: a testament to deception.

Cleft looked at the metal frame of the gurney. It was painted bright yellow, but some of the paint was chipping off, revealing the cold gray steel underneath. *Yellow*, he thought. *She hated yellow . . . except forsythia.*

His eyes, like weary travelers on a mountainside, climbed down her body—from her chest, to her stomach, to her legs, and then to her feet: her tan socks. That's where his gaze rested. The socks were thin and nearly worn through on the heels, a quarter-sized hole calling his attention to her left foot. A nail had been sticking up in the oak threshold of their front door, and he'd hammered it back in two days ago, after his wife had gotten her sock caught on it when letting the dog back inside. She liked to wear the same pair of socks for a few days. "My feet need to get used to the fabric," she would say. But she hadn't said that for a long time, not since the Alzheimer's had advanced.

A lump lodged in Cleft's throat. He wanted to take the sock from her foot now. That hole in the heel—it was precious, a mark of what's missing, a portrait of his life at this very moment. He knew that as soon as they left the room with her, he would regret not taking it. He would long for that sock, like a black and white picture from another era. But embarrassment froze him. Regret ached beneath the lump in his throat. He couldn't bring himself to move.

"Sir?" Ben asked again, snapping Cleft out of his reverie. No response. "Sir, who's 'you'? Are you talking about your wife?"

"Ben—the name. We just need the name right now," said Janet, irritation bleeding through her voice. "Do you have a piece of paper and a pen yet?"

Ben turned back to Cleft. "Sir, my name is Ben. Can you tell me your name?"

"You, you, you, you, you, you, you," Cleft whispered as he looked at his wife on the gurney. Forty-five years. Forty-five years of words, of stares, of touching skin and making love, of listening and looking and sleeping and waking, of her gloriously simple presence, his Jane. And now the silence reigned, a cruel king who refused to speak to any subject, bold or meek.

Cleft shifted his eyes to Ben's contracting right hand. His head felt as if a brick were tied to the top. But he tilted it up to mirror Ben's face, making the boy lean back in discomfort. Ben stared for a few seconds, soaking in Cleft's countenance. To him, Cleft looked like an old, tired bird: his long, straight nose; his pleading but somehow blank stare; the set of wrinkles next to each eye, leading away from the outer corners like tiny roads that disappeared in the smooth field of each freshly shaven cheek. Ben reached into his pants pocket and pulled out a chewing gum wrapper. Then he took a pen out of his other pocket and offered it to Cleft.

"Here. You can write down your name on this."

Cleft stared at the gum wrapper and pen. Then he released his knees, letting the blood return to his knuckles and fingers, his calves and feet—a warm, rolling liquid stretching back into his extremities. Both hands were shaking like leaves on an aspen tree.

He took the pen, set the wrapper on his knee, and scribbled something before handing it back. Ben felt relieved as he received the gum wrapper. It gave him an excuse to look away from Cleft. But his relief turned to puzzlement when he saw the inscription.

Ben was about to say something to Cleft but then turned back towards Janet instead. "His name's Cleft," he said, slipping the wrapper back into his pocket.

"Last name?"

"Oh, yeah. It's Warrington." Ben didn't tell Janet what was written on the gum wrapper. In jagged print, he could make out the words "Job 1:20."

"He wrote that down?" She obviously doubted Ben, and her frustration was building like a storm cloud.

"No . . . I just know. He's the pastor of the church in town. My mom goes there."

Janet glared at Ben, then shook her head. *There* was the judgment. Ben was suddenly back in pre-school, clutching an empty bottle of Elmer's glue as his teacher wagged her head at him. His hands contracted again.

"Please just do what I'm asking you to do, Ben. I'm trying to train you." Ben nodded as he walked over to the bedroom window overlooking the backyard.

And then he froze. The hair on his neck stood up, and the lump that had been lodged in Cleft's throat a moment ago now found its way to his.

"Janet?" He said her name as a child, as if asking his mother about something in the stars. Janet didn't respond. She was busy writing on her clipboard.

"Janet." Ben's voice came louder and more defined.

"What, Ben?"

"Can you come here?"

She let out an audible sigh as she walked across the room, still reading something on her clipboard. At the window, she picked her head up and met Ben's face. And then she realized he was staring not at her, but outside.

"What is *that . . . that thing*?" Ben asked.

Janet nudged him aside with her shoulder and looked down at the backyard. Her eyes squinted. Her head tilted. And as if a tiny wave of water were washing over her profile, her tension melted. Her furrowed brow went smooth. The exhaustion evaporated from her eyes, and the irritation disappeared from her voice. The corners of her lips even turned up. "What in the world."

They both stood gazing, mesmerized. Just beneath the surface of the grass, in a large puddle shape, was a moving light. It was gold—the hue that paints the underbellies of clouds with the last light of the setting sun. But the gold grew brighter and whiter in some places, nearly breaking through the thin hair of the grass. And it was always moving, forming and then shifting like water, ebbing away from the tree line at the edge of Cleft's property as if rolling back from an incline.

Neither of them said anything for several moments. They couldn't tell how long they stared. Once Janet took in a breath as if to speak, but then she let it out. Silence was all they could say. Behind them, Cleft had picked up his head. His lips offered a knowing smile.

***

A voice from downstairs fractured the moment.

"Janet! We're all set. Need anything else?"

Janet broke from her spell-bound gaze and looked at Ben, first with hesitancy and then with resolve. "We need to deal with *this* right now." She nodded at Cleft sitting on the floor.

She didn't want to stop looking. Even as she spoke, she was pulled back to the window, like a magnet drawn to its opposite pole. Seeing those lights had pulled out and evaporated her tiredness, her looming concerns about a thousand unnamed things. At that moment, her whole life seemed to grow warmer, lighter, like a wet bathing suit set on a summertime fence, heated and dried in the grinning sun, everything cold and heavy soaked up by serenity. She wanted desperately to look again. The looking was lovely, but more important than that: it seemed to make *her* lovely. Everything inside her felt charged towards it. But she fought the urge—an urge more powerful than any she'd ever had—and tried to help Cleft to his feet.

"Do you . . . *like* them?" Cleft said as he struggled to stand. It took Janet a second to realize that Cleft knew what they were staring at, and yet he spoke as if the light under the grass was part of his landscaping. Janet and Cleft looked into each other's eyes, she with wonder and he with patient assurance. "If you could just see *under* them," he said, "from the *inside*, from the inside is . . . is . . ." He trailed off, lost in exhaustion.

Janet was speechless as her eyes locked on his, but her rationality slowly shook the awe away, like a cloud cutting in front of the sun. *This is grief-stricken delirium*, she thought to herself.

"You feeling okay to walk?" she said. Cleft reached out his left hand and grabbed onto her arm, struggling to pull himself forward. He wobbled like a buoy in the ocean. Ben went to his other side to steady him. They brought him slowly down the steps to the landing by the front door. The red lights of the ambulance were no longer flashing on the walls. Janet and Ben turned his body like an old boat, leading his drifting legs down the hallway to the dock of his kitchen table.

By the time the ambulance was out of the driveway, Cleft was calm, sitting at the table next to his best friend: a white-faced golden retriever with deep brown eyes—Roland. The dog's muzzle rested on Cleft's leg, both of them mourning the silence with silence. Cleft felt almost weightless, as if his bones were hollow. He could now do the one thing he had left to do. He just didn't know how, or for whom to do it.

Cleft's father, a furniture maker, had built the kitchen table for him and Jane as a wedding present nearly forty-six years ago. It was pine—an odd choice of wood for a kitchen table. The soft wood was a map of human movement, aged with a thousand gouges and scrapes from forks and bottles and teeth, a scrawling and scratched story sitting in the room like an ancient book. The surface was plain but for the center of the table, where initials had been carved and inlaid with ivory, which had faded into a smoky white: CJW. Cleft took his index finger and ran it up and down the curve of the "J."

"You," he said quietly. "Just you."

***

Janet closed the front door quietly until the latch locked into place. As soon as she heard the click, and she and Ben were on the front porch alone, Ben broke the silence.

"Can we go back there . . . in the backyard?!" he asked in a whispered scream.

"No, Ben. We can't," she said sharply. "That man just lost his wife. We're not going to tramp through his backyard to look at some lights."

"Oh, come on! 'Some lights'? Were you even looking at the same thing? . . . I mean," Ben said, fidgeting with a toddler's enthusiasm, "can we come back tomorrow, then? I can ask him." Ben was pleading like a child for a trip to the park.

"No, Ben!" Janet, broken out of her previous serenity, was baffled by the impropriety. Her mother had always taught her formality. "Let people be until they ask to be bothered," she'd say. Janet would never act as Ben was acting right now, not even for this. That was the source of her irritation: his juvenility, his lack of awareness of life's clear rules.

"But you *felt* something, didn't you?" Ben said, begging her to look at him. Janet lifted her head and met his eyes despite herself. The hair on the back of her neck raised, and her throat felt tight. But she said nothing.

"I felt it, too," Ben said. "It was, it was . . . I don't know. It was different . . . but *good*, like it was calling us to itself."

"Let's get through tonight, first. Then we can talk about it. But you know we can't just wander back onto someone's property like that. When you're in that uniform, you have a character to maintain. You're not just 'Ben.' You're an EMT."

"I know, I know. But . . . did Cleft say anything about it, about the light?"

Janet paused. And even later she couldn't explain why she lied.

"No . . . He didn't say anything."

***

Skulking in the woods at the tree line on the edge of Cleft's property, watching the ambulance drive away, stood a man dressed all in black. His face was pale and thin, his dark hair shoulder length and stringy, as if every follicle had begun to die the moment it left his skin and met the open air. He looked more like a standing corpse than a human. His skin was wrapped too tightly around his bones, making all his move-ments tense and forced. Something in his eyes betrayed a wandering, listless vagrancy, as if all he did was walk up and down the earth, pole to equator, equator to pole—traipsing over the terrain looking for something he could never name. On the top of his right hand was a green tattoo of a simple, unadorned circle.

The man stared menacingly through the downstairs window at Cleft, still sitting at his dining room table.

"At last I get you. Now we'll see just who you are, preacher man."

Then he mumbled a song to a dull tune, all while staring at Cleft, his eyes burning through glass and skin. But his throat constricted, as if he sang unwillingly, nearly choking on the sounds that dribbled off his lips.

> Yours is the light.
> Mine is the smoke.
> I cannot get back.
> I cannot get back.
>
> Yours is the day.
> Mine is the night.
> Mind the shadow.
> Mind the shadow.
> Mind the shadow.
> Sleep.

He smiled for the last four lines, at home in his purpose. But then he fell on his knees and threw up a thick black liquid, gurgling it out onto the dead leaves. He spit out the remainder and wiped his lips. His arms were shaking, but he grabbed a hemlock branch and stood back up—still staring at Cleft through the window. The man closed his pale eyelids as if to concentrate. A faint aura seemed to glow from him in the night. He opened his eyes again, turned, and disappeared into the dark woods.

2

THE FINDING

ONE MONTH LATER

S ETH'S FEET FELT AT home on the blanket of amber pine needles and decaying leaves at Childs Park, a tapestry of death beneath the living. He had some quiet sense that he was standing on an *offering* of the woods, holy but long dismissed. There usually wasn't anyone else there. Silver Lake Road, branching off a meandering Route 739, was mostly quiet at this hour. What cars there were swished by occasionally like lost thoughts. And Park Road was deserted—given over wholly to the mourning doves and the red-tailed hawks perched as lords in the high boughs of the hemlocks.

The solitude of Childs Park sifted Seth's thoughts. It made him feel like he wasn't striving to exist the way he usually was with his anxiety. Anxiety made each day an upside-down jigsaw puzzle, where he had to jam pieces together to make some semblance of a shape. But the life he found in these woods was unhindered, free, confident as the current in Dingmans Creek. The woods and the water invited him into their foreign contentment, asserting with their mere existence that life wasn't a problem; it was a path. He never fully accepted this invitation, but it was nice to have it.

Childs Park had no strict rules. Though Seth had always found comfort in rule-following, he liked the idea that he could go where he wanted, that he didn't have to stay on the wood-plank paths that hugged both sides of Dingmans Creek as it rolled down several waterfalls. Each time he went there, he would go to the last one, Deer Leap Falls, and let his feet dangle over the edge of a smooth sedimentary rock shaped like a giant's fingernail. From there he watched the silvery-white water plummet to a pool at the bottom: roaring riches falling into a placid face that Seth wished had eyes to see him. Yes—that was it: he wanted the water to see him. He wanted the trees to see him, and the rocks and the riverbed, every stick and stone. He knew they couldn't, but he still longed for it like a child. His hand went instinctively to his right pocket, where he rotated the two marbles around each other. Those were worlds he could move, while he walked in a world that moved him.

Ever since he'd watched his father die of cancer fifteen years earlier, anxiety had taken the reins of his life and never let his mind settle, always pushing him over the rockiest terrain. Time and movement seemed chaotic and uncontrollable, as if the days were rapids trying to roll him. That lack of control was the black hole from which his anxiety disorder emerged. And yet sitting by this waterfall, resting next to a coursing current, he finally felt like a still point in the turning world, resting while all else raged. The absence of control faded into the background. He almost accepted it. And the sound—a thundering hiss—silenced all protest.

It was mid-March and had just rained the night before, but it was only a few degrees above freezing. The orange-gold sunlight was pouring through the pine boughs, making the wet stones blush with patches of dryness. But the bark on the hemlocks was still soaked with mist that trickled down the grooves of their skin. To Seth, the woods seemed more sincere when they were wet—somehow more alive, as if the trees were beckoned into breathing by the mist.

He came to a shallower part of the creek where three boulders poked their heads out above the current. The moss hadn't covered their surface yet, so he could hop across them easily enough. He was about to hop to the third stone when he saw it: a dark orange ball of fur spiked with muddy water—a dead cat. Seth's heart sank in his chest.

Crouching down, he pulled a twig from a pile of branches and leaves in the waterway. He pressed the twig into the cat's belly but jumped back when the cat's head snapped towards him. A heat flash set his heart thudding as the cat's yellow eyes stared into his own with alert agitation. The cat held the stare for several seconds, then laid its dirty-white chin down on the stone again and closed its eyes. This was their introduction.

The sensation of heat and pressure still surged through Seth's chest before climbing up his neck and cresting at the top of his head—his fight-or-flight instinct. The heat flashes had been getting better over time with the Prozac, but they were still there, lacerations tearing open to reveal the deeper fault lines in his mental kingdom. He swallowed, looked up at the sky through the canopy, and did his 5-5-5 breathing exercise: five seconds inhale, five seconds hold, five seconds exhale. His thudding heart slowed like a heavy train. Oxygen flooded his veins. He recited the lines his counselor had given him, which he only ever said when he was by himself.

> This is my body, alert and awake.
> I can control the decisions I make.

In the open air, his words sounded alien. But he'd been trying to get more comfortable with them. The embarrassment he first felt when saying them out loud had faded, but it wasn't gone. The words had, however, helped him see that he wasn't going crazy and that this was the way his body and mind seemed to react to . . . things. It was his tortured sensitivity.

When he looked down again, he saw the cat was staring at him. And something had changed. The mop-like ball of dirty fur now seemed more familiar to him. He'd assumed the cat was a stray, probably a barn cat from one of the farms nearby. There were several not far from Childs Park. But now he felt an inexplainable sense of ownership. This was *his* cat. The thought was so visceral that Seth didn't question the assumption that they would be coming and going together from now on. He would look back on this moment with curiosity, since he'd always considered himself a dog person. He didn't mind cats but didn't feel the same deep, almost spiritual pull toward them that he did for dogs. His family had always had golden retrievers, and he was at home in their deep brown eyes. He felt slightly younger every time he pet them and watched their tails thud against the carpet. A similar sentiment rose in him now as he stared at the cat.

"Rough night, huh?"

The cat raised his head again at the sound of Seth's voice, but now its eyes were only half opened, slowly blinking with trust and relief. The cat laid his head down on the stone and shut his eyes once more, either resigning himself to his fate or inviting more interaction. Seth couldn't tell which.

He knelt down and gently picked it up, shuffling his hands beneath the lumpy wet blanket of its body. The cat's eyes were open now with hyper-vigilance as it clawed Seth's wrists and forearms for stability, its ears pressed flat against its head. Icy brown water shot down Seth's forearms and under his shirt sleeves, and the shock of it nearly made him drop the cat, but it clawed his flannel shirt and found footing. Once Seth held it firmly, the cat settled and began to close its eyes again as Seth picked off chips of bark and grit from its sopping-wet fur. The cat reeked of old pond water and decayed leaves. It shared the same ancient aroma as the woods.

Seth bundled up the cat with the bottom of his flannel shirt and started walking back to his truck. The cat barely moved when Seth awkwardly opened the door of his red Ford Ranger and placed it on the cold black leather seat. He gently shut the passenger side door, staring for a moment to see if the cat would bolt. Then he got into the driver's side, turned the key in the ignition, and cranked up the heat, pointing a vent towards the cat, who was already asleep. Beads of dirty water ran over the seat edge and onto the floor mat. Seth unbuttoned his shirt, wrapped it around the cat, and pressed it gently into its fur. The water began to seep through the fabric, and the smell of pond filled the truck.

"That should do 'til we get home."

***

As they turned out of the park entrance, Seth went about a quarter mile farther down Park Road before pulling over onto the shoulder next to the Davidsons' old barn. The Davidsons were a local farming family who had been in the area for generations, but rumor had it that they left abruptly several years ago when their son Patrick died of Leukemia. In a town this small, an event like that etches itself in the memory of every resident. Patrick's parents had allegedly sold their acreage to the state in order to pay for his treatment. But the land remained undeveloped. Their giving up of land followed the pattern of George W. Childs' widow, who had turned over their property—what was now Childs Park—to the Commonwealth of Pennsylvania in 1912. There is always a time when giving is better than keeping, or at least a time when keeping is fruitless.

In chipped gold paint, the words "Elysium Hills" were nestled into the faded red boards, the letters happily asleep in their sunken bed of wood. It was part of Seth's routine to stop at the barn on the way back from the park. Each time, he'd get out of his truck and walk around the perimeter, looking and lingering. It started as curiosity. He wondered how long a barn like this would stand before beginning to collapse. But habit made it different. The barn became a testament to the unnoticed aging of the world—the falling of trees, the fading of families, the slow letting go of all things. He wanted to *notice*. He wanted to see how the details would bend and break with time. And he was happy whenever it seemed that they hadn't. Not everything gets lost all at once.

He left the truck running while he walked around, jingling the two marbles in his pocket. He checked for new bird nests and holes borne by last summer's carpenter bees. Barn swallows danced lightly across the peak of the roof, as if trying not to wake the barn. He liked the eastern wall the most, where the sun hit first. Engraved on one of its boards at eye level were the words, "Death made me a traveler. YCGB." The message was poetic and strange. And the English major in Seth loved it. He taught composition at the local community college and was always writing. No one in town, he thought, appreciated a beautiful turn of words more than he did. He'd tried to write a few poems that began with this sentence, but they always turned out stale. He figured YCGB were initials, but that wouldn't match any of the Davidson kids.

The sentence resonated deeply with his own experience of losing his father. Ever since then, he felt as if he'd been looking for something, always just beyond the horizon of his consciousness. Death really had made him a traveler. He just didn't know where he was going.

A few years ago, when he first began coming to the barn, the message was marked in raw deep brown, contrasting with the weathered gray of the other boards. Someone had spent at least a few hours carving it, pulling away strip after strip of rain-worn oak, pushing grooves down and then across the grain, etching a holy message that lived out its days in the quiet pattern of rising and falling light. Since then, the rain and sun had welcomed the engraving to the weathered neighborhood.

Seth ran his fingers over the initial "D" as he thought about his father—those final three breaths counted out by the hospice nurse. No one had ever counted to three like that before. And no one ever would.

"Death," he whispered as his fingers traced the belly of the "D." He stared into the wood, looking but also listening, as if the wood were singing a song just below the decibel range of his hearing.

The sound of another car on Park Road pulled him back to reality, and he remembered the cat was still in the truck. He needed to get it home soon. He climbed into the driver's side and breathed in the smell of warm pond. The cat's stomach rose and fell, rose and fell—a bodily hymn of peace. Seth stared at him for a few seconds and then put the truck in gear.

"Death almost made *you* a traveler," he muttered.

***

Seth's wife, Shannon, would be up by now, and the kids would be awake soon. That's where Seth's wandering thoughts halted as he pulled into their development off of Silver Lake Road. He hadn't stopped to think about what they would do when they saw a muddy cat wrapped in flannel. It wasn't until he turned into the driveway, next to their navy blue Chevy Malibu station wagon, that his lack of forethought surfaced. As the realization settled in, he bit down on his lower lip.

Seth lumbered up the steps of the front porch in his white undershirt, blotted with brown creek water, holding his dripping wet flannel ball. Through the window of the front door, he could see Shannon's look of confusion as she stepped out of the dim kitchen light. She opened the door and met him with a furrowed brow.

"Seth, I made eggs . . . but . . . " She was standing in her bathrobe, a coffee cup in one hand and a plate of eggs and potatoes in the other. "What is *that*?"

Seth smiled at his stupidity, his lack of awareness for others in improvised situations like this. His mother told him he inherited it from his father. Seth didn't mind when she said this, since she said it with a smile. But standing on the porch now in front of Shannon, he hadn't the slightest clue what to say. Seth's little improvised decisions happened often enough that Shannon stopped being offended and started to accept it as part of his personality.

"Ahh, it's a . . . cat." As he watched her face, he could feel her response gather like a wave of water.

"I'm *allergic* to cats. Why would you bring home a cat?" She wasn't angry, just legitimately confused. And for the moment, so was Seth.

"Oh, yeah. I was . . . I found him at the park; he was washed up in a ball at the bottom of the creek. He's still alive! Isn't that crazy? Here, look at him." Seth opened up the flannel shirt and held out the lumpy mass of muddy, orange fur. The scent of pond water and damp moss filled the air between them.

"Seth, it's filthy . . . and it reeks!" She inspected its face for a few seconds. "He's alive?"

"Yeah—watch his stomach; he's breathing. He's just asleep." Shannon loved animals. Seth knew her compassion would win over the agitation at his shortsightedness, eventually.

"My God . . . should you even be holding him? I mean, he could be hurt. Here, put him down on the doormat." Seth hesitated. The doormat, which read "Welcome Back" in bold black letters, was caked in mud, dried leaves, and hay from a bale left there since October. "Here, put him down," she said. "What's the matter?"

"I just didn't want to, uh . . . that's covered in mud."

"Oh, geez. You're right. We should put it on our bed."

"Well, I could put a blanket down first so he wouldn't get mud on the new comforter."

"I was kidding!" Shannon couldn't help laughing, and this eased Seth's tension.

"Well, what if I get a blanket and we put him right inside the door?" Seth said. "I don't want to leave him outside. It's cold, and he needs to dry off."

"What are we supposed to tell the kids when they get up? They'll be up any minute."

"I hadn't really thought about it," Seth said with a pleading sigh.

"Yeah—I'm sensing a pattern here. Would you like to ask your allergic wife what she thinks about it?"

"I'm sorry, Shannon. I wasn't thinking. I just saw him there and felt terrible. We can bring him to the SPCA in town on Monday."

"Fine. Just get a blanket from the closet, and we'll put him inside the front door. But the kids *can't* touch him. We'll have to put a baby gate around him; can you get the two gates from the basement?"

"Yeah. Can you hold him for a second?"

"Let me put this down."

She walked back to the kitchen, where Seth could hear the quiet clang of ceramic on the marble countertop, and chimes of silverware hitting the plate. In hindsight, it went much better than he'd thought. When she came back, she had a tan dish towel in her hands.

"Alright—just be really gentle with him," Seth said.

"I know, I know." She reached under Seth's arms as if she were taking a precious family heirloom and brought the cat closer to her body, keeping an inch of space between herself and the wet flannel shirt.

"Smells like an old pond," she said, wrinkling her nose.

"Yeah. That's how my truck smells."

"Well, I'm getting retested next week for allergies, so I'll find out then if I'm still allergic. If I am, then I really don't think we can keep it. We can bring it to the SPCA in the meantime. At least they can make sure he doesn't have any injuries. And maybe someone's looking for him."

"Alright." Seth hesitated. He knew asking the question he had in mind wasn't appropriate, that the timing was off, that he should say *anything* else. And yet he couldn't hold back. It was a problem he had since he was a kid: perseverating on something when the timing and context told him to let it go. He opened his mouth despite his better judgment.

"And what if you're not allergic? Then can we talk about keeping him? Do you like him?"

"Seth, his eyes are barely open; it's hard to tell. We'll talk about it. Cats usually aren't friendly."

"He *seems* very friendly." Seth twiddled with the marbles in his right pocket again.

"He's barely conscious. Let's see what he's like once he has some food in him and a little sleep—maybe a lot of sleep. Now, can I put him down so you can have breakfast? I made eggs, and I can hear the kids asking to go downstairs. Why don't you get them? I'm sure they'd love to see their daddy on Saturday-Dadurday."

Seth's five-year-old son, Will, came up with "Saturday-Dadurday." It was the first day of the week that Seth didn't have to go to work at the community college. Will loved animals, and so did his three-year-old sister, Olivia, whom they called Livy. So, Seth was excited to tell the kids about the cat.

He kicked off his boots, grabbed the two baby gates from the basement, set them up around the cat by the front door, and then climbed the stairs to Will's room. "Will 'n Livy, Will 'n Livy" he sang as he came to the top of the landing. Squeals and bedsprings sounded from each room. He stopped at the top of the stairs, just for a moment, unwrapping the gift of his kids again.

"Eye-na go downstaiiiiiirrs!" Those were always Livy's opening words in the morning. He got Will first.

"Is it Saturday-Dadurday?" Will said with swollen eyes and a smile.

"Let me think . . . YES!" Seth said as he helped Will out of his bed. Will bounced up and down in circles around his dad.

"Let's get Livy," Seth said. "And then I have a really big secret to tell you guys."

"Livy!" Will shouted. "Daddy's got a sacred . . . uh . . . sacrit?"

"Sec-ret," Seth said smiling, enunciating the last syllable.

"Oh, yeah—Daddy's got a secret for us!"

Livy stood at the edge of her white crib, holding the railing with one hand and sucking on her two fingers with the other. Her eyes—big, brown, and innocent, absorbing the whole world like sponges—closed slightly to accommodate her rising cheeks. Seth lifted her up as she nestled her head in his neck and clung to her tan and white blanket.

"Guys, guess what?" Seth said. In a split second, Will and Livy were silent and serious, pressing for an answer with their stares.

"What?" said Will. Seth smiled at the giant puff of hair on the top of Will's head, wild and fully bloomed.

"Daddy was at the park this morning—"

"But Daddy . . . why didn't I goed . . . go?" Will interrupted. Self-correcting his grammar was a recent development, which made Seth and Shannon both proud and a little sad. No one wants to see a pure language die.

"Well, you were still asleep, and I didn't want to wake you up."

"But maybe today we can go to the park, and I can come with you?"

"Yeah, maybe. But Daddy's trying to tell you something. So, Daddy was walking in the park, and I walked across the stream and—"

"Wiv yul wain-boots?" said Livy, still keeping her two fingers in her mouth.

"Uh . . ." Seth was interpreting the sounds and piecing together the sentence. "No, I had my hiking boots on, but let me tell you what I found."

"I have rain boots. They're gray and . . . and blue," Will said.

"Yes, I know, buddy. But let me tell you what I found. I looked down at my feet. And guess what I saw?"

"What? What, Daddy?" Will chirped.

"I saw . . . a kitty."

"Was it . . . was it died?" said Will.

"No, it was still alive!"

"Daddy, 'cause when I eat grapes now, I can't die," said Will.

"What?" Even though Seth was accustomed to Will's wandering logic, he was genuinely puzzled by this one.

"Mommy doesn't have to cut grapes in half for me anymore. Because I chew them up. So, grapes can't make me choke, so . . . so I can't died . . . die."

Seth tried to hold down a laugh behind his smile. "Wow, that is *great*, Will. But I'm not finished with my story yet."

"Eye-iv gapes?" asked Livy, staring up at Seth with her saucer-sized eyes.

"Yeah," Will cut in to answer for Seth. "But mommy still has to cut up your grapes, Livy . . . cause you can choke." Will had taken a parental role lately, which was annoying at times, but Seth was trying to interpret it as maturity. Livy looked to Seth for confirmation and seemed embarrassed at being three, which Seth hated.

"That's okay, Livy. Will, be nice to your sister in the morning. Guys, listen. Daddy decided to bring the kitty home to make sure he would be okay. Do you want to see him?"

Will squealed and raised his eyebrows. Livy mirrored his facial expressions and rocked her body back and forth in Seth's arms, still sucking on her two middle fingers.

"Alright, but listen. You *can't* touch the kitty, okay?"

"But why?" said Will.

"Well, the kitty is really, really dirty, and he needs to get cleaned first. So, you can just look at him. Okay?"

"But maybe when he has a bath, I can pet him," Will said.

"Sure, bud. When he's had a bath you can pet him. Okay? Alright, let's go downstairs and see Mommy."

Will ran down the stairs ahead of Seth, chanting. "Mommy! Mommy! There's a kitty and—" Shannon and Seth watched as Will tried, with bated breath, to recount the whole story Seth had just told Shannon. Seth picked Will up, and Shannon grabbed a snuggling Livy, both parents holding them over top of the baby gates so they could get a peek at the cat.

"Heeth duddy," said Livy.

"Yeah, he is dirty, isn't he?" Shannon said. "He was swimming around in the dirty water, Livy."

"I kin . . . fwim," said Livy with extra effort on the last word. She was staring into Shannon's eyes, looking for validation.

"You *can* swim—like a fish, with your floaties on," Shannon said. "Now, Livy my fish, do you want some breakfast?"

"I want a bagel with butter and peanut butter," said Will. "Butter on one half, peanut butter on the other," he said dancing around one of the kitchen chairs.

"Coming right up, bud," Seth said. "Livy, do you want some cereal?"

"Yeah!" she said, kicking her legs and rocking her body out of Shannon's arms.

Shannon and Seth gathered their own breakfast by the counter and whispered while the kids ate.

"The SPCA is open from 12 to 4 on Saturdays," she said. "So, we could even take him today."

"Okay, well let's wait until he's woken up."

"Okay, but . . . why? They could clean him up better than we could."

"Well, I wanted to at least consider the possibility of keeping him."

"Seth—"

"I know, I know. We have a lot going on right now with your business and the kids and my work and writing, but they *love* animals. And cats basically take care of themselves."

"I'm not saying yes," she said sternly. "At least not until after I get retested for allergies. You know I love animals, Seth. But I've never had a cat, so I don't know what to think of it. I just want to make sure it interacts with the kids okay—and that I can, you know, *breathe*."

"Yeah, that makes sense. Let's see how he is with the kids. Your appointment is on Thursday this week?"

"Yeah."

"Okay. We can keep him in the garage with a space heater until then. I can make an appointment with the vet on Monday to just get him checked out and make sure he doesn't have major injuries."

"Or rabies."

"Yes, or rabies." Seth rolled his eyes. Shannon jabbed him in the ribs with her finger.

"Alright," she said. I need you to hang out with the kids while I get some work done."

"Sure."

It took effort, but Seth didn't tell her about the heat flash he'd had at the park when he found the cat. He was managing his anxiety well lately, with the medication. He hadn't been to counseling for two weeks, but he'd been using what he was learning—assessing his limits, learning his triggers. He didn't want to add to her worry right now. Eventually, he would tell her. He *had* to. Holding anything back from her made him feel weak and small. It was honesty that had always been their bedrock. And with honesty came intimacy. He could never bring himself to threaten that with her. He would hold off telling her for a few hours, at best. But then he'd pour everything out before he went to sleep for the night. That was their time to connect after the kids were in bed.

For the remainder of the day, he managed to keep Will and Livy away from the cat intermittently, after the initial thrill of having an animal in the house. They wandered over to the baby gates every few minutes, trying to touch him, picking the dirt off his fur. Livy made it her job to remove specks of "dolt" (dirt) from his coat. "Nudder one dolt," she half whispered while laying on her belly next to the sleeping pile of orange calico fur. "Nudder one dolt. Annn . . . nudder one dolt." Shannon kept pulling her away and washing her hands, but eventually she gave up.

Will was the supervisor, telling Livy when and how she could touch the cat.

***

Later that evening, Seth and Shannon sat on the couch, just after they got the kids into bed.

"You didn't name him, did you?" Shannon asked, nodding towards the front door where the cat was still sleeping. "The whole attachment thing—you know."

"Well . . . no. I thought it would be fun to call him by a human name, though. Maybe Christopher or Ronald."

Shannon laughed as she bit into a pretzel. Seth watched the tiny crumbs dust the top of her black t-shirt. "Human names for animals are ridiculous," she said through a smile. "Like my aunt calling her dachshund Timothy."

"Hey, did you see the news last night?" She asked, shifting the subject. Seth shook his head.

"Pastor Cleft's wife passed away," she said. Shannon's father had been a pastor, like Seth's, but they hadn't been to church for a while. They'd attended Cleft's church for some months before, and then Seth asked if they could take a break. It was a cause of conflict, and Seth usually lost the arguments and went to church reluctantly. But Shannon had given in for a bit, trying to allow him some space.

"Why would something like that be on the news? They don't report local deaths like that unless it's a homicide or something."

"Yeah, I know," said Shannon. Seth thought she was going to say more, but she didn't. She just let the silence hang in the room as they both thought.

"They showed a couple of cop cars outside their house . . . and a big white van," Shannon said, breaking the silence.

"You think there was a homicide?" Seth said.

"No—they just said they were looking into a report of some strange activity. Someone said they saw some lights . . . underground?"

Seth shook his head. "This town needs something to happen so they have *actual* news to report." Shannon smiled and nodded.

"Didn't she have Alzheimer's—his wife?" said Seth. "I thought I remember the pastor referencing that in one of his sermons."

"I didn't think you were *listening* to the sermons," Shannon said with a teasing smile.

"Hey, give me some credit," Seth said as he walked back out to the kitchen. "Maybe I'll call the local paper and tell them I found a cat up at Childs Park. See if that gets on the news."

"Why would *that* get on the news?"

"Never mind."

"Seth, please make sure that cat stays inside the baby gates. I don't want him wandering around the house and peeing in all the corners of the rooms."

"He shouldn't be able to get out. He's got no energy, anyway."

"Okay," Shannon said, though her tone suggested she didn't believe him. "I've got some work to do. Beth is asking me to help her plan out some new displays for the nursery this week."

Shannon worked part-time at a local nursery called Kingsfoil which specialized in exotic flowers and shrubs. Beth was the owner and Shannon's best friend since high school. Shannon was sketching out squares on her yellow notepad, using a red pencil, snapped in half by Will's heel earlier that week.

"Alright. I'm off to bed then. Gonna try to get up early to write," Seth said as he climbed the cream-carpeted steps. But then he paused.

"Oh, by the way: had another heat flash at the park. Almost a panic attack, but I got control over it."

"Oh, geez, Seth. I'm sorry. I hate that. Did you practice the saying your counselor gave you, and the breathing exercise?"

"Yes, dear," Seth said with a roll of his eyes, lightening the mood.

"Hey—just checking," she laughed, taking Seth's joke as a good sign. He never joked when his anxiety had taken over.

"I'm glad it helped. That's big."

"Yeah. I guess it's progress. Alright. Love you."

"Love you, too. Hope you get some good writing done in the morning."

Seth had been trying to write a little bit each day in a sort of memoir about his father. As a teenager, he'd watched his father die of cancer in their living room, taking his final breaths in the presence of his family. Seth's counselor said it might be therapeutic to write about how that experience continued to shape him. "I'm treating you for PTSD," she told him. "From watching your father die." She peered at him over the rim of her broad, boxy glasses. Seth balked at the idea of writing about his dad, but he knew deep down that fear is what pushed him away. Writing would force him to face the life-draining, mind-bending reality of death. Now that he had a family of his own, he wanted to focus on them and forget that part of his past—the ugliness of bodily corrosion, the smell of hospitals and astringents, the mention of morphine or "quality of life." That was his past, and it was dark. He wanted his present to remain well-lit.

But then he found writing about it actually did help. He was starting to see how much his dad's death affected his anxiety, his fear of one day not existing, his attempts to remain in safe places, to keep pushing forward rather than staring—even for a short time—at what had happened and what it meant: *that he couldn't live forever*.

And so writing had become a morning ritual: a notebook with unlined paper, a pen, and a mug of black coffee. He could only handle a small cup each day, or else his anxiety got the better of him and made him feel detached and hyper-vigilant.

Each morning, he would start writing, and the words flew onto the page, effortless as ash falling to the earth from a fading fire. He didn't know where the words came from or where they were going. He could just feel them pulling . . . pulling bits of his past up from the dark riverbed of memory. And he examined each bit like a child turning a creek stone around in his hands, looking at the edges and bumps, checking for fossils. There was more to his past than he'd thought—more beauty and pain and color. He'd just been sprinting in the present so long that he'd been ignorant of his own life. And yet the previous morning he'd recalled a quote from his father he couldn't stop thinking about: "In your past is buried the present and the future." His father had said that to him at some point, but when? He couldn't remember.

Seth also realized that writing regularly helped him teach. Composition teachers, he reminded himself, should actually *compose* things sometimes.

He padded up the stairs to the bedroom and set his alarm for 5:30 am. He read a few pages of *The Brothers Karamazov*, which he'd just started again, but after dropping the book several times in the middle of a paragraph, he set it on his nightstand, settled onto his right side, and fell asleep. The words of Smerdyakov were lodged in his mind as he drifted off: "If there is no God, then everything is permitted."

"And if there is a God," Seth said to himself, "then there's a war."

3

A GROWING STRANGENESS

S UNDAY WENT MUCH THE same way—Seth and Shannon trying in vain to keep the kids away from the dirty cat, who slept most of the day. On Monday, when they were planning to call the SPCA, Seth woke at 7:00 am. His 5:30 alarm didn't go off. Yellow irises with black slits caught his bleary-eyed attention, pulling him from the cavern of unconsciousness. Somehow the cat had gotten out of the baby gates again and was padding across their comforter. He knew Shannon wouldn't like that—the cat was still caked with the bits of mud Livy hadn't picked off. A few hairline twigs and leaf fragments were knotted into his fur, bits of earth that refused to let go and fall back to their native stillness. But his purring was strong and soothing, so Seth didn't make any sudden moves.

"Hey," he whispered. The cat's ears bent downward at the sound of Seth's voice. And his look was that of a toddler caught trying to steal an extra cookie. But the ears rose again in a moment. The cat interpreted Seth's silence as permission. It walked farther across the comforter, testing its boundaries, then met Seth's waiting hand on the edge of the bed, arching and then lowering its back like an accordion to receive its first real pet. Seth touched his fur—he could see it was a male now—and felt content. His palm and fingers registered the softness of the fur as Seth lifted his eyes to notice the gold sky waiting behind their tan curtains, illumined now like angel skin. He lay there just petting the cat and staring at the angel-skin curtains for what seemed like an hour.

He nearly forgot Shannon was still in the bed next to him. She stirred and rolled over, staring at the cat for a moment before sitting up and whisper-screaming.

"Ugh, Seth! What's he doing in our bed? Get him off."

Seth came out of his daze, slowly enough for Shannon to squint her eyes at him.

"Oh, come on. He's happy. Look at him."

"I *am* looking at him; he's still covered in . . . pond filth. Go wash him off before the kids get up. But be quiet, and use the downstairs bathroom. I want them to sleep in. Will doesn't have his pre-K program today."

Seth rolled his legs over the side of the bed, slid his feet into his slippers, and picked up the cat, who didn't seem opposed to being carried. He stepped softly downstairs, wincing at each whining step. Then he set the cat down on the linoleum floor, grabbed the can opener from the second drawer by the fridge, and opened a can of tuna from the pantry. He set it before the cat and watched.

"Go ahead."

The cat pounced on the can, his teeth chomping into the pink meat, and Seth could've sworn he heard a human-sounding "Mmm" come from the cat. As he pulled out the wet fish, his tail danced and curled, from bending reed to shepherd's staff. Seth started to make the coffee while the cat ate.

Then he remembered why he'd come downstairs. He dreaded washing the cat. He'd known cats hate water, but he'd never bathed one himself. He thought about using a tiny bit of dish soap and putting the cat in the kitchen sink, but that didn't seem right: the "grease-fighting power" of dish soap probably wouldn't work wonders on cat skin. He started the coffee and then tiptoed back upstairs to Shannon's bedside.

"Hey . . . Shannon."

"Hmmm?"

"I'm gonna run into town to get some cat food and shampoo."

"What? No one's even open. Just use some of our shampoo."

"Bill's shop is open early on weekdays."

"Fine . . . just get back before the kids are up."

***

Bill Watson's gray truck was the only other vehicle in the parking lot when Seth pulled in. Bill had owned Pets' Place ever since Seth could remember. He had a round face, slightly pink, hedged in on every side by peppered gray hair and a matching beard—one of the thickest beards Seth had ever seen, and a good ten inches long. Seth hardly ever talked to him, but later realized he was one of his favorite people in the town—something about his meek and contented demeanor. Bill never seemed to want anything—not even his own voice to be heard. He looked genuinely content every time Seth saw him. It was something he envied.

The bells on the door jingled as Seth walked in with the cat in his right arm. Bill was in the back corner of the store, sprinkling something on the surface of a large aquatic tank. He didn't turn when Seth came through the door. Contrary to all business advice, Bill always waited for the customer to come to him—and it seemed to work, given that most people in town knew enough about him to initiate the conversation and then prepare for a long pause while he thought about his response.

"Hey, Bill."

"Oh, mornin' to you, Seth. Didn't expect to see you in here, unless something's changed." A few years back, Seth had talked with Bill at a community college basketball game. In an attempt to be conversational, he went into some detail about how his family always had golden retrievers when he was a kid. "Good dogs . . . *real* good dogs," Bill had said. But he could tell Bill was slightly disappointed when he learned Seth didn't have any animals—especially after he told Bill about his young son and soon-to-be-born daughter. "Kids are good for animals . . . and animals are good for kids," he'd said. The wording had stayed with Seth.

Bill apparently retained all of this, though he still hadn't even turned to look at Seth. How did he know Seth's voice that well after just one conversation years ago?

"You doin' alright?" Bill asked, still not looking up from his fish-feeding.

"Pretty good," Seth said. "I mean . . . different—but good." Bill finally took his eyes off of the tank and looked over at Seth's face, and then down to his arms where the cat was lazing comfortably. Its eyes were tracking the movements of the rainbow fish in the tank right next to Seth.

"Looks like you got 'different' in your arms," Bill said with a chuckle.

"Yeah, I found him bunched up at the bottom of the falls over at Childs Park—thought he was a beaver or something."

"Looks better 'n a beaver . . . and looks better 'n I'd think he would. How long you had 'im?"

"Just found him early yesterday morning, and I haven't convinced Shannon to keep him yet."

"Oh, she'll give in once she sees him cleaned up a bit."

"That's my thinking, too. I wanted to give him a bath and get him some food in the meantime."

"Mmm. Welt, cat food 'n groomin' supplies are in aisle three. Gimme a holler if you can't find somethin'.'"

"Will do."

Bill wore a pin-striped blue dress shirt and old blue jeans. The exact same outfit, in fact, that he'd worn to that basketball game a few years ago. This wasn't coincidental; Bill wore the same clothes multiple times a week. There was a hole the size of a fingertip in the right shoulder of his dress shirt where an old white undershirt poked through, and around the waistline the shirt had several pulls where thick stacks of keys dangled, one on each hip. His leather belt had a faded Native American design embossed on it. His moccasins were broken in like a baseball glove used every day for a decade. Seth knew you couldn't really place people by their clothes, but he wanted to do that with Bill. It would be a good place, like one of those old general stores that clings to a town's main street long after slow rhythms have passed.

Bill made his way back to the fish tank as Seth turned toward aisle three. He grabbed the first bag of food he saw and picked up a bottle of shampoo that was supposed to be sensitive to animal skin. The cat pictured on the front of the bottle had obviously not just been given a bath.

As Seth walked back up to the front register, a toy duck caught his eye. Its body was fat and its wings were thin, so if you raised and lowered it quickly, it appeared to fly. The only reason he stopped to look at it was because he owned it—actually, he owned several. Before his father died, they had a golden retriever who loved that same duck—enough to tear its head off and pull the stuffing and squeaker out each time Seth bought her one. Near the end of his dad's life, when he had come home for hospice care, Seth would call their retriever, Allie, over to his dad's bedside. Sometimes his dad would have a faint smile when he saw her march into the room, tail wagging, mouth stuffed with a mangled duck. That was enough for Seth to call Allie in almost every time he went to check on his dad.

One of Seth's most vivid memories of those final days was when Allie brought her duck over to the hospice bed, which they had set up in his parents' living room. The irony of his father *dying* in a *living* room wasn't lost on Seth, but he never said anything. The point had come up a few times in his morning writing, though.

As his dad lay dying, Allie dropped the slobbered duck into his lap, and then picked up her head and gazed at him, her pupils black and full, her tail thudding against the metal bed frame, as if death weren't boding in the corners of the room. But his dad's motor skills had left him. His two hands lay nearly lifeless next to the bed railings—champions of hammer swings and handshakes now laid to rest. After a few moments, Allie's tail slowed, and she bowed away sadly when she realized that the hand in which she'd placed the duck didn't have the ability to grab, lift, or throw. His father's thick fingers were memorials too, relics from an era of page turns and pencil holds. These things were the past, not the present. It's a sad day when a dog can't play.

"Don't think he'll be needin' that." Bill's voice snapped Seth out of his memory.

"No . . ." Seth said after a moment, treading the waters of thought. "Though I imagine he wouldn't mind toying with a bird. I think I'll get it anyway, as a keepsake." This was the third time Seth had bought one since his dad passed. And he knew that Bill knew as well. Bill had sold him the other two. And yet Bill didn't say anything or make any gestures. They both set a cloth of silence on top of the mystery. Seth was thankful for that and respected Bill all the more for not asking questions. Bill seemed to have a sense of when things should lie fallow.

Seth kept the other ducks, still new with the tags on them, stored in the garage in a big Rubbermaid container along with the tennis rackets and old basketballs. Shannon saw them once when they were cleaning out the garage. She asked why they had dog toys with the tags still on them. Seth shrugged and said they must have been left over from a prior move. But then after a moment, he told her the truth. And she understood, as she always did—without offering a reason or response. It was one of the many things he loved about her—the ability to let others be themselves in her presence, without scaring them off by judgment or critique. In conversations, Shannon was like a soft summer breeze running through newly risen bee balm flowers, moving around the delicate purple crowns without coercion. She never pushed. But she was fully present and receptive to the smallest of movements.

"Now, that cat's gonna' eat that food, right?" Bill said, raising the pitch in his voice to show that he was going somewhere.

"Yes . . ." Seth was not in the frame of mind to follow implied reasoning.

"You know what he's gonna' do when he eats it?"

"Uhhh. Be happy?" An ear-to-ear grin spread over Bill's bearded face.

"Close. He's gonna pass it."

Seth's mind tripped onto the train tracks of logic. "Oh, right—I need a litter box."

"Good idea," Bill said with a wink, his light blue eyes hugged by wrinkles.

"Now, Seth," Bill said as he rang Seth up at the register. "Where'd you say you found this cat?"

"Childs Park, towards the bottom of the last fall."

"Deer Leap?"

"Yeah."

"No collar? No tags?"

"No. I found him just like he is now . . . surprised he was even alive."

"Well, you take care of him, and he'll take care of you."

"That's a nice thought," Seth said, a little puzzled by Bill's choice of words.

"It oughta' be," said Bill. "It oughta' be."

They exchanged smiles before Seth pushed through the door, ringing the bell again.

Bill stood alone at the cash register, shaking his head. "Now that's a shame. He's young yet. But we don't get to choose." As he spoke, he looked up towards the ceiling. Then he watched Seth's red Ford Ranger roll out of the parking lot. Seth glanced at the store from the road as he pulled back onto Silver Lake. And for a split second, his eyes met Bill's. And they both noticed that they were looking at each other.

***

When Seth pulled into the driveway, he put the stuffed duck into the container with the others in the garage. He noticed the cat staring at him as he stood in the entryway of the house—waiting for him to put his food down.

"You just wait on me for everything."

His purring grew audible as he rubbed himself against Seth's leg. In a few seconds, he was crunching on the food Seth poured into a little white bowl, his sharp ivory teeth breaking it into bits. When he'd finished, he tried to jump onto the couch in the living room, but Seth grabbed him before he had the chance. Seth picked up the bottle of shampoo and headed to the downstairs bathroom. He'd only have a few minutes before the kids were up.

The cat dug his claws into Seth's forearms as he tried to set him in the tub, his ears braced to match the flat top of his head. If the cat could speak, profanities would be flying.

"It's water—for cryin' out loud; it's not like you don't know what it is. You almost drowned in it." *Probably not the best association*, Seth thought. "It's just water; get o-f-f my arm." His claws had already begun to draw blood. Seth pushed him down into the tub but then had to hold him there, his right hand on its back, the cat's shoulder blades jutting out between Seth's fingers.

"Now . . . . stay here." The second Seth lifted his hand, the cat bolted out the door and towards the kitchen. "Step one," Seth mumbled. "Close the door to the bathroom." The cat was now underneath the navy blue wingback chair in the living room. Seth had to pry him out from beneath it as he clawed and bit his knuckles. "Geez! Draw blood, why don't you!"

As he pulled at the cat's body, he thought he heard something—a noise that sounded strangely like a voice. Was it the words, "Just stop"? Seth paused but passed it off as a hissing sound (and there were plenty of those). By the time Seth got him into the warm bath water, the spigot still running as his two hands pressed the cat to the floor, blood was streaming down his forearms, diluted with bath water. The hairline lacerations filled with dark purple blood, then washed clean with water, and then filled again.

He held the cat down the whole time, pulling one arm out to squeeze a blob of shampoo onto the tub's rim, before swiping it awkwardly into the same hand and rubbing it into the cat's fur. After he dried him off and dabbed his own forearms with toilet paper to stop the bleeding, he opened the door. The cat shot to his fortress under the wingback chair and began licking his paws and forearms. Seth realized he'd need to put a long-sleeved shirt on to hide the scratches so that the kids wouldn't see them. They were red and raised, like curse words branded into his skin.

The cat peered out at Seth from under the chair, yellow eyes fierce as fire. "There was no need to maul me," Seth said. He set his hand out before the cat, who smacked it with his right paw. Again, Seth heard a hiss that sounded humorously like the word "stop." He laughed to himself and then left the cat alone. As Seth sat on the carpet and looked around the room, the cat crawled slowly over to Seth's forearm, sniffed at it, and began licking the bloody scrapes with his sandpaper tongue. Thus ended his baptism. It would be the last time Seth attempted to bathe him.

***

Seth managed to sneak upstairs and pull on a long-sleeved shirt just before the kids woke up. Shannon looked over at him as the sound of the fabric brushed against his shoulders and back in the dim light of their bedroom. The sun was up now. Their bedroom curtains, which had been gold with the dawn behind them, were now silvery gray.

"Did you wash him?" she said. Seth nodded.

"He didn't like it, but I washed him. He's downstairs."

Shannon brushed the hair off of her forehead. "We need to be with the kids whenever they go near him. We still don't know how friendly he is." Seth agreed as he touched the long scrapes under the shirt. The pain was like a dull ringing in his skin. The kids woke up a moment later.

As Livy and Will crunched on cereal and dueled with their spoons, Seth switched on their radio to hear the local news.

> Still quite a bit of attention is on Dingmans Ferry this week, where a report of strange lights *under the ground* has been drawing curiosity from locals and a few out-of-towners. The house of one resident is allegedly the source of the commotion, where police cars and other vehicles had been stationed for several hours. Very little is known right now, other than that someone claims to have seen glowing, white lights *underneath* the ground in the backyard of the property. Law enforcement has said they were merely investigating the report as a courtesy. But that hasn't kept a few locals from snooping around the property. Police are asking residents to respect the privacy of the owner, and they say they are planning on

arresting anyone who trespasses on the property.

In other news, in Bethlehem, a large turnout is expected for the second year of 'Musikfest,' which promises to showcase several local bands and—

Seth switched off the radio. This was the second time the underground lights had come through the news, and he couldn't help his curiosity.

"Lights under the ground," he said to himself. "That'd make a good story."

4

A RACE TO THE WHITE DOOR

THE CAT TOOK UP permanent residence beneath the wingback chair and kept to himself for the next few days, as much as Will and Livy would let him. He wasn't averse to being pet, but he didn't seek out attention. Shannon and Seth both decided to give up on calling the SPCA, but neither of them said this directly. It was a decision that dissolved into acceptance with time.

Seth taught two classes at the community college on Tuesday, an introduction to composition and then a research and writing course. He brought the cat with him to work and snuck him into his office early that morning. His office door was close to an exit, so he didn't have to dodge anyone on the way in, and he usually got there before the campus officially opened. The cat lay on his desk for an hour, sleeping and purring loudly as Seth scribbled down some words in his journal about his dad.

The hardest thing about death is the silent waiting. There's a long pause after the leaving. And you stay around to hear what's next. A voice? A vision? But nothing comes. The silence sifts your thoughts like flour through metal mesh. What's left is the pure powder of wonder. And that powder is you—frail dust that could blow away and get lost in the wind. And maybe that's what maturity is about, real wisdom: learning to be okay with the wandering wind that takes things where it will.

Seth set down his pen and took out the two marbles he kept in his pocket. "2,200 degrees," he said to the cat. "That's how hot these used to be before a machine cut the liquid glass into slugs and rolled each one around cast iron rings. They have to be burning to be shaped." The cat looked at him as he spoke, but was then distracted by the sunlight coming through the window, which struck the marbles and sent shards of refracted light onto the desk. The light shards shivered as the marbles moved in Seth's palm.

The cat tried to pounce on the light dancing on the desk. Then Seth rolled the two marbles onto the brown carpeted floor so the cat could bat them around while he went to teach his first class. He was introducing paragraph structure, and then he'd let the students write for a while. "Stay here and out of trouble." He shut the door and locked it.

When he returned, he braced himself for a mess, or the smell of cat urine. But he found neither. The cat had left the marble with red, orange, and white swirls in the corner by the door. It was focused on the clear glass one, slapping it into the spring-loaded door stop. Seth ate a granola bar and graded a few student essays before his next class. By then the cat had fallen asleep on a rectangular patch of sunlight warming the carpet. Seth crept out of the office and again locked the door.

The research and writing class was always a tough sell to students. He found it better to keep lecturing to a minimum and get them all into the library to look up books and articles for their chosen topic. The librarian—Edith Calloway—was happy to see Seth and work with his students. She always wore a burgundy cardigan, with a long skirt leading down to her thin feet, wrapped in black pumps. Her attire earned her the nickname "Cardigan Calloway." But the students hardly ever teased her; she was so soft-spoken and unassuming, working with grandmotherly patience, regardless of each student's sincerity. She often found little ways to encourage Seth in his own writing, too. "Any words come your way lately?" she'd ask. And Seth would talk about whatever he'd written of late. And he was refreshed simply by Edith's eager listening. She was genuinely interested in what he said, not just waiting for her turn to speak. As he was leaving the library with the class, she softly touched his elbow to get his attention.

"Thought you might enjoy this. We've got several copies already, and it was just donated again."

"Oh, thank you, Edith!"

"Have you read it?"

"Not yet. It's been on my list though."

"*East of Eden* is a true masterpiece. Worth every word."

"I bet it is. Thank you, Edith."

"You're welcome, dear."

Seth opened the front cover and found a name in fine, cursive script: Jane Warrington. He tucked the well-worn paperback under his arm and walked to his office with a spring in his step.

Back in the office—when Seth's eyes were glazed over from reading papers that began with dictionary quotes—the cat left the marbles and started batting around a tin soup can filled with pencils on the top of the desk. After he knocked it over twice and spilled all the pencils onto the carpet, Seth fought the urge to clean them up. He resisted for a few seconds, so the cat raced around the office slapping the pencils under the desk and against the wall. Seth watched him, smiling. How could a creature have so much fun batting sticks around a room?

Seth knew the answer. It was *play*, the same sort he did whenever he shot baskets in their driveway. Whether slapping pencils or bouncing a ball, the principle was the same: toying with the objects in the world. Not thinking about death, or loss, or food, or commitments. Pausing all concerns and pouring attention into something that had no refined purpose besides joy in the present. Maybe play had more meaning than he'd thought, more power.

It was in these little moments that Seth began to see the world from the cat's perspective. And it was oddly moving. It closed some invisible gap between them. The same thing had happened the day before when he heard the cat crunching on his cat food. Seth had crunched through cereal shortly after that and thought of how loud chewing could be. These moments of overlap, of sharing, deepened his attachment to the cat. He was growing more and more akin to an animal he hadn't named yet.

He was thinking about names as he sat at his desk when his head began to drop. That was his signal that office time was finished. He felt bad picking up the pencils and putting them back into the tin can, sort of like deconstructing a swingset in front of a toddler. The cat was still batting them around and stared at Seth with confusion as he set the full can back on the desktop. The cat bolted up to his chair and then quickly onto his desk, poised to swipe again when Seth wrapped his hands around the cat's belly and lifted him up to his chest. "No, no, no. Pencils are done." The cat gave an audible growl.

Seth grabbed his briefcase, burgundy leather with brass hardware. It had belonged to his father. He stuffed his papers inside and grabbed his keys. "How bout a trip to Childs Park before we get back home?"

The community college was on Route 739, a few miles up from where Silver Lake Road branched off, so it was a short way there. Given the cat's water trauma, he wouldn't dream of taking him with him into the woods; he'd leave him in the truck with the window cracked.

The air was cool and the sun was bright. Seth hadn't felt the urge to get to the park this badly before. It was stronger than his desire to eat or sleep. It was a compulsion, a pulse rising from his heart and running into the back of his throat. He walked out to his truck and only passed one student on the way.

"Awww! Is that your cat?" she said. Seth kept moving toward the truck as he smiled back at her.

"Yup," he said tersely with a forced smile. The girl turned away hesitantly. Seth knew she wanted to pet it, and it was an awkward encounter, but he had to get to the park. At least she wasn't one of his students.

When he pulled into the gravel lot on the edge of the park, he jumped out of the truck and smacked the top of his head on the door frame. He pressed down on the pain with both hands, running into the woods. Even with the pain throbbing on the top of his skull, he felt wild; something thudded in his blood—an ancient eagerness, a long-buried hope of discovery. It was so strong that he started to smile. And that just made him run faster.

When his feet landed on the path next to the creek, he looked around, trying to figure out which direction to go as he caught his breath. And then he spotted a pin-striped blue dress shirt moving through the brush and branches in the distance. He squinted and stared. He'd know Bill Watson's lumbering walk anywhere. And Bill only ever really wore *one* shirt.

"Bill!" he yelled, immediately embarrassed by his loudness. He quickly lowered the right hand he'd waved in the air. Bill turned toward him like a deer caught crossing someone's yard.

And then . . . Bill *bolted*. Seth frowned and hesitated. Something was off. He could feel his stomach drop inside him. His knees quivered. His heart came forward in his chest and began drumming like a door knocker against his muscle and skin. This was it: fight or flight.

And then Seth surprised himself. He fought.

His legs felt somehow heavy and light at the same time—pushing anvil blood along hollow bones. He tore off into the woods after Bill. As he ran, questions flitted through his mind like crazed birds. *Why'd he look at me like that? Why's he running? Maybe it's not Bill.* As the questions jumped and settled, he wondered at his own body chasing after an acquaintance on impulse. His anxiety was rising, and disassociation was setting in. His feet and legs looked alien, as if he were watching his body from a few feet above.

Bill was on the other side of the creek, so Seth would have to find a crossing. He darted up the path that hugged the north side of the falls, climbing towards the next bridge. He had no idea the cat had squeezed out of the open truck window and was sprinting after him, padding silently on the path.

At last, with his heart rate soaring and sweat beading on his forehead, he crossed the bridge where he'd seen Bill and paused, spinning around in every direction, taking in the colors and the shadows, the quietness of the woods in eerie contrast to his drumming heart. He was scanning—looking for anything that didn't belong, but mostly for the blue amidst the brown: Bill's blue shirt behind the thick undergrowth of the trees and the labyrinthian fence of their trunks.

And then he caught it—a sliver of the pin-stripe blue weaving through the tree trunks, but it was more than a hundred yards ahead of him. He'd have to choose again: walk back and forget the crazed chase or continue pursuing the mystery. The choice only gave him a few seconds to catch his breath. He realized he'd already decided as his legs began moving before his mind could catch up. He sprinted uphill, with iron pumping in his thighs and fire burning in his lungs. He knew the main trail ended not far ahead of where he'd seen Bill. When he finally reached the top of the trail, he could see the path disappear into random birch and maple saplings. He clutched his kneecaps and tried to catch his breath. He'd have to choose a third time: into the wild or back to the world. He pulled the two marbles from his pocket. The clear blue one slipped back in. He wrapped his fist around the fire-in-a-teardrop.

But before he began walking into the unmarked woods, he decided to let his voice do some of the work now. "Bill! It's Seth!" he yelled, bent over. No answer. He went slowly into the woods, crunching on the dead leaves and holding his right fist against his heart. That's when he heard crunching behind him and saw the cat padding up to him. "Agh! How'd you get out of the truck?" He was worried the cat would run, but it didn't. Seth picked him up and walked further into the woods, pressing the cat against his heaving chest while he still clutched the marble in his right fist.

"Bill!" He called turning in circles, searching for traces of the blue shirt again through the tapestry of tree trunks. Nothing. He couldn't even hear footsteps. The silence was a screaming invitation. He didn't want to accept it and go any farther, and yet he did. He needed to.

The cat clawed at him and sprang out of his grasp, but it didn't run away. Instead, it sat for a moment in front of him, swishing its tail, staring up at him. Then it slowly turned as it walked forward, pausing to look back at him. Was it . . . *leading* him? As it padded across the dry leaves, Seth followed hesitantly, still scanning for any sign of Bill. The hair on his neck was raised now, and his anxiety was in high gear. He felt a balloon expanding in his throat. About fifty yards in, the cat hugged the side of a great boulder a few feet taller than Seth. On the other side of the boulder, it stopped and sat, swishing its tail again, and then holding it in the shape of a shepherd's crook.

Seth looked down at the cat, but his peripheral vision caught something that pulled his eyes away. There, embedded *in* the boulder, was an old white door. It had a brass handle, and the paint was chipped and discolored with age, as if the weather had held a one-way conversation with it for decades.

And then he saw the ground beneath the bottom of the door. A soft, white glow broke through the blanket of dead leaves. He stepped back from it, lifting his feet as if he'd just stepped on hot tar. A heat wave surged through his spine and up to his head: his trigger for a panic attack, but he took a deep breath, held it for five seconds, and then slowly let it out. As he felt the oxygen flood his brain and wash over his face, his thudding heart slowed. Bill was still nowhere to be seen.

What in God's name was he supposed to do with a door guarding daylight? It was fight or flight again. But this time,

Seth's courage faded. It was all too much. He'd chosen to fight three times, had won three battles. Now it was time for flight. "Come on," he said to the cat. "Let's get outta here." The cat stared at him. And then Seth heard a voice.

"You could go in."

Seth backed up and spun around, looking for the body that belonged to the voice, for Bill, or a hiker. Anyone. But there was no one.

"*I said . . .*" came the voice again. "You could go in. What's to be afraid of?"

Seth looked down at the cat. There was no way—no way. His anxiety must have broken his brain. He looked around again, furrowing his brow in search of a human. He looked up into the canopy. He circled the boulder. He scanned the perimeter several times. No one.

5

THE CAT SPEAKS

S ETH FINALLY BROUGHT HIS eyes back to the cat. Again came the voice.

"Is it so strange . . . " said the voice, "for words to come from me? Equally as strange for them to come from your lips, isn't it?"

Seth's heart raced. This had to be a trick, or a nervous breakdown, or a brain tumor. The last option was particularly terrifying since that's how his father died. That was a *real* possibility. His anxiety took over. The tips of his fingers began to tingle as he started to hyperventilate.

"It's alright," came the voice, steady and calm, like a man with eighty years behind him. And this time Seth only looked down at the cat, trying to accept the absurdity. "There you go. It's me. It's *my* voice. Don't be afraid."

"I gotta . . . we . . . gotta get back to the . . . truck." Seth was too aware of his teeth, lips, and tongue. He was an alien in his own skin, his mind and body completely disassociated. Was he really doing this, talking to a cat? He kept looking around to make sure no other human was present.

"Okay," said the cat, consoling him like a parent. "Back to the . . . *truck*. Not a very nice-sounding word, is it? It's that voiceless velar stop at the end, like a crow's caw."

"I can't do this right now. I can't—" Seth was giving in to the hyperventilation. The tingling sensation was working up his hands and into his forearms. The cat jumped up towards his stomach, forcing Seth to catch him, and then he dug his claws into Seth's arms to bring him back to reality. Seth liked the pain in the moment. It was the slap in the face he needed, taking his attention off the anxiety.

"Look at me. *Look* at me," said the cat.

"Please . . . just please stop talking," Seth said, gasping for air. Sweat began to gather at his temples. His throat was blocked. "I can't breathe!" He started sprinting back down the path to his truck, dropping the cat in the process. The cat matched and then surpassed his speed with lightning-quick bounds. He landed a dozen feet ahead of Seth and forced him to stop.

"Fine. You don't have to look at me. Just five seconds in," he said. Seth stopped and clutched his kneecaps again. He took in the air through his nose. "Good. Now five seconds hold . . . and five seconds exhale." Seth obeyed and then picked his head up to stare down at the cat as the oxygen flooded his bloodstream and slowed his heart rate.

"How'd . . ." he began, but he was still trying to catch his breath, from the anxiety and the sprinting. "How'd you know about my breathing exercise?"

"I was *made* to know about you, Seth. You are why I'm here."

"This is . . . psychotic," Seth was looking around towards the truck, searching for a sign that he was dreaming, that he was in a trance, anything. He grabbed his chest hair and pulled hard. The pain was real.

"Maybe I have . . . a brain tumor. I've read that you can see things or hear voices if you have a . . . a tumor pressing down on certain parts of your brain. My dad had a brain tumor and—"

"I know," the cat interrupted. "I know he did, Seth. But you don't have a brain tumor. I promise. You just have *me*."

"God—how are we going to afford the medical bills for whatever's wrong with me?! I mean, I have benefits, but I don't know if they'll cover *this*. God, please . . ." Seth began walking to the truck now, and the cat walked beside him. As he reached it, he dropped his head onto the hood. "God, please . . . talking animals. My life isn't *Chronicles of Narnia*."

"Hmmm. But that's a great story. And more fact than fiction when you really get down to it."

"Oh, you're well-read, too? That's . . . that's good. If you weren't versed in the classics, I was going to drop you at the SPCA."

"Ah, a joke. That's good, Seth! It means you're starting to calm down." The cat licked his paw. "Let's just say that I come to you fully equipped. I know all of your experiences. Anything you know, I know."

"Mmm," Seth muttered. He really didn't have a response at this point. His analytic reasoning had burned up in the flames of his panic.

"Whatever you've been through," said the cat, "I've been through. I know where you've come from, who you've been, what you've seen. I know *you*. That's the job of a *steward*."

"A what?"

"A steward. That's what I am."

Seth looked around again to see if anyone else might be able to see him talking to the cat.

"Would you . . . explain what that means?"

"I can, but we should probably get back to Shannon and the kids soon."

"Right. Yeah, we should." Seth paused. "Please . . . and don't take this the wrong way, but please don't talk to me when we get to the house. I just . . . don't know what to say to Shannon, or anyone. About this. Until I figure out what's wrong with me—"

"There's nothing wrong with you, Seth," the cat interrupted. "In a sense, you might say there's something very *right* with you. And, if I can be so bold as to quote your father, 'God has big plans for you.'"

A lump settled in Seth's throat. His father would say that to him all the time when he was a kid. He never appreciated it or really thought about what it meant. Back then, the words seemed so light and airy. They fell into the moment and then slipped away with the wind as he went back to doing whatever he was doing. Now the same words were heavy, soaked in a sincerity christened by death. In his father's absence, he felt the words' presence. He didn't know if they were true now, or even what words so general could mean, but at least he was open to the possibility of accepting them, of holding them in his hands like precious stones. He felt a warm tear run down his cheek.

"It's alright, lad," said the cat. The word "lad" made Seth feel as if he were talking to someone much older than himself. "You've been holding that in for *way* too long."

Seth knew this was true. He'd bolted and barred the door to grief for years since the funeral. He would get choked up occasionally at intense moments—the birth of his children,

Christmas mornings, the sound of his father's favorite hymn playing on distant church bells. But for the most part, Seth leaned heavily against the door to his grief, afraid of the depth and darkness inside. Now he felt how foolish that had been. Letting the tears fall freely lifted a weight from his chest and shoulders. It exposed his soul to the raw air, which stung and settled him at the same time. The cat held its paw against Seth's leg as he gave himself over to weeping. After a long minute, he took a deep breath and wiped his eyes clean.

"God, that felt good, I have to say. My counselor has been talking about suppressed emotions."

"Mmmhmm," the cat agreed. Seth broke out in laughter. His talking cat could sympathize and practice active listening.

"Sorry—did I say something odd? I'm still trying to find my feet in the world of humans."

"No, no. I'm sorry. I just . . . Well, never mind. She talked to me about suppressed emotions from my dad's death, but I never thought it would be a talking cat to draw them out of me."

"Yes, well. As they say, God has his ways."

"So, you believe in God?"

"Well, technically speaking, belief doesn't have as much to do with it as people think. I mean, it's important, of course. It's life-or-death important. But God is God whether I believe in him or not. That's the grandest thing about him, really. He doesn't depend on me for validation."

Seth had never thought of it that way and never heard anyone speak with such quiet confidence. Not, at least, since he heard his dad preach when he was a boy. And back then he understood so little. In his hyper-sensitivity to pretty much everything, the world seemed like a moving fantasy. He could barely keep up with the moments, let alone consider the meaning.

"Well, we should go . . . back home."

"Yes, off we go. Could you just heave me up to the seat, then? I'm afraid I can't get back up to the window from down here."

"Yeah, sure." Seth gently picked up the cat around its rib cage and set him on the black leather seat. It was strange to do this to an animal so self-conscious and articulate, like lifting up a senior citizen. Seth felt extremely awkward. "Is that okay? I didn't hurt you or anything?"

"No, no. I'm fine. Thank you."

"Okay. Well, just remember what I said about not talking when we get to the house. I still think something is deeply wrong with me."

"Understood," said the cat. "But, since I'll be hanging around for a while, you might want to think of a name for me."

"Oh, you don't have a name?"

"No, my friend. That's one of your jobs."

"My jobs? There are multiple jobs?"

"Yes, but we don't have to get into that yet. Just figure out what you'd like to call me. Naming is an important act of ownership. In fact, it's a theological reflection of what God had your ancestors do in Genesis 2. Did you know that naming is a trinitarian—"

"Can you not?" Seth cut him off, feeling badly the moment the words hit the open air. "It's just, I can't wrap my mind around this yet. My head feels like it's exploding, along with my heart. Ugh—sorry. That last part sounded like a line from a Hallmark card."

The cat chuckled. "It's quite alright. I understand. We can talk theology later if you like. Just a name will do."

"Ummm, I don't know," Seth said, looking outside at the sky as he started the truck.

"Just . . . close your eyes and let the name come from your depths."

Seth felt silly and self-conscious doing this, just as he felt when uttering the little poem his counselor had given him. But no one else was around, and he didn't have much energy left to oppose a talking cat. He shut his eyes for a few moments and then opened them.

"*Narnia*. I'll call you Narnia."

"Ah, I like it!" said the cat. "Instead of *The Horse and His Boy*, we'll be *The Cat and His Man*, eh?"

Seth laughed in exhausted amazement. Less than an hour ago, he had a normal barn cat that only knew how to bat pencils around or slap a marble. Now he had a literary, theologically-inclined companion. And possibly a brain tumor, though he tried not to even think of that phrase, knowing full well that it would throw him right back into panic.

"Alright, I have to . . . well, *we* have to get back to the house. Just remember what I said about the talking."

"Will do. Not a word . . . though you and I were made *in* the Word, *by* the Word, *for* the Word—"

"Please," Seth said. "I don't even know what you're saying. If we could just be quiet, I think that would help my heart to settle."

"Sorry. I can explain later . . . *if* you want. Don't have to."

The cat curled up on the passenger seat, rested his head on his paws, and looked through the front windshield, like any human would.

6

TRAVIS AND THE GERIATRIC

TRAVIS WAS A SMART kid in his own way, but the kind of smart you only recognize after months of irritation, repulsion, and judgment have worn off. He'd been a few years ahead of Seth in school, but the separation hadn't kept Seth from hearing stories about him, and from seeing Travis in action.

Once, as Seth was walking through the gym during a middle-school basketball game, he watched Travis curse out a referee without flinching. Everyone's jaw dropped at the profanity. Seth had never heard so many f-words, neither did he consider how many parts of speech it could take—verb, noun, adjective—each with screaming clarity. He was so self-conscious of what people thought of him; he could never imagine doing something like that. But Travis seemed impervious to judgment. He swaggered off the court that day in his oversized uniform, pulling off his jersey to reveal his pale, lanky frame. Even then, based on his middle-school strut and lifted chin, he was pretty proud of his build, if you could even call it a build. Seth remembered in that moment being embarrassed *for* him and thought that was a strange feeling.

And here Travis was walking up the Park Road hill towards Childs Park as Seth was speeding away with his talking cat. Within a few weeks, Seth would get to know Travis very well, and if he knew at this point what he would know then, he wouldn't have been so surprised to see him on the side of the road with a bloody nose and a puffy red eye. Still, what he knew about Travis made this a lot less surprising than it would have been for someone else. Seth fought the impulse, and his panic seemed to turn his legs into stone, but he still slowed the truck and rolled down the driver's side window.

"Travis?" Seth said, putting the truck in park as he checked his rearview mirror. Travis stared at him for a few seconds before a smile of familiarity broke on his thin face.

"Seth, son of Adam!" he said. That had been an annoying descriptor for Seth in high school. He'd never liked it much and wondered why it caught on in the first place.

"Seen better days, huh? What happened to your face?" Seth said. Travis crossed the road and came up to Seth's window, noticing the cat on the passenger seat. The blood from his nose had crusted over, turning red-brown, and his eye looked even worse up close, raw-pink and swollen to reveal a crack where his eye could still let in light.

"Well *he's* been in a scrap," said Narnia. Without turning his head, Seth lifted his hand toward Narnia to signal silence.

"What happened?" Seth said, trying to regain focus. Travis put his hands in his jean pockets and settled in to tell his tale.

"Got my ass kicked by a senior citizen," he started. *Yes*, Seth thought, *Travis would do that*. In the moment, Seth was grateful to Travis for helping him forget his anxiety. He had learned over and over again that anxiety lives and breeds only with the oxygen of attention. Change your focus to something else, and the adrenaline and cortisol levels drop back down, like great trees settling into stillness after a gale.

"You're serious?" Seth said.

"Yeah, some old guy . . ." Travis shook his head and started to laugh.

"You got beat up by an old guy?"

"Yeah, so . . ." Travis started. Seth checked the rearview mirror again and then leaned back, happy to settle into whatever wild story this would turn out to be.

"This old guy with an Abe Lincoln beard started staring at my girl—Cassie—for like a whole minute, over at the gas station, and then he walks over and whispers something to her and walks away, and she starts crying."

"What'd he say to her?"

"I didn't get it from her yet. I was inside the store paying for gas and cigarettes when I saw him out the window. So, I chased after the guy and asked him what his problem was. And he wouldn't turn around—wouldn't even look at me. So I pushed him. Not hard, just to get him to stop. And I guess he was too old to keep his balance or something, so he fell down on the side of the road."

"So you pushed a senior citizen to the ground?" The question made Travis chuckle. "And then?" Seth was fixated.

"Yeah, so then the psycho starts humming something while I'm trying to ask him if he's hurt. Cause, like, I felt bad after he fell over. But he just kept humming."

"What was he humming?"

"Oh, just wait—you'll love this. Cause you go to church and all." Seth didn't feel like clarifying his churchgoing status, so he just smirked. "But as I get down to the ground by his face, he grabs my neck and pushes my head into the gravel. Look at this!" Travis turned his head and showed Seth a brush scrape on his forehead, caked in gray dirt and dried blood. "Then he punches me three times. The first one I gotta hand in front of, but the second two got me here and here." He pointed to his nose and eye. "Guy stunned me for a good few seconds before he walked away."

"And you didn't go after him?" Travis shook his head. "Nah. I mean, I was a little freaked out from the humming, and he *was* an old guy, so . . ."

"So what was he humming?"

"Oh, yeah. Get this—the whole time he's taking shots at me he's humming 'Amazing Grace'!"

"What!?" Seth had a wide smile now, with raised eyebrows, responding to Travis's giddy chuckle. His anxiety had dissipated.

"I know, right? What kind of psycho-geezer sings 'Amazing Grace' as he's punching a kid?"

"Well, you're not exactly a kid anymore," Seth said. They both wagged their heads, and then there was an awkward moment of silence while Travis looked around at the woods and then down at the cat next to Seth.

"Hey, is that your cat?" Travis asked, nodding toward Narnia.

"Sort of—I just found him the other day in the park and cleaned him up."

"'Sort of'?" Narnia said, offended. Seth wagged his finger at Narnia to keep quiet and looked down at the cat with a begging expression. Narnia huffed a breath through his nose and looked out the window away from Seth.

"Look—" Seth said, regaining focus. "Do you need a ride somewhere? I'm going through town to get back home. Why are you walking anyway? Didn't you say you were getting gas at the station?"

"Oh, yeah. I told Cassie to take the car back home. She needed it to bring her mom to the hospital for a nursing shift. And my uncle's place is just up the hill here anyway. Supposed to help him with a house project."

"You sure you don't need a ride?"

"Nah, I'm good."

"Alright," Seth said and let a pause linger in the air. "Well, keep an eye out for geezers on the way."

"Yeah," he said, with a noise that was part laugh, part grunt. Seth put the truck in gear, said they'd catch up soon, and started pulling away. But then Travis turned and said, "So, you come up here a lot?" Seth put the truck back in park.

"Yeah, I do. It's peaceful. I've always liked it. No people. No rules."

"Yeah, that's cool." Travis's coarseness softened in the presence of animals. He was staring at Narnia.

Seth noticed and added, "I'm guessing he's a barn cat or something."

"Oh, good lord. I'm a *steward*," Narnia mumbled with irritation. "Barn cat . . . Do people call you a house human?" Seth ignored him.

"Yeah," Travis said as he stared. "Probably."

"Alright, well, I'll let you go," Travis said as he tapped on the hood of the truck. "Maybe I'll see you around here sometime."

"Maybe," Seth said. He put the truck in gear again and rolled down the Park Road hill toward Silver Lake, unaware that he'd just crossed paths with the person who would become one of his closest friends, even if the unlikeliest.

7

COMING CLEAN

WHEN SETH GOT BACK from Childs Park, Shannon was wrestling with Livy and Will on the family room carpet. Livy's giggle was pure, almost light-bearing. It drifted through the air like wildflower petals. Will was the rule-keeper and superhero, always trying to help her get free from the tickle war.

Seth stood by the door and watched them for a moment, holding Narnia against his chest. He was smiling, but it was a brittle smile, ready to break under the weight of his secret. How in the world was he going to explain this? A talking cat? The theory of a brain tumor causing auditory hallucinations was lodged in his mind. That was the much more plausible explanation. But that explanation also threatened to crush him—an unbearable thought as he watched his family's innocence and remembered the ghost of his father.

Anxiety slithered back into his consciousness, thinning his throat as he breathed and swallowed. But he clung to momentary contentment in the doorway, staring at these people he knew and loved so deeply, who didn't have to fight back nerves all the time, who could just exist in the world without trying. He envied them for this. He envied everyone for it.

"She *loves* you . . . and she'll understand," Narnia said softly through a steady purr. "But it will take time."

"Yeah," Seth scoffed. "A lot of time, if she doesn't commit me to a mental institution first."

"Has she ever doubted you before?"

"No . . ." Seth said, pondering the answer he'd just given, letting it work on him.

"Seth!" Shannon called from underneath Livy and Will. "Get in here!" she yelled. That broke him out of his daze. He set the cat down and jumped into the mix of rolling bodies, sharply remembering how easily both his kids could rip out his chest hair in a wrestle. But he didn't care. The pain was almost pleasant, pulling his mind into the present and roping it down.

"Daddy, guess what?" Will chirped, trying to catch his breath.

"What, bud?"

"Mommy tickles Livy, and then I . . . then I'm the one who has to set her free, and then guess what?"

"What?"

"When Livy gets away, mommy grabs my ankle, and then guess what?"

"What?"

"Livy *tackles* Mommy on the back!"

"Woah! Livy's crazy!" Livy looked up at them with wildness and pride.

"Where's the cat?" Shannon said. She answered her own question before Seth could. "Back to his favorite spot."

"He loves that wingback chair," Seth said. Conversations that hovered on the commonplace always helped to calm him down. He never expressed this, but Shannon understood. They were both good at studying each other. They'd done this even before they were married. Now, almost fourteen years in, they were experts. Shannon already knew something was bothering him.

"He does, doesn't he? It's like his little lair," she said. "How was work?"

"Oh, you know," Seth sighed as Will grabbed onto his ankles.

"Daddy, pull me!"

"Hold on, bud. Daddy's trying to talk to Mommy, and then I'll pull you." Seth regained his focus, even as Will jabbed his clammy feet into his ribs. "It was fine . . . overly ambitious student essays, incoherent ramblings peppered with sentence fragments, forced references to *Catcher in the Rye*—the usual."

Shannon smirked and nodded. "Same old, same old."

"Hey, I stopped at the park after work. I'll have to tell you about it after the kids are in bed."

"Oh, okay. Anything I should worry about?" Shannon knew that topics introduced this way usually meant Seth had a run-in with anxiety.

"No, not really. Just strange. And I saw Travis with a bloody nose and a black eye."

"Travis . . . from high school?"

"Yeah," Seth grinned. "He's always got a story."

"Okay," Shannon said. She seemed uneasy but was trying to mask it for the kids. Will jumped back into the conversation.

"Dad, you said *bloody*!" Will was paranoid about blood. The tiniest scratch on his hand required a band-aid. Seth and Shannon had voiced the "No band-aid unless there's blood" rule, but it didn't take. If he saw redness under his skin from a bump or scrape, he'd plead with them, "See!! There's blood!"

Seth frowned for a moment before realizing that "bloody nose" had caught Will's attention.

"Yes, I did. But it wasn't bad. He was okay." Will wasn't satisfied.

"But . . . did he get hitted? Was he . . . did he have a band-aid?"

"No, bud. He didn't need one. It wasn't bleeding when I was talking to him. He was okay."

"But he should still get a band-aid. . . . I hope I never bleed my nose." Seth and Shannon grinned at each other, trying to hide their expressions from Will.

Livy broke into the moment by jumping on Shannon's back and wrapping her arms around her neck. And the next skirmish ensued.

***

After they'd gotten the kids into bed, Seth and Shannon sat on the couch.

"So, what happened at the park?" Shannon asked. They both sighed as they settled into a conversation that wouldn't be interrupted. Until that moment, Seth had thought of not mentioning the cat's voice. That was stranger by far than the door in the boulder emitting light. And he hoped—he *prayed,* which he hadn't done for a long time—that the voice might go away as a hallucination. Or maybe he'd just hold off on telling Shannon until he could see his doctor or counselor. But his mind threw its hands up in the end. He could never hold things back from her. It never helped anyone. In that tiny moment, he prayed once more that she'd accept him, as she always did, that she wouldn't look at him strangely or treat him as someone with a terminal illness (and maybe he had one, for all he knew). *God, please don't let this change us*, he said inside. But he felt at the end of his sentence that God had already responded . . . with a resounding, "Too late."

"Alright—this is gonna sound weird," Seth began. "So, please just hear the whole thing and know that I'm telling the truth."

"Seth, when have you ever *not* told the truth? It's your defining quality," Shannon said with a smile. But the smile faded quickly, like sunlight behind a cloud. "The fact that you're even saying that is freaking me out. Why would you—" Seth cut her off.

"Because this is *so* weird! Beyond weird. This is ridiculous. And I just need to know that the one person I love most isn't going to think I'm a nut job."

"Seth . . . I promise not to think you're a nut job, at least not any more than I already do." Her joke didn't have the impact she wanted, which reinforced her worry.

"Alright. Alright. Here it goes. So, you know Bill Watson, the pet store owner?"

"Yeah."

"Well, I'm pretty sure I saw him at the park. He was at least fifty yards away, so I guess I can't be sure. But I waved to him, and then he started running."

Shannon squinted. "Like, just running, or running *away*?"

"It felt like he was running away from me. So, I ran after him a little ways into the woods, just to see what was up."

"Okay." The tone of Shannon's voice rose at the end with expectation.

"And then I lost him. I couldn't see anything. But . . ."

"But what?"

"This is so weird."

"Seth, you know I hate being creeped out—just say it fast." Shannon was holding her knees. She'd jump even when Seth came into a room unannounced. Eerie stories weren't her forte.

"Alright, there was this big, this big boulder . . . and there was a door . . . like, *inside* it. Pushed into the rock—this old, white door."

"A door in a rock?" Shannon had expected something stranger for some reason, which immediately made Seth feel better, but he hadn't gotten to the cat yet.

"Yeah. It was white and . . . weathered, with this brass handle."

"Please tell me you didn't open it," Shannon said, growing noticeably more uncomfortable.

"No—God, no. You know me. I almost had a panic attack right there."

"Why?"

"I don't know. It just came out of nowhere. It does that sometimes." They both paused for a few seconds.

"Anyway, the ground, the dead leaves all around the crack of the doorway . . . something was . . . I don't know—*glowing* or something?"

"Glowing?" Shannon leaned in.

"Not, like, bright glowing, but . . . some kind of soft, whiter light. I don't know. This sounds so stupid now that I'm saying it out loud."

"No, it's not stupid. I didn't mean to—" Shannon started, but Seth cut her off.

"I know, I know. I'm just saying it sounds so weird. But that isn't the weirdest part." Seth looked under the wingback chair at Narnia, who was swishing his tail, eyeing them as if watching a play unfold.

"What's the weirdest part?"

"God, this is so . . . ridiculous. But you *promised*."

"Seth," Shannon said laughing. "It can't be *that* weird. Just tell me!"

"Alright. Alright. I started hearing a voice . . ."

"From Bill?"

"No, I couldn't find him anywhere. The voice was coming from . . . *him*," Seth said, pointing to the cat. Shannon tilted her head, trying to see if he was joking with her.

"Seth . . . if you're trying to joke with me—"

"Shannon, I'm not! I swear!"

"Cause I know this would make a good story for your writing, and sometimes writers try to convince themselves that their little fictional worlds are real and—"

"I'm not, Shannon. I'm not."

The two of them stared into each other's faces for what seemed like minutes. Then Seth put his head in his hands and took a deep breath. The smile that had been pulling at the edges of Shannon's mouth relaxed in seriousness."

"You're not joking," She said, not asking him for confirmation but stating a fact. Seth looked up and shook his head, staring into her eyes. "Well . . . the only things that come to mind are your counselor, and then maybe the doctor?" She looked at Seth for confirmation.

"Yeah, that was my thinking, too."

"You don't have any other weird symptoms—like odd smells or fatigue or—"

"All the stuff that would come with a brain tumor?" Seth interjected. "No, I don't. I feel fine. Everything seems normal except for this. But a brain tumor was my first thought . . . and my worst fear." He stared down at the carpet.

"Okay . . . well, let's start there," she said. Silence filled the room, expanding like a balloon. Seth put his head back in his hands.

"Hey," she said with a sincerity that drew Seth's head up. "Whatever this is, you're not doing it alone. We'll get through this."

Seth nodded. Shannon crossed the room, and they embraced. Seth was so grateful for this woman, this person who always met him where he was and promised to walk next to him—through grief, through crippling anxiety, through . . . whatever this was. He took a deep, cleansing breath and squeezed her body tightly against his chest, feeling the warmth of her skin and the floral scent of her straight, brown hair.

"See, I knew she would get it." Narnia's voice rolled out from beneath the wingback chair. Seth raised his eyebrows and tilted his head forward, as if scolding a child. "Oh, fine. But she is a wonderful woman, isn't she?"

Despite himself, Seth smiled and nodded his head ever so slightly. Shannon patted his back and then held his face in her hands. "I love you, okay?"

"Love you, too," he said.

"Anything else you need to tell me?" she said, more in jest.

"Well, I never ended up seeing Bill. I think it was Bill. It was like he disappeared into the woods."

"That's so weird. . . . I hate that," Shannon said, settling back into normalcy.

"I know you do," Seth said. He was well aware of her discomfort with anything paranormal, sci-fi, or, in her words, "just creepy."

"Wait . . ." she said, frowning in thought. She was connecting dots.

"What?"

"That news story, the one on the radio the other night—they said something about glowing lights under the ground."

Seth was surprised he hadn't made the connection. He didn't *like* the connection, but it was obvious. Lights under the ground, light under a door in the rock . . .

"Hmmm. This just got weirder." He took a deep breath.

"You okay?" Shannon could see already that this had caused a lot of anxiety and that more was on the way.

"Yeah, I guess." He swallowed audibly. "Anyway, I ran back to the truck after that. Had to get back to you and the kids. And . . . oh—that's when I saw Travis. Remember him?"

Shannon was happy to move the conversation to something else. "The one who always lost his temper and cursed like a sailor?"

"Yeah. Well, listen to this. He says he got beat up by a senior citizen."

"What?!" Shannon's enthusiasm showed how much more comfortable she was switching the topic.

"Yeah, he said some older man whispered something to his girlfriend that made her cry. And—"

"What'd he say?"

"He didn't get to that . . . but he said he chased the guy down the street and pushed him."

"He pushed an *old man*?"

"Well, I don't know if he was really old or not, but yeah. That is pretty low, now that I think about it. Anyway, he said the guy was humming 'Amazing Grace' when he got up and started punching him! Hit him in the eye and on his nose, and then he walked away while Travis was recovering."

Shannon's mouth hung open in disbelief. "Well, I'm kinda surprised Travis let him walk away," she said. She'd heard a few stories from Seth that gave her the impression that Travis wasn't one to let things go—especially that story of him cursing out a referee (and the entire team) during a basketball game.

"Yeah, me too. But I guess he did. That's all I got from him, and then I wanted to get back home, so I didn't linger."

"Okay." The tone was serious again as the swell of the story settled back into calm waters.

"So, are you gonna report that stuff, to the police—what you saw?" she asked.

"I don't know. You think I should? It doesn't really seem like a thing you tell the police."

"No . . . " Shannon agreed hesitantly. "But if that news story is already covering something like that, then maybe they'd be interested?"

"I guess. It just feels stupid."

"I totally get it," she said. "But even if it's nothing, it would be good to report it, in case something's in the water or the ground or something."

"What do you mean?"

"I don't know," Shannon shrugged. "I mean, if there's something weird in the ground that's making it glow or something."

"Like a chemical?" Seth said.

"Yeah, maybe. I don't know. I don't really have a science background, but maybe there's something there. Gotta be *some* explanation."

"You would think. I'll see if I can get over there tomorrow and let them know what I saw, but I'm gonna feel so stupid."

"Don't feel stupid. You didn't do anything weird. You're just telling them what you saw. Maybe they know what that door's doing there. That's *so* weird, by the way. But it could be for park equipment or . . . something else."

"Yeah, it could be. Anyway—that's all. I should clean up the kitchen before I head to bed."

"That'd be great," Shannon said. "Seth?" she said.

"Yeah?"

"Promise me you'll tell me if you start getting any other . . . symptoms or feelings or whatever."

"I will," Seth said. And then he turned to the kitchen for cleanup.

Seth found comfort in cleaning, in putting everything in its right place. Cleaning had always been his coping mechanism for anxiety—a way of setting the external world in order amidst his internal chaos. He washed the dishes and pots, enjoying the feel of the hot water on his hands as he scraped at dried food with his fingernails and then watched the hot water melt away the stains of egg yolks and peanut butter. When everything was in the drying rack, he wiped down the counters and took a deep breath as he surveyed his work. *Good*, he thought to himself. He hung up the dish towel and shut off the light.

When he got into bed, he opened the nightstand drawer to put his watch inside, like he always did. There, in the back right corner, was his dad's Bible. He'd always kept it there, but he seldom read it, not since the year his father had died. He picked it up, curious at his own interest in the moment. The black leather was soft and smooth from years of use. He opened it to the place where the black ribbon wedged itself like a memory in a tired, papery heart. There was a passage heavily annotated and highlighted, holding all the faded glory of an old map. It was the only passage he ever seemed to read before putting the Bible back in its place, 1 John 2:9–18. He read it again.

> He that saith he is in the light, and hateth his brother, is in darkness even until now. He that loveth his brother abideth in the light, and there is none occasion of stumbling in him. But he that hateth his brother is in darkness, and walketh in darkness, and knoweth not whither he goeth, because that darkness hath blinded his eyes. I write unto you, little children, because your sins are forgiven you for his name's sake. I write unto you, fathers, because ye have known him that is from the beginning. I write unto you, young men, because ye have overcome the wicked one. I write unto you, little children, because ye have known the Father. I have written unto you, fathers, because ye have known him that is from the beginning. I have written unto you, young men, because ye are strong, and the word of God abideth in you, and ye have overcome the wicked one. Love not the world, neither the things that are in the world. If any man love the world, the love of the Father is not in him. For all that is in the world, the lust of the flesh, and the lust of the eyes, and the pride of life, is not of the Father, but is of the world. And the world passeth away, and the lust thereof: but he that doeth the will of God abideth for ever. Little children, it is the last time:

and as ye have heard that antichrist shall come, even now are there many antichrists; whereby we know that it is the last time.

The words met his eyes, but Seth couldn't welcome them in. They were strangers sitting on the page, vagrants asking for a home. But he didn't have a vacancy. At least, he couldn't find one inside himself. And he suddenly felt exhausted. He closed the Bible, put it back in its spot, shut the drawer, and laid back down. He stared at the ceiling for a few minutes, muttering the phrase "the last time."

The final thought that crossed his mind before he drifted off to sleep was how awkward it would be to go to the police station the next day to report a door in a rock.

8

AT THE POLICE STATION

T HE POLICE STATION WAS in the center of town on Silver Lake Road, about a mile and a half south of the community college where Seth taught. He'd never been inside the dull brick one-story building. It was only a landmark for him, a birthmark on the long arm of Silver Lake Road, and Seth never paid it any attention.

He brought Narnia with him and left him in the truck. It had quickly become a habit to bring Narnia with him everywhere. And when they were alone, they talked as candidly and casually as best friends. In fact, to Seth's delight, their conversations quickly turned literary, especially when Seth mentioned his students writing about *Catcher in the Rye*.

"I've always thought," Narnia said, "Holden Caulfield had so much . . . potential; he just found himself in a world that measured things in all the ways he wasn't willing to compete with. It's as if the one thing he was most prepared to offer was the one thing no one was interested in—at least, they didn't know they should have been interested in it."

"Yeah," Seth agreed. "He's got . . . well, I guess I would call it a sort of 'pure heart,' but it was wrapped in defiance of the status quo—which everyone else seemed caught up in like some kind of current. And he'd made all these mistakes, but look at what he really wanted in the end: to keep other people from making the same ones. Of course, he couldn't, because that was a dream. But I've always been encouraged that he wanted to try, and he wanted that *more* than the alleged success of the rest of the people in his world."

"Yes. Well said. And it's tied deeply to the death of his brother, isn't it? His desire to lead and protect comes from loss. You think to yourself, 'If I can't stop something so ugly and evil as cancer, I must be able to stop *something*.' So, maybe it's also a longing for control. Alas . . . the human condition."

"Human!" Seth said with a laugh. "Says the cat."

"Well, am I wrong?" Narnia said, with his usual calm confidence. "Isn't being one of *you* nearly always about trying to come to grips with the lack of control you have—over anything? And what do you do with that? All sorts of things. You rebel. You seek what you think you can control (though that's an illusion). Or you stuff your life with whatever thrills the senses or strokes the ego. Only to realize it isn't what you thought it was. And then you're back to the truth of God, standing at his doorstep and lamenting your limitations. You fall into a relationship with him as if you had no other choice. Or else you kick dirt on his door and run back out into the wild." Narnia went silent for a few moments.

"Geez. That's kinda cynical."

"Sorry. Can be a bit of a downer when I drone on like that."

"It's okay. You make a good point. My dad was a preacher—"

"I know," Narnia interrupted. Seth nodded, still bewildered by the truth that Narnia really did know everything about him.

"Well, he always acted like God *wasn't* a last resort . . . the only option left when we'd exhausted our limitations. But . . . I never got it. I didn't understand." Silence filled the truck cabin again.

"He was a special man, your father."

Seth hadn't cried since the other day in the park. But before that, it had been a long time—years. He was freshly aware that he'd nearly forgotten how it felt: the swelling of the throat, the shift in breath, the warm rush of water to the eyes. He let the tears roll down again. And it felt *so* very good, as if his soul was taking in the mountain air.

Narnia said no more until they pulled into the police station.

"It shouldn't be too long," Seth said, wiping his nose and eyes.

"Take as long as you need. You never know where friends are hiding. I'll just sleep in the sun. It's what I do."

Seth locked up the truck and walked towards the double doors of the brick building. He was nervous. An officer was a few steps ahead and pulled open the door for him. Seth nodded, "Thanks."

The officer offered a closed-mouth smile. He was a few inches shorter than Seth, with a small belly that hung over his black belt just enough to suggest that he had some glory days behind him. But the way he walked made it apparent that he didn't mind this. He was comfortable in his own skin. Seth was jealous of that comfort, once again, and this registered with him in the moment. Whenever he saw someone who seemed completely comfortable, he thought about what that might be like: to simply *be*. His anxiety almost always kept him from getting there. He had to *try* to be comfortable in his own skin, which meant that he never really was.

The officer followed him into the station, where Seth walked up to a broad desk hedging in a receptionist who had her head down and was filling out a form.

"Morning, Gladice," the officer said as he walked past Seth and went into a room about ten feet past the desk on the left. Gladice picked her head up and noticed Seth.

"Hey, Tom." Her cheeks lifted in a tired but familiar greeting, the lines around her mouth etched in by years of habit. Then she turned immediately to Seth. "I'm sorry. Didn't see you come in, dear. What can I help you with?" Seth realized he hadn't thought about what to say before he got there, which made him awkwardly silent for a few seconds. He also realized he hadn't been called "dear" in about 20 years. At diners and restaurants around Dingmans Ferry, he was "Hun." But never "dear."

"I, uh . . . I guess I need to fill out an incident report. I'm not sure. I saw something strange, and my wife thought it would be good to come down here and report it. So . . ."

Gladice nodded and grabbed a clipboard from the side of her desk. She placed a form on it and then held a blue Bic pen to the top with her thumb. Seth looked at her thumbnail, ivory with age. His grandmother used to collect seashells of the same color and fill glass lamp bases with them. He still had one in the attic somewhere. Seth didn't move his hands out right away to take the form.

"Fill this out, then, dear. And we'll take a look. Any immediate danger or threat that we should be aware of?"

"Oh . . . no," Seth said, almost apologetically. "Nothing like that."

"Okay," said Gladice, smiling. "Good. You can just fill that out with a description. Make sure you add your phone number so we can reach out when we need to." Gladice's blue eyes, though tired, were sharp and attentive behind her clear plastic, square-rimmed glasses. Her skin seemed thin, nearly translucent in places, but glowing. For an older woman, she had striking vitality, an irenic yet lively presence wrapped in a weathered body. He could see the veins on the tops of her hands, little green pipes pushing themselves upward. They reminded him of his grandmother's hands, which he'd always thought were strangely silk-like. The sound of Gladice's voice was soothing—as comfortable in the room as the rest of the furniture. She'd been the secretary there for twenty-five years.

Seth took the clipboard and sat down on a brown upholstered chair in the corner. He hadn't figured out what to write where it said "Incident Description." He tapped the pen on his knee while he thought about how he could *not* sound ridiculous. The officer who had opened the door for him waltzed back up the hallway with a white, empty coffee mug. He met eyes with Seth, nodded, and said, "Name's Tom—Tom Regent." He held out his free hand toward Seth, who dropped the pen as he tried to figure out which hand to use for the handshake.

"Seth . . . uh, Seth Logan."

"Oh," he said smiling. "Any chance you teach down at the community college?"

"Yes, I do, actually," Seth said, bending down to grab the pen. "Why do you ask?"

"Well, my son, Ethan, he's one of your students. In your creative writing class, I think. Your name rang a bell. Don't know any other Logans around here." Tom's smile was widening and becoming more friendly.

"Yeah, Ethan! He's one of the few students I don't have to remind to keep his head off the desk," Seth said.

Tom chuckled. "Yup, he's always liked writing. My wife and I actually encouraged him to take a creative writing class—thought maybe that would give him an avenue for his talents. She passed about a year ago though."

"I'm so sorry. But . . . that's great about Ethan," Seth said. But his face was starting to hurt from smiling. He was trying to figure out how to stop smiling without losing the friendly spirit of the conversation. "They have their first short story draft coming up this week—"

"Oh, I know," Tom interrupted. "He's been hard at work this weekend. 'Don't go puttin' your mom and me in there,' we tell him—I mean, *I* tell him. Ain't done nothin' bad to you." Tom laughed at his own joke.

"Oh, I'm sure I'll get some interesting things. I always do."

"I bet," said Tom. He'd taken his police cap off, and the fluorescent lights were shining off the top of his bald head, speckled with short, brown, and gray hair. "Course, he won't share his stuff with us—I mean, with me. What kid wants to show his writing to his parents? But we always—I mean I always, sorry—see him scribbling in these composition notebooks we got for him at the grocery store. . . . He's a quiet kid."

"That's a good thing, I think," Seth said, surprised at his own comment. "I mean, I was a quiet kid and spent a lot of time writing, and my parents said it kept me out of trouble."

"Yeah, that's a good point," Tom said. He glanced down at his empty coffee mug, then raised it with a nod. "Well, I'll let you get back to it. Would ya' like any coffee?"

"No, I'm okay. Thanks. Already had my cup this morning."

"Alright, well you let me know if there's anything I can do for you."

"Will do."

Seth looked back at the blank lines on the form as Tom meandered down the hall towards a little room with a coffee maker and refrigerator. "This is going to sound crazy," he wrote. As soon as the words were on the page, he regretted starting that way, but he was at a loss and just wanted to get to the college as soon as he could. He was curious about Tom's son now. He finished the rest of the description, feeling more and more embarrassed as he wrote. Reading it over, he thought about throwing it away, or taking it with him back home, to look less awkward. Before he could decide what to do, Gladice picked her head up and noticed that he'd stopped writing.

"Finished?"

"Um . . . yeah. I think so."

"I'll take it and have someone look over it. Anything else you need, dear?"

"No, I'm okay. Thanks. Have a good day."

"You too," Gladice said with an extra big smile, as if she were truly happy that Seth had come in. "That cat yours, in the truck?" Seth felt a heat flash go through him. How did she know he had a cat in his truck? But his heart settled back into place when he looked out the window and saw Narnia lying on the dashboard, in plain sight.

"Oh . . . yes. Found him at the park a few days ago, actually."

"Oh." The smile fell from Gladice's face, and her tone of voice shifted, from cheerful to almost melancholy. She put her pencil down. "Just found him in the woods, did you?"

"Yeah. He was in a ball at the bottom of one of the falls—"

"In Childs Park?" Gladice interrupted.

"Yeah," Seth said with curiosity. "Do lots of animals get found there?"

"Mmmhmm," Gladice said, fading into thought as she stared into her tea mug on the desktop, wafting up steam toward her big glasses. After an awkward few moments, she looked up at Seth, as if emerging from a memory. She whispered something, but Seth couldn't make out the words. It sounded like "Suyung-yit."

"What's that?" he said.

"Oh," Gladice chirped as she realized she'd spoken out loud what was meant to be an internal thought. "Sorry, dear . . . just talking to myself. You'll find you do that a lot when you get older," she said, softening the moment back into normalcy. Seth tried to take the opportunity to recount how he found the cat. As he spoke, Gladice's eyes were fixed on his, unwavering. This made Seth squirm a bit, but he assumed it was more politeness than anything else. Seth finished, and she nodded, still without smiling.

"Well, you take care a' him, and he'll take care a' you," she said. Seth nodded and smiled. As he turned to leave the station, he realized that Bill Watson had said the exact same thing, word for word. Seth thought it must be a local expression he wasn't aware of. But an eeriness started climbing up the back of his mind. He got into his truck and started the engine.

"All good?" Narnia said.

"Yeah . . . I think so," Seth said. "Time to get to work." He put the truck in gear and rolled toward the edge of the parking lot, gazing up and down the street before pulling out.

The sun was bright now. The town was starting to wake and move, the brick and aluminum siding on the older homes warming in the gold light. His second favorite color was sunlight on old brick. The sight of it pushed the eerie feeling away. A few people, like ants emerging from an anthill, meandered out of their houses and sat on their front porches as Seth drove by, as if on cue.

"Must be a town thing," Seth said to himself.

"The porch sitting?" Narnia asked.

"Yeah—look at them all. Just sitting in their rocking chairs, like it's their job."

"Mmmm," Narnia said. "Ritual is the hearth of comfort."

"Who said that?" Seth asked.

"Oh, me I guess. It's not from any book I can remember."

"Hmph," Seth said, happy with the expression. He shook his head when he realized he was talking to a cat again, but he also became aware that this was feeling more and more commonplace—as if everyone *else* were crazy for not holding discourse with dogs and conversations with cats.

***

At the closed front door of a light blue house just a few hundred yards before the community college, Bill Watson peered out from behind a white curtain, staring at Seth in his truck until he was out of sight. A voice broke the silence as Bill closed the curtain.

"You gonna tell him yet?" Bill was still as stone as he stared through the curtain, holding his black, chipped coffee mug in his right hand, while his left hand rested on his hip.

"Nah . . . Cleft will tell him when he's ready."

"We're gonna need help," the voice said. "Not a day goes by when I don't see that fella showin' up where he's got no business—starin' at people. It ain't right. And people keep disappearin' to only God knows where. That boy William ain't the only one."

"I know, Dad. I know. But we still don't have a plan."

"Plan is to get him outta this town!" the old man grunted.

"That's not a plan," Bill said with his typical calmness. "That's a goal." He let the swish of another car passing the house fill the air before he finished his thought. "A plan starts with figuring out why he's here in the first place."

9

MEETING CLEFT

ONLY ONE DAY HAD passed before Seth got a call from the police station. It came right before dinner, which is what Shannon called "the witching hour," when the kids started to get restless before they ate.

"Hello?" Seth pulled the ivory cord of the phone toward the counter by the sink while he cut up tomatoes.

"Hi, is this Seth Logan?"

"Yeah, this is him. Who's calling?"

"Daddy! Look! Look at Livy!" Will yelled. Livy had a blanket on her head and was spinning around in circles. "She's a ghost!"

"Will, hold on, bud. Daddy's on the phone." He turned his body towards the wall. "I'm sorry, sir. Kids." The voice on the other side chuckled.

"It's okay—got one of my own. I get it. Course he's much older than yours, by the sound of it."

"Sorry, who's calling?"

"My apologies. This is the police station in town. This is Tom. We talked the other day when you stopped by to fill out your incident report. My son Ethan is in—"

"Oh, right. Yeah. Sorry I didn't recognize the voice right away. So . . . is there anything you need from me?"

"Well, we just wanted to thank you for bringing it to our attention. You've probably seen or heard the news by now, that something odd was reported at a local residence."

"Yeah, my wife and I heard that on the radio the other day. Honestly, I don't know if I even would have reported what I saw if it wasn't for that. Thought maybe my eyes were just tricking me or something. Anyway . . ."

"Well, we thought we'd offer you the chance to have a sit-down with the gentleman whose house was in that news story. If nothing else, we thought it might give both of you some closure. And we don't really want reporters getting too involved with it. So, if you'd like to come into the station and just have a sit-down with this gentleman and explain what you saw, we wanted to make that available to you. Course, it's up to you. And we'd need you to sign a confidentiality agreement, to protect the other resident and whatnot . . . and yourself, too."

"Protect him from what, exactly?"

"Oh, just from getting unwanted attention from some of the reporters and thrill-seekers around here. You'd be surprised how interested people get in stuff like this, in a small town without much to do."

"Right, umm." Seth paused and looked over at Shannon, who was trying to break spaghetti noodles in half over top of a steaming pot of water while Will and Livy crawled between her legs. She frowned and whispered, "Who is it?" Seth just shook his head and wrapped his finger around the cord of the phone a few times.

"Umm, sure. I can do that, if you think it'd help."

"Okay. Well, how about tomorrow morning. That work for you?"

"Well, I've got to teach a class—the one your son is in, actually—at 10:00am. So, as long as it's before that."

"Okay. How about 8:00am?"

"Sounds good."

"Alright. I'll get that set up, then. And we'll see you here tomorrow morning."

"Okay, Tom. See you then." Seth hung the phone up and turned to Shannon, who was trying to move between the stove, the kitchen sink, and the pantry with Will and Livy clinging to her ankles.

"A little help here?" She said, and then noticed Seth's serious expression. "Everything alright?"

"Yeah. Just the police station. They wanted to know if I'd be interested in coming by to talk to the other resident in town about what I saw at the park."

"The other resident?"

"The person from that house we heard about on the radio the other night."

"Oh. Pastor Cleft? That's whose house it is?"

"Yeah. Rumors travel fast, I guess."

"You're gonna do it?"

"Yeah, I think so. Tomorrow morning. If nothing else, it'll let us both get some closure or something. . . . I don't know."

"Seth, would you—" She nodded to her feet again as Will and Livy started pulling at her jeans. There was now a mouth mark in the denim where Livy had been biting her ankle.

"Oh, yeah. Sorry." Seth tickled Livy's ribs to get her off Shannon's legs. Her giggles shot into the room like butterflies set loose in a field. Then he crouched down and waved his fingers in the air. Will recognized this immediately and tried to warn an unsuspecting Livy.

"Livy! Run! Daddy's coming!" They squealed and bolted out of the kitchen and into the living room. Narnia sat still and silent under the wingback chair, occasionally chuckling, but quietly enough not to be noticed by the kids or Shannon.

"Now, if *I* bit someone's ankle, it'd be completely different, wouldn't it?" Narnia said quietly to Seth.

"Yes, it would," Seth whispered. Shannon glanced in through the kitchen doorway.

"Who are you talking to?" she asked.

"What?" Seth said out of breath as Will dug his fingers into Seth's calf. He glanced down at the wingback chair. Shannon saw Narnia underneath. Then she took a deep breath and nodded to herself as she stepped back into the kitchen. Seth could see in that moment how it bothered her that he wasn't just making up the story about the talking cat. He wondered if Shannon was giving more credence to the idea of a brain tumor. He thought it better to leave that conversation until later. A change of subject was needed.

"Hey guys!" Seth shouted. "Everyone—I have a name for our cat."

"*Our* cat, huh?" Shannon said with a smirk.

"Well," Seth said, "Your allergy test didn't show a cat allergy anymore, so I thought maybe we could—"

"That's another conversation," Shannon cut him off. "But go ahead—it just better not be a human name." Seth smiled, realizing that this meant Shannon's approval.

"Okay, okay. Listen up. Will, you remember the story Daddy read you last month?" Will released Seth's calf and rested on his knees, catching his breath.

"Yeah . . . the . . . conticles—"

"*Chronicles of Narnia*," Seth finished for him.

"Yeah, the chronticles," Will said, emphasizing the 'r.'

"Well, I think we should call the cat Narnia. What do you think?"

Will's eyes swelled with enthusiasm, and Livy matched his body language, though it was clear that she didn't know why this was exciting.

"I actually like that," Shannon said from behind him. "Never would have thought of it . . . but I like it." She smiled at Seth and walked back to the stove to check the pasta.

"Nar-ni-a! Nar-ni-a! Nar-ni-a!" Will chanted, approaching the wingback chair. Narnia's ears flattened as he realized that this energy was headed for him.

"Ah, yes," Narnia said, uncomfortable with the attention. "That *is* me, but you don't have to—"

Before he could finish his sentence, Will had picked him up and was awkwardly cradling the cat's body under his two arms, leaning back to put the cat's weight on his chest.

"Oh, Will—that's okay," Seth said. "I don't know if he likes that."

"Might as well," Narnia said under the din of Will's chant. And Seth noticed that the tone of voice suggested amused happiness, which he'd never heard from Narnia. "Kids will be kids, and cats will be cats." As he finished the last part of the sentence, he tried to shift his body in Will's arms. His bottom end was hanging off Will's forearm. "Like a broken accordion," he said. Will heard none of it because he'd now added a march to his chant.

"Hey, better you than me," Seth said.

"Who are you—" Shannon started but then stopped.

"Alright, go wash up for dinner," Seth said. As Will and Livy thudded down the hallway to the bathroom, Seth went into the kitchen to help set the table.

"Hey, umm," Shannon started. "Maybe this week at counseling you can bring up the voice thing with your counselor and see what she says."

Seth took a deep breath as he realized again the potential seriousness of hearing a cat speak. "Yeah," he said. "Yeah, I will."

"You still feel okay otherwise?" Shannon asked.

"Yeah, I feel . . . *good*, actually."

"Good," she said curtly. "And you'll tell me if you feel off?"

"I promised I would, Shannon. Really, I will. And I'll bring it up at counseling this week."

"Thank you."

She drained the pasta in the sink. Steam rolled out of the pot and filled the air. Seth stared at her there for a few seconds, watching her hands move and her eyes focus on the elements at hand, shifting between the strainer and the white ivory bowl filling with noodles and steam. He realized all over again how beautiful she was—her silky brown hair, straight and settled into perfect place; her green eyes, sharp and kind; her slightly pointed nose marking her profile and leading gracefully down to her lips and chin. Shannon started to put pasta on plates when she noticed Seth staring at her.

"What?" She said.

"Nothing," Seth replied.

"That wasn't nothing."

Seth smiled. "I still catch myself staring at my wife," he said. "That's all."

"Oh, brother." Shannon rolled her eyes.

"Don't you oh-brother me. I'm in love with my wife."

Shannon smiled without looking up at Seth, blushing slightly. Seth kissed her head and looked into her eyes before Will broke the moment wide open.

"I want six meatballs!" he yelled as he pulled open the drawer for the silverware.

"And I . . . and I want . . . and I want," Livy struggled to put the sentence together, piece by piece, like an ant trying to gather crumbs. "And I want . . ." she paused and held up her little hand, showing three fingers.

"You want three, Livy girl?" Shannon said. Livy nodded and went to the drawer to pull out her fork.

"Of all the things to name food," Narnia said from the kitchen doorway, "Only humans would come up with 'balls of meat.' I understand the reasoning, but it's still beastly."

Seth chuckled without looking up from pouring water into the glasses. "Meat . . . balls . . ." he said to himself. Will heard him and jabbed a meatball with is fork, turning it around and examining each side. "Meatball," he said in a dazed wonder. Then he connected eyes with Seth, and they both started laughing. They kept going until Seth's ribs hurt and Will had to run to the bathroom to avoid an accident. Neither of them could explain to Shannon and Livy what was so funny.

✳✳✳

Seth arrived at the police station at 7:55 am. He left Narnia in his Ranger. He'd had to sneak him out that morning. Shannon noticed that he'd been bringing the cat with him everywhere, and Seth didn't want to make it an odd thing because he seemed to rely on it so heavily. It was a security measure he couldn't explain, sort of like carrying around his little pill case with Xanax. He hardly ever used it, but it was nice just to know it was there. Something strangely similar was going on with the cat. He needed Narnia to be with him—everywhere. But this was getting impossible to maintain, now that Shannon and the kids were growing more attached to Narnia. Shannon hadn't yet asked him why he took Narnia with him when he left the house, but Seth was waiting for the question, like a deer waiting for dawn in the dark. It was just a matter of time.

The brass bells inside the police station door jingled as he stepped through, and Gladice met his eyes with a warm smile. The steam from her coffee drifted up before her face, giving her a mystical aura. "Hello, Seth," she said, as if they'd been neighbors for a decade. It caught Seth off guard. He had been expecting, "Good morning."

"Um . . . hi, Gladice," he said, staring down at the nameplate on her desk. In white letters on a black background, it read "Gladice Shoemaker." Just behind her nameplate was an open Bible. Seth noticed this and tried not to be obtrusive, but she caught him.

"My father's practice," she said, as if she'd had to deliver this defense a hundred times. "Always up early with the Lord." Those words—*up early with the Lord*—loosened something inside Seth's chest. They were the exact words his father had used to explain what he was doing each morning, when Seth found him hunched over his Bible with a mug of coffee, steam spindling up toward his heavy-bearded face—a black book before a black-haired man.

"No—that's . . . that's great," Seth said, shaking off the reverie. "My dad was a pastor, actually. So, I get it." A broad grin stretched across Gladice's wrinkled face, like sunlight expanding over a field. Seth regretted mentioning it; he didn't want to get into conversations about his dad. It still made him feel anxious, especially since his counselor told him he was likely suffering from PTSD, and mentioning his dad almost always meant mentioning his cancer.

"That's wonderful!" she said, her cheekbones were still raised high with joy. Seth nodded and then looked up and around the station to avoid eye contact. Tom's lumbering stride down the hallway ended the moment. He raised his left hand to say a wordless hello, sipping coffee from his mug with the other hand. He looked carefree, and the light yellow stain on his left shirt pocket made Seth feel more at ease, as if the circumstances weren't so serious.

"Sorry—mustard stain," Tom said smiling. "My wife never knew how I could put mustard on a breakfast sandwich," he said, sticking out his left hand for a handshake. Seth had already extended his right hand, but then pulled it back and stuffed it in his pocket.

"Neither do I," said Gladice, still glowing from Seth's announcement.

"Sorry—should've given you my right hand." Tom chuckled the way he had the day before.

"No, that's okay," Seth said. They all stood for a few seconds, letting their smiles fade.

"The other gentleman will be here any minute—"

"Oh, 'other gentleman,'" Gladice said, amused. "Come on now, Tom. It's just Cleft."

Tom nodded. "I suppose it wouldn't hurt for you to know his name by now: Cleft, Cleft Warrington." Shannon was right.

"You know him?" Tom asked.

"Sort of. My wife and I have been to his church a few times, some months ago."

"Well, I'm sure he'll be glad to hear that." Tom brought his mug to his mouth so he wouldn't have to add anything to his sentence.

"Such a kind heart," Gladice said. Tom nodded slowly. "Just lost his wife, too, only a month ago. Forty-five years . . ." Gladice shook her head. "She had Alzheimer's." Seth nodded, soaking up the information. Gladice rested the side of her face in her hand, with her elbow on the open Bible. Seth noticed she had it opened to 1 John 2.

"Wow, I was actually just—" Seth began, with Gladice's full attention. But before he could finish the sentence, the bells on the door jingled. They all turned to see Cleft, dressed in khaki pants and a blue Oxford shirt.

"Am I being ambushed?"

Seth thought he was joking, so he smiled, but then his smile was swept away by the seriousness in Cleft's face. But Tom chuckled, which brought out a smirk from Cleft, and the smiles spread all around.

"Oh, Cleft. Where's your jacket?" Gladice said, her voice full of maternal instinct. "It's only March!"

"Ah, I'm okay like this, Gladice. Almost April. And the sun's out. It's warmer than you think out there now," Cleft said.

"Not warm enough for no coat," Gladice said matter-of-factly.

"Can I get ya some coffee, reverend?" Tom asked.

"Thanks, Tom. That'd be great. Just black."

"Got it."

Cleft turned his body towards Seth, who was expecting a greeting but then quickly decided to make the first move.

"Seth . . . Logan," he said, offering his hand.

"Cleft Warrington. Happy to meet you." His smile was deep and kind. Seth thought he looked like an old bird, wise and wide awake—his long and noble nose, the straight, sharp ridge of his eyebrows, the smooth, long plains of his cheeks. Cleft took Seth's hand and stared directly into his eyes, so intently that Seth felt looked *into*, not just looked *at*.

"We should talk," Cleft said. Tom, who had been sipping his coffee in observance of the greeting, lifted his left hand from his hip and pointed down the hallway on the other side of Gladice's desk.

"Just this way, if you like," Tom said. "Got a nice little room for you, and I'll grab your coffee. Anything for you, Seth?"

"No, I'm okay. But thanks."

Cleft led the way. It wasn't until he brushed past him that Seth noticed a black Bible tucked underneath Cleft's left arm—the same way his father had carried his Bible. They sat down in a room with wood-panel walls, along with two mustard-yellow upholstered office chairs, each on wheels. An old collapsable table sat in the center of the room, the dark walnut veneer peeling away on the corners. There was a window on the outer wall, but besides that the room was bare.

"I'll get that coffee for you, Cleft," Tom said again. "And then I'll let you two be."

"Thank you, Tom," Cleft said, smiling. As Tom walked down the short hallway, Cleft turned his attention to Seth, who was already tapping his toes on the floor, growing anxious.

"So, Seth, before we talk, why don't you tell me a bit about yourself."

"Oh, okay." Once again, this caught Seth off guard. He thought they would just exchange stories and leave it at that.

Cleft, like Seth's own father, seemed interested in building a relationship with every stranger. This had always annoyed Seth as a kid, but now that his father was gone, he didn't mind it as much. He almost admired it, as a tendency that he'd never have, but as somehow more human, more settled into life, more alert of bridges that needed building. Seth was never comfortable enough around other people to take that sort of initiative, except with Shannon. He felt unprepared and awkward.

"I teach writing over at the community college. My wife, Shannon, and I have been married about fourteen years. Got two kids—Will and Olivia. Will's five; Olivia's three." The mention of his kids brought out remembrance on Cleft's face. Seth noticed his teeth, ivory with age and stained from years of black coffee, but straight and clean.

"You have kids?" Seth asked, feeling a bit embarrassed for throwing the question out so bluntly.

"Oh, yes," Cleft said. His smile slightly faded, from remembrance to reality. "Three—all grown now, and out in the wild world."

Tom stepped back in with a white mug of black coffee. "Sure I can't get you anything, Seth?"

"No, I'm okay. Thanks, though." Tom nodded and turned back down the hallway to his office, leaving Cleft and Seth alone with the silence and the steam.

"Sure you don't want some chamomile?" Cleft said. "It helps with nerves."

"Oh—do I look nervous?" Seth said. The words came out defensively, though he didn't mean them to.

"Just doing the foot tapping. My wife—she was a foot tapper. Chamomile was her go-to every afternoon, with a little bit of honey."

"Sorry . . . No, I'm good. But thanks."

"So . . ." Cleft said as he took his first sip of coffee. "You and I are supposed to talk, huh?"

"I guess so."

"Well, why don't you start? News travels fast in a town with nothing but a shopping center and a waterfall park. Plus, I'm just a crazy old preacher." Cleft took another swig of coffee.

"Okay," Seth said. Having only told Shannon about what he saw, he felt a renewed sense of embarrassment.

"Well, this is pretty weird, but I guess it is what it is and—" Seth started, but Cleft cut him off.

"Hey, by the way, do you have a cat?" A flash of heat ignited in the back of Seth's neck, spreading through his chest and arms.

"No . . . well, not really. But we—" He found himself unable to finish the sentence. Seth hadn't told anyone but Shannon about the cat. And the fact that his cat was talking to him made him instinctively guarded about the topic.

"Not really?" Cleft said with a grin.

"I mean . . . I found one several days ago. Not sure if he's *mine* yet, but he might be. I mean, how'd you know?"

"Just thought I saw a cat in your truck as I came in. Nice Ranger, by the way."

"Oh, yeah," Seth said with immediate relief. The heat flash subsided. "Thanks. I figured I'd leave him out there for this."

"You could've brought him in if you wanted to. Folks around here—they love animals." Cleft's smile grew more pronounced. "Sorry I interrupted you. I've gotta dog in my truck outside, Roland. Been with me fifteen years, 'bout as long as my truck, actually."

"Wow—that's . . . that's a long time for a dog," Seth said.

"Yeah, we go everywhere together. Thick as thieves," Cleft said as he raised his coffee mug to his lips again. "Anyway—sorry. Please, keep going."

"No—it's fine," Seth assured him. His foot, which had been tapping the whole time, relaxed and settled into place. "Anyway. I actually found the cat at Childs Park, which is where I saw this *thing*." Seth stared at the table as he spoke, rolling his index finger over the curling walnut veneer on the table corner, trying to grip the peel with his fingernails. Cleft set his mug down and gave Seth his full attention. "The other day I went back, just for a walk. And I saw—at least, I think I saw—Bill Watson out in the woods. Do you know him?"

"Bill Watson!" Cleft erupted with a chuckle. "I love Bill. Such a character, isn't he? I see him at least once a week when I pick up some things for Roland at Pets' Place. And in church. Gotta love his oddities. Think he's worn that blue dress shirt for twenty years!" Cleft slapped his own knee.

"So you know him pretty well?" Seth asked.

"Oh yeah—he's been coming to my church for about twenty-five years now. Probably should have led with that. You know I'm a pastor, right? People get all fidgety when they find out they're talking to a pastor, so I don't lead with it." Cleft stared into his coffee mug, still smiling. "It's like they think I'm some voodoo holy man looking for their latest sin or about to predict the end of the world . . ."

"Oh, no—I knew that. Shannon and I have been to your church."

"Oh, you have?!" Cleft's grin was authentic and curious. "That's great. Well, anyway. Just didn't want you to feel weird. But go ahead. I keep interrupting you."

"No—it's fine. I didn't know Bill went to the church. Anyway, I think I saw him in the woods, and I waved, but he didn't see me, so I went farther in to say hi." Seth didn't mention anything about Bill's strange look and the fact that he sprinted after him, off the path. But he noticed that the smile had left Cleft's face. He was serious now, studying Seth, which made Seth's anxiety rise like an ocean swell.

"Where was this, at the park?"

"Yeah, just above Deer Leap Falls—don't know if you know where that is, but—"

"Oh, I know," Cleft cut him off. "Been to that park so many times it's like my backyard." Cleft shifted his gaze to the table, staring into some reservoir of memory. He didn't lift his eyes when he spoke next. "So, you were at the top of it? Hmmm. . . . Gotta stay on that path," Cleft said, shaking his head. Seth found the comment strange but didn't say anything. It felt like Cleft was lost in a painting, and Seth didn't want to be the one to call him out of it.

"Yeah, well . . ." Seth said after a few moments of silence. "I went off the path a little and—"

"Oh, you did?" Cleft's face lifted from the table and set itself square with Seth's. In that instant, he had grown even more serious, almost concerned, his smile fading back into his broad cheeks like wind leaving a forest.

"Yeah, just to see if Bill was there," Seth said, almost apologetically. "But I didn't find him."

"No." Cleft replied, as if he knew that already. His gaze returned to the table, though his eyes now drifted to where Seth was fingering the curl of walnut veneer on the table corner. "Did you see anything else?"

Seth didn't know whether he would mention the white door or not. His palms started to sweat and his throat tightened.

"Well, that's the weird thing. . . . I, uh . . . saw—I saw some kind of . . ." Seth knew the word he needed to say but didn't want to utter it.

"Yeah?" Cleft was fixated on Seth's face, and Seth could feel it, even though he had followed Cleft's lead in staring at the table.

"This is really weird, but I saw some kind of light under the leaves?" Cleft looked down at his coffee cup and nodded, as if Seth had just mentioned seeing something routine, something *expected*. Seth went on, "I don't know how else to describe it. It was some kind of white light under the leaves, and that's when I ran back."

"Didn't see anything else?" Cleft asked. Seth froze. Did Cleft know about the door?

"No . . ." Seth decided to lie, but he didn't know why. "That's it. Anyway, I told the police what I saw, just because Shannon and I had heard the news about . . . about your house."

Cleft nodded and smiled. "Yeah—that's something, isn't it? First time I've ever been on the news," he laughed. Seth let out a sympathizing half-chuckle, relieved to be out of the previous subject, like a rabbit free from a tangled thicket.

"So . . . what did *you* see?" Seth asked, surprising himself. And as soon as the words left his mouth, he felt he was being too forward. Cleft took a long sip of his coffee, finishing it up, setting the mug gently down on the table. He looked at Seth with resolve.

"I'll tell you what. I've gotta get back home. Something I have to take care of that I forgot about. But why don't we do this: if you've got anything to add, why don't you stop by my house tomorrow afternoon, say 3:45 pm?"

Seth frowned but tried not to make it obvious. Why did Cleft ask him about *adding* to his story? After a few seconds of awkward silence, Seth said, "Oh—well, I thought we were gonna exchange stories. Did you not—"

"Well," Cleft interrupted. "I don't know if what I saw differs much from what you saw, but I'll lay it all out for you tomorrow afternoon if you like," Cleft said, rising from his seat.

Seth got the sense this wasn't up for negotiation, so he nodded.

"Okay. I can do that."

"Sorry to cut our time short. I just realized I forgot to do something. You know, old man's fading memory and all that." He smiled as he stood. Seth offered his hand. Cleft looked at it with a smile and shook it firmly.

"I'll see you tomorrow then?" Cleft said.

"Yeah, sure. I'll try to stop by."

"Okay," Cleft said as he turned and meandered down the hallway in no hurry.

Gladice looked up at him from her desk and said, "You take care, pastor."

Cleft smiled widely. "I will, Gladice. See you Sunday. Your devotions going well?" Cleft added as an afterthought.

"Oh, *so* well. Been reading John's first epistle, chapter 2—"

"That's my favorite!" Cleft burst in.

"I know! I know!" Gladice was brimming with joy. "I started just last week and said to myself, 'Now, Pastor Cleft's gonna love this!"

"Well, I do. My favorite book, you know."

"Oh, mine too, but I think I told you that," Gladice said. "And John's Gospel, too. My sister and I used to listen to our father read it to us."

"Oh, that's special. Well, how bout we share stories this Sunday after church?"

"I'd love that," Gladice said, clearly thrilled at the offer. Seth watched all this, mesmerized. It dawned on him again that he had been reading 1 John 2 a few nights ago.

And then, out of nowhere, Seth felt a cloud of sadness descend on him. He paused in the hallway as he searched his pocket for his keys.

***

Seth climbed into the truck. Narnia looked up at him, like a doctor checking on his patient.

"Are you . . . are you alright?"

Seth shook his head slowly. "Yeah . . . just a little sad."

"Why's that?"

"It's weird. I was fine until I heard Cleft and the receptionist—this older woman named Gladice—get all excited to talk about the Gospel of John."

"Mmmm," Narnia said with passion, as if he'd just tasted his favorite food. "Wonderful book. John's a real poet."

"Yeah," Seth said, half laughing. "Cause you've read it."

"Remember," Narnia said in a patronizing voice. "I know what you know."

Seth shook his head again. "Well, it's been a very long time since I read it."

"Of course, how could you not be excited to talk about that?" Narnia added quickly. "John's Prologue is like lightning on the dim sky of human history. Everything so gray and tired—full of faithless failings and shortfalls. Everyone just waiting for something to change, for some light to break the fatiguing weather of the world. And then the Son of Almighty God, the maker of light and life, he comes *here*. He makes himself a tent from bones, muscle, and skin. He gets *inside* the world. Inside it! Oh, it's enough to split history in two—it really is!"

Seth gawked at Narnia's rant before turning the key and churning the truck engine into motion. Narnia stared through the windshield at the bright blue sky, painted with wispy cirrus clouds. And then he spoke hesitantly, as if gauging whether or not he could jump across a great puddle.

"May I . . . offer a theory about why their conversation—Cleft and Gladice—made you feel sad?"

Seth was guarded at the suggestion, but tried to allow room for the conversation. "Why not? You know what I know, right?"

"Well, here it is—just a theory, mind you. In your family and your work, you have lots of little moments of joy, beautiful but fleeting things, from your enchanting children and your wonderful wife. But these things feel like drops of rain, don't they? They soothe for a moment; they comfort, but then they dry. And you're left still looking for the next one, looking for more water. And there are looming questions behind everything you can touch and taste and see. And that's where the trouble lies. Deep down, where no light journeys, ever since your father died, in the dark mystery of who you are and why you're here, you haven't had something joy-giving to stand on, a place to plant your feet even as the rain of your experience comes and goes. You know your life is lingering riddles and passing rain. And something is keeping you from asking the deeper questions. Those inspired conversations other people have, like the one for Cleft and Gladice? They remind you of that—"

"Alright . . . that's enough analysis for now," Seth said, obviously irritated, but also shaken.

"Remember, it was just a theory—"

"It's enough!" Seth yelled, surprised at his own anger. Narnia's ears went flat against his head. "It's enough," he said, trying to regain control of his voice. His heart was thudding like a drum. His anxiety slithered back into focus, wrapping itself around his neck.

Narnia looked the other way and put his head on his paws, and Seth took a deep breath and tried to settle into thought as he threw the truck into gear and pressed the gas pedal. He had a *good* life. He loved his wife and kids fiercely, and he usually loved his work. He had it far better than most people did. But . . . something was missing, something he couldn't name. And Narnia's words pressed down on that like fingers on a raw nerve ending. Whatever that something was, Narnia was right: Gladice's comment had awoken it. And for a split second, he imagined himself sitting in the pews with Gladice and Cleft, talking and laughing.

But the thought immediately embarrassed him, and he shook it off. The irritation he felt from Narnia's comment continued to gnaw at his insides, for the rest of the day and into the night—to the point where he opened his old Bible that evening and read 1 John 2 again. He'd read it a dozen times. The words hadn't moved, of course. But something inside of him had. Something was growing, deep in the black and silent soil of his soul, where all the leaves and limbs of time and memory decayed into the richness that leads to warm, dark homes for seedlings of change. Some seed had sprouted. Its shoot was weaving its way through the cracks and crevices, longing to be noticed. But the noticing hurt. That's where his anger had come from.

He wanted something he didn't have. And for the first time in a while, maybe even since his father died, he knew it was something he *should* want.

***

Seth pulled into Cleft's driveway the following afternoon. He'd told Shannon about it, and she said it made sense. "Cleft's a good man," she said. "I'm sure he's just checking in with you. And who knows," she said with an impish grin, "maybe he'll convince you to go back to church."

Cleft's white colonial house was nestled between two great Douglas fir trees. The landscaping was neat and clean, with fresh dark mulch covering the feet of evergreen bushes. A few tulip bulbs had sprouted as March was bowing down its head before April raised its shoulders, encouraging everything in dark homes of waiting to poke their green beginnings into the open air. "Must have a landscaper," Seth mumbled as he walked towards the navy blue front door. He took his hand from his pocket to ring the doorbell, but before he could, Cleft opened the door, greeting him with a soft smile.

That was the moment Cleft knew: *This is the one.* He was so relieved in that instant, as if he could finally drop the boulder he'd been carrying for years. He had been looking for what he called "the Seeker." But it would be a while before Seth knew what that meant.

"Hey, Seth. Come on in." He turned and walked down the main hall by the entryway, not waiting for Seth to follow, letting his brown leather slippers scuff the brick-colored tiles as he went.

"Thanks again for . . . uh . . . having me over," Seth said.

"Well, it's nicer to talk here than in a police station, I think." Cleft walked over to the coffee maker by the sink and filled his mug. "Coffee?"

"Oh, no. I'm okay. Already had my one cup. I can't handle too much caffeine. Makes me anxious."

"Me neither," Cleft said. "Not this late in the day. It's decaf."

"Oh . . ." Seth paused long enough for Cleft to look at him again. "Don't think I've ever even had decaf coffee. I'll guess I'll have a cup." Cleft raised his eyebrows in surprise and nodded.

"You take it black?" Cleft asked with his back turned. "Cream and sugar? Just cream?"

"Black is good. I like things the way they are," Seth said, but then wondered why he added the last line.

"Mmm. Me too. That anxiety—that a constant thing?"

"Pretty much," Seth admitted. It felt good to be this open with a stranger.

"That must be tough," Cleft said, looking down at the dark marble countertop.

"Yeah, well . . . that's another discussion, I guess." Cleft nodded and then poured a cup of black coffee into an ivory mug.

"Well, anyway, I take my coffee black, too. Don't know if I like things the way they are. But I like them the way they will be."

"Not a sugar guy?" Seth asked, bypassing Cleft's comment.

"No—quite the opposite, actually. Once I get a taste of sugar, it's hard for me to stop. So, I just do my best to stay away from it."

Seth took a sip and let the earthy, nutty taste of the coffee sit for a few seconds. He opened his mouth to let the liquid shift to the back of his tongue. Then he swallowed and noticed Cleft staring at him, which almost made him gag.

"Good?" Cleft asked. Seth nodded slowly.

"Yeah," he said. "Good."

"Good," Cleft said. "Very good." He was smiling to himself, still elated at having found *the one*. He had grown weary of seeking. He knew his time was almost up.

Seth took another sip and looked down at the table in front of him. He'd been looking at it since he entered the kitchen. The wood was stained dark and mapped with scrapes and gouges. But the ivory initials, "CJW," inlaid at the center, were what held Seth's attention. "This is a beautiful table," he said.

"Yes. Yes, it is." Cleft's voice housed pure and simple agreement. "An *old* table. Lots of history in it . . . and on it . . . and around it." Cleft stared almost through the table, burying his mind in memories like old leaves.

"What's the J stand for?"

Cleft took a deep breath in. "Jane." He said it resolutely, as if he were repeating a sacred name from history. "Jane was my wife."

Seth picked up on the past tense. "I'm sorry. Didn't mean to—" But Cleft cut him off with a polite head shake.

"It's okay. You didn't know. She just passed of Alzheimer's a month ago actually, but it was . . . a long time coming."

"Geez," Seth said. "I'm really sorry." Sympathy flooded Seth's mind. Ever since his father died, he had an immediate connection with anyone who lost someone. Loss is a club no one wants to join, but once a member, every person keeps his card close.

"Me too," Cleft said, staring back through the table again. Cleft was comfortable with the silence, treating it as a house guest. He would have been content to let it linger for more than a few moments, but Seth's audible swallow reminded him that not everyone felt that way.

"So," Cleft said, taking in another deep breath. "You want to talk about what you saw?"

Seth matched his deep breath. "Yeah . . . well, I think I said everything at the police station."

"Well, you didn't mention the white door." Seth's head shot up. The same wave of heat he felt at the police station went through his body. He gripped the coffee mug and shifted in his chair.

"I don't . . . Well, I didn't—"

"Oh, I know." Cleft's words were like a parent's who had to reprimand his kid a dozen times for the same disobedience. He offered a knowing smile. "I don't blame you. I probably wouldn't have mentioned it either, in your position. A white door in a rock, leaking light from beneath—sounds more like a dream than reality. . . . It's crazy. But, Seth, I'm gonna be straight with you, since that'll be easier for both of us."

Seth forced another swallow and took in a deep breath to settle the waves of adrenaline.

"This town is . . . *special*. It's been that way as long as I've lived in this house, which feels like an eternity now. People always waking up or . . . disappearing. Things happen here that I can't explain, that no one can explain. And I stopped trying to explain it a long time ago. Explanation is . . ." Cleft paused, searching for the right word. "Overrated. But it all starts with that door you saw in the woods. Now, I'm not gonna tell you to walk through it. That's your call. But if you decide to, I'll be here for you."

Seth was trying to process all of this, along with the embarrassment of having lied to a pastor. What did he mean by "waking up" and "disappearing"? And those words—"I'll be here for you"—were the same words his father had written to him in a letter before his first major brain surgery, when Seth was only eight. He felt his father in Cleft's voice. The next sentence Seth uttered was a surprise even to himself.

"Have *you* walked through it?"

Cleft almost laughed. "Yes . . . yes I have. Thank God."

Seth waited for him to continue, but he didn't. "What's in there?" he asked.

Cleft pulled his coffee mug to his lips as he petted Roland on the floor, whose golden head and white face were at his feet. Seth hadn't even noticed that a dog was in the room. As Roland's tail began to smack the kitchen floor with the excitement of being noticed, Cleft said, "Can't tell you that. Not my business. This is Roland, by the way. Best steward a man could have." Seth caught the word "steward" like a fish in a net. He'd heard that before . . . from Narnia. He stuffed the connection into his memory for the moment. He had too much to process.

"But Bill went through it, in the woods that day?" Seth asked.

"Can't tell you that either," Cleft said with resolve.

Seth took a deep breath, trying to decide if this was a prank of some kind, or something eerily more serious, maybe even cultic. He didn't know what to say, but he wanted to leave. Now. He felt like a rabbit caught in a cage. He was staring down at the table, trying to figure out how he could exit without being impolite.

"Think it over," Cleft said. "There's no rush."

Seth nodded, still dazed, and pushed his chair back. But Cleft's voice suggested he leave the chair where it was.

"Roland's been with me almost fifteen years. I take care of him, and he takes care of me."

Seth reached down to pet the dog's back. He was met with Roland's white, happy face and his dark eyes, coal black and beautiful.

"I've got my cat in the truck," Seth said.

"You name him yet?" Cleft asked.

"Umm, Narnia," Seth uttered.

"Now, *that* is a great name!" Cleft said with an enthusiasm that made even Seth smile. "You've read the stories?"

"Well, my dad read them to me as a kid. I don't remember much of them."

"Oh, well you'll have to read through them again. Hey—" Cleft paused, struck by sudden genius. "Read them to *your* kids. It's a perfect time. What are your kids' ages?"

"Will is five. And Livy is three. So, she's not quite ready."

"Yeah," Cleft agreed. "Three is too young. But Will might be able to follow most of them. 'Further up and further in,' aye?" Cleft stared at Seth for a response, but Seth just nodded and tried to avoid eye contact. "Sorry—you might not remember that. My favorite line. Been a sort of mantra for me for years." He trailed off into silence, lost somewhere in a thought country Seth could only stare at from a distance.

Seth couldn't keep himself in his seat another second. "I should . . . probably get going. I have one more evening class to teach at the college."

Cleft nodded. "Well, you're welcome anytime, if you want to drop by. God knows I love the company. So quiet in here without Jane, though she wasn't exactly talkative . . . towards the end." He said this with a wilting expression that made Seth's heart fall like a cannonball. "Towards the end"—he hated those words. He'd heard and spoken them so often with reference to his dad. And yet he didn't realize he hated them until that very moment, the way the sounds of the words pointed to some door no one could walk through except the one destined for leaving.

Cleft walked Seth to the front door and watched him climb into his Ranger, next to Narnia, sleeping on the dashboard. Seth didn't see Cleft nod at the cat, who lifted his head up and nodded back.

Once in the driver's seat, Seth clutched his bottle of Xanax as he turned out of the driveway and back towards Silver Lake Road. He couldn't think about anything other than what was right in front of him. He gripped the steering wheel and tried to keep breathing. Five seconds in. Five seconds hold. Five seconds out. His heart rate started to slow. Narnia stared at him.

"You alright?" Narnia said, his voice soaked in sympathy.

"Not really," Seth said, somewhat relieved at his own honesty. His doctor said, "Take the Xanax when you need to," and yet he always felt like a failure when he did, as if he were taking a step backward. But in the moment, the feelings and adrenaline were too strong to push through. At the next stoplight, he split a pill in half and swallowed the bitter crumb. "Teaching will help," he said to himself. "I've gotta do something."

"You *will* be alright," Narnia said.

"I know," Seth said, trying to believe him. "I know."

***

In the dark of his bedroom, Cleft turned on a bedside lamp and pulled a thick leather journal from his nightstand, turning to the last page. He scratched his chin as he stared at the page.

"Now—where are you, William? Where are you?"

***

Seth's evening class was a writing lab. Students had to construct a narrative that helped readers *feel* something. He could let them write for a good half hour without saying anything. That brought some solace. But he also knew that teaching was one of the best ways to take his mind off of anxiety. Maybe he'd analyze an excerpt with them first... Martin Luther King's "Letter from a Birmingham Jail." That had plenty of imagery and parallelism in it and could keep Seth talking for a while. He decided on that, and his nerves began to ease as he thought about the words, the way some of them group themselves together like children playing the same game at recess. "We still creep at horse and buggy pace toward gaining a cup of coffee at a lunch counter." He repeated the words out loud, grouping them into their little families. "We still creep / at horse and buggy pace / toward gaining a cup of coffee / at a lunch counter." He was still whispering the words as he walked into the classroom.

"Alright," he said resolutely, as much to himself as to his class. "We're going to look at an example, and then we're going to write for the remainder of class."

"Aww! I didn't know you had a cat," said a girl from the front row, lifting her head from the pen drawing she was inscribing on the top of her left hand. Seth noticed the shape etched into her skin—a door with a thin, slightly curved handle. His head burned with embarrassment as he realized he'd brought Narnia in with him.

Everyone looked up. Conversations fizzled out. Attention focused on Narnia, held by the chest in Seth's right arm, staring blankly at the students.

"Calico, man. Sweet calico," said Dustin, one of the students whom Seth hardly ever understood—in speech or writing. A few of the students acknowledged Dustin's comment, but most just stared at Seth, waiting for a response.

"I . . . I didn't want to leave him in the truck. If anyone's allergic, I'll take him back out." The students shook their heads as Seth scanned the room. Then he set Narnia down on his desk in the corner. Above the desk was a plain poster with a quote from Roald Dahl.

> Above all, watch with glittering eyes the whole world around you because the greatest secrets are always hidden in the most unlikely places. Those who don't believe in magic will never find it.

Seth let himself be distracted by the words for a moment as he processed the strangeness of his own behavior. Why? Why was he bringing Narnia with him *everywhere*? Why was there a white door in the woods? Why did Cleft say people were disappearing? He was rich in questions and poor in answers, and that stirred up more anxiety. But he took a breath and pushed words out with effort.

"We're going to look at Martin Luther King Jr. and his 'Letter from a Birmingham Jail.' He paused to see the students' reactions. There were none. They had no idea what he was talking about.

"Ah, the parallelism," Narnia mumbled, half to himself and half to Seth. "Beautiful—like mirrored dances between sounds."

"They don't—" Seth started but stopped abruptly, realizing he was talking to the cat that no one else could hear. Several of the students frowned, noticing that Seth's face had turned to address the cat on the desk.

"Dude, were you talking to your cat?" Dustin's voice came from the back. It lit a fire in Seth's face. Someone noticed. What should he say? *What should he say?* His composure was about to shatter like a glass vase. But before he could answer, Dustin addressed his own question and broke the awkwardness.

"I talk to my dog, like, every day. Petey—the guy's so mellow. He doesn't *answer* me, but I think he, like, knows what I'm saying . . ."

The class was staring at Dustin now, who realized in the moment he wasn't ready for that attention. He quickly looked down to end the monologue. Seth was strangely happy at Dustin's reaction, his embarrassment and discomfort, as if he'd finally come out of the strange world of self he'd lived in all semester, an invisible cocoon always sealing him off from Seth and the other students as he mumbled song lyrics amidst discussions of symbolism. There was a chance in the next few seconds that Dustin might actually hear something Seth said. And Seth took this as his escape route from the anxiety.

"Dustin, would you read the paragraph aloud that I'm passing around?" Seth pulled a stack of papers from his briefcase and started circulating them.

"Uh, yeah. Yeah, I can read," Dustin said, still uncomfortable.

"*Can* you?" came a jibe from the back row. Several students laughed. Dustin tried to ignore the joke, but it obviously hurt him. For the first time, Seth was noticing someone who had been practically non-existent this semester. And he thought then that maybe this boy, whom he'd utterly dismissed as disinterested, actually had something he wanted to say to the world.

And then came the reading. Dustin surprised everyone. His voice was bold, passionate, measured.

> For years now I have heard the word "wait." It rings in the ear of every Negro with a piercing familiarity. This "wait" has almost always meant "never." It has been a tranquilizing thalidomide, relieving the emotional stress for a moment, only to give birth to an ill-formed infant of frustration. We must come to see with the distinguished jurist of yesterday that "justice too long delayed is justice denied." We have waited for more than three hundred and forty years for our God-given and constitutional rights. The nations of Asia and Africa are moving with jetlike speed toward the goal of political independence, and we still creep at horse-and-buggy pace toward the gaining of a cup of coffee at a lunch counter. I guess it is easy for those who have never felt the stinging darts of segregation to say "wait." But when you have seen vicious mobs lynch your mothers and fathers at will and drown your sisters and brothers at whim; when you have seen hate-filled

policemen curse, kick, brutalize, and even kill your black brothers and sisters with impunity; when you see the vast majority of your twenty million Negro brothers smothering in an airtight cage of poverty in the midst of an affluent society; when you suddenly find your tongue twisted and your speech stammering as you seek to explain to your six-year-old daughter why she cannot go to the public amusement park that has just been advertised on television, and see tears welling up in her little eyes when she is told that Funtown is closed to colored children—

At this line, Dustin's voice cracked and a tear rolled down his cheek.

. . . and see the depressing clouds of inferiority begin to form in her little mental sky, and see her begin to distort her little personality by unconsciously developing a bitterness toward white people; when you have to concoct an answer for a five-year-old son asking in agonizing pathos, "Daddy, why do white people treat colored people so mean?"; when you take a cross-country drive and find it necessary to sleep night after night in the uncomfortable corners of your automobile because no motel will accept you; when you are humiliated day in and day out by nagging signs reading "white" and "colored"; when your first name becomes "nigger" and your middle

> name becomes "boy" (however old you are) and
> your last name becomes "John," and when your
> wife and mother are never given the respected
> title "Mrs."; when you are harried by day and
> haunted by night . . .

Dustin paused. "Harried by day and haunted by night," he whispered to himself. Everyone watched him, but he seemed not to care about the attention now. He was somewhere else, somewhere *in* the words. He continued a few seconds later.

> . . . by the fact that you are a Negro, living con-
> stantly at tiptoe stance, never knowing what to
> expect next, and plagued with inner fears and
> outer resentments; when you are forever fighting
> a degenerating sense of "nobodyness"—then you
> will understand why we find it difficult to wait.

Dustin's head dropped. Seth was amazed at the lyrical passion in Dustin's voice. Whispers echoed from the same corners of the room that had questioned Dustin's reading ability. "Why's he crying?" someone said. Dustin kept his head down.

This was the most beautiful thing Seth had experienced in a classroom. The words *worked*. And a person was painted before his very eyes. Dustin had always been there in black and white, faded by apathy. Now he was in color. The words had awoken him.

Seth didn't want to leave the moment, but he knew he had to. "Thank you, Dustin. That was . . . that was powerful." Dustin kept his head down and avoided eye contact.

"What Dustin just read had a lot of repetition in it, *intentional* repetition of grammatical structures, helping us see the relationships among the ideas. Did you notice that?" A few in the class nodded. Everyone seemed to be paying attention—a true miracle. And it was enough to background Seth's anxieties about the white door and his talking cat for the first time. He was in the moment, full of joy for the present. And that, he knew deep in his bones, was not something to pass up.

10

THE DECISION

T HE REST OF CLASS went by like a blur. Questions were asked. Comments were made. The enthusiasm for the topic was strangely palpable. Who knew community college students could care so much about parallelism? At one point, lost in the teaching moment, Seth looked down at Narnia on his desk and raised his eyebrows in surprise.

"Amazing, isn't it?" Narnia said. Seth was aware of his surroundings now, so he just nodded. "You know," Narnia said pensively. "Life is all about *this* for *that*."

"What do you—" Seth started but caught himself. He let the words roll around in his mind for a few moments. His right hand went instinctively to the two marbles in his right pocket. He rotated them around each other. Then he took them out and rolled them in his palm. He was starting to see more beauty in the fire of the one marble. And then Dustin's raised hand drew Seth's mind out of his pond of pensiveness, where he was still searching under the surface for the meaning in Narnia's words.

"So . . ." Dustin started, wheels turning. It was the first time he'd spoken since his reading, and class was almost finished. "I was just thinking. Is *waiting* a kind of suffering?" Seth was still stunned. Who *was* this kid?

"That's a great question, Dustin. Yes, I think it can be. I guess it depends on what's happening while you're waiting, and what you're waiting for."

"So then, the suffering could start to end if someone, anyone, decided *not* to wait anymore?"

"Well, yes. That could be true. Do you have an example in mind?"

"Yeah—yeah, I do."

Just then the other students looked up at the clock and started packing their notebooks and papers away. Dustin started to do the same. Seth wanted to ask him about his example, but he didn't want to pry. He banked on having another chance to ask. Who knows what sort of doors were opening up for this kid? Seth was genuinely, purely thrilled at the miracle that had happened in the last hour.

Seth gathered his things into his briefcase, trying not to monitor the girls petting Narnia. "I'm gonna have to take him now."

"Aww. What's its name?" asked one of them—Shirley Metcalf, who seemed to be oblivious to . . . well, nearly everything that was going on in class. She often took the lead in singing Cyndi Lauper. She kept stroking the cat under its jaw, mesmerized by the softness of the fur.

"Narnia," Seth said, trying not to sound rushed.

"Sweet," came Dustin's voice from behind Seth. "A cat from another world. I wonder if he can like, sing things into existence, like in *The Magician's Nephew*."

Honestly, Seth thought again, *who is this kid?*

"What's a Nernia?" Shirley asked. Dustin coughed out a laugh and walked past the group. Seth scooped up Narnia with a hand under his chest. "See you guys later this week."

Narnia mumbled as they went out to the hallway. "What's a 'Nernia'? What do these kids do if they aren't reading?"

"Sounds like something an old man would say," Seth said, catching himself and looking around to see if anyone else noticed. But he was in the clear as he approached the back exit of the community college.

"Maybe I *am* an old man. *You're* an old man, after all."

"What?" Seth said.

"You've been going to bed at nine o'clock since the ninth grade. Very geriatric. Nothing wrong with it, of course. I love an early bedtime."

Seth was fighting the urge to defend himself but decided to wait until he got inside the truck. As soon as the door shut, he blurted out, "Look, first, you've got to stop talking to me when I'm around other people. It's really hard not to respond and look clinically insane. Second, going to bed at 9:00 is just . . . healthy."

"Healthy?"

Seth stared at the cat for a moment but couldn't keep the smile from expanding. And then he started laughing, uncontrollably. Narnia belly-laughed and turned on his back, the fur of his chest rising and falling in pulses. Seth laughed until his ribs ached and his eyes watered. He didn't really know why it was so funny, and he didn't care. In that moment, as his heaves of laughter started to slow and he regained his breath, he realized that *this*—moments like *this* one—were what made his life a gift. Even with his grief and anxiety and plaguing self-doubt, life was better than the trouble; it was *more* than the trouble.

It wasn't all rain and riddles. It was, deep down at the foundation, an unexpected, often unopened and usually discarded *gift*. *Maybe there's something there*, he thought.

He drove back to the house feeling as if his soul had wings, as if he was only driving because he chose to. And if he really wanted to, he could fly.

***

He burst through the front door, setting Narnia down on the landing. Shannon was playing in the living room with Will and Livy, all dressed in their pajamas.

"Mommy," Will said with resolution. "I'm the only one today who listens . . . who was listening to Mrs. Lamping. All the other kids were breaking . . . they were rule-breakers!"

Shannon nodded sincerely. "You are *very* good at following the rules." Will nodded, as if the whole world already knew this.

When Shannon's eyes met Seth's, she could sense his joy.

"Good day?"

"Mmmhmm," Seth said with a grin. "Very good day, for no reason in particular. Just happy to be who I am and have what I have."

Shannon mixed her smile with a frown and then nodded with approval. "Well, get in here. These kids need a new horse to ride before bed."

"Daddy's home, guys!" Will and Livy rushed over and grabbed his legs.

"My Will and Livy! Are you hugging Daddy's tree legs?" They giggled and refused to let go. Shannon clapped her hands together to get their attention.

"Who wants to watch Fraggle Rock before bed?" she said. Seth stared at her in confusion. "It's a Muppets thing," she explained. "It's a little weird but harmless." Seth nodded. "It'll give us a few minutes to talk. I can see something behind that grin," Shannon said. Seth mirrored her smile.

Will and Livy pounced onto the couch. Will turned the knob on the wood-paneled Zenith TV as Shannon pushed the tape into the VHS. The TV and VHS were both fairly new. Seth had protested that they didn't need them, but Shannon wanted it for the news and thought the kids would love having a fun movie on weekends. The kids using it for the Muppets was a new development, but a very effective distractor.

The theme song from Fraggle Rock filled the room as Shannon and Seth stepped back into the kitchen. Seth was still staring at the orange-headed, pink-haired muppet running through a cave in the wall when Shannon broke his gaze.

"Hey, talk to me."

Seth smiled again at how beautiful his wife was, and it seemed one more gift added to the life he had just laughed about on the way home. *I am rich*, he thought. And he fully believed it.

Seth gathered himself with a deep breath, remembering that his trip to Cleft's house happened before his teaching high with Dustin. But he didn't have to sort out what he would tell Shannon because he always told her everything. He had learned early on in their marriage what freedom and peace there was in that approach, even if it got him into trouble sometimes.

"I went to Cleft's this afternoon. And . . . he knew about the door."

Shannon frowned. "Well, didn't you tell him about all that at the police station yesterday?"

"Well, I forgot to mention the door—"

"Seth," she interrupted, "that was like . . . the whole reason you went in."

"I just . . . I just felt weird about it, and so I didn't say anything."

"I don't know why you wouldn't—"

"I know, I know. I should've told him. But, anyway, it didn't matter. He already knew about it. And he knew that I didn't mention it."

"He thought you were lying?"

"I don't know. I think so," Seth said. "Anyway . . ." Seth paused for several seconds.

"What? What is it?" Shannon was growing concerned.

"He said . . . he said that people have walked through it—the door. He kind of hinted that Bill went through it. I think. And he said *he* went through it, too."

"Cleft said that?" she asked. "He said 'through'? Not 'in,' as if the door was just something the park used to store stuff?"

"Yeah."

"Okay . . . So, what's *through* the door?" Shannon knew it helped Seth's nerves if she tried to ask questions calmly.

"That's the thing: he wouldn't tell me."

"He wouldn't tell you?" Confusion and humor spread over Shannon's face. Seth couldn't tell if it was surprise or incredulity.

"No. He just said something like, 'You can walk through it if you want, and then talk to me.' He said the town was *special*."

Shannon's face lifted. "Seth, he used to say that in *all* of his sermons. That's just his way of making people feel valued."

"No, this was different. This was ... I don't know. It was like he was saying the town had a secret." They both looked down at the kitchen floor for a few seconds.

"Is that all he said?" Shannon asked. "Maybe there's just a really nice garden through that door?"

Seth answered with an eye roll. "Well, I started to have a panic attack on my way to the evening class, and I didn't know why, but—"

"Oh, Seth." Shannon's voice was weighted with sympathy. She walked over and wrapped her arms around his back. Seth returned the hug, despite his agitation at being interrupted.

"I'm sorry," she said. Seth was always amazed that this simple response made him feel less anxious.

"Just take it easy tonight, okay? I don't think there's some weird secret about our clunky little town out in the boonies. Cleft just likes making people feel like they have a purpose. And he's good at it."

Seth disagreed with certainty—about the door, not about Cleft. But he saw there was no way of moving the conversation forward—at least not yet. So he just nodded.

"Anything else?" she asked.

"Oh!" Seth blurted. "I had this amazing class tonight!"

"Really? I don't think you've ever described a class as 'amazing.'"

"I know, but there was this kid—Dustin—who always seems out in left field. But he got really emotional reading a passage from Martin Luther King Jr. And started making comments and asking these questions that were . . . just *incredible*. It was like watching words work on someone, like . . . like a kind of magic. And then the other students got involved, and it was like, 'Yes! This is why I teach.'"

"Awww! That's awesome," Shannon said. He always felt she was a better listener and enthusiast than he was.

"Yeah, it was really great."

"Well, let's think about things like that for now and not some weird door in the woods."

"Right," Seth said, happy at the suggestion but utterly unconvinced it would work for longer than one night.

"I know you don't agree with me," she said smiling.

"Well, I just—"

"Look, I don't know what this door is or where it goes. Just stay away from it. . . . They do have caves around here. You know, like the Lost River Caverns down near Bethlehem. Maybe that's all that's on the other side of the door. Don't overthink it."

"Yeah," Seth said. He hated the truth—that this was so obviously *not* what was on the other side of that door. There was too much depth in Cleft's voice for there only to be a cave, and what cave would emit light? And what did it have to do with people waking or disappearing? None of it made any sense.

Besides, to his own surprise, Seth was feeling that there was only one thing he could do to put this whole thing to rest: walk through the door. Even though Shannon had told him not to, he could just open it, look inside, and then ask for forgiveness later. There couldn't be anything really abnormal on the other side. There couldn't be. Dingmans Ferry was far too dull to have any secrets.

***

Seth didn't have class the next day until 1:00 pm. That would give him the whole morning. He could leave for the community college around 8:30 am and stop at Cleft's house—not to talk, just to tell him that wanted to know what was on the other side. Even though Cleft had made it clear that he wasn't going to tell Seth anything, he figured his persistence would at least get Cleft to go there with him. And that settled his nerves a bit. If Cleft was willing to go with him, then at least someone would be there if anything weird happened. "Unless . . ." he told himself. "Unless Cleft is in on it." But Seth revoked the thought right away. There was no *it*. This was just a door. He only needed Cleft there because Cleft knew what would happen when Seth turned the handle.

The plan settled his nerves until he pulled his Ranger into Cleft's driveway the next morning. Seth's throat was tight and his heart thudded like a drum, as expected. Before he opened the door, he glanced down at the bottle of Xanax in the middle of the seat and took a deep breath. He was not impulsive. He was not brave. He was not adventurous. What was he thinking? Doubt and dread made his limbs heavy as he opened the door and swung his legs off the driver's seat.

Cleft was sitting on the front porch in an old rocking chair, a cup of coffee resting on the right armrest. He looked at Seth as a passionless observer, as if Seth were a blue jay that just happened to drop down on his lawn. As Seth walked closer, he realized that Cleft wasn't looking at him. He was staring past him. Seth looked over his shoulder in the same direction and then looked back at Cleft.

"Cleft?" Seth's voice broke Cleft out of his daze. Cleft blinked several times and then turned his eyes toward Seth, lighting up with a smile. *Did he really not see me?* Seth thought.

"Seth! Good morning! I was hoping you'd come by."

"Yeah, well . . . Thought we should talk again."

"Hmm," Cleft agreed. "Yes. Yes, we should. I'm sorry if our conversation the other day was off-putting. Didn't mean it that way. After you left, I thought about what you said about your anxiety, and then I felt badly about it."

"Oh, it's okay. It's just how I react—to pretty much everything. I was born into the world with tortured sensitivity."

Cleft smiled at the wording. "Hmm. Me too . . . me too. Still, I hope you'll accept my apologies."

"No apology needed," Seth said.

Cleft nodded and tapped the armrest of the rocking chair next to him. "Have a seat," he said. "Unless you'd prefer to stand."

"I like rocking chairs, actually. I'm a foot-tapper (like your wife was), so it gives my feet something to do," Seth admitted. Cleft smiled as Seth made his way up the porch steps and into the rocker. It was a little closer to Cleft than he would've liked, but he thought it would be awkward to move it. He let his body rest in the old, gray wood, softened by years of rain, shadow, and sun.

"So," Cleft said. "Where do you wanna walk?"

"Walk?" Seth asked.

"Oh, sorry. It's just an expression my father used all the time. He said a conversation was like taking a walk through the woods. Whenever we talked, he'd start by saying, 'Where you wanna walk?'" Cleft smiled in reflection.

"Hmm," Seth nodded. "I like that image."

"Yeah, my father loved words. Loved what they did. He said they were magical. In fact, that's probably one of the reasons why I became a pastor. I just *love* words." Cleft paused.

"Me too," Seth said contentedly.

"Oh, that's right!" Cleft said. "You're a writer! Well, you're in good company."

"How did you know I was a writer?" Seth asked, not bothered, just puzzled.

"Well, I make it my business to know what people love in this town. When you and your wife started attending the church some months back, I asked around just so I could get a handle on things."

Seth nodded. He didn't really want this to turn into a discussion about church, and it seemed to be drifting that way.

"So," Cleft broke the short silence. "Where you wanna walk?"

"That door," Seth said as Cleft stared off into the distance in front of them. "You won't tell me what's on the other side. . . . But would you, would you go with me?"

Cleft smiled. It was a smile that immediately reminded him of his father, and in that moment, he felt like a child. Cleft took an audible breath filled with parental compromise.

"I'll walk with you up to the door if you like. But I can't go through it with you. We each go through alone, but you won't be alone after you go through. I can promise you that."

Seth stared at Cleft, waiting for him to say something else, but that was it.

"I am the door," Cleft almost whispered.

"What?"

"John 10:9," Cleft said. Then he tilted his head back and closed his eyes. Seth tried to breathe softly so that he wouldn't give away his awkward discomfort. "Think about that one, before you decide to walk through. Okay?" Cleft said.

Seth nodded slowly. He had no idea what that meant, but he didn't want to look like an idiot, so he said nothing. Then he glanced down at his watch.

"I've got class soon, so I should probably get going."

"Sure," said Cleft. "Was nice of you to drop by. You're always welcome."

Seth believed him, and he thought of how strange it was that he would believe someone who said something so personal, and yet he barely knew Cleft. Something was different about him, but Seth couldn't label it. And he didn't want to either. He was comfortable with the mystery of knowing that another person welcomed him for no reason, especially when that person reminded him so much of his father.

***

His first class that day was slow: Research and Writing Methods. This wasn't the student-driven, emotional high from the previous class. Students lacked motivation, as they usually did. And there was no Dustin to pull them out of a stupor. A few girls at the back hummed Cyndi Lauper on repeat. Seth tried to hide his annoyance. Surely, something better had to be on the radio two years later. He'd had "Shout" from Tears for Fears stuck in his head, off and on that month. Why couldn't they hum *that* song? But no—it was "Girls Just Wanna Have Fun" . . . over and over. Seth was angry with himself for getting "Just-a-wanna" lodged in the rocks of his memory.

He'd asked them to start researching the background to one of their favorite songs, thinking that would be a way to get them into the research process. He wouldn't make that mistake again.

One of the guys in the front row scribbled out a rant against the latest Journey song, claiming that everyone has to "just stop believin'." Seth was pretty sure he wouldn't be able to read through a first draft of that one.

But the time wasn't all diluted. Every class, Seth had started a practice of choosing one student's essay from a previous session, reading it thoughtfully, and writing comments before returning it to that student at the end of class. Some students didn't care about this, and his comments ended up in the trash. He wondered why students didn't have the decency to at least throw it out in a trash can *outside* his classroom. But the few real writers in each of his classes loved when he did this. And Seth had started to choose only their essays to read over. He'd felt guilty about it at first, but then he gave up caring. Was it favoritism to give time only to those who wanted guidance? Maybe.

The essay he'd chosen for that day was from his advanced creative writing course. It was from Ethan Regent, the policeman's son, titled "The World Beneath," and Seth was enraptured with it. This kid had a gift. The introduction sent him off into a sort of trance.

The World Beneath

by Ethan Regent

I like the world beneath because it speaks without speaking. It tells a story that no one listens to but everyone needs. No one praises the dirt, but everyone is part of it; everyone stands on it. We need what lies beneath us. And maybe if we found a way to listen to its story, we'd be . . . awakened.

Ethan had written much about nature in his other essays. His prose had an earthy feel to it that Seth loved. But this essay was mysterious—something in it evaded him when he tried to pin it down. He also couldn't help associating it with that report of underground lights at Cleft's house, the one he and Shannon had heard on the radio. And there was that word again: awakened.

Seth read the introduction again and then set it down on his desk. He looked at Ethan, who was scribbling away on his yellow notepad, the pencil lead scraping the surface with wild enthusiasm as he etched his presence into the concrete world. Seth knew the feeling: the muse. He smiled as he packed up his things.

"Alright. That's all for today. Remember to have a list of five sources you found that provided some background on the song you chose, in addition to a sentence about the reliability or authority of each source. We'll use that for some discussion next—" Seth stopped short. No one was listening. They filed out of the door like ants going to find better food elsewhere. All of them rushed out oblivious to his words, except for Ethan. He was still trying to gather his things into his backpack, but he looked frantic, disheveled, anxious.

"Ethan, do you have a minute?" Ethan picked up his backpack as he finished zippering it, stepping to the side of the rush, obviously embarrassed.

"You didn't do anything wrong," Seth said with a smile. Ethan just nodded. "Your essay on the world beneath has really been working on me. Thought-provoking." Ethan stared down at his shoes and nodded with a bashful smile. "I'll let you know when I have comments ready, okay?"

Ethan nodded again (his default communication). He turned to leave, but Seth couldn't resist.

"Hey, Ethan?" And this time Ethan picked up his head, brushed the hair away from his eyes and looked right into Seth's face. And Seth could see some unrest living there. "I was just thinking . . . your essay reminded me of that news story the other week. Have you heard about it? The lights underground?" Seth said all this with a smile, but Ethan immediately turned pale, as if someone had drilled a hole in his heart and let every ounce of bravery drain to the floor. Seth noticed and immediately lost his smile. Ethan swallowed and nodded.

"It was just a random association, I guess," Seth said. Ethan nodded again and looked back at the floor. "I'll let you go. Keep up the good work, okay?" Ethan walked away, more briskly than Seth had seen him walk down the halls. Ethan's usual walk was more lumbering, like a tree shifting its rooted feet back and forth. But this was different; this was panicked. This was disturbed. There was a story in his steps.

***

As Seth drove home with Narnia sleeping on the seat next to him, he thought about the door in the woods. He hated that he couldn't stop thinking about it, because every time he did, his throat would swell up and adrenaline would start pumping. But the thought kept coming back like a cut in his mouth that refused to heal. He'd made the decision to walk through the door already; he just had to commit to it. *Nothing weird will happen*. He kept repeating that to himself. Though he had planned on keeping his decision from Shannon until afterward, he thought better of it now. He couldn't keep things from her. He'd run the idea by her and see what she thought. She seemed to like Cleft, so Seth didn't anticipate any resistance. *It's just a door*, he repeated in his head. *Just a door.*

He walked into the house and set Narnia down, who waltzed over to his den under the wingback chair. Will and Livy ran out to him, bouncing with enthusiasm. Will was bursting with news.

"Daddy, listen to what I told Livy. I taught her this!" Will said, glowing with pride. Livy took a deep breath and prepared for the recitation.

"Daddy, did you know that swaps . . . that waps . . . that, that *wasp* don't die when they sting you, but . . . when bees die . . . when bees . . . when bees" Livy looked over to Will for support. Will whispered in her ear so she could finish. "When bees sting, they die?"

Seth was disturbed by their continual references to death, as if it were a casual event like skipping a stone. But he tried not to let that dampen his praise.

"Wow, Livy! I *didn't* know that! You are *so* smart." She looked down at the floor, smiling while lifting her shoulders up in confidence. She always did this little shoulder shrug when she was confident. It was one of Seth's favorite gestures. He felt the whole world rise up when she did it, like a boat lifting on a wave.

Will was quick to intervene. "Daddy, *I* taught her that."

"That's really great, Will. I'm so glad you're being a good older brother to her. Hey, where's mommy?"

"Oh, she said she needed some quiet time. She's in her room. Me and Livy are gonna build a pillow fort. Wanna come inside?"

"*Yes*, I do! But let me say hi to your mommy first, okay?"

Seth padded up the stairs as softly as he could while Will began barking orders to Livy about what pillows and blankets they would need. Livy was happy to comply with one hand (the other was needed for finger-sucking).

"Hey," Seth said softly as he opened the bedroom door. Shannon was laying on the bed. "Everything alright?" He could see she'd been crying.

"Yeah . . . Just got some bad news."

"What happened?"

"Beth . . . just found out she has cancer today."

"Oh, geez. I'm so sorry, Shannon. My God . . . "

"We talked this morning for a while on the phone; we both were crying. It's breast cancer . . . early stages, so that's good. But . . . her kids and her husband—I just can't stop thinking about them."

Seth sighed. Cancer was a truth for him, part of the world's ugly, decomposing landscape ever since he lost his father. It wasn't as shocking to him anymore, that people actually died this way, but that did nothing to shed his discomfort and fatigue at the mere mention of the word.

"I can give Dale a call tomorrow," Seth said. "It's been a while, but maybe we can do something to help them." Dale was Beth's husband—a tall, thin, quiet man with glasses and a crew cut. His joints always seemed thicker than his limbs, but he was a carpenter and surprisingly strong given his lanky appearance. Seth had helped him demo part of their house a few years ago. He remembered being impressed with Dale's ability to sledgehammer a wall over within a minute or two.

"They didn't give their kids details, I'm guessing."

"No," Shannon said, wiping her cheeks and gaining her composure. "They said mommy has a special sickness that she needs hospital medicine for. Ryan and Amber don't know more than that." Ryan and Amber matched Will and Livy in age, and Shannon frequently took them on playdates together. And then there were occasional afternoons at the nursery when the four of them would explore the greenhouse and look for salamanders under the rocks that hedged in the perennials in the back of the shop.

"God, I hate cancer," Seth said.

"I know you do. I do, too." Shannon got up and wrapped her arms around Seth's back.

"We'll help them through this, okay?" Seth spoke with resolve. If cancer did nothing else good, at least it made people intentional.

Shannon nodded her head against Seth's chest. Seth knew this wasn't the time to bring up going to the park with Cleft on Saturday. Though it was consuming his thoughts, he'd save it for later that evening.

***

After the kids were in bed, he found Shannon on the couch and sat down next to her.

"Hey," he whispered. Shannon was holding a pillow with both arms and looking out the window. "I think I'm gonna meet Cleft at Childs Park on Saturday, have a look at that door together."

Shannon turned towards Seth. "Really? You feel like doing that?"

"Well, I think so. Cleft seemed to think it might help."

Shannon raised her eyebrows.

"What?" Seth said.

"Nothing. It's just that I haven't known you to be adventurous like this."

"Hey, I can be adventurous."

"Buying a different brand of pretzels doesn't qualify as 'adventurous,'" she said. They both chuckled.

"Good for you," she said. "Cleft's a good man."

"Yeah . . ." Seth said, realizing the truth of what he was about to say. "He is. Reminds me of my dad in some ways."

"Oh yeah? How so?"

"Well, some of his facial expressions, and always carrying around that black leather Bible, like my dad used to."

Shannon smiled and rested her head on Seth's shoulder. "I wish I could have met him."

"I know," Seth said. "He would've loved you. I have no doubt."

Seth went up to bed a few minutes later and checked on the kids. Will was sprawled out like a starfish, as if his whole body were ready to embrace the world. Livy still had her two fingers in her mouth, clutching a blanket in the other hand. He stared at her tiny profile, the little forehead curving towards her eyebrows, the small bump of her nose, the tiny impression above her upper lip, leading down from where her nostrils met. And those tiny, delicate lips. He stared at her for a good thirty seconds. Then he stared at Will. He was trying to impress the images on his memory, to keep something that he could return to, like a shell taken from the ever-moving ocean.

Seth often felt that his life was like a shore. He was never fully comfortable in it, fully at home. And the shoreline was always shifting as he tried to memorize it. That was the primary assault of his anxiety: making him an alien in his own skin by foisting his lack of control in front of his eyes. He wondered again what it might be like to not think of his surroundings all the time, to not have his mind constantly darting off into fears, insecurities, and even daydreams. Everyone else around him seemed to be more settled. He wanted that so badly. But he never really had it. And he'd started to give up hope that he ever would. He began accepting his "tortured sensitivity." But that was just a poetic way of saying he was constantly unsettled, like a bridge on top of ceaselessly stirring water. *What might it be like to be still?*

He climbed into bed thinking about that Saturday. "It won't be a big deal," he told himself. It was just a hike, with a pastor. And yet he knew that this was only an attempt to quiet something that was coming, an unexplainable dark or light that could be either nothing . . . or everything. The lump in his throat told him to brace for the latter.

11

TRAVIS'S GRANDAD

Travis hadn't seen the old man who'd given him a black eye since the day it happened. He'd been back to the part of town where the skirmish took place, but he never saw the old man there again. He'd been staying at his uncle's house for the last few days, sleeping on the leather couch in the family room, next to a coffee table littered with old newspapers and spy novels. There was a giant candle the size of a milk carton sitting in the center of the coffee table. His uncle had made the table from maple wood back in his high school shop class. On the underside were carved the date, 10/13/1973, and a few initials.

Travis was running his fingers along the carving under the table as the light poured in through the bay window that morning. Bill Watson's footsteps creaked on the floor, making Travis's head shoot up from the couch. Bill was wearing the same blue dress shirt that he had on the day before, and the day before that.

"Gotta open up the shop. You wanna give me a hand?"

"Yeah . . . just lemme eat breakfast."

"Your eye looks better this morning. That bruise is starting to fade."

"Still hurts."

"I suppose it will for another few days or so." Bill turned to walk towards the kitchen, mumbling, "Guess he's still got it."

"What?" Travis said with sleep in his voice.

"Oh, just said he's still got it."

"Who?"

"Your grandad."

"My grandad?"

Travis's mother, Tara, told him years ago that his grandad was dead, that he'd died from a heart attack. His mother and father had been separated for a few years, and he spent more time with his mother. So, he took her word as truth. Lately, he'd been coming around his uncle's place in an attempt to gain more independence. His mother was fine with it, though she knew her brother was quirky. But she had forgotten about the lie she'd told Travis. It was so long ago, and Travis never asked a follow-up. The truth had slipped between the floorboards of the ever-moving present. But Bill had a way of grabbing secrets by the corner before they fell through the cracks. This was one of those moments.

"Hold on—are you saying that grandad is alive?"

"Mmmhmm." Bill didn't even look up from washing dishes in the sink. Travis stood up and marched into the kitchen.

"And you're saying that my grandad gave me a black eye?!"

"Mmmhmm."

Travis stared with wild eyes at Bill, who was using his fingernails to scrape a remnant of runny yolk from a plate under the steaming faucet water. Travis was at a loss for words. Why wasn't his uncle surprised by this? Why didn't he tell him sooner? Where did his grandad even live? Travis had a mind to find out so he could pound on his door and ask for a second round.

Bill finally shut off the faucet, put the plate in the drying rack next to the sink, and looked at Travis as he dried off his hands with an old red towel. His eyes pierced Travis's confusion and anger, making Travis step back in discomfort. Travis didn't often look straight into Bill's eyes. There was a strength there that he wasn't comfortable with—some kind of authority built to an imposing height from invisible blocks of time, and it made Travis feel smaller.

"Your grandad . . . he's a strange man, but that's because he's seen some strange things."

"What kind of things?" Travis's brow was still furrowed in confusion and anger.

"Well, that's not for me to tell you. He can tell you if he wants."

"Well, where does he live?"

Bill chuckled to himself. "I don't know."

"You don't know? You don't know where your dad lives?"

Bill's chuckle was rolling into a laugh. "I'm sorry—not tryin' to rile you up or anything. It's just that he went AWOL a few years back and then refused to tell us where he was living when he showed up again." Bill was wiping his eyes from tears of laughter.

"Why is this so funny to you?" Travis was growing annoyed.

"He's just odd is all. Like I am, I guess. Got it from him, I suppose. He's always been that way. It makes me laugh just like it did when I was your age. Your grandma always called him an odd bird, God rest her soul."

"You're not at all offended that he punched your nephew in the face?"

Bill regained composure. "Oh, no. No, no. I talked to him about that straight up. Told him he had no business doing that."

"And what'd he say?"

"Well, he said he did it for your own good."

"My own good?! What the hell kind of grandad punches his grandkid in the face!?"

"Now, settle down a minute." Bill gestured with his hands toward the couch, but Travis was beyond consolation. He was already pulling on his jeans and searching for his sneakers.

"No! I'm gonna go find that bastard! I can't believe you knew about this."

"Where are you gonna look?" Bill still showed no signs of alarm or surprise.

"I don't know . . . down by the gas station where he punched me. What do you care?"

"Well," Bill said, "You come on by the shop after that if you like."

"Think I'll take a rain check on that," Travis huffed.

"Suit yourself," said Bill.

***

Bill's keys jingled merrily as he waltzed across the pet store parking lot. The sunrise was gold and brilliant, bathing the asphalt and the red bricks. Bill paused, looked towards the mountain ridge in the east, and took a long breath in. Then he held it for five seconds and let it out slowly. As the oxygen rushed to his head and eyes, he smiled. He stood there for a few moments, just feeling the sun warm his cheeks, his wrists, and his fingertips. "Amen. Amen. Amen again." That was his routine praise before he went inside the shop.

He unlocked the door and turned around to twist the lock closed again. But he knew someone was in the store already. He could hear a faint breathing. And he knew that breathing.

"Dad . . . how'd you get in here without the key?"

Sitting on a pine bench beyond the checkout lane, under the front store windows that faced Silver Lake Road, sat Lemmuel Watson, Bill's father and Travis's grandad. His hair was a brilliant white, curling several inches out from his Gatsby cap, resting mid-cheek on his matching white beard, which extended far enough below his chin that a gentle wind would move it. His face was pink, his eyes a sharp blue (like Bill's), and something in his demeanor was both wild and wise.

"Can still pick a lock as good as anyone, son."

Bill nodded and smiled. "Why'd you come by?"

"Wanted to check on my grandson."

"And you thought he'd be here?"

"Well, you let him open with you on some days. I took a shot."

"Yeah, well he isn't coming today. Too angry . . . at *you*."

"Thought he would be. So you told him?"

"Course I did," said Bill. "Can't have him thinkin' the town is laced with old men lookin' to pick a fight. Plus, it was just time he knew. And you better watch yourself. Kid's gotta temper and fists to go with it."

"I can handle myself. But I'm glad to hear he's a fighter. I have a feeling we'll need him."

"What are you talking about *now*, Dad?"

Just then the doorbells of the shop jingled as Travis pushed through the entryway and turned around the closed sign. "Nothin' to do in this town this early in the morning any—" Travis froze and his face went first pale and then red with rage.

"The hell are you doin' here?! Didn't know I was related to a senior version of Michael Spinks." Travis didn't know what else to do after this remark. He'd thought of it a few days ago, but he never figured he'd be face to face with his adversary to deliver it, let alone follow it up with . . . what? Another punch? A demand for an explanation?

"Just settle now, son. I was only—"

"I'm not your son! Didn't even know I was your grandson til this morning. What kinda grandad gives his grandkid a black eye while he sings 'Amazing Grace'? You're crazier than my uncle, and that's saying something."

"Hey, now. Don't bring me into this. I had nothing to do with anything," Bill said as he straightened a display of red dog leashes.

"I only sang that song," Lemmuel said, "because that's what I was givin' you: grace."

Travis's eyes looked like they might shoot out from his face.

"Grace!? Are you kidding me?" He stepped forward and got close enough to taste Lemmuel's breath—the stale smell of old cheap coffee. Lemmuel stood taller and clenched his hands into fists. The two were poised this way for a few seconds before Lemmuel broke the silence.

"She tell you . . . what I said?" Lemmuel asked, without breaking his gaze.

"No—Cassie didn't say anything because I'm sure it was messed up and perverted."

Lemmuel stared deeply into his grandson's eyes. He wanted the words that were about to leave his mouth to sink in, and they did.

"I told her what I told her grandmother after I came back from the war."

At this, Travis's demeanor changed. He pulled his face back from his grandad's. His eyes settled and searched Lemmuel's face. He had missed something.

"What's that?"

"A poem, the one that's etched on her tombstone.

> All I wanted were the eyes that held me
> When my eyes could hold no more.
> I will follow you, my dear, sweet Maggie,
> Through every closed and open door."

Travis's body relaxed as he took a step back. He'd misjudged the situation, and there was nothing for him to do now but stay silent.

"Cassie was very close to her grandmother, and I loved her grandmother fiercely. So, it was fitting that I tell her I wrote the poem she'd memorized from a thousand trips to the cemetery, where she faithfully lays flowers by her grandmother's grave. But then you came along with your ego puffed up like a sail in the wind."

"Well, what was I supposed to think?" Travis said, anger returning to his voice. "Some old man I don't know whispers something to her and then she starts crying. What would you have done?"

"Maybe ask a question or two."

"Yeah, but *your* solution was to punch me in the face? Your own grandson?"

"Only after you shoved an old man to the pavement, remember."

Travis breathed out a smile and looked up toward the ceiling, shaking his head. He really was caught in this one, with no way out.

"And the humming of 'Amazing Grace'—what was that about?" Travis's voice was calming, filled more with curiosity now than with rage.

"Ah, yes. You see . . . Travis," said Lemmuel. And at this first mention of his name, Travis finally felt the kinship and respect he should have had for the old man. "Most people think grace is a calm and quiet thing—a warm embrace, a pleasant gift. But *grace* is the thing that strikes your soul so violently that it turns in the best direction." At this comment, Bill stopped fidgeting with the dog leashes and smiled at the wisdom of his father. *Always had a way with words*, he thought to himself.

"Grace is amazing, grandson, because it forces you to go a different way. It is an act of love both *healing* and *hard*." Content with his expressions, Lemmuel closed his mouth and stared at Travis for a few moments before sitting back down on the bench.

Travis was silent. He turned and looked at Bill, and then back at his grandad. "So," he said with the most earnest voice he'd ever uttered, "What's the different way I'm heading in now?"

Lemmuel looked at Bill, who nodded in mysterious agreement. Taking in a deep breath through his nostrils, which drew Travis's attention, Lemmuel spoke three words that Travis would never forget.

"To the door."

12

WHAT HAPPENED TO ETHAN

O NE DAY EARLIER, ETHAN Regent sat on a stump with his fishing pole resting in Dingmans Creek. His father had just taught him how to catch crayfish. Now he was hooked. In a plastic yogurt container filled with an inch of creek water, three of them gently swished on the bottom. He had just hooked a fourth when he heard rustling in the leaves behind him. He turned to see in the distance a man walking uphill towards a great boulder. He recognized the man but couldn't place him. What caught his attention was that the man went behind the boulder but never came out the other side.

He set his fishing rod in the dry leaves and started walking towards the boulder. "Hello?" he called. No answer. *He has to be there*, he thought. "Hello?" He came to the edge of the boulder and walked around to the opposite side.

His heart stopped. There on the ground, an old man was lying unconscious.

"Hey, mister! Hey!" He bent down and slapped the man lightly on his cheek. "Hey, you okay?"

The man's eyes opened slowly as he stared up at Ethan. "I left it . . ." The man mumbled.

"You left what?"

"I left it . . . open."

At this, the man's head fell back down onto the leaves. Ethan followed the man's arm to where his hand rested, in a crack . . . in a weathered white door cut into the boulder. Light streamed out and warmed Ethan's face. He stretched out his fingers as he bent over the man's body, took a deep breath in, and started to smile. His whole body began feeling warm, as if a heated wave were washing over him, pouring sunlight into his veins. He was grinning now, ear to ear, basking in the light, holy in the heat. Slowly, he stood and stepped over the body beneath him. As if pulled by some great magnet, he moved forward, pushed open the door, was enveloped by the light, and vanished.

***

Ethan woke up staring into the canopy. He felt strangely calm, as if he could lay there for days. He heard leaves crunching and slowly turned his head. The man who had been unconscious was now looking down at him. He wore old khaki pants and a flannel shirt. His hair and beard were bright white, and two piercing blue eyes gazed into Ethan's from beneath the brim of an old Gatsby cap.

"You okay, boy?"

Ethan stared back into the man's face with no intention of speaking. Speech felt unnecessary. He seemed drugged into calm acceptance. But he wasn't dazed; he was lucid. Something was deeply different. It was his *perspective*. That's the word he would use later. His perspective was reborn, awakened. At the moment, it was as if the old man, a complete stranger, was more known to him than his own family, as if this man *were* his family.

"I shouldn't have left it open," the man said thoughtfully, his mind drifting elsewhere like a cloud scudding toward the sun. "I just had to stare at it again." He paused for a moment, the wrinkles around his eyes showing a shift in mood. He was coming back from some distant place and landing in the present moment. "Listen, boy. You can't go back. Now you're part of us."

Ethan pushed himself up onto his forearms. "Back where?"

"To who you used to be before you went through that door," the man said. He offered his hand to help Ethan up. Once standing, Ethan brushed the bits of leaves and pine needles from his arms.

"But . . . I didn't go anywhere," Ethan said. And yet somehow he knew that wasn't really true. He *had* gone somewhere. He had been someplace. Where? He could only remember how he felt when his body was engulfed by the white light and he stepped through the door. Where had he gone?

The old man was about to speak but then thought better of it. He took a deep breath and said, "Name's Lemmuel. But you can call me Lem."

He put out his hand to shake Ethan's. But Ethan raised both of his hands and looked at them, as if seeing them for the first time. He turned them around in the sunlight and then pushed his right one out to take Lem's hand.

"Ethan," he said calmly.

"Well, Ethan," Lem said as he turned away. "You're a gazer now."

Ethan frowned. "Where are you going?"

"Home," Lem said. "I'm going back home for now. But you should go and talk to the reverend. He makes pancakes on Saturday mornings. You'll like those." He smiled and walked towards Park Road, hidden behind the trees.

Lemmuel was going to his cabin, a mile up the hill on which Childs Park rested. But he paused at the Davidson's old barn and meandered back to the eastern wall. On the boards, he traced his fingers over the carved letters. YCGB. "One day, Maggie," he said. "One day . . . but not yet."

***

Ethan walked slowly back to his bicycle resting against a hemlock tree in the gravel parking lot. He felt thoughtless, not machine-like, but purely functional, unhindered by distraction or concern. It was the first time he truly understood the word "peaceful"—not just the dictionary meaning, but its shape, its scent, its contours as a chair finely crafted for a sitting soul. There were no intruding thoughts, just the moment and his body within it. He smiled, feeling the muscles in his legs as he pedaled the bike down the Park Road hill towards Silver Lake. Holding the handlebars made his hands tickle. He gripped harder and smiled—all the way back to his house about three miles from the park. He rolled into the driveway as his father was getting out of his police car.

"Well, you look happy," his father said. "Didn't do anything you shouldn't, did you?" He chuckled before Ethan could answer. That had been the second time this week he'd said that. Ethan shook his head and ran past him to the front door.

"What's the hurry, son?"

"I need to write something down."

Ethan pushed open the door, sprinted through the living room, and made his way down the hallway. He felt his hands would explode if they didn't get to a pen and paper. He pulled out his journal, turned to the last blank page, and without even knowing what he wanted to write, began scribbling words. What he wrote at first surprised him, then puzzled him, and then made him nervous.

Unless a seed falls, awake and alert,
Down to the dark and waiting earth,
It remains forever alone and asleep,
Awaiting a seeker to rise and reap.

He finished scribbling the last word just as his father knocked on the door.

"Everything okay at school this week?"

"Yeah—just normal."

"Still enjoying your creative writing class?"

"Yeah, sure. Professor Logan even said I should call him by his first name . . . but it feels too awkward."

"What's his first name?"

"Seth."

"Well, I'd probably do the same thing in your position. Always called your grandad 'Sir' growing up." Tom smiled in recollection. "You sure you're feeling alright? You've been awful quiet ever since you went searching for crayfish at the creek."

A surge of heat rolled down from Ethan's head, across both cheeks, and down his back. He swallowed and almost coughed as he answered.

"I'm good. Just thinking and writing a little more, that's all."

"Okay . . . well, I'll leave you to it." With that, Tom waltzed back down the hallway to the kitchen, whistling to himself. He always whistled when he was uncomfortable. He didn't even like whistling, but he never knew what else to do.

Ever since his wife Karen had died a year ago, he'd been losing the ability to have deeper conversations with Ethan. There was no bad blood between them, just a growing foreignness, as if each of them were developing into circles on separate pieces of paper, both of them growing more aware of their isolation.

***

It wasn't until later that afternoon that Ethan had his first "vision," as he later described them to Cleft. The sun was setting, the sky a pale pink mingled with gold on the bellies of the clouds.

His dad was standing on the lawn, watching the neighbor cut the grass with a new Petty Blue riding mower, a large "43" decal painted on the front. Tom didn't hate his neighbor; he was just irritated by him in every possible way. Robert Gurssel was just five years older than Tom but always made sure he mentioned his age as a factor in his financial ventures. "Takes time to learn this stuff." That was his go-to line. And he always used his latest purchase when Tom just happened to be outside. Some weeks ago it was his charcoal gray Audi 5000S Turbo. He waved casually to Tom out the passenger window as he drove towards town. Robert Gurssel—with his blond floppy hair and his stupid, clear plastic aviator glasses pressing into the sides of his rotund face.

And here he was mowing his half-acre lawn with a Petty Blue. Tom had just over an acre. He could've used that more than Robert, no doubt. In fact, it was ridiculous for Robert to have one. But everything about Robert was ridiculous. Tom stood there with his hands on the metal handle of his Snapper Craftsman push mower, staring with irritation.

Ethan glanced out the window. That's when he saw it. At first, he didn't even know what he was looking at. Was it a big black puddle, running across the front of their house? No. It was moving. It was *slithering*.

Ethan sprinted down the hallway and through the living room. In a panic, he looked towards the kitchen. He'd need a weapon, something big. He went to the corner of the granite countertop where they kept the knife set and pulled out a chopping knife the size of his forearm. Then he burst out the front door, yelling louder than he thought he could.

"Dad, look out!"

Tom jumped back, tripped over his own feet, and fell onto the lawn next to his mower. "What?! Ethan, what is it?!"

The only word Ethan got out before he started chopping was, "Snake!!" He swung the knife down again and again on the black, scaled body, three times as thick as his own neck. But then he paused and stood back. His knife had been cutting through it too easily, as if he were cutting through the air, through nothing.

"Ethan . . . what the hell's gotten into you? What . . . what are you doing?" Tom was more bewildered than he'd ever been in his life. His son—his quiet, thoughtful, patient, artistic son—was chopping at their lawn with a kitchen knife. Robert glanced up from his Petty Blue and then shut down the mower.

"Tom, you alright? Ja' fall or something?"

Tom didn't answer right away. He was still trying to come back to reality from what seemed like another planet. Was his son losing his mind? Did he have a mental breakdown? He read that artistic types can do that. But all he could do in response to Ethan was stare with his mouth hanging open.

"I got divots and groundhog tunnels a bit over there," Robert called from across the way, pointing to the front corner of his yard. "Tripped myself a few times when I wasn't payin' attention. Always gotta watch your step in this grass."

"Yeah," said Tom, pulling himself off the ground.

"I used to have an old Snapper like that one, too. Sometimes my sneaker tip would get caught under the hull when I stopped to clean the blades off and had to rest it on my foot. But you gotta clean them blades or the mower won't last. Learned that the hard way. Takes time to learn this stuff."

Tom just nodded and walked over to Ethan. "Let's go inside a minute." Robert started up his Petty Blue, shaking his head and smiling. Once Tom and Ethan got inside, it was uncomfortably quiet.

"You wanna tell me what's going on?"

Ethan was dumbstruck. He saw it. He *knew* he saw it. But when he walked slowly back to the front window and looked, there was nothing.

"Ethan?" Concern hung in Tom's voice.

"I thought I . . . I thought I saw something . . . in the grass."

"Something you'd kill with a kitchen knife? Was it a rat? A groundhog? What?"

"It was a black snake."

"Gardner snake?"

"No. Bigger. Much bigger."

"Well, if it was black, it coulda' been a rat snake."

"I must have thought it was . . . I don't know. I'm sorry." Ethan was as mystified as his father was now.

"Hey, it's okay. No need to apologize. I just want to make sure you're okay. Scared me half to death."

Ethan nodded. He walked into the kitchen and put the knife, caked with dirt and grass roots, into the sink. "Sorry, Dad."

As he walked towards his bedroom, Tom stayed in the living room, staring after him. Ethan sat down at his desk, his arms and legs still tingling with adrenaline. What had he just seen, or *not* seen? In his mind, the snake was like a mutant reticulated python. But it was black, blacker than midnight in a cave, blacker than the dread of death. But what haunted Ethan now were the red eyes—dark and deep, like the color of blood. He'd only seen them from a distance, but it was enough to give him goosebumps. He looked down at his arms. His hair was still raised.

That's when he remembered the words of the old man he'd found by the white door. After Ethan had regained consciousness, the man said, "You should go talk to the reverend." Ethan only knew one reverend, since there was only one church in town. And he knew exactly where he lived. It was Friday. The man said something about pancakes, which Ethan always associated with Saturdays. He'd go tomorrow, early. He'd heard the preacher say more than once that he liked to wake up before dawn.

With his dad still asleep the next morning at 7:00 am, Ethan wheeled his red Schwinn Bantam out of the garage and began coasting towards Cleft's house. He had no idea what he was getting into, what he had gotten into already simply by walking through that door. But for the moment, he tried only to think of pancakes.

13

THE BEGINNING GLORY

E THAN PULLED HIS BIKE into Cleft's driveway around 7:30 am. But he wasn't the only guest. Seth had parked his red Ranger next to the front porch and was sitting in a rocker beside Cleft holding a cup of tea. But he rose to his feet when he saw one of his students randomly show up at the last place he expected. What would a college kid want with Cleft?

Cleft, however, seemed unsurprised at the chance meeting and stayed in his rocking chair, sipping black coffee and smiling.

"Ethan? I didn't know you were coming here."

"Hey, Professor Logan. Sorry, but I didn't expect to come here either." At this remark, Cleft leaned forward and grew more serious.

"Everything alright?" Cleft asked.

"Um . . . not . . . not really. But I didn't know you'd have company." Ethan seemed ready to turn his bike handles in the opposite direction.

"It's alright—you don't have to go. In fact, Seth and I were just about to take a ride up to Childs Park. We'd be happy to have you join us."

"Yeah, that's actually what I wanted to talk to you about. I'd rather not go, actually."

"Oh, I think you should come. Might find some answers. As Jesus said, we just need to stand at the *door* and knock." Cleft raised his brows at Ethan, whose face went red. He knew the emphasis in Cleft's voice was no accident. And that made Ethan even more terrified than before. He felt a golf ball in his throat and thought he might vomit right there on Cleft's front lawn.

"It'll be a short trip, and I'll drive." Cleft spoke as if he were taking two children to a playground. "Hop in," Cleft said as he pulled his car keys from his pocket.

Ethan wheeled his bike over to the bushes in front of Cleft's porch and set it down slowly.

"No kickstand?" Cleft said.

"I took it off. Didn't want it there." Ethan was visibly anxious and gave no hint of light-heartedness at Cleft's remark.

Cleft noticed immediately and let the smile fall from his cheeks like rainwater. "Son," he said, pausing until Ethan looked at him in the eyes. "You're *gonna* be alright." Ethan nodded and meandered over to the backseat of Cleft's hunter-green Ford Escort. As they pulled out of the driveway, Ethan stared at his bike, convinced that he should have followed his gut and driven back to his house. Whatever was coming next wasn't something he had prepared for.

***

Cleft pulled into the gravel parking lot at Childs Park, shut the car off, and then turned his body to face Seth and Ethan.

"Listen up." He spoke like a father, but Seth and Ethan were anxious enough to happily submit to his tone. "I'm gonna tell you some things, and I'm gonna give you choices. You each make your own choices from here on out. I'll be a guide and resource for you, but that's all."

"A *guide* and *resource*? To what?" Seth said, realizing that his comment came off somewhat defensive. "I mean . . . it's just a door?"

"Don't go through it, Professor Logan." The words slipped off Ethan's lips before he could stop himself, but he also was certain that these were the words he *should* say. Whatever was happening to him since he'd gone through the door, it wasn't normal. It was beautiful at first, until the mutant snakes.

"Now, Ethan," Cleft said, sounding more and more like a parent. "Seth can make his own choices. It'll just be the three of us; there's no pressure for anyone to do anything they're not comfortable with."

"Looks like we've got company," Seth said. A maroon, wood-paneled station wagon pulled up beside Cleft's Escort. In the back seat was Travis. Lemmuel was driving, and Bill was in the passenger seat. Cleft took a deep breath, acknowledging that everything had just gotten more complicated. Everyone opened their car doors and stepped into the warming sunlight, their breaths visible in the late March morning.

"Lem," Cleft said with a nod. "Bill. What brings you out here?"

"Initiation for Travis, here," said Lemmuel, as if he were taking his grandson fishing for the first time. Bill was content to be quiet.

"You've got some yourself, I see." Lemmuel let his sharp blue eyes rest first on Seth, then on Ethan.

"We're just taking a walk," Cleft said. Lemmuel let out a soft chuckle.

"Bet you are . . . Why don't you all get a head start? We've got some things to talk about with little Travis here."

"Don't call me little, *Grandpa*," Travis snapped with sarcasm. Lemmuel just raised his hands in self-defense, still smiling.

"Alright you two," Cleft said, turning to Seth and Ethan. "Let's take a walk."

"Wait. Seth, what are you doing here?" Travis asked. "You know something about this?"

Seth was about to open his mouth when Cleft cut him off.

"We'll just take our walk, and then you take yours. We can talk afterward at my place. Okay?" Everyone nodded in agreement. Seth followed Cleft into the woods, and Ethan followed Seth. It would be the last time he saw the woods this way, saw them as *mere* woods.

***

Cleft didn't turn aside from his path the whole time, and Seth and Ethan were too timid and anxious to question him. They arrived at the boulder with the white door and all turned to look at each other.

"Seth, this is your decision. You don't have to do anything you don't want to do. I'm not going to tell you what happens if you go in there. I'll just tell you that I'll be here to talk to you afterward and that you'll be okay."

"Are you going through?" Seth asked Ethan, realizing immediately how juvenile he sounded.

"I . . . already went in," Ethan said. "That's why I said you shouldn't—"

"Ethan," Cleft cut in. "Don't write your story into him. He has his own pen and paper. It has to be his decision, of his own free will."

Ethan was obviously conflicted. He could either stand up to protect his favorite teacher, defying a pastor whom he was now afraid of, or he could stay quiet. And he wasn't aggressive enough to do the former. He swallowed and stared at his feet.

Seth watched Ethan with concern and then looked at Cleft.

"Look—I don't want any trouble from this, and this whole thing is creeping me out. I'm gonna call it quits for today." Ethan's face settled with relief.

"That's fine," Cleft said. "That's fine. I'm just gonna ask you a question. Why'd you really come up here with me?"

Seth felt defensive again. "What do you mean? You asked *me* to come with you."

"Actually, if memory serves me right, you asked *me* to come with you." Cleft had a point, and Seth wasn't in a state of mind to get into an argument. His feet were begging him to turn in the other direction and go back to the parking lot. His anxiety swelled. His lungs felt like sponges full of water. He couldn't get in the air he needed.

"Seth, I'll level with you. The only question you need to ask yourself before you walk through that door is this: Do I want the truth?"

Seth knew he was right, though Cleft's words struck and stung his mind. All this time, ever since he'd found Narnia, mystery had been scratching at him. There was more to this town than he'd thought, and it bothered him that he didn't know. It kept him awake. It shook him out of his routined life. He loved Shannon and Livy and Will—more than he loved himself, which was a feat of personal growth he'd slowly realized and become thankful for. But thankful to whom? Where does thanks go? He didn't chase down that question. He mostly enjoyed his job teaching and the quiet life he'd been cultivating. But there was something missing—something that eluded him. He couldn't name it. But he was growing more confident by the second in realizing that this door might tell him what it was. He was thinking, for some reason, of Beth and Dale, of the specter of cancer and death that always hung behind his waking days, of his anxiety that seemed bound to it. He wanted to do *something*, just one brave thing, to assault the evil and corrosion of cancer and death, to stand up, to be brave. Up to this point, "brave" was just an adjective, and it always described others. "Brave" was not a word he could hold in his own two hands.

He stepped forward towards the door and reached for the handle. Ethan moved to get his attention, but he caught Cleft's fatherly glare and submitted. Seth put his hand on the brass handle, took a deep breath in through his nose, and pushed the door open just a crack. Light flooded out, assaulting his eyes. All three of them squinted.

"To enter is to see," Cleft said.

Seth turned and looked at Cleft, who looked more and more like his father in this moment of faith. Then Seth surprised himself by pushing open the door and stepping through the threshold before his mind could catch up to his body. The light enveloped him, held him like a heavy heated blanket. It made him close his eyes in some kind of silent, trustful prayer that tilted him forward. He felt himself falling into the open space, but not falling over. Was he . . . flying? Waves of euphoria washed over him and flooded his insides. He was consumed by whatever luminous glory this was—potent, pure, ancient. He gave himself over to it, letting his body fall forward. And that beautiful feeling—falling into the light, while being wrapped in light and filled with light—was the last thing he remembered.

When he opened his eyes again, he was lying on his back, staring into the canopy of hemlock trees, full of marvel and . . . something else. Was it *meaning*? He had no word for it yet, but it was a good, strong feeling, a directional feeling. He knew at that moment that these were no mere woods. There was no "mere." The whole world was somehow turned inside out. Everywhere his eyes scanned, he saw the pith and marrow, an inward sanctity that silenced him. He had seen and experienced beautiful things before, jewels scattered among the duller stones of experience. But this was the world all-jeweled. He could do nothing but gaze.

"Seth," Cleft said from somewhere far above him. "I'm right here. You're okay."

"Yeah," Seth mumbled with utter calmness. "I know." A smile was blooming on his face, like a flower opening its petals to the sun. It was a smile of newness.

Ethan and Cleft took Seth's hands and helped him to his feet. Seth could feel the warmth of their skin, the creases in their palms, the loving bones of their fingers gripping his.

"Where did I go?" Seth asked.

Cleft smiled. "Here," he said. "You went right here." Ethan and Seth both stared at Cleft, waiting for him to say something else, but he didn't. Instead, he led them both back down the path toward the parking lot. Seth walked so slowly, like a toddler waltzing dazed in a city of dreams. He felt the feathery limbs of the hemlock trees. He smelled the rich dirt, almost sweet. His toes pressed into every rock, feeling its shape and sturdiness. He picked up pebbles and rolled them around in his palms.

And then he pulled the two marbles from his right pocket. He'd felt something there and had forgotten what it was. The clear marble held all the colors around him and seemed to gather the light in its rim. The other—the fire in a teardrop—almost made Seth cry. And then he did cry. But he didn't know why. He wasn't sad or mournful or upset. He was overwhelmed. The red, orange, and white swirls inside the marble were overpowering. They were full of story—saying something in a language he didn't know. The tears rolled down his cheeks and met the edges of his lips. He tasted the warm salt.

"Seth!" Cleft called from somewhere far ahead, beyond the sanctified moment. Seth jerked his head up, jolted by the noise. He put the marbles back into his pocket and wiped his face as he walked forward, deeper into the dream that was now his day.

***

Travis, Lem, and Bill followed the footsteps Cleft and the others had made, right to the same spot at the boulder.

"Still don't know why you're bringing me to some damn door," Travis said.

"You don't have to say 'damn,' just 'door,'" Lem said calmly.

Bill smiled at the irony. His dad used to curse like a sailor—every foul word and wretched combination of curses would shoot from his lips like arrows from the unsteady bow of a drunken archer. But that was before he went through the door. That was how Bill first noticed something different in his father. His speech was different, cleansed somehow—not in a stiff or mechanical way. It was just that Lem seemed to pause before he spoke, searching for words like a boy looking for fish from a river's edge.

"Whatever," Travis mumbled. "Just show me whatever it is so we can go back home. I'm hungry."

Bill smirked at Travis. Ever since Bill had gone through the door himself he'd developed a fondness for simply observing. He didn't judge or analyze or dissect; he just observed, watching to see how people would change in the subtlest of ways. With Travis, he noticed that words of hostility would rise like an ocean swell but then fall back down into the depths. Travis was like a little boat on the open water; anger and hostility were momentary. And when the waters settled, there was a depth in him that Bill longed to see someday.

Cleft had trailed behind them but was almost caught up. As they reached the boulder, Travis turned towards his uncle and grandfather.

"So what now? I just walk in?"

"Not before I tell you something," Cleft said, announcing his presence. "If you choose to go through that door, Travis—and it is *your* choice—you will not be the same afterward. I won't tell you what will be different. I will only tell you that we will be here for you." As he spoke these words, he looked at Bill and Lem, nodding. The three of them peacefully agreed on some secret creed.

"Okay . . . Whatever. It's just a door," Travis said.

"Ah," Cleft said just before Travis grabbed the handle. "How *dull* life would be if that were true."

Travis huffed at the remark and then grabbed the handle. As he turned and pushed, the light assaulted and then blinded him. "What the . . ." He moved his left foot back and stared at the others, now clearly marked by fear. The others nodded in harmony. Travis took a deep breath, rolled his neck around, lifted his shoulders, and then settled them, the same stretching routine he did just before he took a foul shot in his basketball games. Then he faced the door, leaned forward, and fell headlong into the white light.

***

The four of them walked back to the parking lot, Travis moving much more slowly than the others, pausing every few feet to touch a tree or press pine needles through his fingers, as if they'd come from another planet. Seth and Ethan waited patiently, leaning against Cleft's Escort, both smiling without realizing it. The fears Ethan had about the door and Seth entering were gone now. He felt surrounded by family—by those who *knew*.

"This is a good day," Cleft said, matching the smiles around him. "A very good day." Seth, Ethan, and Travis exchanged glances.

"You who were on the outside are now on the inside," Cleft said. "There's a lot to say. But I want to leave you some time to reflect. And please, each of you, come to the service tomorrow at 9:00 am. You'll want to hear the words I have to give. Because as bright as this day is, I'm very troubled by someone getting nearer."

Seth was surprised to see even Travis shake his head in approval. *Travis, go to church?* he thought. *It's a strange new world.* But it was a world he liked . . . even a world he *loved*, though he didn't understand why. What had changed? What had the door done to them?

Then Cleft, Lem, and Bill spoke together the words that all of them would soon have memorized like a morning greeting, a snippet from a Henry Wadsworth Longfellow poem.

> Life is real! Life is earnest!
> And the grave is not its goal;
> Dust thou art, to dust returnest,
> Was not spoken of the soul.

With these words, they all bowed their heads, as if in prayer. Then they turned to their cars and slowly rolled out of the parking lot, into a world that was entirely the same and entirely different.

14

THE MAN WITH THE CIRCLE TATOO

AT THE SAME TIME on that Saturday morning, Gladice Shoemaker was on her way to the post office on Silver Lake, shuffling down the sidewalk in her little white pumps, like a pigeon on its unhurried morning routine. She was singing an old hymn to herself, just barely audible.

> Long my imprisoned spirit lay
> Fast bound in sin and nature's night;
> Thine eye diffused a quickening ray,
> I woke, the dungeon flamed with light;
> My chains fell off, my heart was free,
> I rose, went forth, and followed Thee.

With the last line, she crashed into someone who came out from an alley, knocking her to the ground.

"Woah, woah," said the man. "Didn't even see you there, little lady. Let me help you up."

"Oh, that's alright. We all make mist—" Gladice stopped speaking when she looked up into the man's face. He had dark, stringy black hair, pale skin, and cold, unreadable eyes. He looked both sickly and strong. Her heart skipped a beat. He was dressed all in black. But what she noticed most of all, after turning away from his face, was the tattoo on his right hand: a plain, green circle. But the skin around the circle was red and raised, swollen and infected. Flecks of dried, yellow puss hung on the rim of the red skin. She stared for a split second as the man reached his left hand down to help her up.

"You okay there, little lady?"

"I'm . . . I'm alright. Eh . . . thank you. Don't think I've seen you around before."

"Oh, I've been around. Don't come to town much, but I've been here since—well, beyond memory. Name's Skotos."

Gladice's brow wrinkled as she shook off a chill. "Scott-us?"

"No, Mam. Two long vowels: *Skoe-tose*. I know it's a bit strange. What was my mother thinking? Am I right?" He laughed to himself, but then dark clouds drifted over his countenance. His cheek muscles and lips relaxed. He stared off into the distance behind Gladice and whispered, "I don't have a mother."

The hair on Gladice's neck was still raised. She couldn't shake off the chill, the cold. It clung to her. "Skotos," Gladice repeated, hoping to draw him back into a normal conversation. "Well," she said, gathering herself with a nervous smile as Skotos still stared off into the distance, looking deeply into some invisible country. "I'm off to the post office. It's nice to meet you."

Skotos snapped back to the present and locked eyes with Gladice. "I didn't get your name," he said with an eerie seriousness. Gladice was reluctant to give it. She searched in the moment for a way around the situation but saw none.

"Oh, me? I'm . . . I'm Gladice. Gladice Shoemaker."

Skotos nodded with approval, as if she'd surrendered exactly what he wanted.

"You watch your step, now, when you're near the road. Some people drive like maniacs."

Gladice nodded and quickly turned toward the post office, relieved to be out of the conversation. But then she stopped, caught in a net of horror. Those words—those *exact* words—were the ones she'd uttered to her sister twenty-five years ago to the day before her sister went out to the store for groceries and was struck and killed by a drunk driver. They never found out who.

Gladice stopped and turned around. But the man was gone.

She crossed Silver Lake, between a hobble and a run, going right past the post office, and turned on Milford Road, which she knew would bring her to a trail through the woods that led right to Cleft's house. By the time she reached his door, she was breathless and frantic, punching the doorbell several times before Cleft tore it open, clearly irritated until he saw the look on Gladice's face.

"Gladice? You alright? What's going on?"

"Pastor—I'm so sorry to barge in on you like this, but I couldn't wait." She struggled to catch her breath.

"Come in, come in." Cleft held the door open for her, his face wrinkled with concern. Gladice sat herself down in a burgundy wingback chair in the living room. Cleft sat opposite her on the navy blue couch.

"Now," he said. "What's going on?"

Gladice was still trying to catch her breath. "I saw someone . . . someone I've never seen in town before." Gladice's voice was shaking with the little breath she had left in her lungs.

"Well that's hardly something to scare you," Cleft said with a friendly grin, but the grin faded when he saw how disturbed Gladice was.

"No—pastor. This man was *different*. He was . . . he was pale and sickly and . . . and *cold*. Just plain cold! And he had this tattoo on his hand. It looked infected—a raised green circle."

At these words, Cleft's face turned white. Fear washed over him like an icy wave, and Gladice noticed.

"Oh, pastor . . . you *know* this man? You've seen him?"

"Only once," said Cleft. "The tattoo—you're sure it was a green circle? And was he dressed all in black?"

"Yes to both," Gladice nodded earnestly. "When did you see him?"

"I saw him . . ." Cleft started, before taking a deep breath in, as if readying himself for a plunge into water. "The night Jane died. . . . He was on the edge of the property as the ambulance took her away. The whole house was dark and the night had already fallen. He shouldn't have been able to see anything in our house, but he was *looking*. He was looking straight into my eyes and mouthing something, some words I couldn't make out. Or maybe singing. I was too put off in the moment to focus. I went to phone Tom Regent over at the police station, but by the time I got the cord for the phone over to the window for a description of the guy, he was gone. And Tom didn't pick up. So I let it go. But I was really put off by the whole thing."

"Well, of course, you were," Gladice said with a motherly tone. "But you haven't seen him since?"

"No. Haven't seen or heard of him until now. But it troubles me. I know everyone in this little town. But this man . . . this man is . . ." he trailed off into silence for several seconds.

"He's what?" Gladice asked, fixated.

Cleft shook his head. "He's just . . . off. Doesn't feel right."

"That's not all," Gladice added. "He said something to me, something that made me run straight here and push your bell like a madwoman."

"What?" Cleft asked.

"Well, you know I lost my sister many years ago."

"Yes—car accident, right?"

"Yes . . . well, a drunk driver. They never found out who it was. Happened on Silver Lake not far from where I was walking."

"Mmmhmm. I remember now. They thought it was a kid, didn't they?"

"Well, no matter. That's beside the point. I said something to Genine that night, and it was exactly twenty-five years ago *on this day*. I said, 'You watch your step, now, when you're near the road. Some people drive like maniacs.' Those were my *exact* words. The last words I ever spoke to her."

"Okay," Cleft said. "And?"

"Well, those are the very words, to the letter, that this man said to me at the end of our conversation."

"You don't think it's a coincidence? Those words aren't so uncommon," Cleft said, trying to convince himself that what was going on wasn't as strange as he knew it was.

"No, no. His face, when he spoke, it was like . . . like he *knew*, about her, about me, like he was . . . *taunting* me. Oh, when I say it out loud it makes me sound paranoid."

"No, it's alright. It doesn't. That experience marked you, and it's right that you remember those words. If I hadn't seen the man before, on the night Jane left us, I don't think I'd be as concerned. But putting the two together . . ."

"Glad I'm not the only one. I guess fear likes company as much as misery does," she said. Cleft nodded, his face still set in deep thought.

"Oh, and one more thing—his name," Gladice said. "Strangest name I ever heard."

"Yeah? What was it?"

"He said his name was *Skotos*. Not Scott or Scotus. I've heard both before, though the latter not for some time. But he said two long vowels."

Cleft found it hard to swallow, and Gladice noticed. "What is it, pastor? What?"

"I studied Greek when I went to seminary all those years ago. I'll have to look it up to be sure, but I'm almost certain it means . . ."

"It means what, pastor?" Gladice's eyes were wide and her breathing was growing more frantic. Cleft took another deep breath.

"It means *shadow*."

At the mention of that word, both of them got goosebumps. The temperature of the room seemed to drop, and each of them hugged their arms and rubbed. They noticed each other doing the same thing, which raised their alarm even more. Cleft tried to shatter the eeriness of the moment with a question.

"You didn't say which way he went, did you?"

"That's the thing, pastor. I turned around when he said those words about being safe. I turned around, and he was gone. Vanished."

The two of them stared at each other for an uncomfortable moment. Cleft nodded. "Probably an alley close by, though. He could've gone down one of those."

"That's true," Gladice nodded, somewhat relieved. "Though I don't remember hearing footsteps."

"Okay. Well, Gladice, thank you for telling me. You know you're always welcome. Would you like to stay here for a bit, have some tea?"

"Oh, that's kind of you, but no. I'm okay. I just had to tell somebody," she said with a grateful smile.

"Well, I haven't had my walk yet today. So, let me walk you back to the post office and then to your apartment. After that, I'll stop by the station to let the guys know about all this."

With that, the two of them headed towards the door. Cleft did as he promised. As he left Gladice's apartment, he said, "Now, you hear or see anything that's off, you call me."

Gladice nodded. "Thank you, pastor. Thank you so much for your kindness, and for listening to a crazy old woman."

"Oh, come on now," Cleft said. "We're all crazy, you know." He smiled, and Gladice matched him as she closed the door. He went back to his house before going to the station. He'd left his front door open and unlocked, so he waltzed in, grabbed the phone from the wall mount by the kitchen and dialed Bill's number.

"Pets' Place. What can I do you for?"

"Bill, it's Cleft."

"Oh, hey Cleft! Need anything for Roland?"

"No, no. Roland's good. Too many chew toys to know what to do with, and they're scattered all around the house."

Bill chuckled. "Well, what can I help with?"

"Bill, I'd like it if you and Lem came by this afternoon, if you could. Something isn't sitting right with me, and I want to run it by you two."

"Okay. I can close up here around 4:00 pm, and drop by after that. Dad's been hanging around the store today, so I'll let him know, too."

"Great. That's good. Okay, I'll see you both here in a while."

"Sounds good."

Cleft hung up the phone and then got in his car and drove to the police station.

***

When he walked into the lobby of the station, Tom was just headed down the hallway but turned back when he heard the door.

"Hey, Cleft. Didn't expect to see you here. Everything alright?"

"I hope so, but, like I always say, can't be too careful."

Tom nodded. "Well, how can I help you be careful?"

"I just wanted to fill out an incident report, I guess. But . . . maybe not. The problem is there hasn't really been an incident."

"Well, that would seem to be a problem, wouldn't it?" Tom was chuckling, and something about the merriment of his red face made Cleft smile despite himself.

"Yeah, well . . . it's something that doesn't sit right with me. And I just wanted you all to have someone on your radar."

"Okay. Well, shoot."

"Have you ever seen a man around town, dressed in black, thin, stringy long hair, with a . . . a tattoo on his hand? The tattoo is just a plain circle."

Tom shook his head slowly. "No, can't say that rings any bells. He cause some trouble?"

"Well, I never said anything about it the night Jane died . . ." At the mention of Jane's name the room seemed hushed by a sacred energy. "But I saw this fellow in the woods near my house . . . just skulking around, staring through the windows."

"Well, that's trespassing, at least. And it's just plain creepy."

"Yeah, well, he just had a run-in with Gladice, too."

"Gladice?" Tom's voice rang with protection. Gladice was like a grandmother to him. And the thought of anyone causing her harm filled his bones with anger—in a way he hadn't felt since he punched Billy Snyder in the lip.

More than twenty years ago, Billy was the high school bully who'd taken away a Twix from a girl named Sarah. Sarah had Down syndrome and was always trying to hug those who showed an ounce of kindness to her. As she tried to hug Billy in the cafeteria one day (Because Billy had said, "Hey, I love Twix!"), he pushed her away and then took her Twix and held it high above her head, telling her to get lost, pushing her back with the other arm.

The whole cafeteria was enraged, but it was Tom—quiet, respectful, warm-faced Tom Regent—who got up and marched towards Billy. Ever since childhood, Tom had been built solid and strong. He didn't just have broad shoulders and a raised chest; every part of him was filled with unyielding muscle, woven from years of work on his father's farm. He had a gravity to his steps, an intention to his movements. But Billy was so fixated on teasing Sarah that he didn't notice.

Tom got within arm's reach before Billy turned and said, "What the hell do you—" He didn't get to finish the sentence. Tom's fist busted his bottom lip in two and sent his whole body flying backward. He lay on the floor, blacked out, the Twix still wedged in his left hand.

The adrenaline had coursed through Tom's veins so fiercely that he wasn't fully aware of what he'd just done. As the awareness set in, he was scared—terrified of what his father would say or do in response. But before his fear got too far, the cafeteria began swelling with applause. Billy never returned to school after that. And Tom earned the name "Thunder Fist." He knew his dad would hate the title, and he would have several belt lashings to prove it. Tom's father was a Presbyterian with a passion for physical punishment. But in the end, Tom believed deep down that what he did was worth it. It was that very feeling that pushed him towards becoming a police officer in the first place. Sometimes people needed a busted lip to see straight. And if Tom had to suffer his father's anger to make it happen, so be it.

All of this welled up inside his chest as Cleft mentioned Gladice's name. In fact, he noticed his hand had bunched itself into a fist, white knuckles threatening the air around him.

"What sort of run-in with Gladice?" Tom stepped close to Cleft, and Cleft noticed the intensity growing.

"Well, easy Tom. Nothing that bad, just strange. I'm not asking you to charge off and find him."

"Right. Sorry. Go on."

"Well, he bumped into Gladice and helped her up. But he said something to her, said some words that she hadn't heard for twenty-five years, to the day."

"What'd he say?"

"He said the same words to her that Gladice had said to her sister the night she died."

"Gladice had a sister? I didn't know that."

"Well, it's a painful subject for her. Apparently, they were very close, but Genine was struck and killed by a hit-and-run drunk driver, right in town."

"And this fella said the exact same words to Gladice?"

"Exact same ones."

"That *is* strange."

"Yeah, it's strange. And I don't think I'd report it if I hadn't seen the same guy in the woods the night Jane passed. But putting the two of them together . . . just makes me feel off. Something isn't right."

"Well, sure sounds like it. If you don't have an official incident to report, best I can do is make a note and share it with the rest of the squad. We'll keep an eye out for him and let you know if something comes up."

"I think that's all I'd like at this point. Thanks, Tom."

"Sure, Cleft. Anything else?"

"No, that's all. I've gotta get back to the house to meet some friends. But keep me in the loop."

"Will do. . . . Oh, and Ethan said he got to take a hike with you and some other guys earlier this morning."

"Yeah, we did," Cleft said. "He's a good kid."

"Yeah, he is. Don't always see things eye to eye with him, but he's got a lot going on inside; I can tell. Anyway, thanks for taking him with you. I think that meant a lot to him."

"Glad to help. If he's ever looking for company, we share a love of books, so he's welcome to stop by."

"Yeah, that boy *loves* to read . . . and write. I'll let him know."

With that, Cleft turned and opened the door to leave the station while Tom pulled out a yellow notepad and started jotting down bullet points from their conversation.

***

When Cleft got back to the house, Lem and Bill had just pulled into his driveway. Lem seemed aware that something wasn't right.

"What's going on, reverend?"

"Thanks for coming over, guys. I want you two on the alert. There's been two sightings of some fella that doesn't seem right. The same character, Lem, that you've encountered over the years. I saw him the night Jane died, skulking around in the woods over there." Cleft pointed to the tree line behind his house. "And then Gladice ran into him—literally—this morning."

"What'd he say to Gladice?" Bill asked. Everyone was concerned about Gladice. She was like the town's grandmother.

"Well, apparently he spoke the exact same words to her that she spoke to her late sister, Genine, twenty-five years ago to this day."

"What were the words?" Lem asked.

"Well, they're not as important . . . some warning to be cautious with crazy drivers. But it didn't sit well with Gladice. And it doesn't sit well with me—someone bringing up the past like that."

"But how did he know Gladice said that? Maybe it was just a coincidence," Bill suggested. Cleft nodded but obviously wasn't convinced that this was a possibility.

"Listen," Cleft said leaning in closer. "This man—he dresses in all black; he's got longer, stringy hair, a pale face, and—most notably—a circle tattoo on his right hand. If you see him, I want you to let me know so I can have it reported to the police station."

"But we can't do nothin' if he hasn't done more than say some strange words," Lem said. "But I'm sure he's been takin' people."

"Dad, we don't know for sure that he's taking people or even that people are disappearing," Bill said. "A boy like William could've easily wandered off."

"There's plenty of others!" Lem said defensively.

"There *are*, Lem. I know," Cleft interjected. "But we can't link that to this guy just yet. Anyway, we can at least keep an eye out. Something in my gut tells me this guy isn't here to see the waterfalls. Doesn't belong here." Lem and Bill nodded, both feeling a heightened sense of their duty to protect Gladice, and, somehow, the rest of Dingmans Ferry.

"Oh, and one more thing," Cleft said. "He said his name is . . . *Skotos*."

"Skotos?" Lem said. "What kinda name is that? Sounds European."

"It's Greek," Cleft said.

"Ain't had nobody from Greece in these parts," Lem said with a laugh.

"Yeah, well . . ." Cleft hesitated to complete the sentence. "In Greek it means . . ."

"What?" Bill said, with gathering anticipation. Lem was locked in, too.

"It means *shadow*."

At the mention of that word, all three of them chilled, with hair raised on their forearms and neck—tiny follicles stretching into the air to grab any passing warmth. But there was none. Bill looked down at Cleft's arms, and then at Lem's, noticing what had just happened.

"I don't . . . did you feel that?" Bill started.

"Pay no mind," said Cleft. "The air's just cool is all."

Each of them took a turn swallowing as they stepped away from their tight inner circle.

"You just watch for him, okay?" Cleft said.

"Sure thing," Bill said. They turned and walked back to Bill's green truck.

***

Deep in the woods, about a hundred yards back from Cleft's property line, Skotos leaned against a Hemlock trunk, staring. He could see Lem and Bill pull out of the driveway.

"Yes," he said with a whisper. "You watch. . . . It's time to gather." He sang his song quietly again, but only the second half.

> Mind the shadow.
> Mind the shadow.
> Mind the shadow.
> Sleep.

The chorus ended, as it always did, with coughing—a deep, raspy cough that seemed to pull from the fathoms of his gut, scraping the rim of his insides. He choked up more of the black, bitter sludge and spit it on the ground. Then he wiped his mouth and the sweat from his face. He rested his back against the tree trunk and sighed out a sentence.

"No—I don't have a mother."

15

SUNDAY SERVICE

THAT SUNDAY MORNING, THERE was a full sanctuary at Trinity Presbyterian Church. Seth's wife was still surprised (but quietly encouraged) that Seth had asked if they could all go to church that morning. She wanted to do whatever she could to foster a relationship with him and Cleft, whom she respected as her own father. Will and Livy had already made their way to Sunday school. Will took up his role of protector and encourager.

"Livy, I'll be with you the whole time, and we can color . . . I think," Will said with his little arm around her shoulder.

"My God, they're so sweet. I can't take it," Shannon said with an ear-to-ear grin. Seth took a calm, deep breath. "They're beautiful," he said. Shannon glanced at him for a moment, wondering at his choice of words. He'd been speaking differently ever since he'd gotten back from his meeting with Cleft yesterday. His words were simple, direct, and intentional, and yet somehow effortless. His voice sounded above the din of internal conflict and distraction, as a bird call at the top of the canopy: unhindered by the bark and the branches. His voice was *free*.

Seth and Shannon made their way toward the front of the sanctuary. "Seth, do we need to go this close?" Shannon asked, never wanting to be the object of anyone's gaze. "Yes—I want to hear everything clearly." He spoke with the same simple directness. He wasn't sharp or demanding. His voice had only soft edges. Shannon sighed but gave in. They sat in the pew right behind Lem, Bill, Travis, and Tara, Travis's mom. Shannon looked at Travis and made sure Seth saw her. Then she raised her eyebrows in surprise. Seth just smiled and shrugged. Tara looked behind herself and muttered a quiet, "Mornin'."

Tara's eyes looked sleepless, her face pale and weathered, but strong. Her hair was dark brown and wavy, pulled into a tight bun, and she clutched the handle of a thermos mug of black coffee. Her white knuckles made it clear she wouldn't put it down without a fight. Travis leaned closer toward her.

"Are you gonna be able to stay awake after your night shift?" he asked. She took another swig of coffee.

"Slap me if I fall asleep," she said with a straight face. Travis started laughing and then put his arm around her.

"What's with you? Askin' me how I'm doing and huggin' me all the time? You fall off a cliff yesterday and bang your head?"

"No, Ma," Travis said with the same calmness that was in Seth's voice. "Just seein' things better."

"Quit saying that. You're creepin' me out."

Travis chuckled and squeezed his mom's shoulder. She acted indifferent, but Shannon noticed in her eyes how much she loved Travis's altered demeanor, how she seemed to hang around it like a long-lost friend. She seemed awkward in Travis's presence, but only because she'd been distant from him for so long, since before her husband left. That's when Travis developed a well-balanced approach to life—with a chip on both shoulders. This was the first time Tara saw consistent compassion in her son, a gentleness she thought had frozen in the cold of adolescent disenchantment. But it hadn't. It had only gone dormant. And the white door had awoken it again. Shannon's heart swelled when she noticed Tara's head drift slightly to the left and rest on Travis's shoulder. It was her quiet way of asking permission to enter the once loud arena of her son's life—where curse words careened through an atmosphere of apathy. But now it was quiet. The arena was all sand and sun. The stands had emptied. Travis had room now, for others.

After they sang several hymns, including Gladice's favorite—"And Can It Be"—Cleft waltzed confidently up to the oak podium in his khaki pants, navy blue blazer, and royal blue tie. Seth always noticed the shoes people wore, since he'd worked as a teenager in two different shoe stores—G.H. Bass and Clarks. He was a lover of leather for its deep earthy scent, for the way it held old stories in its grain, for its openness to holding new stories in creases and folds. Leather was made for the cartographer in every human soul. He saw the burgundy penny loafers on Cleft's feet and smiled. The folds and creases in the toe box told him the shoes knew the man, and the man knew the shoes. His father had worn the same loafers, the same color.

Cleft opened his black Bible, laid it flat on the podium, and took off his watch, placing it to the right of his Bible. And then he began his sermon.

> I'm so glad to see all of you here this morning. It's
> always good to have a full house for God. And
> the text we're going to look at this morning . . .

it's deep and defining. It's going to show you who you are, or who you're not. And if by the end of this sermon, you want to be someone *other* than who you are right now, you come and talk to me.

Seth was fixated on Cleft's face, and Cleft set his eyes on Seth's and nodded before continuing. In that moment, contentment again washed over Cleft. He had indeed found *the one*.

Turn with me now to 1 John 2, verses 8–18. And read with me.

"Again, a new commandment I write unto you, which thing is true in him and in you: because the darkness is past, and the true light now shineth. He that saith he is in the light, and hateth his brother, is in darkness even until now. He that loveth his brother abideth in the light, and there is none occasion of stumbling in him. But he that hateth his brother is in darkness, and walketh in darkness, and knoweth not whither he goeth, because that darkness hath blinded his eyes. I write unto you, little children, because your sins are forgiven you for his name's sake. I write unto you, fathers, because ye have known him that is from the beginning. I write unto you, young men, because ye have overcome the wicked one. I write unto you, little children, because ye have known the Father. I have written unto you, fathers, because ye have known him that is from the beginning. I have written unto you, young men, because ye are strong, and the word of God abideth in you, and ye have overcome the wicked one."

At the mention of "wicked one," Cleft looked up to notice someone standing at the door of the sanctuary in the back—dressed all in black, glaring at him. Skotos didn't need to announce his presence. He could be *felt*. Cleft cleared his throat and continued, but not before he noticed the smug look on Skotos's face, and the black smudge trailing off the edge of his bottom lip.

"Love not the world, neither the things that are in the world. If any man love the world, the love of the Father is not in him. For all that is in the world, the lust of the flesh, and the lust of the eyes, and the pride of life, is not of the Father, but is of the world. And the world passeth away, and the lust thereof: but he that doeth the will of God abideth for ever. Little children, it is the last time: and as ye have heard that *antichrist* shall come, . . ."

Cleft looked up again. Skotos slowly placed his hand over his heart, displaying his raised and swollen circle tattoo. A tired smile pulled the left side of his mouth up as he turned toward the doors of the church. Cleft nodded to Lem in the midst of his awkward pause. Lem turned and noticed Skotos leaving. The congregation could sense something awry, and the murmurings began to lift like starlings taking flight. Cleft cleared his throat again to regain their attention, as Lem stood up and made his way to the end of the pew, smiling calmly at Tara, whose look asked him what he was doing. "Bathroom," he whispered. He walked quickly with his head down, on the edge of the sanctuary, toward the church lobby. All this happened as Cleft continued.

> "Even now are there many antichrists; whereby we know that it is the last time." The grass withers and the flowers fade, but God's word stands forever. Amen.

As the people settled in for the sermon, Cleft saw Lem, with his curled white hair, open the doors and follow Skotos out. This rattled him. He had no idea what Skotos was capable of, and he had no intention of Lem being a test case. Cleft tried to get Bill's attention, too. But Bill had fallen asleep. Travis elbowed him in the ribs to rouse him. At the moment, Cleft thought it better to continue, though Travis was whispering something to Bill.

> Now, I wasn't going to preach on this passage today. In fact, I had a whole sermon prepared on Deuteronomy 6. But I think many of us need to be reminded of who we are this morning . . . or who we *can* be. The light of God can change us. It can make us . . . *new*.

Cleft looked down at Seth and Travis. Shannon noticed and stared at Seth with confusion, waiting for him to respond to her, but he didn't. He was locked in on Cleft's words and nodding in agreement. A knot grew in Shannon's stomach, a fear that there was something Seth wasn't telling her. But Seth told her everything. At least, he always had.

> It can make us so new, in fact, that the people who used to know us do a double-take. They might not recognize us at first. But that's because we're new creatures—not just different . . . but *reborn* into a new world. The psalmist once said of God, "In thy light shall we see light" (Ps. 36:9). But for those who believe in the light of the world, we don't just *see* light; we *become* light. That's why Paul says in Ephesians 5:8 that we *are* light in the Lord, and we must walk as children of that light. Now, our passage this morning draws out many things—and I can't touch on all of them. But I want to offer three points about our being light. First, our *love* is the mark of our light. If we're struggling to love, that's no small thing. It suggests we're dimming, darkening . . . becoming less. Love is a light. Second, the realm of darkness is the realm of hate.

At the end of this sentence, Cleft looked up at the sanctuary doors to see Lem standing there shaking his head. Cleft nodded in acknowledgment and continued.

Hate is always taking things. It takes advantage. It takes time. It takes emotion. It takes relationships. It takes life. And above all these things, it takes the light of love, the very light living inside those who believe. I don't want to rile anyone up, but the hate we see in the world around us—that's not something to ignore or sidestep or sleep through. It's something to fight. Light wages war against darkness. Wherever it is, whomever it possesses—that's a battleground for the children of light, for those who have fallen into the unexplainable mystery of God's illumination.

He glanced down at Seth for a split second. No one noticed, except Shannon.

Third, the one thing that needs to draw out our deepest, most passionate love is the will of God. Now, I know what you're thinking. "Pastor, how in the world am I supposed to know what the will of God is?" Well, of course, that's in here. [He held up his black leather Bible.] But there's a lot in here. How can we know all of God's will—not just in this book but in our own lives, with all the tiny decisions we make each day? Well, here's one way to summarize things. God's will is the work he wants done. And Jesus once said, "This is the work of God, that ye believe on him whom he hath sent" (John 6:29). Believing in the *light,* helping other people believe in the light—that's it. That's the sum of God's will for us in this world. Now that'll look a bit different for each of us. But in every case, it'll be thinking and acting in a way that does one of three things: affirming the truth, loving others more than yourself, or enjoying the God-given beauty right in front of you. Truth. Love. Beauty. These are the marks of light, and the marks of all those who believe in it. Let's pray.

It was a strikingly short sermon, maybe a quarter of the usual length. But everyone seemed to be listening, bent on every word, like birds staring at their king before some grand migration. Cleft came down from the podium and walked towards Bill and Lem in the church entryway as the piano notes began to fill the sanctuary.

"No sign of 'im," Lem said.

"I don't like this, fellas. Don't like it all. I want all of you on high alert."

"What about me?" Seth joined the group from behind, with Shannon trailing him.

"You, too," Cleft said. Shannon crept up closer.

"You guys doing something together?" Her voice was timid and scared, like a squirrel making noise next to larger animals.

"Hey, Shannon," Cleft said with a warm smile. "Just keeping a lookout to make sure everyone's safe."

"Safe from what, exactly?" She was looking now at Seth.

"I'll have Seth explain things to you. No need for alarm. Excuse me for a minute." Cleft walked briskly back into the sanctuary, sternness in his eyes. In the last pew, three teenage boys were laughing hysterically, all focused on Cain Shoemaker (Gladice's grandson)—their ringleader who was drawing something in one of the pew Bibles. He was dressed in a denim bomber jacket with matching light jeans. His blond hair bobbed in front of his face as he laughed and kept sketching.

"Care to share the joke?" At the sound of Cleft's voice, the heads of the three boys snapped up, though Cain's face quickly took on a sneer of rebellious joy. "You wouldn't be drawing in the pew Bibles, I know. Because that's not permitted."

"How were we supposed to know?" Cain retorted, puffed up with his own confidence.

"Because it says so . . . right there," Cleft said without skipping a beat, pointing to a sign on the back of each pew. 'Please do not mark the pew Bibles in any way.'

"Yeah, well, guess I don't read signs, then," Cain said. He'd wanted to say something snappier, given his audience, but nothing else came to him.

"Mmhmm. Well, you can ask your folks for $5 to replace that one," Cleft said as he turned to leave.

"Don't got any folks, pastor—not any folks with money."

"No?" said Cleft, irritated at having to continue the engagement.

"Nope."

"Well, then hang around for a few minutes in the lobby, and I'll figure out a way for you to pay for it."

Cain just laughed, prompting the other two boys to join in as Cleft walked towards the church doors to say goodbye to everyone else. Cain and his crew walked out a side exit door into the parking lot to avoid Cleft, laughing and punching each other. In the woods at the edge of the parking lot, behind the wide trunk of an enormous oak tree, Skotos glared and grinned at Cain.

"Oh, my boy . . . my boy. You're the one."

***

Seth buckled the kids into their car seats as Shannon climbed into the driver's seat of their Chrysler station wagon. It had been a hand-me-down from Shannon's parents, who were always upgrading their vehicle since her father owned a dealership outside of Pittsburg. Seth rubbed his thumb on a white scratch along the wood paneling of his door before pulling it open and climbing in.

"You want to tell me what that was about?" Shannon said with a blend of irritation and concern. Seth hadn't prepared anything to say, but he felt strangely okay with that and started speaking immediately, without a filter.

"That door in the woods—the one I told you about?" Seth said.

"Yeah, what about it?"

"I went through it." Seth let his words sit for a few seconds.

"And?" Shannon asked, searching for more. "You went through a door. That's it?"

"Well, Cleft had gone through . . . and Bill and Lem . . . and one of my students. So I wasn't the first."

"But why is this a thing? What's on the other side of the door?"

"I'm not sure."

"You went through a door, but you're not sure what's on the other side? Seth, what's going on?"

"It's hard to explain. I just . . . opened the door and saw this . . ."

"This what? Seth, you're starting to freak me out."

"What's a freak-me-out?" said Will.

"Nothing—sweetie, mommy and daddy are trying to talk about something." Shannon started the car and began backing out of the space. As she put the car in drive, Seth answered.

"I saw this really bright light. That's all I remember."

"What do you mean, 'That's all I remember'? You act like you passed out." Seth didn't reply right away.

"Well, *did* you pass out? Was it your anxiety again?" Shannon's voice was growing with concern.

"I don't know. I just remember Cleft and Ethan there. And then Bill and Lem and Travis were in the parking lot, and I felt . . . *different*. But not in a bad way. Just different. Calmer. At peace. Awake."

Shannon was about to say something but swallowed her words, shook her head, and pulled the car onto Silver Lake. Seth's choice of words was only making her more concerned. It was the concise, intentional directness.

"What's axiety?" Will asked.

"Sweetie, Mommy and Daddy are talking, okay? Can you ask Livy what she learned at Sunday school?"

Will turned to Livy and started engaging with her on a picture she'd colored of John the Baptist. She had scribbled out his face with red crayon so that only his body and staff were visible.

"I want you to take me there," Shannon blurted out, almost surprising herself.

"What?" Seth said. He wasn't prepared for that.

"I want you to take me to this door so I can make sure it's not . . . weird or anything. For all you know, there could've been some kind of . . . chemical leaking out of the ground there. Or something."

Seth tried to think of a reason to oppose her, but he couldn't. Why shouldn't she be able to see the door? Why shouldn't she have the choice to walk through it? Cleft had given him the choice. He had no rebuttal. But he hadn't thought of walking through the door as a family affair. He'd thought it would be something he could figure out on his own, and then return to the safety of his normal life. He could see now that what he'd done had implications for his family, and he wasn't comfortable with that—not because he was afraid, but simply because he hadn't accounted for it. He'd wanted to protect his family from whatever strangeness was spreading in their little town. But now he could see that there was nothing that could prevent it. And it dawned on him that he no longer thought anything truly strange was happening. Strangeness comes from being on the outside. But now he was on the inside.

There was nothing that could keep everyone from being involved eventually—Shannon or Will or even Livy. Anyone in the town could be involved. In fact, they were already. Everyone was involved with the door—both those who walked through it and those who claimed to know nothing about it. There was no lasting isolation from the door. It stood as the center of gravity for Dingmans Ferry, calling all residents *to* it or *through* it. One by one, they would all choose. And yet, one by one, each had already been chosen. The door itself seemed to harness an energy, magnetically pulling people towards its threshold, or else ushering them away and keeping them at bay.

With all its stock simplicity, its rote and rural normalcy—as a tourist town full of fishermen, farmers, and hunters more concerned with taxidermy than with teleology—Dingmans Ferry saw the world through Seth's clear marble. All was plain. The world was *exactly* as they saw it, and nothing more. Their habits helped them refuse the possibility that Dingmans Ferry was actually the fire in a teardrop. It had been falling into an invisible war—a slow fall, like one of its waterfalls brought to an inching pace. Seth had just dropped over the edge. Shannon was about to follow with Will and Livy.

Because of the door, reality ran much deeper and higher than people supposed. The inside was far greater than the outside. And the ending was working its way backward towards their beginning.

All hinged on the white door. But few of them knew it was not the only threshold in Dingmans Ferry.

16

THE TAKING OF CAIN SHOEMAKER

CAIN'S FATHER, MARTIN SHOEMAKER, worked construction when he was sober, which wasn't often. He stood in the kitchen of their trailer, scraping black residue from a frying pan, the hot water in the sink drifting into his unshaven face. His lips pursed around a half-inch-long cigarette. He spit the remainder into the sink and shoved it down the drain with his thumb. The tiny ember burned his skin, rousing his slumbering (but ever-present) irritation.

"Where's Cain?!" he yelled. A voice came from the bedroom.

"The hell if I know!" his mother yelled back. Tabitha was staring into their tiny bathroom mirror, trying to wax the hair off her upper lip. "Said he was goin' to church with his friends."

"Church?! What's he gonna do there? Pray for money? He ain't gonna get any. Told that boy a dozen times—even if he starts workin', still gonna' be a drinker like his good old dad."

"That's real nice, Martin. Real nice. He doesn't have to be like you."

"No?" Martin yelled. "What's he gonna' do, be like you? Waxin' the hair off his face?"

"Oh, shut up! Just because some of us don't cares about how we look doesn't mean everybody's gotta' look like a slob, Martin."

"I don't look like no slob," he said, shutting off the water. "I'm a . . . handsome devil." He took a swig of beer and looked at his reflection in the window behind the sink, running his hand through his hair to see how far back his receding hairline had gone. He huffed at the image and went to grab his coat.

"Church . . . waste of damn time," he said.

"Wait . . ." Tabitha said. "What day is it?"

"Sunday, isn't it?" Martin said only half paying attention as he searched for his keys. Tabitha walked down the hall with the wax still on her lip and examined a cat calendar pinned to the hallway wall.

"It's . . . it's Tuesday! Where the hell *is* he?"

"Tuesday. Guess I missed some work then."

"As if you could hammer and nail with all that alcohol in your veins."

"No better than you can bag groceries with all that stupid lotion on yer hands."

Tabitha shrugged off his comment. It wasn't worth getting into a fight when she had to get to work in an hour. His antics had led to some nasty house renovations: the hole in the drywall behind the calendar; the crack in their dining room table; the dried grease splattered all over the backsplash and kitchen wall from when he'd thrown a frying pan at her for a comment about his receding hairline.

Wherever Cain was, it must have been better than here.

***

Cain trudged through the woods with his two friends—Patrick and Jesse—Skotos leading them. He'd met them at the edge of the church parking lot on Sunday and asked them if they wanted something that would "rock their world." Cain had only just gotten into marijuana a few months earlier. The thought of a new drug set desire aflame in his veins. Patrick had joined him in his drug dabbling, but Jesse held back.

Much to his disappointment, Cain's friends were less ambitious than he was on this particular morning. Skotos had asked them to hike with him into the woods between routes 739 and 209, on the south side of Adams Creek. Patrick and Jesse went along for part of the hike, mainly because they had nothing else to do. They lost their nerve and interest when Skotos told them they'd have to hike into the woods for a few hours. That creeped them out enough to risk looking like chickens.

"I'm out, man," Jesse said. "Gotta go wake my mom up for work anyway."

"Whatever," Cain said. "Go wake up your mommy. What about you, Patrick? You in?"

"Nah . . . I'm gonna pass." This rejection was more of a blow to Cain since Patrick had wandered with him into the dazed and delirious lands of alcohol and pot. Why was he drawing the line here?

"When did you guys get so soft? This is gonna be big—I know it."

But Jesse and Patrick had already made up their minds and started walking towards 739.

"Don't expect anything when I get back!" Cain yelled.

"You know, your friends . . ." Skotos began, with the quiet confidence of a python, "are not like you. They follow. You lead. And if you really want to lead, what I give you will help you in ways you can't dream of."

"Oh yeah," Cain said, nervous but trying to hide it, swallowing to regain composure. "What's so great about this stuff anyway?"

"It's not stuff. It's a *way*."

"What do you mean? A way to what? I thought we were talking about drugs—like cocaine maybe."

"Mmmm," Skotos replied, as if he'd expected the answer. "And what will cocaine do for you? Give you a feeling, an experience, a revelation that passes into nothing after a few hours? The excitement, my friend, is temporary. I'm offering you something that lasts, something that will truly set you apart, make you the leader I know you are."

"You keep acting like you know me. You don't. And I don't need this."

"I never said you did. The real question is, do you *want* this? Need has nothing to do with it. Want drives us. Want propels us forward. Do you *want* to go forward or do you want to go back?"

Cain locked eyes with him for a moment and then sneered, looking around at the woods and then at 739 in the distance, which carried the swish of a car only every few minutes. He could see the church steeple of Trinity Presbyterian Church—a white point pushing into the blue sky, mocking him with what he'd never been able to have, with what everyone else in that church seemed to *pretend* to have: hope. He hated hope. It always disappointed. What good was a steeple in the sky when storms still came and blocked the sun? He was tired of his tiny trailer soaked in cigarette smoke, tequila, and cheap vodka. His whole life seemed to be going jaundice, shriveling in a yellowed haze. Drugs had provided a momentary escape, but he knew Skotos was right: they didn't last. What he really wanted, though he would never admit it and risk sounding juvenile, was someone to *see* him. He wanted to be noticed . . . because he didn't even know who he really was. And maybe someone noticing him, like Jesse and Patrick pretended to, would help him find himself.

But Skotos was right about them, too: Jesse and Patrick were followers. They could do nothing to bring Cain direction, to help him move forward, to get away from his jaundiced life. That's why Skotos's words caught him like a fish in a net. He couldn't go back. He *wouldn't* go back. Not anymore. There was nothing to go back to.

"Fine. I'm in."

"Good," said Skotos with a controlling smile. "Let's go."

The two of them headed into the woods. Cain only looked back once, at Jesse and Patrick, who were almost to 739 now. Their stride suggested they had something to go back to, and they didn't turn to look at Cain. That solidified his decision. No one was looking at him. No one. But they would.

***

Skotos and Cain huffed as they came over a small ridge and stepped on boulders down the other side, hopping from rock to tree root.

"How much farther?" Cain said.

"Just beyond that rock face." Skotos pointed ahead of them to a great black rock wall, jutting out from the earth as if it had refused to go with the rest of the land.

"Rebel's Rock," Skotos whispered.

"What?" Cain said as he wiped the sweat from his forehead. The chill of March was seeping into the softness of April.

"I call it Rebel's Rock. The door is on the other side. We can camp here tonight. I'll start gathering firewood. You do the same."

"Wait . . . the door? The door to what?"

"You'll see."

Cain was nearing the end of his patience.

"You have a cabin out here or something?"

"Or something," Skotos mumbled.

***

The fire crackled before them, sending orange light to dance on their faces.

"So, Cain. Why did you come up here?"

"You said you had something good," he shrugged.

"Ah, but that's not the deeper reason, is it?"

"What are you, some kind of shrink?"

"Just a conversation partner. See, it seems to me that you had all you needed down there, in that tiny town."

"You don't know anything about what I need."

"So, talk. Who else is here to judge you?"

Cain paused as the truth of the words settled into him.

"I don't . . . have a reason to go back. No *real* reason, anyway. My dad's a drunk, a burnout waste of space. And my mom—she just spends her whole day distracting herself from the fact that she's getting older, and that this is the best it's gonna get for her." He paused, realizing that voicing his thoughts actually made him feel sorry for his mom. She was stuck, trapped in a decaying life.

Skotos stayed silent, inviting more words. Cain looked up at him for a second, expecting him to speak. No one else had ever really let him talk without interrupting. No one else had actually *listened*. So he went on.

"Anyway, there isn't anything worth going back to."

"And what is it you really want?"

"You sure you ain't a shrink?"

Skotos just shook his head, staring at Cain, using the silence as a threshold for the boy's soul, so willing to walk forward. It was confirmation that Skotos had chosen the right person, and he almost smiled.

"I just . . . I don't know. I just want people to know who I am, even if I don't. I guess that sounds pretty stupid. But . . . the drugs, they just give me a break from chasing . . ."

"From chasing who you are?" Skotos finished his thought.

"Yeah."

They sat silently for a few moments in the audience of the embers.

"I can't tell you who you are," Skotos said, staring at the fire. "But . . . I can show you a way forward. And if you really want people to *see* you, then this is the way to do it. Go through the black door on the other side of this rock."

"Yeah, well, you still haven't told me anything about where this door goes."

"The door goes to *you,*" Skotos said, as if Cain should have known this. Cain was about to respond but didn't know what to say. He nodded slowly.

"Come," Skotos said. "The time is ripe."

With that, he arose and started walking towards Rebel's Rock, skirting the bottom of the black stone. Cain followed sheepishly, looking around, and then behind him into the black woods, knowing there was nothing there worth turning to, but wanting there to be. The woods were empty, mirroring his insides—hollow like an abandoned house, longing to be inhabited but fully convinced that the vacancy had been there too long for hope.

Skotos rounded a corner and then turned to wait for Cain. There in the black rock was, somehow, an even blacker door. The door seemed forced into the stone, smashed into place. But when Cain reached for the brass handle and expected resistance, he found none. The handle turned almost effortlessly, and the door felt weightless. And without any explanation, he felt himself filled with euphoria. He even turned to smile at Skotos, who was smirking back.

"Feels good to own your future, doesn't it?" Skotos said. Cain nodded, unable to wipe the grin off his face. And then, without thinking of how wildly dark the threshold was, he stepped through, more confident than he'd ever been before. Skotos closed the door behind him, counted to six three times, and then opened the door. There stood Cain Shoemaker in the shadow: completely the same . . . but entirely different.

***

Martin looked at Tom, who was seated across from him at their cheap fold-out kitchen table. Martin's skin was usually red, but it was even darker, with a vein hugging the left corner of his forehead and running down toward his cheek.

"I said I ain't seen him for three days! Now you gonna do your damn job and find him or keep asking questions!!"

Tom was unphased. He'd dealt with Martin Shoemaker several times, usually for drunk and disorderly conduct, but there was also his involvement in a barn fire nearly ten years ago, and then his lack of a solid alibi for a small-scale grocery store hold-up four years earlier. Martin was the easiest suspect in town, and the hardest to trust.

"We're already working, Martin. Just relax."

"Don't tell me to—"

Martin stopped as he watched his son waltz through the trailer door as if he'd just been out getting groceries. Even now, Martin could tell something was different . . . off. It was in his gate and demeanor, his brisk and confident strut. Cain was *purposeful* in a way Martin barely recognized.

"The hell you doin', boy?!"

Cain got to the fold-out table before Martin could even stand up. He stood an inch from his dad's face and said something Tom would never forget—nor, for that matter, would Martin.

"You listen, Daddio. Listen good. I been in the dark. You sit there like you've been layin' in the light. But I tell you right now: your *light* is my *dark*. And I'm not small anymore. I been where you ain't ever dreamed. And you're gonna see. Understand? Don't call me 'boy.'"

Martin, baffled and confused in the same instant, found no words. He just stared at this person—his son. And yet not his son. Who was this? On Saturday evening, he'd told his teenager to quit complaining about not having anything to do. He said, "Go get lost. Maybe you'll find something then." And Cain had slammed the door without looking back. But even then, Cain meandered, his feet looking for something in their front lawn to kick (and there were plenty of beer cans). He had left that trailer small and uncertain. He had left as a child. And now? Now he seemed somehow older than Martin, older than his own father. And his speech—so certain and focused.

"Where the hell you been, Cain?" Martin said, in a much softer tone, more earnestly curious.

"I been to hell, pops. I been to hell, and it ain't half bad."

Tom cleared his throat, which at least drew Martin's attention, though not Cain's. The other officers looked at Tom for direction.

"Okay, boys. Looks like we got a misunderstanding here. Cain, you alright?"

"Very well, Tom. Thank you for asking. I'm sorry about the trouble. I guess my folks just lost track of me. But we're all okay now."

Tom, almost as dumbstruck as Martin, nodded and looked at the other officers, pointing them toward the front door. After Tom closed the door behind him, silence filled the trailer. Cain put his hands into his jeans pockets and strolled over to the window, staring out with a smile as he watched the police cruisers roll out of the dusty driveway.

Without turning to look at his father, now joined by his mother, who still had a waxing strip on her upper lip, Cain said clearly and coldly.

"The time is ripe."

On the top of his right hand, something that looked like poison ivy was spreading in an arc, bubbling out from his skin with raw irritation.

17

TOGETHER THEY SHALL SEE

S ETH DROVE WITH SHANNON next to him in the passenger
seat, Will and Livy in the back, singing the theme song to
Fraggle Rock.

"I still don't know if this is a good idea," Seth said.

"Why? You did it. Why shouldn't I? You said it was harmless."

"It's not just 'harmless,' Shannon. It's better than that. I just
think . . . I think you oughta want to go through the door for
yourself, not just because I went through."

"Oh, I'm going for you, Seth. I'm going for this family. I
don't know what you've been thinking lately, but ever since you
went through that door and started talking to that cat, I feel like
I'm living with a stranger." Seth was hurt by the word "stranger"
and was about to reply, but she cut him off.

"Look, Seth: I'm not saying it's bad. It's good. You're . . .
peaceful. Calm. Focused. I don't know. I don't know what you
did when you went through that door, but you're not doing it
by yourself. We don't do that, remember?"

Seth smiled. It had been part of their wedding vows:
"Nothing apart; everything together." Shannon brought it up
whenever they were headed in two different directions on

something. But it was usually in a joking sense. This was serious. And Seth hadn't given his decision to walk through the door much forethought—as was typical for him. He didn't regret his decision, but he did wish he'd thought more about Shannon, about the kids. He hadn't just made a choice for himself. He'd made it for them, too. He didn't know it then, but he could see how true it was in this moment. And he now longed for Shannon to join him, and even for the kids, too.

They pulled into the small gravel lot at Childs Park. "Come on, kids. We're going on a little hike," Shannon said, trying to reassure them (and herself) that this was nothing out of the ordinary. Livy waited for Seth to undo her seatbelt and then wrangled her little body out of the car seat and looked for Will to lead her into the woods.

Will was already at the start of the trail, beckoning Livy with enthusiasm. "Livy, stay behind me!"

Seth met Shannon by the hood of the station wagon. "Hey . . . we're okay. We do this together," he said. She nodded hesitantly.

"There's nothing *weird* about this, right? Like, I'm not gonna turn into a zombie? Hey kids, wait up!"

"The most beautiful zombie on the planet."

"Oh brother," she said with an eye roll. But it lightened the mood enough for them both to start walking. When they were several yards from the door, Seth pulled Livy and Will aside. "Can you guys build me a big leaf pile? I want to jump in it." Will was instantly sold on the idea and began scraping leaves together. Livy joined him, kicking the leaves while sucking her two middle fingers.

"God, this is weird. It's weirder than I thought," Shannon said. Tension wrapped her vocal cords. She looked at the door—with its chipped paint and tired brass handle. The handle could have been turned thousands of times, even tens of thousands. What made her throat tighten in discomfort wasn't its appearance. It was something *behind* the door, not just its light, but . . . what was it? It was as if the door were watching her, reading her, sensing her movements. But that was insane.

"You have to decide to go in for yourself," Seth said, breaking her concentration. "There's no compulsion."

Shannon was gazing at the light seeping through the edges of the door. "I know. I just . . . You'll catch me if I fall backward, right?"

"Always," Seth said with a smirk. "But you won't fall backward; you'll fall forwards, and then you'll open your eyes, and I'll be here—head in the canopy."

"What do you mean?"

"Nothing. You'll see. At least, that's what Cleft said: To enter is to see."

Seth smiled confidently, and Shannon trusted in that smile. She put all her weight on it. She took one more look at Seth, her eyes begging for reassurance. Seth nodded his encouragement. She turned the handle, shielding her eyes from the blinding white, and stepped through—a smile growing on her face as wide and full as a mid-day summer sun.

***

The next thing she knew, Shannon was staring up at Seth's face from the ground. He looked *different*. With the canopy above his head and the light pouring in around him, it was almost as if he wore the leaves as a crown, as if he were kingly.

"You okay?" he asked. "It's just me—head in the canopy. See?"

Shannon didn't answer for a few moments. She just stared, marveling in silence, as Seth had when he went through. She held a peace inside her rib cage that she had never known before; it radiated through her veins, replacing the old blood with something she could find no words for. She turned her head to see Livy and Will still kicking the leaves together into a pile. They looked like angels to her, draped in clothes too big for their bodies. She found them so beautiful that she wanted more of their skin to be seen, not covered up in cotton and shielded from the world. The clothes seemed like a barrier between them and the papery leaves drifting in the light that shot through spaces in the foliage. They looked wildly happy, engrossed in their present vitality. A tear of joy rolled down her cheek into the dry leaves. And as it fell, she believed she was watering the earth.

"Amazing, isn't it?" Seth said, offering her his hand. Shannon took it, rolled herself up, and then fell forward into an embrace with Seth. She hugged him for what seemed like a minute before Will noticed.

"Mommy—look at this pile! You can jump it." Will proceeded to demonstrate. Shannon made an effort to shake out of her daze. But it wasn't a daze. It was too deep.

"Wow! You and Livy girl must be *professional* leaf pile makers," she managed to say, but feeling as if it was the first time she'd heard her own voice. "It's perfect! I'm gonna try it." Shannon backed up and exaggerated her efforts to leap over the little pile.

"Mom! You did it! That's really good!" Will said—still in his Livy-encourager mode.

"Aww. You're so sweet, Will." He looked away, embarrassed but beaming. "Shall we head back to the car?"

They all started walking back, but then Will remembered he'd left his sword stick behind him, along with Livy's little twig. (They always had to match.) "I gotta get my sword!"

"Okay," Shannon said. "Hurry up!"

Livy chased after him, but then Will noticed the big boulder and had to investigate.

"Woah! Livy, look at this door!"

Seth and Shannon turned with alarm to see Will reaching for what they knew was the handle.

"Will, hold on sweetie! Don't open—"

But it was too late. Will had gone silent and held the door open for Livy. In a matter of moments, they were both lying on the leaves in front of the door. Seth and Shannon gathered around them, initially horrified, but also quietly hopeful. Their hearts held equal portions of terror and thrill.

"Will! Will, are you okay?!" Seth said. Will just smiled up at his dad.

"Daddy . . . yeah. Yeah. I'm okay. What happened? Your face . . ." Will reached up and touched Seth's unshaven face, his little fingernails brushing over the tiny stubs of hair. Then he pushed with his fingers into his dad's skin. "This," he said. "This is skin."

"I know, Bud."

"Livy, look at mommy! Are you okay?" Shannon yelled, trailing off her volume at the end so as not to scare them. But it wouldn't have anyway. They were both calm and quiet.

Livy shook her head yes, still holding her two middle fingers in her mouth. But she took them out to reach for Shannon with a huge grin on her face. She paused mid-reach, staring at her fingers glistening from her own spit. The light bounced off them as if they were glass. She brought them close up to her eyes.

"Livy?"

"Hole-mee," she said. And the two embraced for a long time, as did Seth and Will. Their whole family lay there before the white door, clinging to each other, but wedded to something that went well beyond them, and yet also inside them. They were part of something, though none of them really understood what. But each felt like a drop of rain called up into the expanse by the long cascading arms of the sun.

***

A great explosion stabbed their moment of peaceful union. This was no shotgun, common in the woods around Dingmans Ferry during hunting season. This shook like disaster, a giant throttling of the landscape.

"What was that?!" Shannon said to Seth, both of them still holding their kids.

"I don't know. But it was big. I think we should get back home."

Shannon nodded and walked briskly ahead to the station wagon, carrying Livy. Seth followed, holding Will's hand.

As Shannon walked back to the parking lot, even though the boom had pricked her fear, she was awestruck by everything around her. It was like she was seeing the world for the first time, or coming back home to a country she'd left centuries ago. The shimmering leaves, the lazy, waving atmosphere of the soft spring wind in the canopy, the happy hush of the stream. She felt somehow more awake. She was reborn to an inside place, to the inner chapel of a great seed. In Childs Park, she moved through the wild womb of this inside world, so grand she couldn't see the top or bottom. Everything around her was laced with an aura she could only describe as "magical."

***

The whole family walked slowly into the entryway of their house, as if entering a holy tent, and removed their shoes. Each placed their shoes in a straight line by the door: Seth, Shannon, Will, Livy. Each of them, without conscious attention, had placed shoes in a neat pair next to the others. Everything was in order. Everything was in its right place.

"Well, look at the humans," came a voice from the living room. Shannon, Will, and Livy looked at each other puzzled.

"Seth, who's here?" Shannon whispered. "Who's in our house?" Seth's only reply was a smirk. One by one, each of them looked at the wingback chair, where Narnia sat, flicking his tail.

"I'd say 'welcome home' to all of you, but I believe you've all felt a home now that's far better than this one. Am I right?"

Shannon looked at Seth with wide eyes.

"It's just me," Narnia said, as if he'd lived with them for years. "Now you know your husband isn't crazy. Well, at least not *that* kind of crazy."

Will and Livy were smiling and slowly walking towards the living room, trying to confirm that this wasn't a dream.

"Much as I'd love to have a cuddle fest on the couch, we need to investigate that boom. Nearly knocked me off the chair."

18

A PRACTICE EXPLOSION AND A DISAPPEARANCE

CAIN ROSE FROM THE ground with ringing in his ears. He'd actually done it. The flames and the smoke billowed up from the small brick remains of the bungalow. Skotos had shown him how to rig up homemade explosives that could take out a small house. The bungalow in the woods was practice. Cain took in his new surroundings as his ears throbbed. He stared at the flames drifting into the upper branches of the hemlock trees. Shattered glass and debris lay at his feet. He shook his head to get the ringing to stop. It didn't help. Skotos was trying to say something, but Cain could only see lips moving.

"What?!"

Skotos came closer. "I said, 'This is only the beginning.'"

"Yeah, well you never told me what the real target is." Cain was still yelling, just so he could hear his own voice.

"It's that chapel in the sky," Skotos said slowly, so Cain could read his lips. He pointed southwest through the woods to the church steeple poking out above the canopy line.

"Woah, woah, woah!" Cain said, starting to hear the sound of his own voice more clearly. You didn't say anything about blowing up a church!"

"Relax, Cain. Believe in yourself. And trust me. No one needs to get hurt. And you won't get caught. It's all in the execution."

"Believe in myself? You keep saying that. I don't even know what you're talking about. But how is blowing up a church supposed to get me any recognition anyway? You said you'd help me make a name for myself. But even though I hate that church, other people love it. If I did take it out, that wouldn't help me at all. It'd just make people hate me."

"No, Cain. It would make them *fear* you. And fear is just as good as love, isn't it?"

"What?"

"If people love you, they still try to bend you to their will. But if they fear you . . . then you can bend their will to yours. That's respect. That's where you build your name. That's where you matter."

Cain was silent as he chewed on the words. He didn't like the way they tasted, but he couldn't bring himself to spit them out. He felt stuck. He touched his upper jaw just below his ear and felt the wetness of blood. He looked up at Skotos with alarm.

"It's fine. Your eardrums just tore a little from the explosion. We'll get you headphones."

"Torn eardrums?! Oh, great. This is great."

"Don't be dramatic. You'll be fine."

"Easy for you to say. You just order me around. Why don't *you* blow up a church?"

Skotos locked eyes with Cain and stared. Cain felt his throat closing up, tightening like a kinked hose.

"I can't breathe! Can't!" Cain fell on his knees and stretched his hand out toward Skotos. Skotos walked towards him and grabbed his shoulder.

"You listen to me, Cain Shoemaker," he said with the calm confidence of a settled psychopath. "You need *me*. I do *not* need you."

Cain's face was starting to turn blue as his body screamed for oxygen. A crazed plea for help radiated from his bloodshot eyes. Skotos uttered one last sentence. "You will do as I say, or you will go as I wish." Then he blinked, changing his countenance in a fraction of a second, emerging from some dark and distant cave to come back to the present. Cain gasped for air as he fell on his back. Every panicked breath was a miracle.

"You're a psychopath! You're a psycho!" He managed to get the words out as he sucked in more air.

"Oh, Cain . . ." Skotos said with a parental smile. "Psychopaths are small. They're little people. They always want something. I only *unwant*." Cain was too busy heaving for air to process the meaning. Skotos let a few seconds go by with Cain staring up at him in horror and confusion. He straightened his back in a leisurely stretch and said, "Cross me again, and I will end you."

"Is that . . . is that a threat?" Cain said, with the tiny ounce of courage he had left, hanging by a spider thread.

"I don't make threats, Cain. Threats are a waste of time. I make promises. And I keep them."

***

Skotos and Cain were long gone by the time the firetrucks arrived on the scene. They had to park on Sproul Road at first, before they found tire tracks that branched off through the woods to the bungalow near Adams Creek. The fire chief, Ezekiel Yoast, was talking to Tom Regent, who had gotten to the bungalow remains a few minutes earlier.

"We lookin' at an electrical fire? Gas explosion? What?" Tom asked, ready to write down notes on his notepad.

"Nah," Ezekiel said, rubbing his burly black beard. "There ain't no gas lines to this place, and we haven't seen anything suggesting the wiring was off. Course, most of it's charred now."

"Okay. What are you thinking, then?"

"Well, it's a bit early to conclude anything, but my guys found some traces of fertilizer, gunpowder, and a bit of hydrogen peroxide. That mean anything to you?"

Tom scratched his cheek. "No. Can't say that it does."

"Those are common materials for homemade explosives."

"You think someone did this on purpose?"

"Can't rule it out at this point," Ezekiel said. "Could be kids with nothin' better to do. It ain't for insurance reasons—I can tell you that much. This place was a dump. I'd seen it a few years ago. Mostly neglected. I'm surprised the township didn't doze it."

"Hmmm," Tom said, writing down the explosives ingredients on his yellow notepad. "Who's the owner, anyway?"

"Some guy named . . . ah, where'd I write it down?" Ezekiel shuffled through some papers on a clipboard. "Oh, here it is: Lemmuel Watson."

"Lem?" Tom said with surprise.

"You know 'im?"

"Well, yeah," Tom said. "He's a local of locals. Been around longer than I have. I didn't know he had a little place like this."

"Looks like no one's been livin' here for years."

"Alright. Well, thanks, Zeek. I'm gonna get some photos and then head back to the office to write up a report."

Ezekiel nodded and then went back to packing up gear for the fire truck. He stopped at the edge of the charred remains, still smoking like an offering, when a glimmer of silver caught his eye from the ground. He bent down and picked up a simple pendant for a necklace. It was four letters fused together: YCGB. Ezekiel turned to get Tom's attention but then thought better of it. Something this little couldn't be of use to anyone. And Lem would have to come around after this incident, so he could give it to him in person. Unless he was part of this. In that case, Lem would never show up. For now, Zeek stuffed it into his pocket and went back to dragging in the fire hose.

***

Cain made no attempt to quietly enter his trailer—not because he was desperate or in a rush, but because he still couldn't hear very well. The ringing hadn't entirely left his ears. All sounds seemed distant. His mother was the first to see him.

"Jesus, Cain! What happened?!" Tabitha rushed over and held her son's face in her hands, examining the blood stains by his ears and the charred marks on his red t-shirt.

"It's fine, Ma. Just was playing with some friends and knocked heads with one of them."

"Knocked heads? What in God's name were you playing? Were you throwing bombs at each other?" She wrapped her floral robe tightly around her chest and searched her son's face for an explanation. But she found none.

"I'm gonna go take a shower. If anyone asks, tell them I was hanging with Patrick and Jesse." Cain walked away before his mother could protest. His dad was out—whether at work or at the bar was anyone's guess. But Cain was grateful he didn't have to explain things to both parents at once. He went into the hot water of the shower and let the brown stains of dirt and pink blood water wash down the drain. As he stared at his feet, he thought about why he'd gotten himself into this, about what might happen next. But the strangest part was that he didn't regret his decision, not after the explosion, or the loss of hearing, or even after nearly dying at the feet of a psychopath. It was as if his life was set on a course, caught in a current he had no strength to swim against. And even if he could fight it, what would he be trying to get back? There was a strange peace for him in this. He didn't have to worry about the direction of his life anymore. That was set now.

He stepped out of the shower and dried himself off with a gray towel that was damp from someone else's use, which disgusted him. Everything in his life was used, soiled, contaminated. He had to get out.

***

On the other side of town, Cleft was spreading black mulch in his front garden bed, tucking the bits of fragrant wood around the shins of a rhododendron. He wiped his brow with his forearm and turned to survey the rest of the lawn.

Ethan Regent was on his bike heading toward Cleft's driveway at just that moment. He skidded to a stop near Cleft's mailbox and began walking his bike the rest of the way.

Cleft went to grab another double handful of mulch, but at the corners of his vision, he saw them: the lights under the ground—the same ones Janet and Ben had seen the night Jane died. They were harder to see in the sun, much more so than on that hallowed night. But they were there: puddled and lazy and beautiful. Cleft stared and smiled, and then began crawling towards them on all fours. He reached out his hand to caress the grass above one of them, as if brushing the hair away from a child's face.

Ethan stopped when he saw Cleft crawling into the middle of his lawn in broad daylight, looking like he was about to catch a frog or a butterfly, delicately poised above something Ethan couldn't see. As Cleft's hand came down and pushed through the grass, a white light enveloped his body. And in an instant, he disappeared.

Ethan's tongue caught in his throat. He turned around to see if anyone else might be there, anyone to confirm the ridiculous impossibility he'd just seen. But there was no one. He was at the edge of Cleft's yard alone. And terrified.

***

Ethan was about to turn and pedal as fast as he could back home when he noticed Cleft, or at least Cleft's body, sitting limp in the rocking chair on his front porch. He dropped his bike on the lawn and ran to the porch.

"Pastor Cleft! You okay? How'd you get up here?" He said as he grabbed Cleft's forearm and shook it. Cleft took a deep breath and sat up straight, as if he'd just awoken from surgery and was gathering his surroundings.

He looked at Ethan, puzzled but not bothered. "Ethan."

"Where..." Ethan struggled to articulate himself. "Where'd you go?"

"Hmm?" Cleft tilted his head, as if this were an odd question.

"You were on your lawn. And then you touched something ... and you disappeared."

"Disappeared?"

"Yeah ... like vanished. Into thin air. I must have imagined it. I must have."

"Oh." Cleft paused in remembrance. "Oh, no. You didn't imagine anything. I just hadn't been for a bit. I wanted to look at it, from a distance, you know?"

"No, I don't know. Hadn't been where? You were on your lawn, and then you were gone. And then you were *here*." Ethan grabbed the arm of the rocker.

Cleft stared at Ethan as if he were joking, or stupid. But he made no response. Ethan swallowed and waited for a reply that never came.

"Ethan, can I help you with something?" Cleft was coming back to reality but still spoke as if he were dazed.

"I wanted to ... just ... no." Ethan eventually decided. "No—I'm okay. I have to get back home."

"You sure? You look troubled," Cleft said.

Ethan huffed as he headed toward his bike. "I *am* troubled," he mumbled to himself. Then he hopped on his bike and rode the three miles back to his house.

***

Cleft went inside and picked up the phone. He dialed Bill's number.

"Hello?" Bill said.

"Bill. It's Cleft. He's coming for the church."

"Hey, Cleft. Umm . . . who's coming for the church?"

"Skotos."

Bill paused for a few seconds, unsure of what to say and where this was coming from. "How do you know that?"

"I just do."

"You went there again, didn't you?"

"Yeah. I did."

There was a long pause of silence that hovered between them, both processing what had happened.

"Let me get my dad and come to your place."

"Bring Seth, too."

"You sure you want him in on this so soon?"

"Yeah. He's got to get his feet wet sometime. Better sooner than later, if this is really going down."

"Okay. Be there in a bit."

***

Cleft hung the phone up on the wall as Roland, his white-faced old golden retriever, sauntered down the hall-way towards him, his bright fur settled around his weighty brown eyes.

"You went there again, didn't you?" The voice came from Roland.

"I did," Cleft confessed.

"You said you'd take me with you next time. It's been too long."

"Ah, geez. I'm sorry, Roland," Cleft said, with the same tone of a parent who'd broken a promise to his child. "Next time."

"Next time. Okay. Who knows how many 'next times' we've got left."

"Yeah," Cleft said, suddenly somber. "I know. Especially now that I've found him."

"What did you see?" Roland said, settling his body into a sitting position on the carpet in the living room.

"Same . . . beautiful place I always see. God, I can't wait to call it home. I would have stayed longer, but something called me back, something I heard."

"Something you heard?"

"Yeah. It was this . . . voice."

"What did it say?"

"It said, 'He's going to build a chapel.' But it wasn't a good thing. It reminded me of something I read in seminary decades ago." Roland waited for him to finish his thought. "Every time God plants a church, Satan builds a chapel."

"Hmm. I think I get the meaning."

"I think our church is under threat."

"Hasn't it always been? Who is it this time?" Roland asked.

"I don't know. Maybe this fella they're calling Skotos."

"Still want me to keep a watch and a nose around the perimeter?"

"Of course. That's been a great help, my friend."

"Happy to do it. We'll fight the good fight together."

"Always have, haven't we?" Cleft said. Roland nodded.

"Yessir. Always will." With that, Roland slowly turned his tired body toward the front door. Cleft pushed open the storm door to let him out. Then he sat in his living room, thinking and waiting.

***

At Seth's house, the whole family stood staring at Narnia, still hunched beneath the wingback chair.

"Did he just . . . *talk*?" Shannon asked, her eyes marked with incredulity.

"You can hear him?" Seth asked but then answered his own question. "Of course you can. You've been through the door."

"Mommy! The kitty, Narna, just talked!! Did you hear it?!" Will shouted, caught up in wonder and dancing toward the wingback chair. Seth looked at Shannon, and they both took a deep breath, as if to say, *We're really doing this.*

"Yes," Seth said. 'Nar-ni-a' can talk now. Or maybe he always could, but you couldn't hear him."

"Oh, yeah," Will said, embarrassed. "I said 'Narna.' Livy, I just called the cat 'Narna.'" Will laughed. Livy smiled and stared with her fingers stuck in her mouth as usual, but obviously didn't know why that was funny. 'Narna' sounded fine to her. She took her two fingers from her mouth and crawled over towards Narnia, joining in Will's contagious enthusiasm.

"Ine . . . I'm . . . Livy," she said to Narnia. Seth and Shannon smiled at what they knew was the cutest introduction in the history of the world.

"Yes, I know. You're such a smart, brave, strong girl," Narnia said. Livy smiled wide and then put her two fingers back in her mouth. She began petting his leg very gently.

Just then the phone rang, ripping through the moment. Seth picked it up.

"Hello?"

"Seth. It's Cleft. I wonder if you could make your way over here—alone. Sort of urgent."

"Oh. Umm. Sure. Give me a few minutes?"

"That's fine," Cleft said before hanging up.

Seth was about to tell Shannon, but she'd heard the whole conversation. She had excellent hearing, which never ceased to surprise him. Before he could get a word out, she said, "We're coming, too." Seth wanted to protest but couldn't think of a reason to. They were all *insiders* now. They might as well come and go together. Narnia too. They loaded into the station wagon and headed for Cleft's.

19

A CRITICAL MEETING

L EM, BILL, AND TRAVIS arrived at Cleft's just a minute before Seth pulled into the driveway in their station wagon. Cleft frowned when he noticed Seth wasn't alone. He walked down the porch steps towards them, exchanging his frown for a welcoming grin.

"Hey! The whole Logan crew! Didn't know you'd have everyone with you, Seth. That's great. Shannon, good to see you again. And who are these little giants?"

Will marched over to Cleft with confidence, having just heard his mom talk about how kind and wise Pastor Cleft was. "I'm Will, and this is Livy." Will put his arm around her shoulder. Livy still had her two fingers in her mouth (when did she not?), but was trying to smile bashfully around them.

"Well it's great to finally meet you," Cleft said, bending down to their level. "I've heard so much about you both. But I gotta tell you: you're much bigger than I thought you were. Do you eat a lot of vegetables?"

"I love green beans," Will answered without missing a beat. "And Livy . . . she likes vegetables, too."

Livy took her fingers out to make an important announcement. "But not bussel spouts." She put her fingers back in her mouth and looked over at Shannon. All the adults were trying to bind the laughter behind their lips. But Cleft managed to disguise a laugh with a cough.

"Well, thank you for being honest. I don't always love broccoli, but I eat it anyway."

Will nodded in serious approval.

"Hey, do you guys like marbles? Because I have some really cool marbles my daddy gave to me, and I wondered if I might be able to give them to you."

Will's eyes lit up, and he looked at Shannon and Seth for permission. Livy just studied Will's face, not having a clue what marbles were.

Shannon nodded to Will. "Just remember that we don't ever put marbles in our mouth. I'm thinking especially of you, Livy girl." Livy shook her head up and down, still not sure why she was being singled out.

"Alright—come inside and I'll show you where they are. You're gonna love them. My favorite one is green with swirls of white." Cleft led the way for the kids while Seth and Shannon followed, exchanging introductions with Travis, Lem, and Bill.

***

Narnia, who had quietly sat in the car, hopped out of the window. Roland, who had been mingling with the legs of all the guests, looked at Narnia and wagged his tail.

"Guess I don't get introduced," Narnia said quietly.

"A steward?!" Roland said, approaching Narnia.

"I am," Narnia said with surprise. "I see you are as well."

"Been years since I've seen another steward. How are things going?" Roland asked.

"Okay, I suppose. My name is Narnia, by the way. And you are?"

"Oh, forgive me. Roland's the name."

"Pleased to meet you."

"Likewise. How long you been with your human?"

"Less than two weeks, actually. I'm still getting my bearings with all of this."

"Ah. Well, I'm glad you're here. I can fill you in. I'm a veteran, I guess. Been with my human fifteen years."

"Fifteen years! My goodness. Is that some sort of record?"

"Maybe," Roland said with a laugh. "Come inside so we can chat. I know a few patches of sunlight that should still be on the carpet."

"Sounds wonderful."

Narnia followed Roland up the steps and in the door that Lem was holding open for them. Roland led them down the entryway, through the kitchen and to the living room. They sat on a braided blue carpet, each in a patch of sunlight breaking through the window.

"Well," Roland started. "I'll tell you what I know, and feel free to ask any questions along the way."

"Sounds good. And thank you for this hospitality. It's so nice to have another animal to talk to. Seth is still getting used to speaking to me, and Shannon and the kids just found out I could talk."

"Wait, *they* can hear you?"

"Yes," Narnia said, unsure of why this was important.

"Then they've been through the door."

"Yes. Yes, they have. All of them now. Is that good or bad?"

"Well . . ." Roland paused. "It's good. It just changes things a bit. They'll be able to see things others can't."

"How do you mean?"

"I'll try to explain it the way Cleft explained it to me. He's sort of the leader of the movement in this town."

"Movement?"

"I'll get to that, too. Everyone in this town—and I suppose everywhere else, too—lives in what he calls *the in-between*. Lem likes to call them *tweeners*. That means they haven't been through the white door yet. Once they go through the door, they become what he calls *gazers*. They start to see things that others can't—things that are here but aren't visible to certain eyes."

"Okay," Narnia said, soaking in the information. "What sorts of things do they see?"

"I guess you would say . . . spiritual things. These things are always here, always around us. But most people don't have the eyes to see them. Entering through the door gives them a new set of eyes. Take human anger, for instance. Everyone might be able to see the anger on someone's face after an insult. But gazers can see how that anger is working on the person, so to speak. And they see it concretely—in the form of something."

"The form of something?"

"Best I can do is give you an example," Roland started. "Are you familiar with Gladice Shoemaker?"

"Ah, the sweet elderly woman. Works at the police station, right?"

"That's the one. Well, some years back, Cleft saw her walking down main street. I was with him. She had this giant necklace around her neck. At least, that's what we *thought* it was from a distance. When we got closer, we could see what it really was:

a thickly woven braid of thistles—many of the points jabbing right into her skin and drawing blood. You could see the pain and anxiety on her face."

"So, you and Cleft helped her take them off?"

"No. We couldn't. Our hands would have gone through thin air if we tried. The thorns were a physical manifestation of a spiritual reality."

"Which was?"

"Gladice had struggled for many years with a fear of death—ever since her sister had died young from a car accident. That fear was constricting her, tightening around her and cutting off all senses of peace and contentment."

"I see," said Narnia. "So, what did you do then?"

"Cleft had to use the most powerful tool at a human being's disposal: *words*."

"Words?"

"Yes. He started asking her questions—short and simple ones first. Then the deeper ones—the sort that drives a wedge down into the soul, breaking apart the ice that keeps it stiff. He asked her—though it was forward of him—why she seemed distressed. And when she didn't answer right away and then tried to dodge his question with small talk, he did the hardest thing for humans to do."

"What's that?"

"He *waited*. He let the silence be a servant. And it served her well. She opened up and started crying. Talked about her anxiety and her grief. And Cleft listened. As he did, we both watched those thorns dry up and break down, the dark brown color fading to pale yellow. The lines between the thorns started to break. And thread by thread, they fell to the sidewalk and vanished into nothing."

"My God," said Narnia, enraptured by the story. "That's . . . that's glorious."

"That's the sort of thing gazers can see on an everyday basis."

"Okay. So, there are *gazers* and there are *tweeners*. And our job—"

Roland calmly cut him off softly. "Is to walk faithfully with our gazers until God calls them home."

"Home," said Narnia, giving the word its somehow rightful royalty. "Yes . . . I think I somehow knew that."

"It's a fairly straightforward and very honorable job for us."

"Indeed," Narnia agreed.

"But there's trouble brewing. And that's why the humans have gathered here. So, it's best we make our way over to the study where they're talking. Oh, and remind me later to tell you about the city."

Both rose from their sun patches and shook themselves off, leaving trails of white hair drifting in the tired arms of the sunlight, and heading back through the kitchen and down the hallway, where voices were waiting for them.

***

Cleft was pouring out a small canvas bag of marbles for Will and Livy while Shannon knelt beside them, her hand on Livy's back.

"Now, Livy. Remember the one rule with these, okay? You *cannot* put them in your mouth." Livy shook her head in agreement, her two fingers still settled inside her lips. As Will and Livy played with the marbles, Cleft sat back in a sofa chair near a floor-to-ceiling bookshelf packed with everything from poetry to commentaries, history and biography, fantasy and philosophy. Seth reached into his pocket and pulled out the marbles he always carried with him.

"Ah, got your own collection there?" Cleft said.

Seth was embarrassed. He thought no one was looking. "Oh, yeah. Just two." Cleft stood up and walked over to examine them.

"Hmm. A drop of rain, and fire in a teardrop."

"That's the exact same way I describe them! Have I mentioned these before or something?"

Cleft was smiling at the coincidence. It made him feel even closer to Seth, as if their hearts held the same type of paintbrush.

"No, don't think so. You know, when they melt the glass to make these, it gets up to—"

"2,200 degrees," Seth finished. They both laughed, thrilled to have found such obscure common ground.

"Guess we share an interest. Always been fascinated by marbles. They're like little worlds, cut and crafted and self-contained."

"I always carry these two with me," Seth admitted.

"Really? Why's that?"

"I don't . . . I don't know. Feels like I'm always choosing between them, choosing which world I see. The clear one shows everything as it is."

"But upside down. The sphere acts like a convex lens. Based on what you're looking at and where the focal point is, you'll see the world turned upside down."

"Yeah. That's right. Anyway, it's easier to see things through that marble. But the other one—that feels like the way the world really is."

"How so?"

"Well, there's a fire right where your eye wants to look. The fire impedes your vision, keeps you from seeing beyond it, but . . ."

"But there's also a beauty to the flame," Cleft finished.

"Yes. Sometimes that's how I see the world—a beautiful disruption. Nothing is as simple and transparent as I want it to be."

"Hmm. You and me both," Cleft said with a smile. He was certain now that'd found the one. No one else had this sort of sensitivity and openness, and was also willing to walk through the white door—not even his own sons. Each of his sons—William, Blake, and Samuel—had left him years before and started their own lives elsewhere. Each had passed off his ecstatic rants about the white door as lunacy mixed with pitiable religious vigor. Cleft had lost them a long time ago. But now he'd found Seth. He nodded to show that the conversation had reached a fitting end. Then he took a deep breath to start the next one.

"Now, Seth," Cleft began. "I was hoping to address those who have gone through the door with this news, but—"

"I have," Shannon cut him off. She'd been listening in to the whole conversation. No words could escape her sharp hearing.

"You have?" Cleft raised his eyes in surprise.

"Yes . . . and so have they." Shannon nodded at the kids.

"The kids?" Cleft was dumbfounded. Shannon was a surprise to him. But the kids going through the white door was baffling. It had never happened before—not with anyone so young. He'd only known adults who went through. "The kids went through the . . ." He didn't finish the sentence. He was sprinting up fields of thought, looking for the implications.

"Is that okay? Should we be worried?" Shannon's maternal instinct kicked in and she looked at Seth with concern.

"No, it's . . . it's fine," Cleft said. "I just haven't seen it before, so I'm surprised—that's all. Have they . . . have they seen anything strange since then?"

"Well, no. But I haven't either. But what's all of this mean, anyway? What does that white door *do*?"

Cleft took a deep breath as he realized he'd be getting into a longer explanation, or story, or both. Lem, Bill, and Travis seemed content to talk about something from Bill's pet shop, a new species of fish he'd ordered.

"Look," Cleft said. "I'm going to be straight with you since I think that's just the best approach. You can take this or leave it on your own. All I can tell you is what I know. Okay?"

Seth and Shannon looked at each other and nodded.

"That door," Cleft began, "gives people entrance into *another world*, for lack of a better phrase. Once you go through it, once you're enveloped by that light, you see things differently, things other people don't see. Strictly speaking, the world is the same. But everything is different. You've probably felt that already."

Shannon immediately thought of the ecstatic peace and awe she felt when she found herself lying on her back and staring into the canopy at Childs Park, how the whole forest seemed alive with a sacred energy.

"I have," Shannon said. And Seth nodded. "But in a good way. I feel more peaceful, and . . . and everything seems more—I don't know . . ." she trailed off. But Seth finished her thought.

"Awake."

"Yeah," Shannon said, both in wonder and relief at having the thought finished.

"What I've told folks in the past," Cleft continued, "is that everything is the same, but everything is different. You live in the same world, but it's like the cloudy plastic film that used to cover it has been peeled off. The color is sharper and deeper."

"Yeah. That's how it feels," Shannon said.

"So, for the sake of simplicity, let's just say that the world we all lived in before we went through that door is called *the in-between*. We're now in the world I call *the land of the living*. It's biblical language that I landed on because . . . well, because I'm a Bible nerd." Seth and Shannon smiled.

"So, what's the real difference?" Shannon pressed, looking down at Will and Livy, who were turning the marbles in their hands with focused wonder, rolling the self-contained little worlds around their palms.

"Well, you may see things, notice things, that other people don't. They tend to be things of spiritual import."

"What do you mean?" Seth asked.

"Think of it as night-vision goggles. Except these are day-vision goggles. You've been given eyes to see things that other people don't have the eyes to see. Those could be good things—moments and images of peace and beauty and grace. And they could be bad things."

"What sort of bad things?" Shannon asked. But at this question, Will looked up from playing with the marbles.

"Well, there may be a better time to get into that. And I will get into it, I promise. At this point, I'll just reassure you that you don't need to be worried."

Shannon was obviously not content with that response, but she let it go for the sake of the group. Lem, Bill, and Travis had trailed off their conversation and were now sitting down and listening in on Cleft's. Travis was pulling dead skin off of his thumb, letting his own questions stir inside. Lem and Bill were patiently listening, obviously more in the know than the others. Will resumed his marble play, showing Livy how to roll them across the carpet.

"So, everyone else is in the in-between right now, and we're in the land of the living," Seth summarized. "Is that all?"

"No," came a voice from the hallway. "There's more."

"Who said that?" Seth said, mildly alarmed. He looked at Lem and Bill, but they shook their heads and began to smile. Roland stepped into the room from the hallway.

"Roland did," Cleft said, holding out a hand for Roland to receive a pet. Roland happily accepted and shoved his head under Cleft's hand.

Seth laughed, at first in disbelief, and then in wonder. "You've got a talking dog?"

"He does," Roland said, before Cleft could answer.

"And you've got a talking cat," said Narnia, strolling over to the loveseat Seth and Shannon were sharing.

"Ah," Cleft said with a big smile. "You've got your steward! Pleased to meet you, uh . . ."

"Narnia," the cat finished.

"Narnia! That's right! I love it. Was that your idea Seth? Oh, it's perfect. Just perfect. Pleased to meet you, Narnia."

"You as well, pastor." Narnia hopped up onto Shannon's lap. She was smiling, still very new to the idea of talking animals, and not yet comfortable with the fact that one of them could sit on her without being self-conscious. That Narnia could speak somehow made her feel less comfortable holding him. "Would you get the right side of my neck a bit? I can never quite get it."

Shannon laughed to herself and then scratched his neck. "Oh, that's perfect," Narnia said, full of gratitude. Everyone in the room started to chuckle.

"I guess this is from the door?" Shannon said, still smiling and marveling.

"Yes, it is," said Cleft. "We can now hear voices where silence reigned." He paused at the sound of his own words. And so did the others.

"But," Travis broke the silence, though he was still baffled by the animals' speech. "If there's an in-between and a land of the living, is there a . . . *darker* side, too?"

Everyone stared at him for a moment.

"Well," Cleft said. "That's sort of why I called you all here. Since the night my wife Jane passed, there's been a man that's been lurking around town. Lem seems to have seen him before, some years ago. He calls himself Skotos—which, not to creep anyone out, but it means 'shadow' in Greek." At the mention of the name, everyone felt a chill. Even the children paused from rolling marbles and looked at Shannon. They had goosebumps on their little arms.

"Lem and Bill have been keeping an eye out for him, and I've already given the police station a description so they can keep watch, too. He's usually dressed in all black," Cleft continued, "with longer, black hair, a pale face, and a plain green circle tattoo on one of his hands."

"What'd he do?" Travis asked.

"At this point, not much of anything. But he was trespassing on my property the night Jane died. And he said some unsettling words to Gladice Shoemaker a few days ago. Gladice works down at the police station, if you don't know her. Sweet older lady—like a mother to anyone who knows her."

"What'd he say?" said Travis, now taking the lead for inquiry, irritation beginning to creep into his vocal cords. If Seth was always battling his fight-or-flight instinct, Travis seemed to have just the "fight" part.

"Well . . ." Cleft paused and looked down at Will and Livy, who seemed distracted enough for him to keep going without disturbing them. "He said the exact same words that Gladice said to her sister on the night her sister was killed by a drunk driver—twenty-five years to the day. Gladice said it was like he knew, like he was taunting her."

"That's terrible," Shannon said, looking for matching expressions of horror in the rest of the room, which she found.

"And then there's," Cleft started but then trailed off.

"There's what?" Lem said.

Cleft took a deep breath, realizing he'd have to keep going deeper down the rabbit hole. But Roland's old, wise voice broke in from behind the group. "Cleft, you'll have to tell them about the city . . . and about us."

Shannon's mouth fell open again at hearing an animal speak. "Umm, hello." She waved her hand as if greeting a small child.

Roland turned towards her. "Hello, Shannon. Pleased to meet you." Shannon responded with a speechless nod and smile. She felt like she was dreaming.

"What city?" she asked, looking back and forth at Cleft and Roland.

"By now," Cleft began, "you've all heard the story on the radio or in the newspaper about strange lights underground, spotted on my property." Seth and Shannon looked at each other with eerie suspicion. "Those lights, they lead to a . . . another place, maybe even the same place that the door leads to, for all I know." Cleft grimaced at the inadequacy of his words. But he went on.

"The difference between the lights, so far as I can tell, is that the door lets you see things *here*, but these lights, they take you somewhere else, to the borders of . . ."

"Of what?" Shannon pressed.

"Of a white-stone city . . . against a golden horizon. I've only seen it from a distance. Roland has, too. My heart tells me it's a place I'll get to enter when . . ." Cleft looked down at the kids again. Will's enthusiastic voice seemed loud enough to cover Cleft's words. "When I die one day. But all this is full of mystery. I can't explain it, and I don't understand much of it. But I'm hoping that together, we'll understand more."

At the mention of death, Will's head snapped up. "I'm going to see heaven when I died . . . dies?" He looked to Shannon for help.

"'Die,' sweetie, but that's not something you need to worry about now."

"Oh, I'm not worried," Will said. "It'll be a good trip."

Cleft smiled at Will's simple confidence. "It will," he said. "A very good trip." At that, Will returned to the marbles, Livy still sucking her two fingers and rubbing the top of a red marble against the carpet with the palm of her hand.

"Anyway, I sort of fell into one of the lights yesterday and had this . . . message, maybe a vision. I don't know."

"Wait," Seth said. "You 'fell' into them? What does that mean?"

"The lights are underground, so far as I can tell, but whenever I've touched one of them, I go there . . . to that place, to the borders of the city. In fact, I'm afraid Ethan Regent saw it happen the other day and was freaked out."

"Hmm. We'll need to talk about him later," Seth said. "He's one of my students."

"Yes, we do. Later," Cleft said. "But, anyway, these lights aren't always there. They come and go, and I can't predict their appearance. I've tried but failed. In fact, the older I get, the less explaining I seem capable of." He paused. "I've written down everything I've seen or thought of in a book. Maybe one day, one of you will read it." As he said this, he met eyes with Seth.

"But what was the message you said you heard?" Shannon asked, holding off on questioning the reliability of the entire narrative.

"This sort of thing hasn't happened before, so I'm not sure what to do with it. But I had this . . . *conviction* that Skotos was coming for the church."

Lem sat up straight. "He tries to take that, then we'll take *him*. Take 'im out." It was clear as Lem spoke where Travis had gotten his fighting spirit.

"Easy, Lem. I don't know how to interpret this yet. I just wanted everyone here to be an extra set of eyes." He scanned the group. "If you see him or anyone else suspicious around the church building, I want you to call the police station right away. I've already talked to Tom about staying vigilant about this. So, he'll be expecting communication."

Everyone nodded and soaked in the threat of the intruder, a splinter in their mental skin.

"That's mainly what I wanted to tell you all, but I do want to have a word in private with Seth and Shannon, outside."

Seth and Shannon looked at each other with worry. But they followed Cleft out the front door as he rose from his sofa chair. Cleft sat on the rocker to the left of the front door, but Seth and Shannon chose to stay standing, still concerned.

"What is it?" Shannon asked. "What's wrong . . . I mean *more* wrong than what you just told us."

"This town is . . . strange. And it's had something strange for a while. And I'll let you two judge for yourselves what you'd like to believe. I'll just let you know what I've seen. Okay?" Seth and Shannon both nodded and took deep breaths.

"For as long as I can remember, whenever someone in this town finds an animal out in the wild—"

"Like I did with the cat," Seth said.

"Yes," Cleft said. "Like you did with the cat. I did the same with Roland. It's a sign, a sign that, that . . ."

"What?" Shannon asked, with growing alarm, but almost knowing ahead of time what Cleft was going to say.

"It's a sign that the end of that person's life is coming into view."

Seth's knees went weak, and he almost fell. He grabbed the arm of the other rocker and sat down.

"You okay?" Cleft asked, grabbing Seth's forearm and watching the blood leave Seth's face.

Shannon rushed over to him. "Seth! It's alright; it's just your nerves."

"Nerves?" Cleft said. "Oh, the anxiety," he said with deep sympathy.

"The anxiety," Seth said with reluctance.

"Now, hear me out first," Cleft said. "There's less reason for alarm than you think. First of all, this is just a theory, something that Bill noticed years ago. And second, I'm not saying anything about imminence, about when this could happen. In fact, I found Roland in the woods nearly fifteen years ago." As if summoned by his name, Roland pushed through the front storm door, holding it open so Narnia could come out.

Seth nodded in desperation, still in the midst of a panic attack. He was taking labored breaths and trying to keep his head up. All he could think about was leaving, absence, parting, losing his beloved wife and precious children. How could he not be with them? How could he not be here? His head spun and sputtered, like a dried-out engine.

"Might actually help to put your head down, between your knees," Narnia said. "Old trick to get the blood back where it belongs."

Seth immediately bent down and put his head between his knees, feeling the warm rush of blood confirm Narnia's words. Cleft put his hand on Seth's back.

"The other thing to remember," Cleft said, "is that all of us have an ending to face. We just do a heck of a job at ignoring it. What may happen to you *one* day, Seth, will happen to everyone *some*day. What you've got is actually special. You've got a *steward*."

At that word, both Roland and Narnia sat up straight, as if called to attention.

"A steward?" Shannon said, her voice still shaking from the revelation. She was doing her best to put her energy into Seth right now and not bury herself in confused grief and panic.

"Stewards are sort of like shepherds," Cleft said, putting his hand on Roland's head. Roland leaned into the pet. "They know all about you, and they go everywhere with you. The best advice I can give you, Seth, is to *talk*. Talk to Narnia as much as you can. Process your thoughts, your hopes, your desires, your grievances. Let the speech flow freely."

Seth picked up his head and took a deep breath in through his nose. His fingers and toes were still tingling—an effect of his hyperventilation. He rubbed them together, then stood and hugged Shannon harder than he'd ever hugged her before, squeezing her back and ribs into himself, smelling her hair, soaking all of her in. She whispered in his ear, "We do all things together. No matter what. Okay?"

Seth nodded as a tear rolled down his cheek, matched by one from Shannon. Cleft bowed his head. Then he turned and invited them back into the house. "You can come back in when you're ready."

A few minutes later, when Seth and Shannon had composed themselves for the kids, Cleft went on.

"Now, listen," he said, with the confidence of a bird leading a flock on migration. "I've told you all a lot, and there's more to tell still. I'd like to meet each Saturday here to regroup and check in with you all. As best I understand it, we're in some sort of war, for lack of a better term. It's something I don't fully understand. But there's light, and there's dark, and there's purpose. And that's been steady since the fall of Adam."

Travis piped in. "So there's good, and there's bad, and there's neutral."

"No," Cleft said with certainty as he looked at Travis. "No, there is no *neutrality*. We are all either *for* the light or *in* the darkness. The in-between is just a place for choosing openly what's already been chosen deeper inside." Travis frowned at the words but didn't pose another question.

"Keep your eyes open for this Skotos figure. Call me or Tom at the police station right away if you see anything, especially around the church. I also want you to let me know what you're seeing."

"What do you mean?" Seth asked, happy to divert his attention away from his own impending death sentence, which he was trying to rationalize and cope with second by second.

"I told you that everyone who goes through the white door starts to see things—spiritual things, things that others don't see. I'd like you to tell me what you're seeing. Like I said, I have a record, a sort of book, of all the things we've seen in years past. And it's important that we keep adding to it." Everyone nodded. "The more we share, the more we understand, despite the pervasive mystery. And I hope you're okay with mystery, because you're about to start swimming in it."

"Mommy, what's a . . . dezbite?" Will asked.

"What, sweetie?" Shannon looked down to see Will and Livy ready to leave with the canvas sack of marbles.

"A dezbite," Will said. Cleft started smiling.

"That was a strange word, wasn't it?" Cleft said, bending down to Will's level. "It means 'even though.'" Will shook his head in seriousness, absorbing the word into his tiny database of sounds. Livy stared at him, still sucking on her favorite two fingers.

"Now, it may seem sort of . . . I don't know, cub scoutish," Cleft said. "But we tend to end our meetings with a piece of poetry from Henry Wadsworth Longfellow." Seth picked up his head from its weighted anxiety and met eyes with Cleft. Longfellow had been one of his favorites since he was in high school. Cleft nodded to Lem and Bill, and the three of them said,

> Life is real! Life is earnest!
> And the grave is not its goal;
> Dust thou art, to dust returnest,
> Was not spoken of the soul.

Seth smiled. "A Psalm of Life" was one of his favorites. Despite everything—the strangeness, the chaos, the threat of death and loss—something felt very *right* about this whole situation, as if he were in the perfect place in a story he didn't understand. White doors. Talking cats. Stone cities through puddles of light. The in-between. Who could understand any of it? But he was here, in the middle, and he had a visceral sense that this was *exactly* where he was supposed to be. He also had a sense that he was going to grow larger, to grow into a shape his heart hadn't wanted before, a shape he would never have chosen for himself.

He was losing control—which he hated. But deep down, he truly believed that this was somehow better. His life, as his father once told him, would be very small if it was only what he could imagine it would be.

***

After Seth, Shannon, and the kids pulled out of the driveway, Lem turned to Cleft.

"So, we gonna talk about who blew up my bungalow?"

20

THE TARGET

I T WAS 2:00 AM on the next Friday. Skotos and Cain were crouched in a shed as Skotos directed Cain with the wiring and explosives.

"I told you!" Cain said with shaking hands, "I *ain't* blowin' up no church. I can't. I don't want to do this anymore!" He was on the edge of tears.

"You need to grow into the shape you chose," Skotos said with coldness. "Stop going back to that pathetic little attention-seeker you used to be. If you want a name for yourself, you have to make it. And we're not blowing up the church."

Cain looked up from his work with relief and confusion. "We're not?"

"No. We'd need a lot more explosives for that anyway."

"Then what are we blowing up?"

"The goal is to remove the church as a place of gathering until we can build our own place for the others. To do that, we need to take out the electricity and plumbing systems. That's what we're going to do."

"What do you mean 'our own place'? And who are the 'others'?"

"Well," Skotos said with a patronizing sigh. "You don't seem capable of handling much more than the present moment. So, I'll answer those questions when you're ready. For now, just finish the bombs."

"What are you going to do?" Cain asked, fear clinging to his vocal cords.

"That's my business. You're trying to *make* a name for yourself. Let's just say I'm trying to *destroy* one."

Skotos went outside of the shed and picked up a gravel stone, scraping it into the rim of his circle tattoo until blood began to seep out, the black-purple liquid mingling with the tattoo green. Then he took some dirt and massaged it into the open wound. He held up his hand, studying it for a moment, as the blood soaked into the dirt. "The infection must take," he uttered to himself. "The infection *will* take."

"What are you doing?" Cain said, peeking out from the shed doorway.

Without turning around to look at him, Skotos said, "Rehearsing a truth despite myself. Now get back to work."

Cain ducked into the shed and kept working until he was finished about forty-five minutes later.

"I'm done," he said, not with an air of confidence but with the remorse of a slave.

"Good. Let's go. The time is ripe."

***

Cleft woke at 3:45 am. The second explosion had been loud enough to do that, given that he was less than a mile from it. He sat up in a cold sweat, and then frantically dressed and bolted down the stairs to find his shoes and keys. He *knew* somehow that it was the church. But he still acted surprised, even to himself.

On the last step of the stairs, his pinky toe landed first and rolled his foot forward. He felt a bony click inside his ankle, and sharp pain came shooting up through his calf. He fell down on the hardwood floor by the front door, grabbing his calf muscle and moaning. "No, no, no, no! Not now! Please—God, not now!"

Roland jumped off the couch, where he sometimes slept when the foot of Cleft's bed became uncomfortable. Cleft was relieved to hear his nails scraping on the wood floor. "Cleft! What happened?"

"Turned my ankle. Twisted it." He grimaced in pain. "Did you hear the boom?"

"Course I did. Thought it might be a gun, maybe a firework."

"No," Cleft said, taking in a breath through his clenched teeth. "No, it was too big for that."

"What can I do?" Roland said.

"Grab my shoes. I'll try to pull them on and then limp to the truck."

"You can't drive. That's your right foot. You need that one for the pedal, don't you?"

Cleft took in a deep breath. Roland was right. The searing pain and inflammation were growing, throbbing. Swelling had set in quickly. A grapefruit was growing above his foot. But he had to get to the church. He paused before his next sentence, not sure he had the courage to follow through with it.

"You can drive."

"Excuse me. Is there someone else in the room, or did you really just ask *me* to operate that big . . . rolling machine?"

"Roland, something's off. I know it. And so do you. We have to get there. And I can't walk."

"So, call someone to drive you."

"No—it's too early. Look, I'll sit in the driver's seat and handle the steering wheel and the brake with my left foot. I just need you to softly push on the gas peddle when I say so. We can coast most of the way."

"This is a textbook bad idea."

"Oh, come on, Roland. It's a mile down the road in the middle of the night. What could go wrong?"

"Well, now you've doomed us."

"Come on, now. Help me up." Roland trotted over so Cleft could use his back as a steadying point while he reached for the stairway railing. "That's it. Now just grab my jacket from the couch. I'll get the keys."

"This is silly, Cleft," Roland said as he hopped into the passenger side of Cleft's truck. "We can't do this."

"Just do what I tell you, and we'll be fine." He turned the ignition and moved his swollen ankle towards the driver's side door so Roland could get his chest and paws closer to the gas pedal. Cleft slipped his left foot under his right leg to reach the brake. "Okay. Now, easy. I'm putting it in drive, and just ease on the gas gently."

Roland stretched out his paw to push the pedal, but it wouldn't budge.

"It sticks a little," Cleft said.

"Yeah. Okay, here we go." Roland punched at the pedal with his left paw. Too hard. The truck jerked into Cleft's front lawn. Cleft's chest banged into the edge of the steering wheel.

"Easy! Easy!"

"But it's not easy!" Roland growled.

"I don't mean that kind of easy. I mean *gently*."

Roland tried again. He pressed the pedal softly this time to roll the truck forward.

"Good! That's it."

Roland stopped. The truck jerked to a halt.

"Why'd you stop?"

"You said 'That's it.' That's all I needed to do, isn't it?"

Cleft sighed and rubbed his eyes. "No, you gotta hold the pedal down for the truck to keep moving."

"Well, that's not very smart. I should just have to push it once. Who designed these things, anyway? Simple commands—that's what you need: *go, stop, sit, roll over*."

"Aren't you supposed to know what I know?" Cleft said with frustration. "You're a steward. I know how to drive a car, so you should know how to drive a car."

"Apparently there are limits."

"Perfect. This is just perfect."

"Settle down, now," said Roland, with wisdom that stretched somehow beyond Cleft's. "Let's just work out a system together."

"You're right. You're right. Okay. When I say 'go,' you ease on the gas. And then I'll keep saying 'hold' for you to keep it where you are. If we need more speed, I'll say 'more.' And if we don't need any more gas, I'll say 'off.' Okay?"

"Okay. What about 'stop'?"

"I'll take care of that with my left foot. Now, let's try this again."

Anyone looking at the truck that morning, jerking out of Cleft's driveway and tripping down the street, would have thought its driver was a toddler under the influence. By the time they hit Silver Lake Road, they were getting closer to a rhythm—gunning forward, halting, gunning forward, halting. Roland rammed his head into the compartment wall beneath the steering wheel several times. And Cleft's chest ended up bruised. But they made it. They rolled into Trinity Presbyterian Church with confusion and dismay buried in the wrinkles on Cleft's brow.

***

"What in the world?" Cleft said in shock. Water was covering the parking lot. And he could hear the sound of spraying in the distance. The foyer of the church was on fire—not a blazing inferno, but strong enough that Cleft couldn't attempt to put it out himself, especially in his condition. He limped towards the building, then turned around trying to figure out what to do. Where was the nearest phone? He scanned the houses across the street, all of them blacked out. No power.

He was about to head back to his house, where he hoped there was still power. "Alright, Rol—"

He stopped when he saw the flicker of police lights down the street. Tom's cruiser rolled into the parking lot, followed by the fire truck.

"Thank God," Cleft said, loud enough for Tom to hear as he rushed out of his car. Cleft leaned up against the truck door and held his right foot off the ground.

"Cleft! You alright?"

"Tom, boy I'm glad to see you. I'm fine. Just got here. But I don't know—"

Tom motioned with his hands for Ezekiel and his crew to start working on assessing the situation and getting the fire put out. He turned back to Cleft.

"Go on."

"I heard a loud boom from my house and tried to rush here—sprained my ankle pretty bad."

"And you still drove?"

Cleft looked over at Roland. "We managed. But I don't know what happened here. And the water . . ." He looked down at his feet, the leather of his loafers soaking up the dirty water.

"Maybe a burst pipe. We'll get in there and start figuring this out. Did you see anybody on the property?"

"No. No one."

"Well, I'm surprised more people aren't on their porches over there. I think that blast could've woken up the whole town. Never heard of an electrical problem causing something like that, or why it would affect the plumbing."

"It was a bomb," came a voice from behind Cleft. He spun around to see who'd spoken.

"What?" No one was there.

"I said I never heard of an electrical pro—," Tom repeated, but stopped as he heard his radio from the cruiser. He shuffled over to give the squad an update.

Cleft scanned the parking lot and bent down to look under his truck.

"I'm not there. I'm *here*." The voice was calm and confident. But Cleft couldn't see anyone, anywhere.

"Every time God builds a church, Satan builds a chapel," the voice said. Cleft kept turning around, trying to find its source. He turned so many times that he got dizzy. He put his hands on the pavement and sat down, his pants soaking in the cold water. But he didn't care. He just needed stability.

"You alright?" Roland said, pushing his wet nose into Cleft's cheek. He'd jumped out the open driver's side door when he saw Cleft spinning around.

Cleft's breathing was audible, his face was flushed, and sweat began rolling down his temple. "He's here." Those were the only two words he got out before things started going dark at the edges of his vision. And then he passed out.

***

Roland barked to get Tom's attention.

"Geez! Cleft!" Tom rolled Cleft up out of the cold water and slapped his face gently. "Hey! You alright?" Cleft blinked and turned his body over, trying to lift himself from the ground.

"No, no—just take it easy," Tom said, keeping Cleft's head in his lap. "We got an ambulance on the way just in case. Let them check you out."

Ezekiel jogged over in his fireman gear and pulled off his helmet. "We got a mess in there, Tom. The fire is under control, but something took out the electrical panel in the basement, and the water heater must have exploded from too much pressure or something. Still looking into that. But that looks to be the extent of it. Just a mess with repairs. Could take a few weeks."

Tom nodded. "Thanks, Zeek. I'm gonna hang here with Cleft for a bit, and then I'll get some of the fellas to help me analyze the situation. You suspect any foul play by what you've seen."

"Don't suspect," Ezekiel said.

"Well, that's good," said Tom.

"I'm *sure* of it," Zeek followed up quickly.

Tom's head snapped up in alarm. "Sure of it?"

"Yes. Found remnants of chemicals for common home-made explosives—the same ones we found at the bungalow, plus some shoddy wiring that looks like it's been done by a toddler. This wasn't an accident, Tom. Somebody rigged this."

"And I bet I know who," Cleft said in a whisper from the ground.

"What's that?" Tom said, turning back to Cleft. "You say something?"

"No. Sorry, no." He thought it best not to speculate, but he *knew*. He'd been told after all—by someone who didn't have to be present in order to speak.

***

"Alright, I did it! It's done!" Cain was out of breath as he made it to the shed in the woods, where Skotos sat calmly in a wooden chair, squeezing the puffy red skin raised around the dirty scrape he'd made on his hand, along the edge of the circle tattoo. As he squeezed, clear liquid began oozing out and gathered into a single drop that ran down the edge of his index finger.

"Hey!" Cain said, irritated at not getting a pat on the back. "I said it's finished."

"I know it is," Skotos said without looking up. "Now we need to find others."

"Others? Why? I thought you said you only needed me. This is how I'm building a name for myself, remember?"

Skotos gave a patronizing huff. "Always the same with you. Yes, you'll get your new name. But we need others to join us. Then we can start building. And I can get back to tunneling."

"Building? Building what?" Cain wiped the sweat from his brow with a dirty hand, setting a streak of brown on his forehead.

Skotos was silent for another few seconds.

"Building what? What are we supposed to build? I thought we'd be done after taking out the church."

"The shadow chapel."

"*Shadow* chapel? You want to build another church? You starting a cult or something?"

"Or something," Skotos said, still refusing to look up from his hand. "It will be . . . bright and beautiful. And everyone will walk right passed the old church to get to it. That will make it easier for us to take them."

Cain was at a loss for words and too tired to argue. He sat on the floor of the shed, still gathering his breath. His legs were tight and sore. He pulled his feet together into a butterfly stretch.

Skotos finally looked up to see Cain stretching. A whispered laugh turned into a chuckle, accented by coughs.

"What? What's so funny?" Cain said, obviously irritated.

"Little Cain," Skotos said coughing out another laugh. "Little Cain doing his stretches after his bomb workout."

Cain paused, still holding his stretch, and then let himself smile. The smile gave way to a rolling laugh. And both of them sat there in the shed, doubled over in hysterical laughter. It was the closest thing to friendship that Cain had felt in a very long time.

But it ended in a warbled cough from Skotos. He coughed out more of the black sludge and spit it into a puddle on the shed floor. Cain pushed himself back in revulsion.

"Eh! God! What is that?! You have . . . cancer of something?"

Skotos calmly wiped his mouth and took a breath after the coughing fit. "Cancer is a cold compared to what I have."

"What is it? That stuff you coughed out?"

Skotos paused as he searched for the words. He found them sooner than he thought he would.

"Charred pride."

21

WHAT ETHAN SAW

F OR THE SECOND TIME, Ethan Regent took his Schwinn
bike across Silver Lake and into Cleft's driveway. It was the
day after the blast. Trinity Presbyterian Church was roped off
with police tape. And behind the doors of their homes, the town
was buzzing with gossip like a public square packed with crazed
pigeons. Speculation is the privilege of the masses.

Cleft sat in a rocker with his right ankle wrapped in a bandage and resting on a bag of ice set on top of a little coffee table
matching the rocker.

Ethan leaped off his bike and left it on the ground. He had
more confidence this time, more repose. He needed answers.
And the last time he came here, he saw a man disappear into
a puddle of light. Before anything else ridiculous happened, he
needed to get *in*—to find someone who could explain what was
going on in a town of illuminated doors and giant black snakes
and puddles of light. Dingmans Ferry was starting to feel more
like one of the stories he'd been writing and less like the boring
reality it used to be. And he knew Cleft was his only way in.
In his defense, Cleft had meant to talk to Ethan, but the events
in the past week had taken his intention and hidden it behind
heavier worries.

"Ethan!" Cleft said happily, without shifting in his rocker. He was glad to have a distraction from the sinister events of the previous day, which were still crystalizing in his head. "Didn't know you were coming by. It's great to see you!" Ethan was puzzled as to why anyone would be so excited to see him. He had been resolved to be stern with Cleft and demand answers, but the greeting threw him off.

"Hey . . . Pastor Cleft."

"Oh, you can just call me Cleft, Ethan. That's fine." Ethan nodded. "I take it you came here for something other than coffee."

"Yeah, I did. But what happened to your ankle?"

"Ah, rolled it trying to get down the steps too fast. Had to get Roland to drive me into town," he said with a smirk, looking down at Roland, who shifted his eyes and sighed through his wet black nose—a canine eye-roll. Ethan, of course, assumed he was kidding and didn't respond to the comment. Cleft was childishly disappointed, having had no one to tell the story to yet. But he didn't push it.

"I'm . . . I'm trying to figure out . . ." Ethan started, struggling to find the right introduction.

"Here," Cleft interrupted, reaching for the other rocker, which was impossibly far away. "Grab that one and take a seat. That was Jane's. She'd love you to take a load off."

Ethan carefully settled his body into the rocker, in respect. Cleft nodded slowly when he saw Ethan's neck and legs relax. He took a deep breath and began easing back and forth, letting the rocker do its work.

"I understand you've got questions, son. So, shoot. I'll give you straight truth, I promise."

Ethan surprised himself with what flew from his mouth next. "I saw a giant black snake but then it vanished." That got Cleft's attention quickly enough. He leaned forward.

"Black snake? Where? At your house?"

"Yeah, right outside the front door. Its body was thicker than both my legs put together, and it had these dark, blood-red eyes." Ethan gulped as he relived the scene. "I got a knife from the kitchen and started stabbing it. It was gonna kill my dad—I know it. I had to do something."

"And that killed it?"

"No—it just . . . disappeared. Gone. My dad probably thinks I'm cracking up."

"Ethan, tell me everything. I mean *everything*. What else was happening before you saw it?" Cleft was locked in like a fighter pilot on a target. Ethan took a breath to gather his thoughts.

"Well," he began. "My dad was trying to get our push-mower started out front, but when I saw him, he was just staring across the street at our neighbor, Mr. Gurssel."

"Why was he staring?" Cleft asked.

"I think he was looking at Mr. Gurssel's new mower. It's a Petty Blue riding mower."

"A Petty Blue?!" Cleft said, almost spitting out his mouthful of coffee. "I've been to Robert's house; he doesn't have but a quarter acre. What in the world does he need a Petty Blue for?"

"He doesn't, I guess. But he's got lots of money, so he seems to have pretty much whatever he wants."

"You and your dad have a little over an acre. Bet *you* could use a Petty Blue."

"Oh, yeah. My dad would love that," Ethan said with a smile, distracted from the seriousness of the moment. "He's always saying, 'One day we'll snag a Petty Blue, and I'll teach you how to ride it so you can help with the lawn."

"So, your dad was just staring at Mr. Gurssel?

"That's what he was doing when I saw the snake—yeah. Where do you think it came from?"

"That's the part I don't think you'll believe so easily," Cleft said, lifting his coffee cup to his lips.

"What . . . like the Amazon or some other place?"

"Oh, no . . . no. It came from your dad."

"What do you mean?"

"My best guess, Ethan, is that what you saw in that giant black snake wasn't a foreign species. It's native to every sinful soul. What you saw was *envy*."

"Umm, I don't . . . I don't know what you're saying. Is that a kind of snake?"

"You said the snake disappeared as you were stabbing it, right?"

"Yeah."

"So it wasn't a normal snake."

"Well, I guess not."

"And it was there only as your dad was staring at that Petty Blue."

"Yeah. But why didn't my dad see it? It was *huge*."

"Because Ethan," and Cleft leaned closer to him as he said the next words, close enough to make Ethan lean away. "He hasn't been through the white door, and you have." They both paused for a few seconds as Ethan's thoughts began connecting.

"So, you're saying I could see this snake just because I went through that door? Nobody else could see it?"

"Once you go through that door, Ethan, you start seeing things that others don't see—spiritual realities that are just as raw and real as anything in the physical world. You could see what your dad was battling even when he couldn't. He was fighting *envy*—that's my best guess. And Lord knows Mr. Gurssel has plenty to be envied. The man's got holes in his pockets—and deep pockets. The bottom line is, Ethan, that to enter is to see."

They both sat in the quiet for a minute, as Blue Jays darted among the evergreen trees in Cleft's yard.

"The truth is, Ethan, you going through that door couldn't have come at a better time."

"What do you mean?"

"You want the whole story? Cause I'll tell it."

"Yeah, I think I do."

"There's something bad brewing. And it's not just the strange thing you just saw. Like I said, all of us who have been through the white door have seen some wild things. And we'll get to that soon enough. But it wasn't til recently that someone dark showed up and started stirring trouble. In fact, I think he's the one behind the bombing."

"Bombing?!" Ethan said with alarm. "I thought the church was just old and had some systems go. No one told me anything about a bomb."

"Well, keep quiet about it. But Ezekiel, over at the firehouse, said the scene was laced with traces of homemade explosive ingredients and novice electrical wiring. Whoever did it wasn't a professional, but *somebody* did it. I just don't know why—at least, not exactly."

"What do you mean?"

"This fella that's been stirring up trouble calls himself *Sko-tos.*" A smaller shiver went through both of them, though stronger in Ethan than in Cleft. "He was here the night Jane died. Then he was lurking around town and scared the life out-ta' Gladice, whom I think you know." Ethan nodded. Gladice was everyone's stand-in grandmother, even for those who had grandmothers. "And then this whole mess."

"Why do you think *he* did this?"

"I heard it from his own mouth."

"He came and told you?" Ethan asked, surprised.

"No, no. I just said I heard it when I was on the scene. I was in a daze, I admit. But his voice was clear as a bell."

"But you didn't see him there?"

"No, I didn't. Didn't see anyone other than your dad, Ezekiel, and his crew."

"Weird. Especially after the whole Cain mishap, too."

"What Cain mishap? Cain Shoemaker? Gladice's grand-son?"

"Ah, geez. I probably wasn't supposed to say anything. Nothing official got reported."

"Not really such a thing as secrets in a town this small, Ethan."

"Yeah, that's what I thought until I went through that white door."

"Hmm," Cleft said, lifting his eyebrows. "Good point. Well, I won't make you say anything you aren't comfortable with."

"No, it's okay. My dad said Cain went missing for a few days after last Sunday. His folks reported it on Tuesday morning."

Cleft thought of the last encounter he'd had with Cain at the back of the church sanctuary. He didn't feel any remorse for scolding Cain and his gang about drawing in the pew Bibles, but he *did* wish he'd said more—something, anything. Kids like Cain, he'd learned, really wanted an invitation, some kind of attention they weren't getting elsewhere. And based on what

Cleft knew about Cain's father, he was certain Cain wasn't getting much attention.

"You talk to him since he's been back?"

"Me?" Ethan said, coughing out a laugh. "No. I'm not really friends with him. Not even in high school. He always chose a rougher crowd, and I'm not exactly . . . well, let's just say I feel more at home with books than with broken rules."

"You and me both," Cleft said. "Well, I'll see if I can get out there to his house and check in with him.

"Okay, well, be careful. I heard some rumors that he's been off ever since he came back."

"Rumors from whom?"

"The only two guys he hangs around with—Patrick and Jesse."

"The goons he brings with him to church?"

"Yeah, I guess so."

"Suppose I should be surprised he even shows up to church in the first place." Cleft paused and there was an awkward silence. "Well, anyway, I'll be careful. Are you alright? You're welcome to come by here anytime, by the way, day or night."

"Yeah, I guess. And thanks. Well . . . there is one thing," Ethan said sheepishly.

"Go ahead."

"Am I gonna see anything else? Like, do people see things every day or . . .?" He trailed off.

"People see things that are there. That's all I can tell you. And you can be sure, with time, you'll be able to tell the difference between a physical reality and a spiritual one. Something inside you will click."

Ethan nodded, not encouraged by the message, but at least understanding. "Not sure what to say to my dad, either. He's noticed I'm off, too."

"Tom's a good man, Ethan. Got a good heart in his chest. Honesty is your best path with him. Even if he doesn't believe you right away, he'll come around when he sees how earnest you are."

Ethan nodded, then lifted up his hand to wave goodbye as he turned. He didn't know what he'd say to his dad yet, but he knew he'd have to say something. If it was a giant black snake one day, what would it be the next? But he paused as he was about to pick up his bike by the handles.

"Hey, Cleft."

"Yeah, Ethan?"

"Where'd you go?"

"What do you mean?"

"The other day . . . when I was here and you—you fell into that . . . puddle. Where did you go?"

Cleft smiled and offered a terse reply. "A city."

"A city?" Ethan asked, looking for more.

"Yeah—maybe I'll take you some time."

Ethan began to smile. It was the first time he'd really smiled since entering the white door and having his world turned upside down. And they both stood there for a moment, just grinning at the possibility of going to this place, this city. If the name Skotos drew out a chill, the mention of this place was like a warm breeze.

Cleft had only seen it from a distance. Roland had seen it also. And Ethan had never been there. But nothing could be clearer to anyone who heard it named in the open air: this place was worth the travel. In fact, it was worth discovering without the intention of coming back.

***

As Ethan pedaled out of the driveway, Cleft groaned and banged his fist on the armrest of the rocker. "Dah! Roland! I wanted to tell him about you and your driving the other day."

Roland picked his head up from the old blue carpet on the porch. "I doubt he'd believe you anyway—and neither will anyone else for that matter. And it wasn't exactly something to brag about."

"Ah, come on, Roland. I was proud of you! First time driving a truck. Probably the first time *any* dog drove a truck."

"Not sure I'd call what we did 'driving.' And I hope it's the last time," Roland said, laying his head back down. "I bashed my head and back more than I can remember. You humans and your *machines*."

"Better to make machines than become them," Cleft said.

"Not sure there's much of a difference," Roland said.

22

WILL'S RIDDLE

Seth, Shannon, Will, and Livy had been with Narnia in the living room of their home all morning—just talking. Narnia could not have come to a better home. After battering him with questions and tickling him under his chin, the kids began looking for other creatures in their house or the front yard that might also speak to them. Their imaginations were on fire. Seth, Shannon, and Narnia stayed in the living room talking about the explosion from the other day. Cleft had called Seth that morning, filling him in on a few details that wouldn't be reported in the paper or on the radio. But he kept his phone call brief.

"It was *him*, Seth. And that takes things to a whole new level."

"You're sure? You didn't see anyone on the scene, did you?"

"Didn't have to. I heard his voice in my head. And Zeek was sure about someone using homemade explosives. Who else would have a motive?"

"Yeah, it's just . . . why would he want to take out the church? And—I'm not trying to be dark here—why not blow up the whole building?"

"Well, in answer to the first question, I'd say this guy is vigorously opposed to anything faith-related. But in answer to the second, I don't know. Maybe he wasn't skilled enough. Probably didn't know what he was doing."

"But Zeek told you that the two explosions were at the electrical box and the water heater, right?"

"Yeah."

"That just sounds sort of intentional to me. Take out the power and the plumbing for a few weeks. It's less ambitious and less likely to ignite, you know, an all-out war between good and evil."

"This is serious, Seth."

"No, I know. Sorry. All I'm saying is that if he *is* behind this, then maybe he knows what going too far would look like." The moment Seth said "he," it dawned on him that he really didn't want to use his name.

"And why wouldn't he want to go too far?"

"I don't know; I'm just speculating based on all the fiction I've read. But . . . let's just say he *was* trying to build his own army of darkness to wage war against anyone who believes in God. He'd need that: an army. He'd need a gathering. And it's easier to grow a gathering when you move incrementally. Move too fast, and you scare people off."

"Hmm. I hadn't thought of it that way. So, you think the bombing was intentionally low-scale?"

"Look, I'm not a detective. It's just a theory."

"Not a bad one. Listen, I don't want to keep you from your family on the weekend. But would you all like to come for dinner tomorrow? I'd need some help in the kitchen, but I thought the kids could play with some old toys I found in the attic."

"Yeah, I think that'd be fun. We don't have any plans, but I'll check with Shannon. You said you'd need help in the kitchen. Not much of a chef?"

"Oh no. Actually, I think I'm pretty handy in the kitchen. But I sprained my ankle the night of the bombing and can't move around so well."

"Ah, I get it. Wish we could stop calling it 'the night of the bombing.'"

"That's what it'll always be in my mind."

"Yeah."

"Let's say 4:30 pm tomorrow?"

"Sounds good. See you then."

Seth filled Shannon in on the details while the kids played outside. They looked out the front bay window as Livy ran circles around Will, who was standing stone-still and staring up at the sky.

"God, they're so happy," she said.

"Yeah. They think the whole world's talking to them. Every kid's dream."

"And yet," Narnia chimed in from the wingback chair, "maybe not entirely a dream."

They smiled. Narnia began purring loudly on his over-sized throne.

"What's Will looking at?" Shannon said. "He's just standing there like a statue."

"I'm guessing it's a game. I'll go find out which one."

Seth went down the porch steps and across the yard as Livy continued running circles around Will, chanting, "Yoy, yoy, yoy, yoy, yoy!"

"Will, what are you doin', bud?"

Will's eyes were glazed over as he stared into the expanse. He didn't respond.

"Will, what game are you guys playing?" Still no response. He got closer and touched Will's arm. Will slowly turned towards him and muttered something in a whisper. "Can't hear you, bud. You gotta speak up."

Will's voice grew a bit louder but was barely above a whisper.

> Heavy as night, light as the air.
> Heavy as night, light as the air.

"Will. Hey, snap out of it, bud. Pause the game." Seth shook Will by the arm, struck by what he'd just heard. It didn't sound like his son. Will took a deep breath in, almost gasping for air as if he'd been holding his breath. He blinked and rubbed his eyes and looked at Seth.

"You okay, buddy? You alright?"

"Yeah, daddy. I'm just playing with Livy." Livy had stopped her singing and was staring at Will with her two fingers in her mouth.

"What did you just say? Do you remember?"

"I didn't say anything," Will said, amused. "I was a statue, and Livy was running around me."

"Heavy as night, light as the air," Seth said. "You don't remember any of that?"

"Nights aren't heavy, Daddy," Will said. Content with his response, he resumed chasing Livy around the maple tree a few feet away.

"Great," Seth said to himself as he stood up. "Cryptic riddles from my five-year-old. As if this town wasn't strange enough." He walked slowly up the steps, then went into the kitchen and grabbed a pen and a notepad, trying to jot down what his son had just said.

"What are you writing?" Shannon asked as she dried the dishes and put them away. "Something for one of your books?"

"I wish," Seth said. He told Shannon what he'd just witnessed. She was obviously disturbed and walked briskly to the bay window to check on the kids. But they were playing normally again, Will chasing Livy and then stopping to pick up a bug and ask where it lived.

"What did he say?" She asked.

"That's what I'm trying to remember and write down. I think this is it." He handed her the notepad.

"Oh, God—that's creepy." Shannon took a breath in, remembering something else. "Wait, wait. He was writing something over at the kids' table while Livy was coloring earlier." She picked up a gray piece of construction paper, covered in Will's five-year-old pen script.

> Heavy as night, light as the air,
> Under the trout, ahead of the bear.
> Falling down when the star rises,
> Ever one through a thousand guises.

"Seth, how in the world . . ." Shannon started.

"I have no idea," Seth said. "My students couldn't even write something like this."

"What is it?"

"Well, it looks like a riddle."

"No—I don't mean that. I know it's a riddle. I mean, what is *this*? A five-year-old scribbling a riddle down on construction paper when he doesn't have the vocabulary or know-how? This is from that door, isn't it? Oh, God. Seth, if we did something to them because of this, I'll never—"

"Hey," Seth paused the train of panic. "We didn't do anything to them, and they're okay. I know this is weird, but at this point, I'm adding it to my list."

"Your list?"

"My list of weird things that happen in this town. We'll ask Cleft about it when we see him for dinner. He'll know what to do."

"I'm not so sure. But fine." Shannon wasn't consoled. She went back to the bay window, staring at Will and Livy, still playing around the maple tree. Shannon's heart was thudding like a drum.

"Shannon," Seth said, sensing her anxiety. "Let's just show it to Cleft tomorrow and see what he thinks. I don't want to get too alarmed right away."

"Hmm. My anxious husband doesn't want to get too alarmed. Sounds like someone's making progress with anxiety," she huffed.

Seth chuckled. "Just finding it easier to trust these days. That's all."

"Trust who . . . well, *whom*?"

"I don't know yet. But nice grammar."

"Well, my husband's an English nerd," she smiled.

Seth found her irresistible in that moment, despite the strangeness and growing uncertainty about what was going on.

He walked over to her, took her face gently but confidently in his hands, and kissed her.

"What was that for?"

"Just because. I love you. And whatever comes our way comes *our* way . . . together. Right?"

"Always," she said, looking into his eyes. She kissed him back. And they held hands as they walked out to the front porch and watched the kids playing as the sun began to set, the golden light picking up dust and dancing bugs as they wove around and through the aura. They felt born into blessing and caught in something grand. Even Shannon could feel it, more than she felt worried about their riddle-wielding five-year-old. Whatever their family had done in going through that door, they were undoubtedly seeing *more* around them. And that truth was a constant whisper of encouragement.

23

DINNER FOR FIVE (HUMANS)

T HE KIDS WERE HAPPY to run around with Roland and Narnia in Cleft's front yard while Seth and Shannon helped in the kitchen. Cleft had been reluctant at first to sit idly by with his ankle on a bag of ice, but he resigned himself to his need for help. He smiled at the renewed realization of his own dependency—something he often preached on from the pulpit but found nearly impossible to live out in his own experience until he was forced to.

"I'm just gonna put the chicken drumsticks in at 350 degrees. Should be ready in about an hour and a half, give or take. You said you had some potatoes?"

"Your husband's already on that," Cleft said. Seth looked up and smiled from his work at the counter. That was a mistake. The serrated edge of the knife cut into his fingertip as he sliced a potato in half.

"Ah! Oh, geez! That was stupid."

"You cut yourself?" Shannon asked with alarm. "Is it deep?"

"I don't think so, just bleeding a lot."

"Oh, I'm sorry, Seth. Just had them sharpened last month. Should have warned you. There are bandaids upstairs in the hallway bathroom, under the sink."

Seth nodded and trotted off to get the bleeding under control. As he padded up the steps to the second floor, Cleft heard a whisper, clear and cold.

"Best not to let the infection spread. It spreads so easily." Cleft knew the voice instantly and sprang forward in his chair, looking around for the lanky figure with pale skin. But there was no one. Shannon noticed him jolt up.

"You okay, Cleft?" Shannon asked.

"I . . . umm. Yeah, I'm . . . I'm okay. Just heard something, that's all."

"Something good?" Shannon said with a hopeful smile.

"Mmm. I wish."

Seth walked back in with a fabric bandaid hugging his finger, the blood beginning to seep through the bandage.

"Crisis averted," he said.

"Sort of," Shannon smirked. "You're leaking there." She pointed to the bloody bandage.

"Dang it. Would you be able to finish the potatoes? I don't want to season anything with my blood."

"Eww. Yes, please don't touch them."

"Interesting metaphor—" the whisper returned to Cleft.

"Huh?" Cleft said out loud, despite himself. Seth and Shannon turned towards him.

"Seasoned with blood. The secret to everything holy, is it not?"

"Cleft are you okay?" Seth asked. Both he and Shannon knew something was off.

"Guys, I'm . . . I'm uh . . . I'm hearing things." Cleft said, and then looked down, embarrassed.

"Hearing what?" Seth said.

Cleft took a deep breath. "Well, not 'things.' Voices. One voice, really. I heard it the night of the explosion, and I heard it just now. It's—" he paused, not wanting to mention the name out in the open, but resolved to speak in a near whisper. "It's Skotos."

A chill went through the room. "I asked you both to dinner partly to talk about it, and partly to check in with you. Is everything going alright with you? Have you noticed anything strange lately?"

Shannon and Seth looked at each other. She nodded to Seth.

"Actually," Seth began. "Will said something the other day that was just plain creepy. He was outside playing with Livy when I noticed him just staring up at the sky, like he was in a trance or something."

"Ugh, don't say 'trance,'" Shannon muttered in the background. "It creeps me out even more."

"What did he say?" Cleft asked. Seth pulled out a folded piece of paper from his back pocket and handed it to Cleft, who immediately unfolded it and read the writing.

> Heavy as night, light as the air,
> Under the trout, ahead of the bear.
> Falling down when the star rises,
> Ever one through a thousand guises.

"He said this?" Cleft asked in disbelief.

"Yeah. Well, he *said* the first line when I approached him in the front yard. The rest he had written down on a piece of paper.

I have no idea where it came from, especially the vocabulary. I don't think he's ever even heard the word 'guises' before."

"It sounds like a riddle, doesn't it?" Cleft said. "Or some sort of . . ." Cleft searched for the right word, "prophecy."

"Ugh, 'prophecy' is even worse than 'trance,'" Shannon said.

"Any idea what it means?" Seth asked.

"Well, you're the English guy. How would you solve it if it were a riddle?"

Seth took the paper back and read the words slowly. "Riddles work with wordplay and perception. So, 'Heavy as night, light as the air' would describe something that *looks* heavy but is really weightless. 'Under the trout, ahead of the bear.' What's underneath trout? Stones? A riverbed? But whatever it is, it has to also be something that can go *ahead* of an animal on land."

"Oh! I know!" Shannon chirped, like a kid with the answer to a math problem. But she didn't shout it out. "You want me to wait or tell you?"

Cleft laughed. "I guess give Seth and me a chance."

Shannon beamed. She wasn't usually ahead of Seth in matters of words.

"Okay. Well, 'Falling down when the star rises.' That must mean the sun. So, it's something that falls down when the sun comes up."

"How have you not guessed this yet, Seth?" Shannon was thrilled to be ahead of the group.

"And then, 'Ever one through a thousand guises.' So, it takes lots of shapes, but it's all the same stuff." Seth thought for a moment and then relief and embarrassment swept over his face. "Oh, my gosh! How did I not see it?"

"I don't know. I really don't," Shannon said laughing as she touched Seth's arm. "You got it, too, Cleft?"

"Oh," Cleft said with a faded smile. "I got it as soon as I read it."

"So, the wise old pastor beat us to it," Shannon said, hoping to get a grin out of Cleft. But she didn't. "Why so serious?"

"I'm sorry," Cleft said. "I'm sorry. Don't bother with me. I'm taking everything too seriously right now."

"The answer bothers you?" Seth asked.

"The answer . . ." Cleft hesitated but then continued. "The answer is *Skotos*. The answer is shadow." His words froze the room in place. The sound of the children's voices playing was all that broke through the eerie stillness.

"Oh my God," Shannon said, putting both hands on her chest to feel her own heartbeat.

***

"Look," Cleft said to break up the fear icing the room in silence. "Maybe after dinner I can show you something that will lift the mood for all of us, given the circumstances."

"The circumstances of my five-year-old writing a riddle about the creepiest figure that's ever set foot in this town? I hope so," Shannon said with a shudder. Seth pulled her into his chest.

"Hey, it's alright. We'll figure this out together," Seth reassured her.

"He's right," Cleft said. "We're in this together, whatever this is."

"What did you want to show us after dinner?" Shannon asked, begging for a distraction.

"Something good. . . . No, not just good—something great and glorious. My favorite place. Feels like I need to see it after the last few days and all of this . . . churning darkness."

Seth and Shannon looked at each other.

"Is it far from here?" she asked.

Cleft smiled. "No. Usually right in the backyard."

"Usually?" Seth asked.

"Well, you can't control it. It comes and goes where and when it wills, like the wind."

"What does?" Seth said.

"You'll just have to wait and see," Cleft said with a parental smile.

Seth and Shannon didn't know what to expect or where this was coming from, but it seemed harmless, and they had an unchallenged trust in Cleft.

Dinner was quiet for the adults, who poured their attention into Will and Livy. Will asked if the chickens knew their legs would be sold at the grocery store. That got a laugh from everyone, except Will, who saw nothing funny in the question.

***

After they'd had dinner and cleaned up, they all stood waiting in the backyard. Cleft was staring hard at the grass.

"Cleft?" Seth said uneasily. "What are we looking for here?"

"Just wait. I think they'll be here."

"You think *who* will be here?"

"Not 'who.' Just . . . just wait."

Cleft looked at Will and Livy fidgeting in their parents' grasp. Shannon was holding Livy, who kicked at Will as he tried to grab her feet.

"There!" Cleft said, scaring all of them as he jabbed his index finger toward the edge of his lawn. "Right there! Do you see it?"

One by one, they all noticed a glowing, puddle-like patch of light, not *on* the grass, but *beneath* it. Roland started wagging his tail. Narnia was prowling and inspecting the shape, padding towards it.

"This is what I wanted to show you," Cleft said, wearing an ear-to-ear grin on his freshly shaven face. "You're gonna love this."

"Love what?" Shannon said. "Is there more?"

"This is just the entrance," Cleft said. He looked at everyone, including the kids, and said, "You only come if you want to. And if you want to, just do what I do. Remember: to enter is to see."

With that, Cleft approached one of the puddles of light that had been drawing nearer to them with the grace and quietude of a lazy fish. Cleft got on his hands and knees, bowed his head towards the puddle, and disappeared.

Shannon almost dropped Livy. "What?! Seth, what just—"

"I don't know! I don't know! He was . . . he was just here and then—"

"Magic!" Will shouted. "He did magic! Mommy, I want to do it."

"My God," Narnia whispered. "Not just magic—it's the *deeper* magic."

Roland didn't need any encouragement. This wasn't his first trip. "You all coming or not?" he said, sounding more like a toddler than his senior self. He bounded towards the same puddle Cleft had bowed into and put his black nose to the ground. Gone.

"You gotta be kidding me!" Seth was still holding Will's shoulders but let go of them to run his hands through his hair. Will seized the opportunity.

"I'm doing the magic too!" Will yelled. "Come on, Livy!"

"Will, no! Wait!" Seth yelled, but it was too late. Will did a summersault, missing the puddle Roland had gone into, but then turned around and tried to grab the puddle. His head touched the grass at the edge of the light. Another one gone.

"Seth!" Shannon said, panicked. "What are we—"

"Ah, geez!" Seth said, knowing what he had to do next. "God, please don't let this kill me." He crawled on the ground towards the puddle Will had disappeared into, and bowed his head, not realizing that Livy thought this was an invitation to ride on his back. She jumped on. Both disappeared in an instant.

Shannon almost threw up and lost her breath at the same time. "It's alright, Shannon," Narnia said. "Might as well go where the good ones have gone. Come. We'll do it together."

They crept toward the luminous puddle. Narnia bent his head to the ground and looked at Shannon, checking to see that she was following. She was, but her arms were shaking. Narnia nodded and said, "On three. One. Two. Three." They both bowed into the light and disappeared.

24

A CITY OF LIGHT

SOME THINGS DEFY EXPLANATION. And for that, they are the greatest blessing. Explanation offers an invitation to the mind. But the *deeper magic* Narnia mentioned before he bowed into the puddle of light doesn't do that. It whisks you away without your approval. It takes you from *here* to *there* without permission. And that's a good thing since we'd never grant the grand and beautiful permission to enter our lives from a distance. From far off, what's beautiful is terrifying. We'd never enter it unless pushed. And that's exactly where these seven stood: a pushed paradise.

There's a place between dreaming and waking, when we feel as if we're between worlds, standing in neither, but drifting beneath and above them. That was the feeling that enveloped these seven as they noticed their feet planted in taller grass at the top of a hill in a new country—so sharp and vibrant that it almost hurt their eyes. There was no sound except for a low humming, deep and almost musical. A gold light fell all around them as if from a setting sun halted on the horizon. One by one, each of them uttered a pure and passionate "My God"—even the children.

Cleft was the first to turn his head from what they were all gazing at. He was going to speak, but then he thought better of it. He just laughed to himself. A tear formed and rolled down Seth's cheek—the warmth and the salt somehow holding decades of resistance finally let go. He took Shannon's hand. A tear was beginning to roll down her cheek as well. Livy and Will just stared, eyes wide as saucers, soaking in everything. Roland wagged his tail slowly but steadily; Narnia let his swish freely. They all were happy in the silence, just staring—a fitting response before something so . . . what was the word? *Holy*.

***

They stood atop a hill. A thin tree line was at the bottom. And beyond that, a rich green country spotted with trees, patches of white flowers (a white that seemed to glow), and glades dotting a forest that rolled down the hilly landscape like a blanket. Where the trees ended, a neat and well-trod dirt road led into the chief object of their attention: a white stone city, almost too bright to bear, as if the light itself were emitted from the stone. It looked so very old and yet showed no marks of time's decay.

"This," Cleft said quietly, so as not to scare off the sanctity of the moment. "This is where my soul flutters. This is where glory lives." He stopped, seeming to know already that he'd said too much. Everyone else remained silent for what could have been a minute, or a century.

"Bird," Will said, pointing towards the city. Shannon looked down at him and then followed his finger toward the city walls. Sure enough, there was a white-winged bird larger than anything she'd ever imagined. At this size, and from this distance, she guessed that the bird might be the size of an elephant. But the size took nothing from its grace, as it glided around the front wall of the city, like some giant bee hovering over its beloved flower. Cleft was fixated, and his mouth hung open.

"I've never seen one of those before," he said, taking a big step forward and squinting. The giant bird arched away from the city and began flying towards them, over top of the forest. Everyone looked at each other. It curved back and forth over the treetops, its huge size becoming more and more apparent. It wasn't the size of an elephant. It was the size of a house. And it didn't have one set of wings; it had three.

Shannon took Seth's hand again. "Seth," she said with some alarm. "I think it sees us." Everyone seemed to snap out of their daze and look around, scanning their surroundings for a place to take cover. "Seth, it's coming right for us."

Seth grabbed Will and Livy but didn't know where to go with them. On the broad top of the hill, the group was fully exposed. They had nothing to do but run, and none of them was committed to that yet. At 200 yards off, they could see the bird was emitting its own light—like the white flowers. They couldn't make out its features, but its size was staggering—dinosaur-like. And then they heard its call: at once thunderous and melodious: "Ooopoe, Ooopoe, Ooopoe." It came in groups of three, loud enough to knock them all down. Will and Livy grabbed onto Seth. Roland and Narnia hid under Cleft as he scrambled to the ground. "Ooopoe, Ooopoe, Ooopoe."

It was nearly on top of them, and as it dove down toward the group, everyone shielded their eyes and covered their faces, filled with fear, but also just an ounce of thrill. The enormous white-winged body blocked their vision as they braced for impact.

***

And then, in an instant, they were back in Cleft's front yard, laying on the grass as they had laid on the hilltop. Each of them felt as if they'd awoken from a dream, looking at their limbs and surroundings to make sure they were really there. Will and Livy still clung to Seth's waist. Shannon was next to them. Roland and Narnia had a good shake as they emerged from under Cleft, who gathered himself to stand up but forgot about his sprained ankle. He put pressure on it.

"Oooh! Geez!" he said. "Yup. Still sprained."

"Mommy, did that bird try to get us?" Will said with a whimper. Livy was silently sucking her two fingers, unwilling to lift her head from Seth's belly.

"Are you okay, sweetie?" Shannon said, crawling over towards Will and wrapping him in a hug. "That was . . . that was something else, Cleft."

"That's never happened before," Cleft said, almost defensively. "I promise. I've never seen one of those . . . things. I don't think it would have harmed us though."

"Not sure what would have happened if it sat on us," Seth cut in. Cleft acknowledged the possibility. "And I've *never* heard a bird call like that. Ever."

Cleft began singing the bird call quietly to himself. "Ooopoe. Ooopoe. Ooopoe." He seemed lost in thought. "Where do I know that sound from?"

"I'm not sure how you *could* know that sound, Cleft," Shannon added. "That thing was otherworldly."

"Ooopoe," Cleft said again. "My gosh," he said laughing.

"What is it?" Seth asked. "What?"

"Ooopoe sounds exactly like a Greek word from the New Testament."

"What's it mean?" Seth asked.

Cleft's face looked as if it was climbing back down from the realization he just had. His smile stayed as he looked up towards the sky. "It means . . . *not yet.*"

25

THE SHADOW CHAPEL

"**F**IND YOUR SKULKING FRIENDS and tell them to meet us in the field behind the church," Skotos said. "And tell them to bring shovels."

It was the Monday after the explosion. Police tape still hung around the perimeter of Trinity Presbyterian Church. Cain and Skotos sat around their old campsite by Rebel's Rock.

"Aren't there gonna be, like, cops swarming that place?" Cain asked.

"We're not doing anything illegal. The land behind that church was for sale. So, I purchased it."

"With what money?"

"With *my* money."

"How'd you get that much money—thousands of dollars—when I ain't ever seen you working?"

"Cain, you're so traditional. Open your mind. Money is just a tool, a bargaining chip to get the better things. You can put in time and energy and servitude to get it. Or you can find someone who has a lot of it, choose a pressure point, and squeeze."

Cain swallowed any other questions. He knew Skotos well enough by now to interpret those words. He hoped it hadn't meant someone's death. But then he thought the person couldn't be dead if he was still a money source.

"So, you bought the land. Why?"

"I told you already. We need a chapel. People always gather around something—even if something is nothing. We'll give them a nice nothing, gain credibility, and then take them."

"Take them where? To that black door? You still haven't told me what happened to me when I went through it."

"I told you all you needed to know," Skotos said, growing bored of Cain's questions. "You went through that door to find yourself. And you did. Now you're just tripping over your old self to understand it."

Cain ignored the comment. "I just think that's gonna be a hard sell to people. It's weird . . . creepy-sounding. Like some sort of dark magic."

"Ah, dark magic is the best kind, Cain. And you're wrong about the people. Humans are mostly stupid, but not for the reasons other people give. They aren't stupid for a lack of intelligence or inferencing."

"Yeah? Why are people so stupid then?"

"Because they always assume they have control over things clearly beyond them. All we need to do is sell them on the control of their destiny. And that sell is *so* easy for you humans."

"Why do you keep talking like that?"

"Like what?"

"Like you're not a human. You're just as human as I am."

Skotos picked his head up from drawing in the dirt with a stick. He looked squarely at Cain's eyes as if he could pierce straight through to his core. Cain's heart rate began to rise. Goosebumps gathered on his neck and arms.

"I am *not* a human—you sickly sacks of bones and flesh. But hear this right now, Cain Shoemaker. Don't you *ever* ask me who or what I am again. You *know*. And every time you pretend not to it makes me want to crush your skull."

"Jesus! Don't take it so—"

"And don't you *ever* mention that name around me! Ever! I swear on my own black heart—I tolerate that name out of compulsion. But if you toss those letters into the air when I'm around, you can be sure I will make you eat them!"

"Alright, alright!" Cain said, backing away from the fire and standing up. "For cryin' out loud."

"Now, as I said." Skotos returned to his cold, calm self. "Get your skulking friends and meet me in the field. With shovels."

***

Cain went straight to Jesse's apartment, trying to think of what he would say to get him and Patrick to come with him. Both of them had already walked away from Skotos once. He didn't think they'd be keen on joining them again.

As he walked down Silver Lake and turned toward Jesse's apartment, he looked for the dogwood tree that would just be budding now in the softness of the April sun. It stood at the start of Milford Road. He had so few happy and peaceful memories. This was one he kept with him.

In the third grade, he and his class took a field trip to Dingmans Creek, a tributary to the nearby Delaware River. It was late spring, and the dogwood tree had bloomed. Its white-pink petals were drifting off in the breeze just as the class marched beneath it on the sidewalk. He looked up and saw the petals spinning down on top of his head. "It's snowing! It's snowing!" Patrick said, opening his mouth to catch the "snowflakes." But one went in his mouth and made him gag. Cain laughed until his ribs were sore. But before moving on at the scolding of Mrs. Cadberry, he looked up once more and followed a single petal as it danced down towards him. He held open his hand, and the petal landed perfectly in the center of his palm. And just for that, he felt special, chosen, selected in the dizzying movement of the day. He put the petal in his pocket. That night, he carefully placed it between the pages of the big King James Bible they owned but never used, shoved beneath the TV set in their trailer to add more height to the screen. The petal was still there. He'd never told anyone.

Now, he stood confused looking down Milford Road, staring at the space where the tree had been. There was no stump, no evidence of changed landscaping. Nothing. The tree was gone. As if it had never been there.

***

Gladice was taking her daily walk down Silver Lake after she'd gotten off of work at the police station. She shuffled her grandmotherly body down the sidewalk with purpose, pumping her little arms, doing her best to do what her doctor told her she should do: get her heart rate up. She had beaten the cancer nearly two decades ago. She could do it again.

She squinted her eyes behind her big, square-rimmed glasses, picking out a trio of boys a hundred yards ahead of her and moving away towards the church. One of them she recognized right away: her grandson.

"Cain! Cain!" she called. No response. "Can never get my voice loud enough. Lord, help me. Cain!"

Cain stopped and turned around in a circle, looking for the voice. His shoulders slumped when he saw who it was—not because he didn't like his grandmother, but because he knew she was the one person who actually cared about him, and he wasn't in a place right now to be cared for. He had things to do. But he could never bear dismissing her.

"Taking your walk, Gramma?"

"Yes," Gladice said, huffing after she'd quickened her shuffle to catch up with the boys. Patrick and Jesse tried to avoid eye contact. "Where you headed?"

"Just walking."

"Oh," she said, with a grandmother's feigned surprise and lack of belief. "Just a walk. You're like me, then."

"Yeah. I guess so. You doing okay?"

"Oh, you're sweet to ask. Yes, I'm doing fine. Just trying to get my heart rate up. Your mother okay?"

"I think so," Cain shrugged. "I haven't seen her much this week. She's been picking up extra shifts at work."

"Well, I raised her to be a hard worker."

"Hmm. Wish you could've raised my dad that way."

At this comment, they both looked down. It was a sore subject and had been for years. When Tabitha married Cain's father, Gladice knew the risks, and had heard the rumors about his drinking and run-ins with the law. She rarely spoke to him, since he had fulfilled all the sad, unspoken prophecies. Now Tabitha—her sweet, sunshine-loving little girl—was locked up in a trailer, their town's version of a tower, and there was no knight to rescue her. The knight was locked in the tower with her, his mind soaked in alcohol and his soul shrouded in smoke.

Gladice had tried so many times to get Tabitha out, to give her the courage to leave. She'd even made up a bed for her in the cramped apartment, next to a couch cluttered with sewing supplies. But it was never to be. Tabitha was stuck—wedged between failed promises and faded hopes. She reigned as queen in a realm of cigarette butts and beer bottles.

"Me too," Gladice said, almost in a whisper.

"Well, I gotta go. Have a good walk, okay?"

"Sure," she said. "You too."

Gladice turned back towards her apartment as Cain, Patrick, and Jesse went farther down Silver Lake, turning right just after they passed the church property.

***

Skotos was waiting for them. Patrick and Jesse looked at each other, both unsure of themselves.

"I told you to bring shovels."

"Ahh," Cain said, kicking the dirt. He looked so much more confident and collected when he *wasn't* in the presence of Skotos. But whenever he was, his demeanor was that of a wilted flower, weak and bent forward. "We—"

"I figured you would, so I brought a few," Skotos said. "Grab one and start marking the corners where I've put the sticks. Then dig a small trench around the perimeter. I'll pay you $100 an hour."

"A hundred bucks an hour!" Jesse said. Patrick matched his enthusiasm. Neither of them had ever been paid a quarter as well as that for any job. But, then again, you could count on one hand the number of jobs that Jesse and Patrick actually did. They gravitated toward watching rather than doing. But the offer from Skotos sent them both marching towards the shovels.

"Are we gonna dig this whole . . . foundation or whatever, for this building? Cause that'll take a long time," Cain said, trying not to let the tone of his voice overstep the boundaries Skotos was always reminding him of.

"No," Skotos said matter-of-factly. "That would be stupid."

"So, what are we . . ." Cain trailed off. He didn't know what he was asking.

"Why are you *so* fixated on the future? Focus on the present. Let me take care of the future."

About three hours later, the boys had dug the trench. And they turned their heads up at the sound of heavy machinery. Rolling towards them was what appeared to be a brand new Bobcat mini excavator in shining white paint. The driver was hunched, with his head slightly down. They couldn't identify him yet. But when he hobbled out of the excavator and limped toward Skotos, they each were taken back.

His face was so swollen and bruised that you could barely make it out as human. There were slits where eyes should be, though he must have been able to see out of them. A trickle of blood dribbled from his lips as he mumbled something to Skotos. Then he bowed—a very strange response, old and servile. He walked past the boys and mumbled something they couldn't understand, pointing to the perimeter they had dug out. He seemed to be explaining what he was about to do. The only sound Cain could make out was something like, "Dags dime tu-lunis tough." Cain nodded and smiled before stepping away from the excavator as the poor creature put it in gear and began the work of digging.

***

Cain, Jesse, and Patrick huddled on the side for the next several hours. Before heading home, they approached Skotos to ask him about payment, but Skotos was ahead of them. He extended three crisp one hundred dollar bills to each of them. They took the money eagerly. Jesse voiced what all of them were thinking.

"Umm, Skotos. This is, umm, just three hundred, but we've been here for seven hours."

"Did you *work* for seven hours?"

"Well, yeah. I mean, we've been here that long," Jesse said, already beginning to lose confidence.

"No one gets paid to watch. You worked three hours and watched for four. If you want more work, be here tomorrow at 8:00am." With that, Skotos turned to have words with the excavator, who had just shut down the machine.

"Be here tomorrow at 7:30 am. Or you get round two."

The poor creature stared down at him from the excavator seat and nodded, pain and defeat written in pink skin and yellowing bruises on his face.

"You'll do well with us if you keep this up. Remember, *it takes time to learn this stuff.*" The man's head hung even lower at those words. He put the excavator in gear and rolled out of the field like a child whose toys had all been broken right in front of him.

***

By the time Sunday rolled around, the foundation had been built up on all four sides with cinderblocks, and concrete had been poured and set for the floor. This made it all the more startling when Cleft showed up, still on his crutches, to check on the church property, which was being prepped for repairs. Even though services had to be canceled for that day, he still wore his traditional khaki pants and navy blue blazer. He frowned as he saw the commotion behind the church and then doubled his pace when he realized how much work was already done.

"Hey!" he called, noticing the man he'd come to identify so easily—his black stringy hair, his pale skin, his bony frame, wrapped in the same attire he always wore (black jeans and a long-sleeved black t-shirt). Skotos did not look up from his clipboard. Cleft had not seen him since he'd heard his voice the night of the bombing, and then again at dinner with the Logans.

"Hey!" Cleft called again as he got within fifty yards. He didn't know that Gladice was out for a morning walk and was now following him from a distance. She, too, knew the icy figure behind the church lot.

Cain was talking to Skotos, who appeared irritated, punching the clipboard with his index finger as they both stood near the edge of the newly set foundation. Cain backed away before muttering something. At that point, Skotos tossed the clipboard to the ground and shoved Cain so hard that his body flew through the air and landed with a cracking thud several feet below on the concrete. This made even Cleft freeze in his tracks. A fall from that height could easily lead to serious injury, even death. And the slapping sound of the body hitting the stone was sickening.

And it was then, in that moment of sharp evil, that Gladice Shoemaker committed herself to justice.

26

GLORIOUS, GLADICE

G LADICE COULDN'T EXACTLY RUN, but she could trot with vigor, swinging her little arms with consequence. Her periwinkle Martha's Vineyard crewneck sweatshirt did nothing to impose fear, but it did elicit a chuckle of amusement from Skotos, who saw her coming a long way off.

Despite her slow, shuffling pace, she passed Cleft on his right as she made her charge (if you could call it that) at Skotos.

"Gladice? Hey, Gladice! Wait!" Cleft yelled, but Gladice didn't even flinch or turn to acknowledge him. She was seeing tunnel vision. She'd never watched anyone hurt her grandson before, and the righteous rage that fumed inside her chest knew no boundaries. She saw only red.

When she was within fifteen feet, she pulled a small canister from her sweatpants pocket. She noticed now that Jesse was standing behind Skotos, panicking about his friend, whom Gladice could now see lying unconscious on the concrete foundation, a small puddle of blood ringing his head like an unfinished halo.

Gladice had *never* been in a situation like this before, so she had no vocabulary ready. She just blurted out the first thing that came into her head. "Damn you to hell!" she said in a wavering yell, aiming her canister of pepper spray at Skotos's face and pressing down on the trigger.

And in that fraction of a second, leaving nothing but the shadow of a sneer, Skotos was gone. They were all stunned for a split second until Jesse started screaming. The pepper spray had found a target, but it wasn't Skotos.

"Oh, dear! Oh, God! Sweetheart, I'm so sorry!" Gladice tried to console Jesse, who was rolling on the ground like a bear grabbing at his eyes. As she tried to put a hand on his back, Jesse flipped over and pushed her hand away, even as he shouted for help. But this gesture was enough to put Gladice's attention back on her grandson, still unconscious on the concrete foundation. She looked at the ladder leading down into it and hesitated.

"Let me, Gladice. Let me," Cleft said, tossing his crutches to the side and stepping gingerly with his sprained ankle on the first rung of the ladder. "Dah!" he yelled, trying to switch to his other foot, but it was too late. He'd already pulled the arms of the ladder off the edge of the foundation and was falling in slow motion towards the concrete bottom, pulling the ladder on top of himself.

"Oh, Cleft!" Gladice yelled, helpless. She'd rushed to the scene and done nothing. Guilt and frustration swelled like a din around her, marked by Jesse's ongoing groans. He was still rolling on the ground, his eye sockets and cheeks all red and scratched. "God, what do I do? What do I do?" She said, half to herself and half to God. She hobbled as fast as she could back towards Silver Lake, praying that Tom might be doing his morning patrol.

He wasn't. She resolved to run all the way down to the police station, three-quarters of a mile. And she did. She burst through the door, jingling the bell, as Tom stepped out into the hallway from the break room where the old coffee maker was still sputtering and dripping. He put his mug down and ran to Gladice, who collapsed in his arms.

"Gladice! Geez! What's wrong? What's wrong?"

Gladice couldn't catch her breath. She'd never in her life attempted to run something close to a mile. The burning in her lungs and the shortness of her breath were telling her why.

"Cleft . . ." she coughed out before heaving for another breath. "And Cain . . ."

"What about 'em? They okay?"

She shook her head. "Church. Behind the church . . . they're hurt."

Tom ushered her with him, almost carrying her, out to the police cruiser.

"You just keep breathing and point to where I need to go."

Gladice nodded, happy to not have to pause her breathing to get a word out. Within two minutes, Tom was pulling into the church lot. He told Gladice to stay put while he ran towards the building site, clutching his sidearm. From fifty feet away, he could see Jesse still rolling back and forth next to the freshly dug foundation, groaning. He could see Cleft on his hands and knees, leaning over top of Cain. Cleft had a nasty gash on his forehead, letting a trail of blood down his cheek.

"Cleft?! It's one thing after another with you now, isn't it?" Tom said, part in jest. He surveyed the scene, saw that no ladder was available except the one next to Cleft, and jumped down to the concrete foundation. He regretted the decision as soon as his body was in the air. He landed like a bag of bricks and turned his own ankle in the process.

"Nah! You gotta be kidding me!" Tom yelled, fully aware that he had done the *one* thing you shouldn't do at the scene of an accident: make yourself another victim. Cleft looked into Tom's face with pained amusement.

"Well, now the help is hurt. What are we gonna do now?"

Tom grabbed his radio from his belt as he held his turned ankle in the air. "Call for more help," he said, wincing with a sigh of disappointment. Within a few minutes, another police cruiser pulled into the lot. They were all unaware, however, that this was unnecessary. A miracle was now set in motion from a place they least expected.

***

Jesse Glattfelter had always been a strong kid. He just didn't know where to put his strength. His legs were lean but packed with natural muscle. His torso and upper back had all the right proportions—all the ligaments and bones wrapped up in mutually reinforcing positions. His shoulders were broad, his chest solid, and his biceps and forearms stuffed with so much muscle that they appeared swollen. No one could ever see this because Jesse always wore long clothes—pants in the summer, and even long-sleeve shirts, except when the temperature went over 90.

He was raised to believe that bodies are best used, not seen. His father, Aaron, managed construction projects and was often away. His mother Emma, a plain but pretty heir of Pennsylvania Dutch work ethic, may have been the source of his strength. No one knew how strong she was because she did so much of her work on a small family farm off of Park Road, where no one watched but God. The trees and the birds saw her might, but no other human. She once picked up an injured calf in the field that weighed some 200 pounds, hefted it onto her shoulders, and carried it to a bed of hay in the barn. Her husband had been so proud that he told the story whenever he had the chance. Emma had superhuman strength.

That was before they moved into their small apartment on Silver Lake. The farm had gotten to be too much work for her without Aaron around as much, and she decided to train as a nurse. Their farming days were over. But Jesse received the same strength in his blood. And while Patrick and Cain knew Jesse was strong, they had no idea how far it went. But they would.

Patrick showed up on the scene after being sent out to get tools from the hardware store. Holding a brown paper bag full of tools with both hands, he surveyed everything with confusion: Cain lying in a heap with Cleft kneeling over him; Tom clutching his ankle and mumbling into his radio; Gladice standing on the side of the foundation holding her elbows and looking helpless. And Jesse, rolling and moaning like a beaten bear on the grass.

That's when something changed in Jesse, when his strength and burning blood surged inside. He forced his eyes open, blinking to get the pepper spray out in tears. He could see blurred figures, watercolor bodies dripping wet on the edges and fading into chaos. He knew Gladice was on his left; he could still hear her mumbling prayers.

He threw himself down to the concrete foundation, keeping his feet and hands outstretched to stick the landing. Then, like a blind gorilla, he crawled around to find the ladder. Gripping the cold aluminum, he used it as a cane to find the edge of the foundation. He jammed it into position, kicking the bottom with his heel so that the upper tips of the ladder wedged deeply in the brown earth just beneath the grass at the top.

He went first for Tom. "Grab my neck," Jesse said.

"Now just hold on, Jesse. You can't lift—"

But Tom could feel the power and control of Jesse's forearms already lifting his 260-pound frame up onto his shoulders.

"Geez, Jesse. Put me down, son! You're gonna break your back!"

"Back is strong," Jesse said as he marched over to the ladder and walked up the rungs, hands-free, setting Tom's body down on the ground as gently as if it were a baby deer. Tom was too stunned to say anything, and he didn't have the chance. Jesse was already back down on the concrete, heading for Cleft.

"Jesse, now, hold on. You're gonna hurt yourself. I'm okay to limp," Cleft said, holding up a hand to stop Jesse. But Jesse just wrapped Cleft's arm around his neck and picked him up like a toddler. As he climbed the ladder again and set Cleft down next to Tom, both men stared at each other in disbelief.

Lifting up Cain was easy in comparison, but Jesse cradled Cain's head like a newborn and brought him over to Gladice, who thanked Jesse and began talking to Cain in whispers. An EMT truck pulled in just as Jesse sat himself down, puffy-eyed and tearing, next to Gladice.

Gladice looked over at him after making sure Cain was still breathing. "Young man, I don't know where you got that strength, but that was nothing short of a miracle."

"Not sure it was a miracle. I was just doing what I was made to do."

"Well, sometimes that's just as miraculous," Gladice said, with wisdom and sincerity in her eyes. She looked not just *at* Jesse, but *into* him. Jesse felt immediately that the only other human being who looked at him this way was his mother—with an attentiveness and love that made him avoid eye contact with her. He was speechless for a moment. And then he said something Gladice would never forget.

"Mrs. Shoemaker?"

"Yes, dear?"

"Thank you . . . for hitting me with the pepper spray. I hadn't been woken up in a long time. I lost my vision, but I gained my sight." He rubbed his eyes again and then held them open so they would tear and cleanse his eyes once more.

Gladice had no response but a smile, and Jesse lifted his face towards the sky, letting the pepper-spray tears roll down his cheeks. But he was actually crying now, not just tearing up from the pepper spray. And it felt *so* freeing to cry. He had forgotten. He had forgotten what it was like for the soul to break a dam.

Gladice left Cain to check on Cleft and Tom, while Janet and Ben, the EMTs who had just arrived, began inspecting Cain. He was starting to regain consciousness. As Ben ran to the truck to fetch the gurney—the same one that had carried Cleft's wife out of his house only a month ago—Cleft looked at Gladice and chuckled to himself. "What a day, what a day."

"Hmmm. Good, Lord. I hope my grandson is okay. Never seen a fall like that before."

Janet overheard her and called out to them.

"It's just a concussion, Gladice. A good one, but he should be okay. We'll have to monitor him at the hospital for the next twenty-four hours, though."

"Of course," said Gladice. "I'll go with him and get ahold of his mother."

"I heard what Jesse said to you, Gladice" Cleft muttered, almost in a whisper. "I know you missed your target, and we'll talk about that soon. But I think you hit the one God intended."

"Seems a strange way for God to work—through pepper spray," she said.

"But when it comes down to it, it's no less glorious than parting the Red Sea. God's work in souls is always glorious, Gladice. Always. We just have our preferences for what we'd like to see. Mark my words: that pepper spray may have saved his soul."

27

HOW DO YOU FIGHT?

THE FOLLOWING DAY, CLEFT called a meeting: Seth and his family, Lem, Bill, Travis, and Ethan. All the gazers. Roland and Narnia were there as well. And he invited Gladice, too. She'd been at the center of the turmoil, and Cleft sensed it was time for her to choose whether or not she would go through the white door. He'd need to have a separate conversation, he was sure, with Jesse.

With a bowl of salted nuts on the kitchen table, the smell of black coffee in the air, and an active robin singing ceaseless *cheerios*, Cleft started the meeting.

"I called you all here because, as most of you know, Skotos is . . . strange. I've heard his voice in my head. Gladice watched him disappear—twice. Just vanish. And—" Cleft paused, bracing the room for what he was about to say. "I think it's time we just come to terms with what we fear, deep down, is the reality. I don't think Skotos is . . . human."

No one said anything for what seemed like a minute. It was as if the words were foisted into everyone's mouth, and all were separately tasting and chewing, not prepared yet to swallow. It was Gladice who broke the silence with a short and sincere, "Oh, dear," punctuated with a heavy sigh.

"When you say 'isn't human' you mean . . . what?" Shannon asked.

"I mean some incarnation of evil—some spirit or demon . . . Satan himself for all I know."

"Jesus," Lem said, scratching his white beard and looking down.

"Isn't that taking the Lord's name in vain, Grandpa," Travis said with an impish grin.

"Not if you're talkin' to him," Lem said, without looking up.

Gladice surprised everyone by voicing the question buried beneath their pondering and panic. "So, how do we fight?"

"Mommy!" Will broke into the room with Livy at his heels. "Look at *this* marble!" Cleft had given them marbles to play with again, and Will had been busy building a little path for them to roll through, using some old Lincoln Logs that Cleft found in his attic.

"Hold on, sweetie. We're in the middle of—" Shannon replied, but Will cut her off.

"There's a whole world inside it! Look!"

Shannon took the marble from her son and held it up to the light. Greens and blues swirled together while a sharp thread of red divided the middle.

"See," Will said. "Up on top of the red line is heaven, and down under it is . . . is the earth."

"That's a very creative way to see it, Will. You've got a special mind."

Will beamed with pride. Livy stood behind him sucking her two fingers. She looked at her mom with her giant brown eyes.

"You too, Livy," Shannon said. "A beautiful little mind." Livy smiled around her fingers and looked down. All the adults were happy to be distracted and stared at the kids as they marched back out to the living room. Gladice voiced her question again when they had settled into silence.

"So, how do we fight?"

"What do you mean?" Travis said.

"Well, I tried to get him with pepper spray and got your poor friend instead."

"He's not really my friend," Travis added.

"He might be yet," Cleft said. "I sense a metamorphosis for that boy."

"And as I always say," Narnia added, "You never know where friends are hiding."

"Well," Gladice continued, "We can't get him arrested. We can't harm him. We can't even keep him in one place. So, what are we supposed to do?"

"If you'd all permit me to speak as a pastor," Cleft said. "Let's consider this from a Matthew 4 perspective."

"What's a Matthew 4?" Travis asked, having never touched a Bible in his life. "Oh, you mean the Bible?"

"Yes. What did Jesus do when he was tempted by the devil three times?"

"Quoted Scripture," Gladice said, feeling a bit like a girl in Sunday school again, quietly proud to have the right answer.

"That's right. And, back in Genesis 4, in the Old Testament, what did God say to Cain before the murder of Abel? Anyone remember that?" The room was silent. Cleft opened his big black Bible and began to read. "This is right after Cain's sacrifice was rejected because his heart wasn't in it. Cain's face fell and he was upset. And God said,

'Why art thou wroth? And why is thy countenance fallen? If thou doest well, shalt thou not be accepted? And if thou doest not well, sin lieth at the door. And unto thee shall be his desire, and thou shalt rule over him.'"

"I don't get it," Travis said, before he'd even thought about the words. The sounds seemed hazy to him, like a fog he had no interest in sifting through.

"God was saying," Cleft replied, with kindness and patience in his voice, "that what was really bothering Cain wasn't a person. It was something inside himself. It was *sin*. It was jealousy and the anger at being rejected. That sin was crouching outside Cain's door, as it were, outside his soul. It was waiting for him, ready to attack."

"So, what was Cain supposed to do?" Travis asked.

"Well, he was supposed to fight it. And that must have been hard for him because we're used to fighting things *outside* ourselves. But this kind of fight had to be against himself, against the painful workings of his own heart. Cain was supposed to engage in what theologians call *mortification*, the killing of sinful thoughts and desires inside."

"And did he?" asked Travis.

"Did he what?" Cleft said, looking up from his Bible.

"Did he kill the sin inside himself?"

"No. No, he didn't. He let the evil win, and then he murdered his brother."

"Geez," Travis said, almost laughing. "The Bible is violent."

"*People* are violent, Travis. And the Bible has people in it."

"So," Seth cut in for the first time, "are you saying we're supposed to memorize Bible verses to respond to Skotos, as

Jesus did with Satan? And that this is, somehow, going to be fighting back against evil, against Skotos?"

"Well, I'm not trying to make things that simple. I'm just trying to start the conversation. It would seem we have to fight darkness with light. Isn't that always how it goes? And the brightest light I know of is Jesus Christ and his word. John called him the light of the world. We're not going to get anywhere fighting against Skotos with physical means—that much is clear."

"Who's John?" Travis said, locked into the conversation, but still lost.

"Geez, Bill," Lem said. "This boy hasn't come within ten feet of a Bible, has he?"

"Maybe more than ten feet," Bill said. Travis shrugged off their comments.

"John was one of the gospel writers," Cleft said. "There are four gospels, perspectives on the life of Jesus."

"Okay, so," Travis started, "I still don't get it. You think this Skotos guy is Satan or something?"

"Or something, yes," Cleft said.

"What's this thing he's building behind the church, then?" Travis asked.

"That's what I don't know," Cleft said. "The other day was the first time I saw it, and it makes me nervous. We've got to do something. I was hoping the police would help, but that was when I still thought Skotos was, well . . ."

"This talk about not being human is really freaking me out," Shannon said.

Lem shifted in his chair. "So . . . Believe. Speak. And then kill," he muttered.

"What?" Travis said, still struggling to find his feet in the conversation.

"We ain't gonna fight against the devil if we don't believe he's real, and we got nothing to fight with if we don't believe in light. So, belief comes first. Then we practice saying the words of God, to ourselves, or to him, if he shows up. So, speaking is second. And then we kill the sin inside ourselves. Believe. Speak. Kill."

"Yes," Cleft said, with a pensive pause. "Yes, that's right, Lem. It's worth a shot, anyway. I don't know how any of this is going to work out. Travis, let me grab you a Bible. Anyone else need one? I've got extras."

"Umm, I'll take one," Shannon said. Everyone else apparently had one. Seth thought of his father's Bible on his nightstand at home. He'd finally be reading it in full. And he knew that would mean he'd be drawing closer to something his father had gathered around for most of his life, a campfire Seth had only ever seen through the back of his father.

"Now, Gladice, if I could have a word with you on the porch while the rest of you mingle," Cleft said, rising up and pushing in his chair.

"Oh, yes. Of course," Gladice said as she stood up. "Feels like we're up against Nazi Germany."

"Honestly, Gladice," Cleft said. "Not sure there's as great a difference."

"How do you mean?"

"We always think we're fighting evil on the outside, that evil is *out there*. But evil isn't out there; it's *in here*," he said, pointing to his chest. "And that makes fighting against it a war within. And not many people are even willing to wage a war like that."

"Why not?"

"Because they're convinced evil couldn't possibly have a home inside them. They think they're all noble savages at heart."

"Noble savages?"

"It was a term from a French philosopher, Jean-Jacques Rousseau. I'll tell you about him later." Gladice nodded as they walked toward the front porch.

Travis cut back into the discussion before they were through the threshold. "What's a Jon-Jack?"

"I'll tell you later, Travis," Cleft said, as his voice faded to the porch.

***

Cain awoke in a hospital bed, white sheets and white walls assaulting his dreary eyes. His head pounded. He reached over and felt the IV in his arm, taped in the pit of his left elbow.

Bit by bit, images and sounds came back to him. As Skotos had given orders to Cain, Jesse, and Patrick, Cain felt the growing irritation of being under an authority he didn't choose—even though he had chosen it. Skotos had said Cain would make a name for himself, but where was the evidence of that? All he'd done was walk through a black door with a sense of euphoria, gain confidence for a few days, and then he was *consumed* . . . consumed with a gnawing sense of dissatisfaction and disgust, as if the whole world had a stench he couldn't stand. He hated his own skin, and the people, objects, and colors surrounding him. He was a rabbit in a steel trap, and the world around him was putrid gray—hardly worth escaping into anymore.

Despite the fact that Skotos had almost killed him before, he stood up to him—half in anger, half in ignorance. "I'm not building some dumb chapel until you tell me what this has got to do with *me*. You stand there and bark orders like a foreman, and you don't even pick up a shovel yourself. Go ahead and kill me if you want to! I'm dead anyway!"

Skotos leaned in close to Cain with icy calculation. "You're right," he said. "You *are*." And with that, Skotos opened his eyes wide to reveal a yawning dark that had no end, as if his pupils were black holes sucking every fiber of truth, goodness, and beauty in, and letting nothing out. Cain had only a fraction of a second to be filled with fear before Skotos jolted his arms forward and shoved Cain into the air, above the concrete foundation. He felt his body float until a hard smack came up from beneath him. Everything went black after that. But just before he landed, as he floated through the air, Cain heard a confident whisper, a single word: "Sleep."

***

Cain shivered as he recollected. And then he couldn't stop shivering. His teeth chattered and clanked together like nails against metal. The nurse came in and checked his temperature. It was only 94 degrees. He was well on his way to hypothermia. They brought in heated blankets and draped them over his jittering body. The doctors checked his vitals, ordered bloodwork, but had no explanation. Amidst their constant entrance and exit, Tabitha came in—lost and terrified as she watched her son shake and moan.

"Oh, God! Cain!"

"Mom!?"

"What happened?" Tabitha leaned in and hugged the shaking body of her son. Cain leaned into her neck, smelling the stale cigarettes and drugstore perfume. He'd always hated the scent. Until now.

"I fell and hit my head, and now I c-c-c-can't—"

"It's okay, baby. Stop talking. Just stop. We'll figure this out."

And for some unexplainable reason, he believed her. He always had, despite all the stains on her character. He could see it in her eyes, ever since he was a boy: she didn't have insight or wisdom or a depth and breadth of experience. She had none of those things. But she had the one thing that he needed most when he was in pain: *sincerity*. He looked into her eyes as she pushed herself onto the bed. And that was when he gulped and tried not to scream.

"Mom! Your eyes! I can't . . . I can't see your eyes!"

"Hold on! Just hold on, sweetie. It's probably just your head." She embraced his face with her hands. A doctor stepped in when he heard the commotion.

"Everything okay in here?"

"Doctor, he says he can't see my eyes. Is that . . . a head injury thing?"

"Blurred vision can accompany brain trauma, yes. Cain, do you have blurred vision of everything in the room?"

"No. I can see everything fine. It's just her eyes. I can't see her eyes."

The doctor stopped and looked at Tabitha's eyes. She blushed. It had been a long time since her husband had looked her in the eyes with any concentration.

"Strange. I haven't heard of blurred vision being localized that way. I suppose it's possible. Let me check on the bloodwork." He turned to leave but then stopped and stared at Cain's body.

"Hey, your body stopped trembling. Nurse, can we check his temp again?" The nurse handed him a thermometer, and the doctor held it in Cain's mouth for him. "Remarkable. Just remarkable."

"What is it, doctor? Is it worse?" Tabitha asked, on the border of tears.

"No, no. It's normal. It's 98.5 degrees. When did this happen?" He looked at the nurse, who shook her head in ignorance.

"Must have been when his mother came in," the nurse said.

The doctor looked at Tabitha's right hand, clutching Cain's hand under the blankets.

"Hmph. Well, I'm glad the temperature is back up. Let me go and see about that bloodwork."

Cain stared into his mom's face. The blurred circles of her eyes were slowly but surely coming back into focus. He had never felt so relieved. She looked at him as if he were five years old again.

"Told you we'd be okay," she said.

The doctor came back in and started talking without looking up from his clipboard. "Bloodwork looks good. We'll keep him overnight just to observe him and be safe. But you should be all set to head home in the morning."

Tabitha let go of her son's hand and faced the doctor. "Oh, God. That's so good. Thank you, doctor." She wanted the doctor to say something more, but he didn't. He turned and left, and so Tabitha turned back to Cain with a sigh.

A wave of heat surged through Cain's body as he looked at his mom's face. The eyes were again two blurry circles.

"Mom, I can't see your eyes again!"

"Honey, I think it'll pass. Okay?" Tabitha was more confident now only because she'd heard the doctor sign off. But Cain was restless. Deep in his bones, he knew this wasn't right, that something was behind this, something deeply wrong. He closed his eyes so he could focus on something else just for a moment, to push the panic away.

"Mom, you remember that dogwood tree I told you about once? Where I caught the petal that was falling during a field trip, to Dingmans Creek?"

"Umm. Sort of. My memory isn't that sharp. I'm sorry, honey."

"Well, it's gone now."

"They cut it down?"

"I don't know."

"Wait—you said the one by Dingmans Creek?"

"Yeah," Cain mumbled, always irritated by his mother's lack of listening skills.

"It's still there, sweetie."

"What?"

"It's still there. I just saw it yesterday morning when I was on my way to exercise class. In full bloom. It isn't gone." She smiled at Cain to reassure him that the world wasn't disappearing.

Cain's brow furrowed. "Then why couldn't I . . ." he started in a whisper before his mom cut in.

"Cain, you gotta speak up, honey. Your momma's not old, but I don't got sonar hearing."

"I don't think that's a thing, mom."

"Well, you know what I mean. Look, you want me to stay with you? I can get someone to cover my shift down at the grocery store."

"No, Ma. It's okay." Cain's Switch from "Mom" to "Ma" signaled to Tabitha that his softness had faded. He was back to the old Cain. And she felt sad in a way she couldn't express. It had felt so nice to be needed. She looked at him for a few more seconds until he turned his head towards her.

"Really, Ma. It's okay. I'm fine. I'll be back in the morning. I'm sure this thing with my eyes will go away eventually."

"I'll come pick you up."

"No. I can walk."

"Cain, it's two miles, and you just had a concussion. I'll pick you up."

"Fine."

"Alright. I gotta run. I'm so glad my little gumper is okay. And stay away from that construction site from now on."

"Don't call me 'gumper,' ma. I'm not three years old."

"Ah, you'll always be my little gumper." She leaned over him, kissed his forehead, and walked out of the room, trailing the scent of her stale cigarette smoke and cheap perfume.

***

Gladice and Cleft walked back into the dining room, Gladice wiping her eyes from a recent cry.

"Saturday," Cleft said.

"Yes. Saturday at 10:00 am," Gladice agreed.

Cleft turned to the rest of the group as Will and Livy continued to chatter and roll marbles across the carpet in the other room.

"Okay, everyone. Let me just . . . recap, I guess."

Lem looked up from stuffing a few salted nuts into his mouth, leaving dust and peanut skins scattered in the white fields of his beard. "Believe. Speak. Kill," he said through peanut crumbs.

"Yes, Lem. But I don't know if everyone soaked in the situation in quite the way you have." He made eye contact with everyone else at the kitchen table. "Look, I don't know exactly what's going on here. I'm doing my best to understand it, but, frankly, it's beyond me. I don't know exactly *who* this Skotos guy is. I don't even know *what* he is."

"I do," Lem interrupted. Cleft just nodded and raised a hand politely.

"But I do know that he's dangerous. And that he's been tooling around with Cain Shoemaker, among others. I still have to make my way over to Cain's house to see what he knows. But until then, I want everyone on the lookout."

Everyone nodded soberly. Will yelled from the other room.

"Mommy! Can we go back to that place yet?"

All who had been to "that place" needed no more information to identify it.

"Oh, not yet, sweetie. We'll ask pastor Cleft about that later, okay?"

"Aww. Okay," Will said, clearly disappointed.

"What's 'that place'?" Travis said, thumbing through the gilded pages of the King James Bible Cleft had given him.

"Maybe next week," Cleft said with a smirk. "Oh—and before I forget, I thought I'd teach you all a few lines of verse that me, Lem, Bill, and now Seth like to say to each other in parting."

"You part of some secret club now?" Shannon said to Seth playfully, elbowing his side.

"The same one you are," Seth said smiling.

"It's just something I find reminds me of a truth that's easy to forget," Cleft said.

"What's that?" Shannon asked.

"That we don't get to live forever—not in the way we think, at least."

Shannon nodded and took in a deep breath.

"Here's how it goes," Cleft said. Then he started the recitation, joined by Lem, Bill, and Seth.

> Life is real! Life is earnest!
> And the grave is not its goal;
> Dust thou art, to dust returnest,
> Was not spoken of the soul.

"Hmm," Shannon said. "I like that."

Will started chirping like a bird from the other room: "Life is real. Life is erness. Life is real. Life is erness."

Shannon started giggling. "He loves the way words sound."

"Just like his dad," Seth said, with obvious pride.

"A boy after my own heart," Cleft said.

"Look," Cleft addressed the group. "Just read one passage from the Bible this week. Let's say, for those who can, do John 1, the first fourteen verses. Start off slow. I'll touch base with each of you this week and see what you get from the passage.

For now, see what words strike you, and keep them close. Read it over and over again. Memorize it if you can."

"Sure Skotos don't like John's Gospel," Lem said.

"No," Cleft said. "I'm sure he doesn't."

28

GLADICE AND JESSE

T HE NEXT MORNING, CLEFT went to Jesse's apartment. Dingmans Ferry was a small enough town that anyone, and certainly the pastor, knew where everyone else lived. Jesse lived with his mother, and sometimes his father, in an old brick apartment on Silver Lake. The brick was a deep red, mostly dark from algae and lichen growth. But there were large patches of brightness, too—places where moisture in the brick traveled to the surface, bringing salts from the stone out to the open air. The mortar between the bricks seemed shrunken, clinging to the crimson rock, but unnoticed, like forgotten family relations. People see the hard things, but rarely what holds them together.

Cleft walked up the cement steps to the white porch door, blanketed in dust from car exhaust on Silver Lake's busier segment. His finger pressed the doorbell, and Jesse was at the door within moments. He looked surprised to see Cleft, since he'd only ever seen him in situations where he, Patrick, and Cain were reprimanded. But he tried to conceal his discomfort.

"Pastor Cleft? Are you here for me, or for my mom?"

"For you, son. And don't worry. You haven't done anything wrong. I just wanted to have a chat with you, if you're willing. Got a few minutes?"

"Yeah. My mom's still asleep, so I'll come out here." He stepped out onto the cement in his white tube socks, royal blue sweatpants, and a faded white t-shirt. He sat in a cheap plastic Adirondack chair, holding out his hand towards the matching one for Cleft.

"I won't take too much of your time, Jesse. I will say that what you did at the church property the other day was—well, it was one of the most impressive feats of strength I've ever seen." Jesse avoided eye contact. He just nodded and stared at his own feet. Cleft waited for him to reply, but nothing came.

"I have to say . . . what you did surprised me, in two ways. For one, I didn't know a grown man could do anything like that, let alone a kid. For two, I can't figure out what brought you to do it in the first place. I saw . . . a change in you. One minute you were rolling around wiping the pepper spray out of your eyes; the next you were charging off to carry three people to safety—walking up a ladder with no hands!" Cleft slapped his knee and laughed, which brought a smile to Jesse's face. His eyes were still red and swollen from the pepper spray.

Cleft waited for Jesse to say something. But, again, he just stared at his feet and let the silence roll on with the morning. Cleft realized this might be the extent of Jesse's responses. So he got right to the point.

"Listen, Jesse. There are . . . *secrets* in this town." Jesse looked up at Cleft's face for the first time since opening the front door. "And I sense that God might be doing something in you, and that you might be ready to experience one of those secrets. Now, I won't pressure you in any way, but I'm going to meet Gladice up at Childs Park in a bit, and you're welcome to come along.

"What's at Childs Park?"

"The secret," Cleft said.

"We'll be there at 10:00 am, so I know that doesn't give you much time to decide. But there it is. If you want to go deeper in this town, you can be there. If you'd rather stay where you are on the surface, that's your choice." With that, Cleft stood up to leave.

"Pastor Cleft—" Jesse started, but then lost his words.

"Yes, Jesse?"

"I don't . . . I don't know if I believe in God. I don't think I do. That mean I'm going to hell?"

"People go to hell when they've decided they want nothing to do with God, not when they're looking for an opportunity to start a conversation. You seem to be in the latter camp. That's why I hope to see you over at the park." Cleft turned and started down the steps.

"Pastor Cleft?" Jesse stood on the top step looking down at Cleft.

"Mmhmm?"

"This thing at the park—is it . . . dangerous?"

Cleft paused and then looked into Jesse's eyes. "Well . . . yeah, in a way. Very dangerous. And very beautiful. The question is, who's put in danger by it? And the answer, I believe, isn't you, Jesse. It's someone else. It's someone I'd like your help to challenge. But you can't see that yet. To enter is to see."

Cleft walked away before Jesse could say anything else. Jesse knew in that moment that he would go. Something inside started rising to the surface, the same something that prompted him to carry three people up a ladder without using his hands, and the same something, in fact, that had told him *not* to follow Cain and Skotos into the woods several days ago.

***

On Saturday, Gladice and Jesse arrived at the small gravel parking lot for Childs Park. Cleft had driven his truck, since his ankle had finally healed enough to put a bit of weight on it. But Roland came with him, as usual. Gladice and Jesse both walked, since it wasn't far from town. In fact, Jesse had gone out of his comfort zone and asked Gladice if she wanted to walk together to the park. He'd seen her on Silver Lake and asked her where she was going, even though he knew. The fact that Gladice was going made Jesse feel more at ease. How "dangerous" could this thing be if Cain's grandmother was doing it? They talked a little, but mostly just walked. The high point in their conversation had the fewest words.

"I never said 'thank you' for saving my grandson."

"Oh . . . I don't think I saved him. I just picked him up . . . for the medics."

"Picking someone up is the heart of salvation, Jesse. I should've learned that earlier. Maybe it would've changed things with my daughter."

"Cain's mom?"

"Yes. We don't talk much anymore. I tried for a while, as that sad excuse for a husband dragged her down into a black hole with all his drinking. Some days I would hope his liver exploded."

Jesse smirked. "That's harsh." Gladice couldn't see the humor and instead felt guilty.

"Shouldn't say things like that—I know. But Martin's always been trouble. Well, almost always. Not at the beginning, but he's taken my Tabitha down with him."

Jesse was silent. Cain never talked about his parents, and Jesse knew better than to ask.

"Well, my dad isn't around much anymore. Sad excuse for a dad, I guess. Says he's always traveling for work. But, I don't know."

"But your mom is okay?"

"Yeah. She's okay. Works a lot."

"That can be good."

"Yeah. I guess . . . I don't really know, like, *how* she is. We don't talk about that so much."

"Might be worth asking her some time."

"Yeah."

By this point, they were both content to stop talking because they were trudging up the steep hill of Park Road. Jesse paced himself so that he could stay with Gladice. They both were breathing heavily when they saw Cleft from a distance. He was outside of his truck, Roland sitting next to him—a noble portrait of faithfulness. Though Jesse and Gladice said nothing, they both noticed that Cleft looked much older. It was something in his eyes, a weariness. And though they both tried to convince themselves otherwise, they could see his hair was graying much more. And they had only just seen him a few days ago. It was as if he had aged ten years. Roland, too, they thought, was whiter in the face than they remembered.

"You made it," he said with a smile. "Had no idea you'd walk here. I could've picked you both up on my way."

"Nonsense," Gladice said. "Walking is good for the soul." The words hit Cleft oddly—at once poetic and prophetic.

"Well, I can put a bit of weight on my ankle now, but I still have to use this to get around." Cleft held out a black cane with a silver handle. The silver was tarnished with a faint yellow, but they could see the paisley design underneath.

"We could wait until your ankle is better," Jesse said.

"Yeah, we could. Or you could just carry me like you did the other day." They all smiled. "No, I think it's time. You two need to see this."

"What is it?" Jesse asked, growing nervous. A tingling sensation in his stomach fluttered and then settled again.

"Well, it's better now to just show you," Cleft said as he used his cane to limp towards the path into the woods. It was a sunny day, and the rays of light were diving through the canopy to illuminate dust and swarms of gnats in crazed little clouds. With Cleft's limping, it took them a while to get to the end of the path, and then to make their way to the boulder. When they got there, Cleft's cane arm was tired and his good leg was sore at the knee and hip. He wanted to sit down, but the leaves on the forest floor were still wet with dew.

"This . . ." Cleft said, still trying to catch his breath. "This is what I wanted to show you."

Jesse and Gladice frowned as they stared at the old white door, light pouring out of the cracks all around.

"What the—" Jesse stopped himself from completing the sentence when he saw Cleft looking at him. "What is that, behind the door?"

"That's what you'll have to see for yourself. Look, neither of you has to go through that door, and I'm not going to tell you what's on the other side. But I'll be here if you need me. And if you—"

He stopped as he noticed Gladice walking straight towards the door and turning the handle. Jesse, out of a protective instinct for his own mother, reached out and grabbed Gladice's right arm to pull her back. But it was too late. He felt the pull himself—a good, strong pull to fall down. And so they both disappeared into the light, faces set with broad smiles. Cleft was grinning too.

The next thing they knew, Gladice and Jesse were holding hands as they lay on the forest floor, gazing into the canopy with ecstatic wonder.

***

Seth and Shannon stood on their porch in quiet observation. Ever since they'd gone through the door, and then seen that city of light, the world around them seemed *awake*. Or maybe they were looking at it with renewed eyes. They couldn't tell which. But they could sense wonder seeping from the edges of every tree, every rise of topography, every face they met eyes with. *More*—that was what they were seeing. More, and too much to take in. Every sense of feeling in control of the world around them was gone, in the most beautiful way. And that was because they both felt more connected to the environment—in all its vibrant and wild detail—than they ever had. If the world had been a still-life painting before, where things and people existed but had no movement of their own, and no perceived meaning, then it was now a story, a moving, breathing, pulsing narrative told by someone they could not see. And they were elated just to be characters.

They had invited Travis over for dinner. He was chasing Will and Livy around the front yard, but they had stopped and kneeled down to look at a caterpillar, shuffling its accordion body through the grass. Narnia was a few feet away, staring and lowering his head to catch every bodily movement of the finger-length creature.

Seth and Shannon thought Travis might need some help in understanding John 1, since it appeared to everyone at Cleft's house that he'd never touched a Bible. So, they offered to read it together. Shannon was making Will's favorite for dinner: spaghetti and meatballs.

They ate together and laughed at Will's intermittent chants of "Meat! Balls! Meat! Balls!" Travis was laughing so hard he had to keep wiping the tears from his eyes. Will was thrilled and amazed to have that sort of comedic power over an adult. By the time they cleared their plates, everyone's stomach hurt from heaving out laughter.

Shannon set up Fraggle Rock for the kids while Travis and Seth laid their Bibles on the kitchen table. Seth had the quiet conviction that his Bible could give him wings.

"Alright," Seth started. "John 1 is one of my favorite chapters, and it was one of my dad's."

"Your dad ain't alive anymore, right?"

"Yeah."

Travis nodded in respect. The room settled in sanctity.

"So, here's the hard part with this. Everyone—or almost everyone—knows the name Jesus Christ these days. But they don't really know *who* he is," Seth started. Travis remained silent. "He was a man, but the Bible in this passage also reveals that he existed a long time before he was on the earth."

"Like, he was in heaven or outer space?"

"Heaven—sure. Not outer space." They both started to giggle like five-year-olds, and Shannon meant to scold them with a look but couldn't keep herself from laughing.

"Jesus is also called 'the Son' of God, which you probably know. In this passage, he's called 'the Word.'"

"Why?"

"Because . . . well, it's a lot to get into. Let's just say God has always been speaking. And the one he's been speaking is the Son."

"So, God speaks *people*, like we speak words?"

"Well, kind of. I mean, yes. But, this is different." Seth could sense how much harder this would be than he assumed. "Let's just say that God is and always has been the Father speaking the Son in the hearing of the Spirit."

"I don't get it. I thought God was just . . . God."

"He is. But the Father, the Son, and the Holy Spirit are the one God."

"So, like, three mini-gods?"

"No . . . umm. This is harder than I thought. I need Cleft."

Travis looked embarrassed, as if he'd done something wrong or didn't measure up to the task.

"Maybe just read the passage," Shannon suggested.

"Yeah. Let's do that. Alright. You can stop me at any point if you have questions. I'll probably have questions, too."

And so he began.

> In the beginning was the Word, and the Word was with God, and the Word was God. The same was in the beginning with God. All things were made by him; and without him was not any thing made that was made. In him was life; and the life was the light of men. And the light shineth in darkness; and the darkness comprehended it not. There was a man sent from God, whose name was John. The same came for a witness, to bear witness of the Light, that all men through him might believe. He was not that Light, but was

sent to bear witness of that Light. That was the true Light, which lighteth every man that cometh into the world. He was in the world, and the world was made by him, and the world knew him not. He came unto his own, and his own received him not. But as many as received him, to them gave he power to become the sons of God, even to them that believe on his name: Which were born, not of blood, nor of the will of the flesh, nor of the will of man, but of God. And the Word was made flesh, and dwelt among us, (and we beheld his glory, the glory as of the only begotten of the Father,) full of grace and truth.

Travis looked like a fifth grader who had just had a calculus problem read to him. Seth was silent while he thought about where to begin. And in his head, he asked God himself for help. He could talk about *Catcher in the Rye* and John Steinbeck or the principles of composition, but this? This was out of his league. And then a moment of clarity broke through the clouds of his overwhelmed inadequacy like a ray of light.

"Okay, so think of it this way." Travis looked at him eagerly, hoping his guide had found a way through the woods of words in front of them. "People wanted God. Desperately. Right? They wanted God. But they couldn't see him because God is invisible, right?"

Travis nodded.

"But here, they get to see God, because God came down to them. The Son, the Word that the Father has always been speaking, came down to earth."

"And he was light?"

"Yes. He helped people see things the way they really are, see *themselves* as they really are."

Travis was nodding, and it gave Seth hope.

"But . . . why does it say that the world didn't know him, or, like, didn't receive him?"

"Because of sin. Sin is like a blindness."

"What do you mean?"

Seth paused to think, but the inspiration was coming to him more quickly than he could process. His mouth opened almost without his permission.

"Are you ever so busy with something, so focused, that you don't see what's going on around you?"

"Oh, yeah. Like, this one time I was in the gym working on foul shots. And a few other guys were in the gym, but then Cassie came in and walked behind the basket, and I didn't even see her. At all. I was, like, completely zoned in."

"Okay, yeah. So, think of that concept in a negative way. People can be so focused on themselves—on what they want, how they can get it, what's in the way—that they don't see something really good for them, something they need more than the other stuff they're chasing." Travis was nodding more earnestly. Seth had broken through.

"So . . . God came to people but they didn't see him because they were focused on other stuff?"

"Yeah, but even worse than that. He came right up to them and stood in front of them, and they turned him away. They said he was getting in the way of what they really wanted."

"That's messed up."

"Yeah. It's *really* messed up."

They both paused and gathered around the truth for a few moments, not saying anything. Seth broke the silence when he heard Travis take a deep breath.

"But not everyone rejected him," Seth continued. "Some people saw him. Some people received him."

"And those people got to be . . . sons of God? What does that mean? Like, divine?"

"No, not divine." Seth searched for a common explanation, and for some reason Travis's mother came into his mind, that moment in the church service when she laid her head down on his shoulder, a portrait of weariness receiving rest. "It lets you be part of the family of God."

"Oh . . . that's . . . that's cool." Travis had a huge grin on his face, and it spread to Shannon and Seth, who had met eyes with one another. Quiet as a breeze, Narnia crept into the kitchen and under the table.

"Sons in the Son—that's what true believers are." His words startled everyone, who hadn't seen him enter.

"Dude, Narnia," Travis said with relief. "You scared the—" and just then Travis paused before cursing. But it wasn't because he thought Seth and Shannon wouldn't approve, or even because the kids might hear it from the other room. He didn't *want* to say the word he was about to say. He felt that the word was a muddy stone, and he'd just washed his hands. The experience puzzled him. He never finished his sentence.

Seth and Shannon looked at each other again, not sure what to do with the awkwardness.

"Well, this was a lot for one reading," Seth said. "I was going to ask Cleft if we could do a little more, but now I'm glad I didn't. This is plenty."

"Could you, like, summarize it for me, or something?" Travis asked.

"Sure. Shannon, you want to try?"

"Me? Oh . . . sure. I can try." She looked down at her Bible and traced the words with her fingernails. Seth stared at her cuticles and the little arc of white at the base of each nail, her smooth skin. He was in love with all of her details and couldn't hold back an admiring smile.

"So, the Son of God, who is the light of the world, came down to earth. But he was rejected by the ones who should've accepted him. Those who did accept him became a part of God's family. That sound about right?"

"Sounds pretty good to me," Travis said. "You guys are good at this stuff. Reading was never my thing."

"Well, what we have to think about," Seth started, "is what to do with this passage when we walk out that door."

"What do you mean?" said Travis. "We just were supposed to read it."

"You remember that little saying your grandfather had: Believe. Speak. Kill?"

"Yeah, he's a wacko," Travis started laughing. "I love the guy, but he's so far out in left field. Half the time I don't even know what he's talking about."

"Well, I think he had something to say this time," said Seth. "I mean, if Skotos walked up to you, what would you do?"

"Punch him in the face and tell him to go back to hell."

"I mean, what would you do with *John 1*? And remember: Skotos doesn't seem to be . . . the same as we are. So, I don't think punching would do much anyway." The room felt chilled at the mention of Skotos.

"Well," Shannon started thinking out loud, "let's just say he *is* evil incarnate . . . that he loves chaos, death, and darkness, and he wants to spread that to everyone. What would antagonize him?"

"All the opposites, I guess," Seth said.

"Are any of those opposites in this passage?"

Shannon's question sent them all back to the words they had just read.

"What about 'Light shines in darkness'?" Travis said, surprising all of them, himself included. "That could be, like, our chant."

"It's pithy and to the point. I like it," Shannon said. "Good job, Travis."

"Yeah," Seth agreed. "Perfect. So, we could say that if we see Skotos again, even if we just say it to ourselves. And we'll keep an eye on how he responds. We'll see what it does."

"Yeah. Okay," Travis said. "Believe. Speak. Kill."

They all nodded, as new soldiers set on a war strategy. Thus ended their first meeting. And they would have to test it much sooner than they would have liked.

***

Cleft led Gladice and Jesse, very slowly, back through the woods to the gravel parking lot. Jesse kept staring at his hands, bunching them into fists, and then extended his fingers out. He felt as if he held stars at the ends of his arms. Gladice's head snapped toward every bird call—swallows, chickadees, cardinals, catbirds, meadowlarks, and a lone mourning dove that whistled his somber "but who" through the thick hemlock canopy. Gladice had always loved birds and kept a feeder outside her apartment window, which she filled religiously. But now the birds were more than an interest. They were—how could she put it?—a sort of distant family. They were calling not just to each other, but to *her*.

Cleft got their attention by putting his hands on their shoulders. "Hey, you remember what I told you? Keep watch. And call me if you see anything suspicious or strange. Welcome to the gazers," he said with a half smile.

"Where are you going?" Jesse asked.

"I've gotta go pay your grandson a visit, Gladice. Find out what he knows."

"You want me to go with you?" Jesse asked.

Cleft thought for a moment. His inclination was to say no, but Jesse might be insightful as one of Cain's best friends. And Cain, no doubt, would be asking questions once he saw Jesse's changed demeanor.

"Sure. Hop in the truck. In fact, Gladice, why don't you hop in, too? I don't want you walking back by yourself. I can drop you off at your apartment."

Gladice nodded, still lifting her eyes up at a cardinal that was darting among the lower boughs of the pine tree above them—an ember of hope dancing in a sea of hallowed green.

29

TALKING TO CAIN

C LEFT PULLED INTO MARTIN and Tabitha's driveway with Jesse in the passenger seat. *Coors Light* cans littered the grass but glittered in the sun—tiny ornaments of decadence. Martin's truck wasn't there, which meant only Tabitha was home. That was a good thing. Martin was harder to reason with . . . because he was usually intoxicated or hung over. Jesse was wearing the same sweatpants and t-shirt he'd had on the day before, not because he forgot to change, but because he loved the feel of the fabric now. The cotton of his pants had a fuzzy exterior of fine threads dangling just above the surface. He rubbed his hands up and down his thighs. Then stared at the tiny fibers of royal blue cotton.

"Will you quit that?" Cleft said as they approached the front door of the trailer. His words and tone reminded him of how he spoke to his sons when they were fidgeting in the grocery store line.

"Sorry. It's just . . . so soft. Don't know why I never noticed it before." Cleft let it alone for now. He knew it was the door—its ever-mysterious way of making people feel they'd just been born, as if the whole world with all its lights and colors and smells and sounds had been freshly cracked open, like a walnut hidden beneath the darkening shell of the ordinary. He remembered how even the air he breathed when he first went through the door tasted like a blend of summer and honey, with a hint of cinnamon. He had kept opening his mouth and closing it for the first few days, letting his tastebuds confirm the miracle over and over and over. It was Jane who had to tell him to stop fidgeting. That was before she'd gotten her Alzheimer's diagnosis.

Cleft rapped on the door three times before Tabitha showed up in her bathrobe. She normally wore a lot of makeup, but she had none on now, and she looked older and weaker than Cleft remembered.

"You guys here for Cain?"

"Yeah. Everything alright, Tabitha? You look troubled."

"Must be the pastor in you." She put her hand to her mouth to try and push back the cry, but it just came out through her eyes instead, and then she allowed herself a few coughs before she could take a deep breath and regain composure.

"It's alright," Cleft said softly. "It's alright. What's going on?"

"He's . . . umm . . . not well. I don't know what's—" she started but then cut herself off with crying. "I'm sorry. I'm sorry. I've just . . . never seen him like this."

"Is he being mean or harsh? Is he sick?"

"Yeah, he's been pretty dark lately," Jesse added from behind Cleft.

"That's just the thing," Tabitha said, gathering herself with another deep breath. "He *was* like that. He was. I don't know what happened, but ever since he came back from that hike in the woods, he's been off. Mean and quiet . . . it's like he had somethin' he was tryin' to do without anyone knowin'. But now? Since the concussion? Now, he's like a little kid. He's so scared and . . . and fragile. I swear it's like he's four years old again."

Cleft and Jesse weren't prepared for this. And though it would have sounded hopeful in other contexts, here it only sowed a seed of suspicion.

"Could we see him?" Jesse asked.

"Yeah, Jesse. I think he'd especially like to see you. He's been talkin' about you and Patrick, draggin' up these memories from grade school. Keeps sayin' you guys walked by a dogwood tree and he caught a petal in his hand."

"Oh, man. I remember that! So weird what you remember."

"But, guys, that's the thing you need to know before you go in there. He keeps saying he can't see things. He told me he couldn't see that tree when he went past Milford Road the other day. But I know it's there. I saw it myself. And then at the hospital, he said he couldn't see my eyes anymore, except when I held his hand. That's what breaks my heart because when he was little he used to tell me I had such pretty eyes—" She lost it again, and all Cleft and Jesse could do was nod and hope that their listening would ease the panic. "Just come in. Come in."

She led them back to Cain's bedroom where he was lying in bed with the curtains closed, but the spring breeze and the light were drifting through the window. Cain was staring at the curtains, but his head jerked towards the door when he heard his mom's voice.

"Honey? Brought some visitors for you." Cleft and Jesse stepped into the doorway. Cain felt a lump in the back of his throat that almost brought tears to the surface, but he shoved them back. Then he heard a whisper.

They will only be in the way. Get rid of them.

Cleft hadn't heard the whisper, but judging by Cain's reaction—a frightened confusion that he'd experienced himself—he knew.

"Cain?" Cleft paused for several seconds before he decided to continue down this path. "I don't know what he just said to you, but I know he said something." Cain locked eyes with him, as if he were a child caught in a burning building. Jesse just looked behind him and then back at Cleft.

"Who said?" Jesse asked. Cleft ignored him.

"Cain, I need you to tell me what happened. Everything. I know about Skotos. I know."

The fear in Cain's face was screaming. He blurted out three words: "The black door—" but then halted, as if someone's hand went over his mouth. He closed his eyes, and when he opened them, something had changed. There was a calculating coldness, a horrid determination. His pupils were twice their former size. Cleft recognized Skotos there, in the bottomless dark of Cain's pupils, swallowing every speck of light. Cleft slowly reached his hand back and grabbed Jesse's arm. He felt like someone had just pushed the detonate button on a bomb.

"Jesse. Go. Now!"

"What? But we just—"

Cain shot up to his feet, standing on the bed and reaching behind him for a Louisville Slugger baseball bat. Jesse's stomach dropped. He needed no additional prodding. In fact, he grabbed Cleft's arm this time and pulled him towards the door. In a second they were both sprinting—Cleft as well as he could on his still-healing ankle.

In half a second, Cain was in the hallway with the bat raised above his head. His mother turned from the kitchen.

"What in the—!? Guys!? Cain?!" She lunged at him and grabbed his waist. Cain was still weak. He hadn't eaten much since his concussion and hospital visit. And it was a good thing he hadn't. Rather than slapping Cleft on the back of the head, he fell on top of their glass coffee table in the living room. Half in anger and half in lost control, he brought the handle of the bat down on his mother's head. Even in his rage, the "thunk" it made scared him. It was much harder than he thought he was capable of. And by the time he could hear Cleft's truck start, Cain was pushing himself off shattered shards of glass. His mother's hair was soaked in blood, and part of the blood was touching his elbow. The wetness of the blood on his own skin brought him out of his violent rage. He was five years old again, terrified that his mother was unconscious on the family room carpet, surrounded by splintered glass.

"Ma! Ma! Get up! I didn't mean it! Wake up!" He slapped her face and then felt her neck for a pulse. If she had one, it was faint. He clawed his way towards the phone on the countertop, cutting his knees on the shards of glass. He picked up the ivory receiver, smearing blood on the back and across the buttons as he dialed 911. But it hit him as soon as the voice answered on the other end.

"911. What's your emergency?"

He couldn't speak. He was still holding the baseball bat in his left hand. He'd clubbed his own mother. She might even be dead. And he was responsible. He did it. The guilt filled his lungs like water.

"Hello? 911. What's your emergency? Is anyone there?"

He hung up the phone, then turned and threw up in the kitchen sink. After he wiped his face with the towel, he went over to his mother's body with tears in his eyes.

"Ma? Mom? If you can hear me—God, please hear me—I'm sorry. I'm so sorry. I didn't mean to. I don't know what's wrong with me. I don't know—" Then came the whisper, cold and clear.

There's nowhere for you now. Meet me back in the woods, by Rebel's Rock. I can protect you.

Cain hated the voice. It rubbed on his eardrums like sand in a fresh cut. But he also knew Skotos was right. There was nowhere for him now. That "thunk" of the bat on his mother's skull had been way too hard. He knew: he had killed his own mother. He'd be wanted for murder. And he was guilty. It was either prison or a life in the woods, at least until he got caught.

He grabbed his backpack and tossed in half a pack of English Muffins, a jar of peanuts, and a few bottles of water. Then he went back to his room to grab sunglasses and a baseball hat, got his coat from the hall closet, and left. He ran along the edges of his neighbors' yards and the perimeter of the forest to get to Silver Lake, staying away from the tree line when he approached 739. He scampered across the street and into the woods where he could make his way to Adams Creek, and then to Rebel's Rock, which would take about an hour and a half. Or maybe longer. He couldn't remember. But he'd get there before dark.

As Cain disappeared in the woods between Silver Lake and 739, Martin Shoemaker drove his green truck down the street towards their trailer, trying hard not to swerve over the double yellow lines. There was still enough alcohol in his veins to get him arrested. But, as usual, he made it back to the trailer and saw the front door open.

"Gonna let all the bugs in, dammit."

He carried a shopping bag with bread, peanut butter, and jelly to the front porch. He pushed open the screen door, looked inside, and dropped the bags where he stood.

30

CLEFT AND JESSE

C LEFT AND JESSE SPED back to Cleft's house after running from a possessed Cain. As they drove back to Cleft's, they tried to make some sense of it.

"What *was* that?!" Jesse started. Cleft shook his head several times before answering.

"I . . . I'm not certain, but let me just say that I've seen wild things in this town for years, but I've never seen something like that. That was some kind of . . . possession, and it had Skotos written all over it."

"Skotos? The guy we were building that chapel for?"

"The what?"

"The chapel—the one behind the church. He paid us a hundred bucks an hour to help him dig and lay the cement foundation."

"A chapel?"

"Yeah. Is that weird?"

Cleft opened his mouth to speak but could find no words.

"I guess I just figured he was, like, religious or something."

"Look, stay away from Cain for now. I know you're freakishly strong, but what's got ahold of him is stronger than you can imagine."

"Okay."

"I can drop you at your mom's, but while we're on the way, have you seen anything strange since you went through the door?"

Jesse smiled. His face was full of childlike joy.

"Jesse?"

"Yeah, sorry. Yeah."

"Yeah, as in you *have* seen something strange?"

"Yeah."

"Would you tell me about it?"

"The other day, I got home and was reading for a while. And then I fell asleep. When I woke up, it was later, after dinner. My mom had just gotten back from her nursing shift at the hospital. She was lying on the couch. But . . . when I saw her—" Jesse paused, searching for words. "She had this—I don't know—this *light* coming from her. It was, like, radiating from her. I kept rubbing my eyes because I thought my vision was blurry or something. But it wasn't. It made me feel like she was holy or something. Is that . . . is that wrong, to say someone is holy?"

"No. People can be holy. They can't be divine, but they can be holy if God grants it."

"Well, then I guess she was holy, lying there on the couch. Do you think—ah, never mind."

"No, go on."

"It's just a dumb idea. I'm not that smart."

"You're probably much smarter than you give yourself credit for. What did you think?"

"I don't know much about God, or religion, or stuff like that. But I know that God *gives*."

"How do you mean?"

"Like, he gives life at creation. He gives peace. He gives hope. And he gives Jesus, and the Holy Spirit. He's—what's the word?—*prodigal*."

"You sure you're not a theologian?" Cleft said with a smile. "Sounds like you know the Bible better than most."

"I've read through it a few times."

"A few times?!"

Jesse laughed. "I read once that the three greatest influences on the English language are the King James Bible, Shakespeare, and *Pilgrim's Progress*. So, I read all of them, just to get a grasp of the language I live in, you know?"

Cleft was dumbstruck. The kid with super-human strength was also an avid reader, and a much deeper thinker than he'd expected. Cleft began to feel silly for ways he'd treated Jesse in the past, when he'd hung with Patrick and Cain and yoked himself with those who seemed only interested in upsetting the order around them.

"Anyway—I was just thinking that . . . maybe my mom had light coming from her because she's always giving. She works crazy hours at the hospital, takes up extra shifts all the time. And I saw her at work once. She was just running around asking what she could do for patients—strangers. And these people were short with her, entitled, and sometimes just mean. But she kept giving. She kept serving. It's like she empties herself of all her energy, giving herself away to all these people, and then she falls asleep. I couldn't see it before. But I see it now."

Jesse grabbed his chest and tried to hold back his emotion.

"It's alright, Jesse. Crying can be like water for the soul—keeps us growing."

Jesse nodded. "Anyway, that's what I thought."

"You could very well be right. In my experience, once people go through that white door—we call them 'gazers' by the way—they start to see spiritual realities they were blind to before. Gazers see *more* than what's in front of everyone else."

"Hey—" Jesse said as they pulled into Cleft's driveway.

"Oh, I'm sorry, Jesse. I told you I'd drop you at your mom's."

"No, it's not that. I can walk anyway. I was just thinking. Remember what Cain's mom said about his vision?"

"His vision? No. I don't—"

"She said he told her he couldn't see that dogwood tree that we passed on a field trip once, when we were kids. She said the tree was still there, but Cain couldn't see it. And then she said he couldn't see her eyes. Remember?"

"Yeah," Cleft said, the wheels of interpretation beginning to turn inside.

"It's like he's seeing *less*—of the good things around him. Like he's slowly going blind, one object at a time." Jesse shuddered at the possibility.

"I hadn't thought of it that way," Cleft said.

"You just made me think of it because you said people who go through the white door see *more* of what's around them. Maybe people who go through the black door start seeing *less*."

"There's a black door?!" Cleft had forgotten the three words Cain spoke before he went crazy and chased them with a baseball bat.

"Oh, yeah. I thought you knew. I've never seen it or anything. But Cain said he went through it, with Skotos."

Panic fell on Cleft's chest like a sack of bricks. But then he took a deep breath as if making a grand discovery.

"Oh my God. Of course! This makes so much sense now. This . . . " Cleft's head jolted up higher as he spotted the lights on his front lawn. He felt like being impulsive. "I have to take you somewhere. Will you go with me?"

"Umm, is it far?"

"No, no." Cleft said, and then smiled. "But yes."

Jesse didn't know how to respond. Cleft pointed out across his lawn.

"There! You see those pockets of light on the grass?"

"The spots of sunlight?" Jesse said, but then he looked up at the sky. It was overcast. The lights couldn't be from the sun.

"Not sunlight. Follow me and do what I do."

"Ah, okay. This feels weird."

"It's the best kind of weird you can imagine—*more* than you can imagine." Cleft's voice was full of an excitement Jesse rarely saw. It reminded him of his uncle and the way he would rattle off stories about hunting trips—his lasting obsession. Cleft was a child again. "Come on!"

Cleft was jogging towards the lights, still favoring his sore ankle, and Jesse followed, but also felt caught up in a bizarre dream. What was he doing?

"Over here! Now, just bow, touch your head to the light, and trust me." He grinned widely.

Jesse laughed. "What?! This is too weird."

"I told you," Cleft said with a mammoth grin. "Best kind of weird you can't imagine." With that, he bowed, touched his head to the puddle of light, and vanished.

"What the—" Jesse looked around, hoping someone else had seen what he just saw. But they were alone. Aside from the Blue Jay rants and Chickadees, all was quiet. He looked at the lights, trembling inside. Then he knelt down, slowly lowered his head to the ground, and disappeared.

***

Cleft was standing next to him at the top of the hill, in the tall waving grass. It was blindingly bright. Jesse instinctively grabbed Cleft's right hand, a child reaching for fatherly assurance.

"What . . . is this?" Jesse asked. He thought he should feel scared, but he didn't. Something suspended his panic. He was observant, settled, focused on the golden light enveloping him, as he stared ahead at the white stone city in the distance.

"I call it the City of Light," Cleft said.

Jesse had nothing to say yet. He just stared, his eyes darting from place to place, sponging in the atmosphere. He saw giant white shapes drifting overtop of the city and watched them turn and bend with inexpressible grace, like great blankets dancing on the wind currents.

"Birds?" he asked.

"No," Cleft said. "If I had to guess, I'd say they were angels, and far bigger than you think. We're a good mile from the city." Cleft couldn't get the smile off his face.

Jesse did calculations in his head. If the flying creatures were this big from a mile away, they were easily larger than houses.

"This—this is what I wanted to show you," Cleft said, kneeling down. A cinder gray boulder had white letters engraved on it.

One door white. One door black.
One leads onward. One leads back.

"In all my years, I never knew what the black door was about. I've seen this boulder for fifteen years. And then you mentioned it today. It took fifteen years to answer one question."

A silk-soft breeze caressed their skin and hair as they examined the writing on the boulder. The script was so elegant—bold but beautiful.

"Angelic calligraphy," they said in unison. They surprised themselves and started laughing.

"What are the odds?" Cleft said. "What are the odds?"

"I don't know how this helps . . . but can we, like, *stay* here, for as long as we want."

"Would be nice, wouldn't it? Maybe someday. That's my hope. My dream is to walk down that path towards the city, knock on those two great doors, and go inside." Cleft was pointing beyond the blanketed hills and toward the well-trodden path leading up to the city gates.

"You've never been inside? In fifteen years?"

"Nope. Not allowed."

"What do you mean?"

"Well, maybe I'll explain that later. For now, we should get back."

"How? Do we have to bend down and touch the ground with our heads again?"

"No, no. Just close your eyes and focus, really hard, on the place we were before this. Okay?"

"Okay."

The next moment they opened their eyes they were in Cleft's front yard. The sun had broken through the clouds, and two robins were exchanging songs across the canopy of the hemlock trees at the edge of the property.

"Woah. That was . . . something else," said Jesse. "Maybe there's more to the fiction."

"What do you mean?"

"Well, people think fiction is fake, and non-fiction is real. That *this* is the most real you can get," Jesse said as he stomped his foot on the grass. "But, in fiction, what we see comes from what we don't see."

"Yeah? And what did you have in mind?"

"Well, *The Magician's Nephew* and *The Silmarillion* for starters. In both creation accounts, the 'real' world is the product of supernatural speech. And that makes that divine speech more 'real' than what we see around us, right?"

"Ah. I think I see where you're going. I'm sorry for misjudging you, Jesse."

"What do you mean?"

"Well, I never would have thought that you've read all these books. Given the company you keep—Cain and Patrick—I just figured you were into other things."

"Oh, no. Reading is my favorite. I don't talk about it in front of Cain and Patrick, cause they don't like to read that much. Maybe they'd make fun of me, or maybe they'd just feel like outsiders. And no one wants to feel like that."

"True."

"But, anyway, it's okay. I'm as guilty as the next person in judging by appearances. I guess reading so much has just made me more aware of when I do it."

"Well, listen. Since you're a reader, I'll share a little verse we say to each other when we part ways now."

"We?"

"Gazers—people who have been through the white door. It's from Longfellow. Have you read him?"

"A bit." But Jesse was being modest. He joined Cleft in the recitation after he heard the first word.

> Life is real! Life is earnest!
> And the grave is not its goal;
> Dust thou art, to dust returnest,
> Was not spoken of the soul.

"Haha! You're fantastic, Jesse. That's great."

Jesse looked at the ground, embarrassed.

"You think that's true—that the grave is not our goal?"

"I know it is, in the fibers of my being, Jesse. We are made for *more*."

"Alright. Well, I'll keep you posted if I see anything else weird. I'm gonna get back to check on my mom, and then maybe do some reading."

"Oh, yeah? What are you reading now?"

"Steinbeck, *East of Eden*."

"Oh, my. Now *that's* a book!"

"Yeah. Maybe we can talk about it when I'm done."

"I'd like that. See you soon, Jesse. And stay clear of Cain in the meantime."

"Yeah. Okay. See you later."

***

Cleft turned to go back inside as the light began drifting further below the tree line. And then he heard a voice—not Skotos, but the most beautiful voice he'd ever heard on earth. It was Jane, but her tone was different—certain, secure and younger.

"Soon, my love."

Cleft spun and looked around, but rather than waste the moment looking for a source, he replied, "Soon? How long do I have?"

"Soon."

"How long?! How soon?!"

But no answer came. The birdsongs filled the air again, weaving a blanket of normalcy over the landscape. Cleft didn't need to ask about what "soon" was referencing. He could feel it in his bones, thudding in his tired blood. Roland came out the front door and pushed his head under Cleft's hand.

"You hear that?" Roland said.

"Yeah. You too, huh?"

"Mmhmm. I'll be with you."

"I know." Cleft petted his best friend and looked out at the sunset. "I know you will be. I'd try to stay, but I think we both know a bigger adventure is coming for us."

"Yes. Yes it is," said Roland. "But for old times sake, how 'bout you throw me that tennis ball a few times? My legs feel like running."

Cleft chuckled. "You got it." He took the tennis ball from inside the rim of a potted plant on the steps, where he always kept it. Then he drew back his arm as Roland poised himself. He threw it as hard as he could and grinned as Roland chased after it like a feather of gold in the dark green grass. They played for almost an hour—throwing and seeking. A man and his dog. An old Seeker and his happy steward.

31

LIGHT IN THE DARKNESS

S HANNON AND SETH WENT to visit Beth and Dale Harbrook. Beth's cancer had progressed, and her chemo had increased to the strongest dosage yet. She mostly stayed in bed, read a little, and slept while Dale and the kids waited on her. Ryan and Amber, matching ages with Will and Livy, had been told that "Mommy was sick and had to take strong medicine." They were unsettled but mostly ignorant, like rabbits in a great wood who had heard rumors of a roving wolf. The kids played with some Lincoln Logs and Matchbox cars in the playroom while Seth and Shannon sat with Beth and Dale in the living room.

"How are you today?" Shannon asked with hesitation—convinced that every question she could ask would fall like a stone in a deep, dark pond.

"Better now. Rough this morning," Beth said in a whisper.

"Kids are good as ever though," Dale added. Seth noticed that, while nothing had physically changed about Dale, his face carried a mask of weariness he couldn't remove, an exhaustion from plodding through a slough of suffering, one heavy foot at a time.

Seth was trying to think of something encouraging to say. In his head, he heard the icy voice of Skotos:

You have nothing to offer them, little Seth. Shut your mouth and get out.

The words echoed with sharpness like a gunshot cutting through silence. He opened his mouth to speak but closed it again. Cancer had been a giant who always struck him dumb. It took his dear father, then his grandmother not long after. Then his favorite high school teacher. Then a childhood best friend. It had an endless appetite. And now it was threatening to take those closest to Shannon.

Seth's mouth felt pinned closed. Everyone in the room seemed saturated with submission. But a holy hatred stirred in Seth, an ember of resistance. And he could choose now, in this moment, to fan it into a flame or let it dim into dust. And for the first time he could remember, he chose the former.

"Light shines in darkness," he said. The words slipped out before he'd had a moment to think. And as soon as the sounds hit the open air, he realized he had nothing to follow them with. Shannon gave him a look—not to embarrass him but as if to ask, "What are you doing?"

"Sorry," Seth said. "It's just something Shannon and I read with a friend, and now I can't get it out of my head."

"Sounds like a professor problem," Dale said with a smile.

"Maybe it is. It's just—" Seth took a deep breath before the plunge. "You both know I lost my father to cancer, and many relatives."

"Seth, I don't think this is the right time to—" Shannon started, but Seth pushed through the resistance. He had something to say. He didn't know where it was coming from, but the call was clear, like sunlight filling the end of a tunnel. He decided to make a run for the light.

"And I know most people would think it's morbid to talk about that at a time like this. But here's the thing: nobody is gone."

Beth looked confused, and Dale matched her, his thin face peering into Seth's eyes, trying to catch the faint color of hope.

"What do you mean?" Dale asked. Shannon nodded. She had no idea where her husband was going with this and prayed inside that it would bring some comfort to her best friend.

Synapses lit up in Seth's brain. Thoughts linked arms. And the truth dawned inside him and shot rays of light through every inch of his body. He knew *exactly* what to say, and he could hardly get the words out fast enough.

"You know how in John's Gospel it says 'the light shines in the darkness'?"

"Didn't know you were a church type," Beth said. She and Dale were faithful church attendees, but they knew Seth hadn't been to church in a while and rarely talked about anything faith-related. They also hadn't seen Seth in church lately because they were home-bound until Beth could recover from the side effects of increased chemo—the fatigue that battered her limbs like waves against a beaten hull, the bruising and bleeding with every bump or trip or stumble, the nausea that seemed attached to her throat like leaches, the throbbing pain in her tongue and throat with every swallow, the intense mood changes—from gratitude to gaiety to grief, as if her soul were a popsicle stick tossed on great currents beneath her.

"Well, I am. I am. And maybe that darkness is like a disease of doubt. It's all around us. It's inside us. We can't seem to get away from it. Because we're so worried that one day—one day we'll be gone. But then . . ." he paused. Everyone was tuned in to his words now, marching after him as children down a wild path in the woods. "Then God comes to us—a light in our doubt, burning away the black. And he tells us that those who have come before us—they're not *gone*. Not really."

"Because everyone is immortal. C.S. Lewis said that, didn't he," Beth's voice whispered, surprising everyone. She was tracking with Seth, holding on to his coattails and happily refusing to let go. "In 'The Weight of Glory.'"

"Yes! Exactly!" Seth had forgotten about that essay, but it jumped into view now, and it was perfect. "And if we're immortal, then we're not gone after death. We just have to choose the direction: light or darkness."

"But God is Lord of the choosing," Beth said with a smile.

"Spoken like a good Presbyterian," Dale said, grinning at his wife.

"Yes—he's in control of everything," Seth said, with the giddiness of a child who's just discovered colors for the first time, who can hardly take in the things around him because the whole world is swollen with meaning and beauty. His heart was like a peony head warming in the sun after a heavy rain—heavy and heavenly.

"But my point is, if God really does shine in the darkness, if the light is who Jesus Christ is, then we'll never be gone. We'll be *with* him, at least, if we follow. He'll be . . . *inside* us somehow."

"The light shines *in* the darkness," Dale said pensively. "So, darkness is just an arena for the light."

"Yes! And the light is our home," Seth said, almost breathless. He hadn't got out everything he wanted to say, in the way he wanted to say it. But, as a writer, he knew that this was evidence that the message was true. It was uncontainable, as it should be. Truth is a wild thing.

They all turned towards the window in that moment, as they heard an intense chorus of birds—thousands of them. A giant flock of starlings swung down in the trees right in their front yard, just outside the window.

"Honey, look!" Dale said. "Kids, come here and look at this!" The kids ran into the room searching for the excitement. Dale pointed out the window. Then he turned the couch a bit so Beth could see. As if on cue, the massive flock lifted like a cloud, the thudding flutter making its drumming felt even inside the house. The giant, circus-tent-sized flock began waving and twisting right above their house. Bending, breaking, gathering, diving. Everyone stood in the living room mesmerized. So very many, all moving as one. It was a great, harmonious, unyielding flag in the blue sky.

"Nobody is gone," Seth said as they stared. "Nobody is gone."

A tear trickled down Beth's cheek. She grabbed Dale's hand, and then Shannon's. And they all watched, as the wild God of the world waved his bird flag for them.

"Light shines in the darkness," Shannon said, grinning at Seth with tears in her eyes. She had never been so proud of her husband, nor so grateful for hope.

32

THE CHAPEL MEETING

M EANWHILE, WITH BEAUTY AND hope rising in starlings on one side of town, a sickening ugliness was building, board by board, behind Trinity Presbyterian Church. No one would know it was ugly, though. The building was bright, clean, and solid, with cream-colored siding and golden shutters hugging the tall windows. The windows, however, began several feet up the wall, so no one could look inside the building from the outside. Inside it was plain, with pews and a pulpit up front. Everything resembled a church in some way. Where a cross would be, behind the pulpit on the wall, there was a simple black circle.

Skotos had hired a crew to work fast—mostly ruffians who had dropped out of construction jobs for one reason or another. And Martin Shoemaker was leading them. He didn't know who Skotos was, that he had any connection to his own son, or that he was filled with a darkness that would make any man choke. Skotos was simply the only one in Dingmans Ferry who knew Martin was a faithful drunk and hired him anyway. Having a job again gave Martin some hope of recovery. It was a hope he was familiar with over the years—quick to rise and even quicker to fade. So, he didn't put much weight in it. But he enjoyed it for the moment. He had a purpose right now, a task that called him up and let him forget for a few hours each day that he was locked inside his own tiny life by bottles and cans.

And in a wheelchair, with a bandage wrapped around her head, sat Tabitha Shoemaker. Skotos's hand was on her shoulder, and he was speaking softly to her.

***

Patrick, despite witnessing what had happened to Cain, was still there, now serving as a foreman directly beneath Martin. He was compliant, amenable, and mostly silent. Patrick had always been the quiet one in the group. Cain was more vocal. Jesse was quiet but interactive and happy to follow along if the idea or joke was amusing enough. Jesse also, as Cleft now knew, had a whole world going on inside his head, molded and marked by literature. But Patrick? He followed Cain and Jesse around not for their company or for their agenda. He didn't think much of either of them. But he also didn't think much of anyone. People were like shells to him. Each had a shape, with contours and colors, visible in the sun. But they were all fragile—weathered into weakness by . . . something. He was never quite sure what. But the words "good," "right," and "love" always hit his ears like wandering house flies. He wanted to swat them out of every conversation. They buzzed meaningless.

Patrick wanted only what touched his skin, or struck his tastebuds, or stimulated his eyes. He knew not to concern himself with anything more than that, because anything more was a fantasy. He went to church with Cain and Jesse just for an activity. But he struggled to stay to the end of each service. And

Cain only went because he had once promised his grandmother, Gladice, that he would go until he was twenty-one. In return, she promised him twenty dollars a service. He didn't really need the money, but it was easy, and he made a point of making fun of the other congregants who sat in front of them. Patrick knew where Cain put the money each Sunday, and he planned on stealing it when Cain had amassed enough. He just needed to develop a plan.

But then Skotos had shown up and offered them a hundred dollars an hour for work that kept Patrick busy and built up much quicker than twenty bucks every Sunday. In one week, he had made almost four thousand dollars—more money than he'd ever dreamed he could make in that short of a time. And it was *so* simple. Skotos handed him straight cash at the end of each day. He could hold it in his hands, touch it, exactly as he wanted to do with everything else in his life. No mystery. No measuring. No fuss. Just money. It was perfect. And Skotos never asked him questions, which was exactly how he liked things. He wanted to sponge up sweetness around him without being checked on.

Patrick laid a bundle of white siding on the grass and waltzed over to Skotos, who still stood next to Tabitha.

"So, ah, who are we building this place for anyway?"

"No one," Skotos said. "And we're not building a place; we're building a lie." Patrick didn't know how to respond, so he said nothing.

Later that evening, when the building was basically finished, he called all the workers over.

"Listen up. You all did good work, and you can collect your final pay tonight. Then I don't want to see any of you ever again. Got it?" Skotos held a small grin on his lips.

The workers looked at each other with amusement. Who did this guy think he was? Cleveland Metzger, a balding, heavy-gutted man whose face resembled that of a tired pig, stepped forward.

"You sayin' you got no more work? After *this* job?"

"Oh, I have a lot more work. But you're too stupid to do it." Skotos was happy to have the challenge. He flexed his neck as he twisted his head in circles like a crazed raptor ready to pounce on its kill.

"You talk like that 'round here, and you're looking for knuckles in your mouth. Wipe that grin off your face before I smack it off."

Skotos's smile broadened. Patrick was watching his eyes. He noticed that Skotos's pupils grew, as if trying to suck in all the light in front of him. It seemed intentional but nearly effortless.

Cleveland's face turned white. His eyes bulged. He fell to his knees grabbing his throat.

"Hey, Cleveland! Cleveland?! You alright?!" His less confident sidekick, a gangly unshaven man whom they all called Butcher Lee, was grabbing Cleveland's shoulder and shaking him. "Cleveland?! Someone call an ambulance!"

"Why an ambulance," Skotos said softly to himself—but anyone within ten feet could just hear him—"when a grave is so much closer?"

Everyone watched in horror and started yelling as Cleveland's body began sinking into the dirt. Five men rushed to grab his arms and pull him up. But it did nothing. Cleveland might as well have been holding the anchor to the Titanic. He couldn't speak, but his eyes—they were burning into everyone's memory. Almost lidless, frantically searching for anything that might help. But he was caught, somewhere in the blackness of Skotos's eyes. His quick tongue had brought him down to the dirt. The mud closed up over his face as the men continued yelling and struggled to pull at Cleveland's hands. When it was hopeless and Cleveland's chin fell beneath the dirt, they staggered back and looked with terror at Skotos, who still wore the same subtle grin. The earth closed up over Cleveland Metzger's fingertips, sealing him in the soil.

The yelling ceased, leaving only the huff and heavy breathing of the other men, who then bolted towards their cars. All of them, that is, except Patrick. He had watched. He had watched the whole time. He felt no terror, no remorse, no sympathy. It was as if he'd just stared at a snake swallowing a field mouse in slow motion. It held his attention. He turned to look at Skotos, who looked back at him and nodded.

Tabitha was still in her wheelchair. Martin had fled without even thinking about her. Her eyes were wide open, and her cheeks reflected tiny streams of tears under the new streetlight Skotos had put outside the building. Skotos left her there and looked at Patrick. "Let's go. Cain will be waiting."

At the mention of her son's name, Tabitha's head tilted up. She tried to mouth words but barely any sound came out.

"Www . . . waid . . . wait." Skotos ignored her and kept walking. Patrick followed his lead.

"Where . . . mma . . . son?" Her voice was fluctuating and broken, cutting in and out like static. "Where's my son?" she said louder. But her audience was the chilling night now. Darkness wrapped her, and she closed her eyes. Her head was starting to pound, as if a dull railroad tie were knocking into her skull. And then she nodded off. She was left there shivering until Martin came back for her at dawn—full of compassion, and full of alcohol.

***

Skotos and Patrick startled Cain as they stomped through the black woods into the campsite by Rebel's Rock. Cain had started a fire, eaten some canned provisions Skotos had apparently brought there himself, and then fell asleep with his back against a tree.

"Patrick?"

"Yeah." That was all Patrick said, content to acknowledge the fact of his presence.

"Patrick is going to be my Aaron," Skotos said.

"What do you mean?"

"Come on, Cain. You know your Bible."

"Not really."

"Moses was an Old Testament prophet who set the people of Israel free from bondage in Egypt. Remember Pharaoh and the plagues?"

"Oh, yeah. So, Aaron?"

"Well, Moses was afraid to lead the people, so God let Aaron be his speaker, his mouthpiece. Aaron was the voice of God through the voice of Moses."

"So, Patrick is going to be your Aaron?"

"Yes. But with me, fear has nothing to do with it. Patrick can do what I tell him while I work on what I really came here to do."

"Which is?"

"Well, you haven't shown yourself trustworthy enough to be let into the inner circle. The disease was supposed to spread in you, but it hasn't yet. Patrick will be better suited." Skotos paused. "And handsomely paid, of course."

Cain decided to hold off on pushing Skotos to reveal his deeper intentions for Dingmans Ferry. He decided to push smaller issues instead. He shuddered to even think about what "disease" Skotos was talking about.

"Where do you get all this money, anyway? It's, like, tens of thousands of dollars."

"No—hundreds of thousands," Skotos said, matter-of-factly. "And I got it from a friend . . . Well, that's not true. I got it from an enemy that I squashed into a friend. And he was happy to give it, once I borrowed some of his oxygen."

"Do I know him?"

"What is this to you, Cain? Are you his keeper? Or is this some sort of mystery game?"

"No, I just want to know who's on our side."

"Fine, then. It's that floppy-haired moron, Robert Gurssel. He's got so much money and so little courage." Skotos was starting to laugh to himself. "His face—when I asked him for the money—it was priceless. Fear and ignorance and incredulity running like oil into the ravines of his . . . fat forehead wrinkles." Skotos lost it and started dry-heaving his laughter. Patrick joined him.

Cain didn't know what to say. He faked a smile and tried to avoid eye contact. He was starting to see the sadism. Why had he not seen it before? Not in Skotos but in *Patrick*? Skotos, he knew, was something different. And he didn't dare ask what. But Patrick had been around him for over a decade. And he hadn't seen it. This quiet follower, tracking him and Jesse like a silent snake. He was always there, licking the conversations with his forked tongue to see if they were worth contributing to. But they never were. Not to Patrick. He only stayed around them long enough to shed his skin, rubbing his life against the rocks of his alleged "friends" whenever he had the itch. In truth, he cared nothing for them because he cared nothing about anything. Or if he did care about something, he had no way of expressing it on the outside. It occurred to Cain then that he didn't even know Patrick's last name. He'd never asked. Now seemed as good a time as any, out in the quiet woods.

"Hey, Patrick?"

"Yeah."

"What's your last name? I never asked you."

Patrick's throat constricted. Cain had unknowingly stepped on a nerve. Patrick was speechless for a few seconds as he stared at Cain. And then his face hardened.

"Doesn't matter."

"Umm. Okay? It's not a big deal."

"No," Patrick said as he walked away. "No. It's not."

That was the closest Patrick had ever come to letting his secret slip. If anyone ever found out what he'd done . . . well, they wouldn't. He had made sure of that. But he still had to be careful. If anyone could trace him back to the Davidsons' farm, he'd be finished. He took a deep breath in as he stared up through the trees, the same canopy under which he had buried them: his father, mother, and younger brother.

"You could have waited and then used the tunnels," Skotos said from just behind Patrick.

"What?"

"I've only just started building a new tunnel, but you could have put the bodies there. Plenty of room, for the ones who don't understand you."

Skotos *knew*.

"I don't know what you're—"

"Oh, let's not do the games, you and me. We see the world as it is. It was your mother and father and brother who didn't. They were blind. And the blind can only be of so much use. There's nothing wrong with what you did. And your secret is safe with me."

Patrick was dumbfounded and relieved and paranoid at the same time. "But how did you—"

"Don't ask that," Skotos said coldly. "Don't ask that." He shook his head slowly at Patrick, who nodded. The snakes understood each other. The dark knew the dark. Patrick smiled deeply for the first time in a long, long while. And so did Skotos.

"But what are these tunnels?"

"Hmm," Skotos said with sincerity. "They are why I am here. I will tell you more soon."

***

The following morning, all the residents in Dingmans Ferry had a letter waiting for them in their mailbox. It was a vanilla envelope with a plain circle on the front. Inside was a card. In an elegant script were the following words.

> If you want something real, something you can feel, come to the white chapel on Sunday at 8:00am.

There was no signature. No return address on the envelope. Everyone knew where the white chapel was because everyone in a town this small knows when a new building is going up. They had watched with pained curiosity as another "church" was being built behind Trinity Presbyterian. What denomination was it? Who was the pastor? Who was leading the project? There were no answers, which meant there was plenty of speculation. People are happy to create false explanations. It offers the illusion of control.

The timing for the meeting was intentionally one hour before services for Trinity Presbyterian. Skotos wanted Cleft's attendees to see them exiting the building, not entering. He wanted questions to swarm like bees around a rotting apple. And he knew they would.

When 8:00 am on Sunday arrived, only a dozen or so showed up. Most people who had any interest were content to watch. They wanted to see others have a taste of the oddity before they sampled it themselves. Among the first were Cain, Patrick, Martin, and Tabitha. Tabitha looked as frail as a dandelion puff. Martin pushed her wheelchair without looking down at her. The handles gave him something to steady his body on, and he needed that after downing a bottle of Jim Bean. He was especially nervous this morning. A fear had been growing inside him—a larva that had eaten enough of his thoughts to turn into a worm, which now wove its way down into his stomach. The alcohol numbed the discomfort in his gut.

The "message" Skotos delivered to them that morning was as cryptic and brief as might be expected by those who knew him. Patrick appreciated it most. It wasted no one's time. Tabitha couldn't bear to look at Skotos's face. He haunted her. She looked away from him whenever she could. And her eyes were drawn to a door on the side of the main room. It was the basement door. She would not take her eyes off it. They burned holes in it while Skotos spoke.

"I won't thank you all for coming, because I honestly don't care that you're here. I will always be candid with you. What you get here will simply be . . . whatever you truly want." People began exchanging puzzled glances with each other. They assumed this was a build-up to some sort of sell.

"Look at this circle," he continued, pointing to the one on the wall behind him. "Do you know what's in here?" He paused until enough heads had shaken. "Everything. Everything you want is right here—in this town, in your home, on the streets. It's all here. I have come to help you get it." There were murmurings, but Skotos went on.

"All you need to do is talk to me. And, in time, you may talk to Patrick as well. He's in training." Patrick smiled with something that resembled pride, but in truth it was more coy sadism. Cain shivered when he saw the look on Patrick's face.

"For the rest of the time we have this morning, I want you to think and talk. Think about what you want, why you're here. And talk to each other about it. I'll come around as you talk. Okay?"

With that, Skotos left the pulpit, but then went back up as if he'd forgotten something. "And one more thing: if you'd like to be a part of this, you'll need the symbol imprinted on your hand before you leave—this circle. It doesn't hurt at all. It's just a mark of your commitment."

"Commitment to what?" said a woman in the back. "What is this?"

Skotos locked eyes with her. "My daughter, why give a name to a thing when names don't matter? What matters is the thing itself."

"But what is the thing?" she asked.

He replied after an intentional pause so that everyone in the room could hear his answer. "Whatever you want it to be—health, money, love, success. Whatever you want it to be. Just be here next Sunday morning to get it. Same time."

That's when the murmuring picked up and rose into open-air conversations. Skotos and Patrick stepped to the side while people began talking. Tabitha worked up the courage to take Skotos's hand. He turned and looked at her as if she were a dog begging for scraps.

"What is it?" he said.

"What's down there?" She pointed to the door leading to the basement. Skotos leaned in so that his lips were almost touching her ears. She was too terrified to move. She waited like a statue for him to speak. And he reveled in the moment.

"Death . . . Now, Miss Tabitha, don't you *ever* ask me that question again." Skotos pulled his head up and wore a smile for anyone who might be watching. And Martin Shoemaker was. He could see from the paleness of his wife's face that something was wrong. But he dare not ask her. Not here. Not when there was any chance of crossing Skotos.

Skotos—who had possessed his family and nearly killed his wife. Skotos—who buried men alive with his eyes. He must be walked around like a landmine, spoken to as a god, and obeyed like the devil. He had made it crystal clear what would happen otherwise. And Martin Shoemaker was in no mental place to question him.

33

WHAT HAPPENED TO TRAVIS

T RAVIS WOKE UP IN Bill's place on what he thought would be a regular Saturday. Bill had left to open up the pet store. The house was quiet. A mourning dove and meadowlark sang outside, their songs drifting in through the open windows like smoke.

He made himself some coffee, pulled on his sweatshirt, slipped his feet into his sneakers, and went out to the back porch. He sat in a cast-iron deck chair, with two faded floral pillows, resting in the sun. He felt his body coming into awareness of itself as the orange-gold light glazed his face and hands. He moved the fingers of his right hand, watching the knuckles bend and the skin draw tightly over the bone. He made a fist. Then he flattened out his hand. Then he spread his fingers out again and waved them in the light. He'd never noticed his hands this way before.

He bunched his fingers into a three-quarter fist so that he could make a cave entrance with his pointer finger and thumb. The little dark door of his pointer finger led the way to the shadow inside. But then he held up his hand to the sun and opened his pinky finger, letting light in the backside of his tiny cave. "Light shines in darkness," he said in a whisper.

At that moment, he noticed the light was being blocked out. He picked his head up to see what cloud had come in the way, but the clouds were all above him, far from the rising sun. He looked through the tree line at the horizon and saw what he thought was the line of mountains in the distance. But it wasn't a mountain. And it was moving.

He stood up and squinted. "What the . . ." He walked to the edge of the porch and squinted harder. The dark shadow was growing taller, definitely moving. And it was coming up around the periphery of Travis's sight. His stomach dropped as he tried to figure out what was happening—trying to make sense of a mountainous shadow rising up into the sky around the whole valley. He turned to run to the back door—the phone was just inside on the wall. But he sloshed his coffee all over his arm. In his panic, he almost ignored the searing burn. He put his coffee mug down on the glass-top table and picked his head up to check the horizon again. The shadow had stopped moving.

He stared to verify. Then ran inside and picked up the corded phone to dial the number to Bill's pet shop. Bill answered in his nonchalant, breezy manner.

"Pets' Place. This is Bill. What can I do for ya?"

"Uncle Bill, it's Travis! Something's wrong, *really* wrong. Look out the window at the horizon."

"Okay. Settle down, now. Gimme a second to get to the front of the store where I can see." Travis heard his feet shuffling and some parakeets in the background.

"Hurry up! Something is off!"

"Okay. Settle down now, Travis. I'm lookin'. What am I lookin' for?"

"See that giant, mountain shadow that's all around the valley?"

Bill was silent for a moment. "I . . . uh, I don't—"

"It's like a massive dark wall, above the mountain ridges. Blocking out the sun."

"Sun is shining fine here. Got that nice white-gold color after it's shaken off the orange of sleep. Beautiful."

"What? Are you saying you don't see it? It's a huge wall—taller than skyscrapers. This is so f—"

"No need to drop the F-word, kiddo. You're still seein' it?"

"Yes!"

"Okay. Well, if you're seein' it but I'm not, then you might be havin' a vision."

"A vision?"

"Remember what Pastor Cleft said about gazers? After you go through the white door, you start seein' things other people won't see. So, just take a deep breath and tell me more about what you're seein'."

Travis went to take a deep breath, but it was broken in half by a boom so thunderous that it shook the phone out of his hand. He saw smoke rising deep in the woods, beyond Adams Creek. He grabbed at the phone with shaking hands, picked it up, dropped it on the wood deck, and then picked it up again. It was like a bar of soap in his hands.

"Travis? Travis? You still there?"

"Did you hear that? The explosion? Do you see anything? It was coming from the other side of town."

"Now, Travis. I'm in the middle of town right now. I didn't hear anything, and I don't see any smoke. Let's try this again. Take a deep breath."

"I tried that already! It's not working!"

"Travis, just—"

"No! I'm not gonna calm down! Something's wrong! I gotta get outta here!" He turned to run back inside and dropped the phone. He stepped on his untied shoelaces and fell forward with all his weight, crashing through the screen door and landing on the hardwood floor inside next to the table. He'd shattered his coffee mug. As the shards of ceramic drifted to a halt on the smooth wood floor, he rolled over and looked up, as if a bear were about to pounce on him. He squinted, then pushed himself off the floor.

"Dah!" A shard of the mug was now wedged into the bottom of his palm. He pulled the bloody piece of ivory clay out of his hand and held his thumb on the cut to stop the bleeding. This distracted him only for a moment, but when he picked up his head to check the horizon again, there was nothing. The sun was shining in the white-gold color Bill had spoken of. There was no wall, only the mountain range hugging the town in a fatherly embrace. The meadowlark and mourning dove were still singing. Travis was dazed and confused. He walked slowly back to the cast-iron chair on the porch outside, resting his body on the structure. He felt as if he'd just run ten miles. Everything was calm and quiet, as it should be. Everything in the outside world was at rest. All of the unrest was inside him.

34

THE BOOK OF CLEFT

J ESSE AND ETHAN RODE their bikes over to Cleft's house. They had each seen something and wanted to discuss it with him. They called for him from the porch, but there was no answer. Ethan rapped on the wood frame of the screen door.

"In here," came Cleft's voice, sounding as if his chest had been rolled over by a train.

"Pastor Cleft?" Jesse said.

The boys nearly lost their breath when they saw him. His hair was almost completely gray. It had been dark brown just a few days ago when they saw him last. Roland was at his feet, with a white face resting in angelic sleep. He didn't even pick his head up when the company came in. Cleft raised his hands as if to assure the boys that he was fine. But it was pointless.

His skin was wrinkled, and the rivers of his veins were lying just below the pale fields of flesh. His eyes were swollen. It seemed thirty years had passed in a matter of days.

"What . . . what happened?" Ethan went to his side and kneeled like a child. "What happened to you? Is this from the door?"

Cleft gave a tired smile. Jesse sat next to Ethan on the carpet.

"I think my number has been called, boys." He needed to explain no more. The boys were speechless. "Sooner or later, we all get our number called. I just hope you boys know what yours is before it comes up."

"Should we call someone?" Jesse asked. "The hospital, or—"

"Oh, no. Hospital wouldn't do much for this. But you can bring me the phone from the end table over there. The cord should stretch. I'll call the others and see if they can come."

One by one, Cleft used what was left of his tired voice to ask his friends to come as soon as they could. Seth and Shannon. Lem. Bill and Travis. Gladice. He ended each conversation with a simple sentence. "It's time for me to leave." That was all.

Within the hour, they were all there, gathered in the living room around Cleft, who sat in a navy blue recliner with blankets draped over his legs and torso. Each blanket was decorated in primitive Native American symbols. Jane had bought them nearly twenty years ago from a vendor at an outdoor market. Ten dollars a piece wasn't bad back then, for a hand-woven blanket. Everyone was in awe of how Cleft looked: transformed somehow, as if the aged body he was given came with the experience behind the wrinkles and ravines curving down from the edges of his nostrils and his straight, bird-like nose. His glasses rested on his face

"There's something you need to see. Seth, I think you should be its keeper for now."

"What is it?" Seth's voice was weak and worn. He couldn't tear himself away from the memory of his own father, lying just like this—quiet, brittle, and frail.

"It's . . . a book."

"Where is it?"

"In my nightstand, upstairs. Top drawer. Bring it down here."

Seth went upstairs in the hallowed dark. The afternoon sun was behind the clouds, and the night was drawing in. He entered Cleft's bedroom and surveyed it closely. Then he went to the nightstand and opened the drawer. A thick, leather-bound journal was wrapped tightly with a leather cord. It must have been over 500 pages. Seth felt the soft leather in both hands, then turned it over. On the back were stamped initials: YCGB.

"What *is* that?" Seth said out loud. The same letters he'd seen on the back of the Davidsons' old barn were here, on Cleft's journal. He walked down the stairs with the journal in hand. Cleft turned his tired face toward Seth and held out his hand to receive it.

"What's YCGB?"

"Hmm?"

"The initials, on the back."

"Oh, that's something of a mantra for Lem and me. It's not initials. It's an acronym: You Cannot Go Back."

"What does it mean?"

"It means, for you, that you're going to have to choose one of those marbles in your pocket (we both know which one). And once you do, you keep moving forward. You keep seeking."

Seth put his right hand into his pocket to jostle the marbles around and pulled them out. Shannon was watching him.

"It's wonderful when life's that spot of rain, isn't it?" Cleft said. "When everything is clear, even though it's upside down. But you know better, Seth. You know what our world is now. We are the fire in the teardrop, the war cupped by the transparent hands of God."

Seth stared at the marbles, and then back at Cleft.

"What's happening to you?"

"The same thing that happens to everyone; it's just happening faster."

Cleft held up the book and everyone went silent, waiting for some new revelation from their leader.

"Everything we know is in here. Everything. Lem wrote a number of the entries. Then I've added my own. But there's plenty of space left."

"The Book of Cleft," Travis said, trying to lighten the mood. It didn't work. Everyone was somber. Cleft ignored the comment.

"You're a writer, Seth. You have to write what you see, what you notice, what you hear. You can read what's in here, but you have to write. You have to write so that you can be written."

Seth wanted to ask what Cleft meant by the last line, but not in front of everyone else. Gladice was starting to cry but tried to disguise her tears as she played with Will and Livy on the floor.

"Okay." That was all Seth could think to say.

"Okay," Cleft said. "Shannon, you think I could borrow your husband for the night? I don't feel all that well, and it would give me peace of mind to know someone else was here with me."

"Of course," Shannon said. "You sure you don't want me to call the hospital?"

"No, no. I'm fine. Fine as a dandelion in May." Cleft smiled at his own words, and his eyes began to close in sleep.

"I guess we should let him rest," Seth said. "I'll stay here with him and keep you all posted if anything changes. It's fine. I'm sure he just needs some sleep."

Everyone agreed and gathered towards the door.

"Daddy?" Will said.

"Yeah, bud?"

"Can I have that marble, the clear one?"

Seth dropped the fire in a teardrop into his pocket and held out the clear marble to Will.

"Sure. You take good care of it, okay?"

"I will."

Shannon kissed Seth good night. "Promise you'll call if you need anything?"

"I promise. We're close. Just a few miles away."

"Okay. Thanks for staying with him."

"Sure thing. I used to do this with my dad when he was sick."

"I know." Shannon offered a sympathetic smile, knowing the depth of that statement, the pain and sickening loss buried beneath the words.

The door closed behind Travis, who was the last one out.

"They're gone now?" Cleft said.

"I thought you were asleep."

"It was the only way to get them to leave. We need to talk."

***

"I don't have much time, Seth."

"Time before what?"

"Before I go and don't come back. Just listen."

"Are you talking about dying? Is that what's happening with your hair and your face? It's like you've aged thirty years in a few days."

"Yes. Roland and I are making our exit soon." Roland walked in from the kitchen and sat next to the recliner where Cleft was. It took Seth a second to realize that Narnia was still there.

"You and Roland?"

"Yes. He's my steward, remember, just as Narnia is yours. We come and go together."

Seth looked down at Narnia and Roland. They looked so noble in that moment, like faithful servants who had committed themselves to another.

"And one day I'm going to die with Narnia?"

"Yes." Cleft let the word settle on Seth. He watched for anxiety to rise. But it didn't. Seth just nodded. Then he took the marble out of his pocket and turned it around in front of the gold light from the lamp sitting next to Cleft's recliner. The red, orange, and white swirls inside the clear glass seemed to spin.

"Seth, this book is important," he said as he held it out to Seth. "But it's not what you need to focus on right now."

"No? What am I supposed to focus on? Putting my affairs in order?"

"No, Seth. You have *much* to do before you go anywhere. *Much.* This book will give you a path to follow, but the path is still unmarked ahead of you, ahead of us."

"What are you talking about? I thought I was just observing and writing down what I see."

"But I haven't told you why. It's become clearer to me that Skotos is the one behind something much darker and deeper than I understood. He's *taking* people."

"Taking people? Taking them where?"

"I don't know. The latest is a man named Cleveland Metzger. He was a construction worker who lived in an apartment on Silver Lake. I didn't know much about him. He never came to church. But I can't find him now."

"So, he's missing? And you think Skotos has something to do with it?"

"It's not just him. There's a list . . . in here," Cleft said, pointing to the leather journal.

"How long of a list?"

"Long. But that isn't the part that creates the most trouble."

"No? What's more troubling than people going missing?"

"The memory of those left behind. See, after someone goes missing, the people who knew them, who loved them, start to forget them—bit by bit. I first noticed it about fifteen years ago with a boy named William. He was a rough kid (fourteen years old at the time), bent on bullying anyone else who came near him. He always wore this red trucker's hat—beat up and dirty. He disappeared one day, and I went to his mother to offer some pastoral consoling. And in parts of the conversation, she seemed to lack memory about basic things she should have known about her son: the color of his eyes, his favorite things to do."

"She didn't just have a memory problem?"

"That was my first thought. But it happened again a few months later to a man named Liam. His wife, Tara, couldn't remember what he did for work or where he was born. She tried in the moment, but it was like she was searching for clothes in an empty closet. There was nothing for her to grasp."

Seth thought for a moment, processing the strangeness. "But what makes you so sure Skotos has any connection? What makes you think these people didn't just run off, or die? The memory thing is weird, but I still don't see the connection to Skotos."

"Yes, well. Like you, my assumption is that the people simply skipped town, or worse. But the memory loss was too odd to ignore. One day, I was at Childs Park for a while and then decided to take the long walk back home. I had more energy back then," Cleft said with a smile.

"You walked all the way there? That's gotta be four miles from here."

"Yes, just about. Like I said, I had more energy back then. In fact, I had so much that I went all the way down Silver Lake to 739. A friend had told me that Adams Creek was a good spot for fishing, and I was curious. So I headed that way. But before I got into the woods between 739 and 209, there was this red trucker's hat on the side of the road. William's hat."

"Probably lots of red trucker's hats out there, Cleft."

"No—this was his. It had a streak of white paint on the left side of the brim. I remember. And that's when I felt sick to my stomach, like I'd just stumbled into a dark secret. I didn't know what it was: murder, suicide—"

"Or just a boy who dropped his hat," Seth said. Cleft glared at him. "What? I'm just saying it's very possible unless there's more to the story. . . . Is there?"

"In one sense, no. But consider what I was up against. The people who knew this kid started to forget who he was. Even the police who had reported him missing. It was like . . . I don't know, like everyone's memory was made of tissues and water was being poured on them. The memories faded and then disintegrated. But not for me. I kept it in the book. William is just one case. There are *dozens* in there."

Seth swallowed and held out his hand to take the journal from Cleft.

"So, what? I'm supposed to find all these people now?"

"You're supposed to search; you're the seeker, just as I was for the last fifteen years. That's when the book came to me, from Lem."

"But if Skotos is involved, then why haven't you seen him until recently?"

"That's the oddest part, Seth. When I first saw him and heard his voice, it was like he wasn't a complete stranger, like I'd *felt* him before—that icy chill we all get whenever we mention his name."

Seth knew the feeling. He rubbed his arms. Cleft mirrored him, and then they both looked at each other, noticing what they were doing.

"See! It's that coldness. That's been around ever since I got this book."

"Look, I get it. I do. But it's tough to make a whole theory based on a feeling."

"People have done far more with far less."

"Maybe. But—"

"Something is in those woods, Seth. I think that's where Skotos took Cain Shoemaker. And Jesse told me the other day what I think it is."

"What's that?"

"There's a black door, and apparently Cain went through it."

"A black door, like . . . the opposite of the white door we've gone through?"

"I don't know what it does. I've never seen it. But that's the puzzle piece I've been looking for. You know what the white door has done to us. What do you think the black door could do to people?"

"I don't know. But it still doesn't make sense."

"What doesn't?"

"Well, you said people keep disappearing, as if Skotos was taking them somewhere, maybe through this door. But if that's the case, then why is Cain back here? Why didn't he disappear like the others?"

"I think Skotos is doing something strange with him, training him maybe."

"Training him? For what?"

"I don't know exactly, but he attacked me and Jesse the other day."

"Attacked?"

"Yeah. We went to talk to him about where he'd been with Skotos. And then this voice spoke to him."

"Voice? You heard it?"

"I didn't have to. I've heard the same voice in my own head. I knew in that moment that Skotos was talking to him, and when I put my finger on it, something changed in Cain—some devilish blackness took over his pupils. He grabbed a baseball bat and tried to get me and Jesse, but we ran out of the trailer, and he didn't follow. It was the closest thing to possession I've ever seen.

"Possession—as in *demon* possession?"

"That's what I'm calling it for now. But something was *inside* him, something dark. Maybe even *someone* dark. And now he's gone AWOL. No one's seen him, including his poor mother, Tabitha, who looks like she's been beaten, probably by that drunk of a husband."

"Cleft . . . I'm . . . I'm at a loss here. Even if all that you're saying is true, I don't know what I'm supposed to do. You still haven't told me anything that suggests these people who have gone missing are still out there, still alive."

"I know. That's more of a gut feeling than anything else. But this new chapel Skotos put up behind Trinity—I'm worried he's trying to gather more people there so he can get them out. So he can take them wherever he's taken the others."

"Have you talked to anyone who's been in that chapel?"

"No, not yet. That will be your first job."

"My first job?"

"Yes. I'm fading, Seth. Fast. In fact, I need to shut my eyes for a bit. I'm so tired."

"Okay. I have more questions, but we can talk tomorrow."

"Tomorrow," Cleft nodded. His eyes closed and he began to snore lightly. Seth found a pillow and some blankets in a linen closet and made himself a bed on the couch. He felt as exhausted as Cleft looked and had so many questions swirling inside him that he figured the best he could do was let them sit overnight. He drifted off to sleep in a matter of seconds.

***

Cleft rose with the robins. It was hard for him to get out of the recliner. His limbs felt like iron. But he managed to walk quietly towards the front door in his slippers, Roland bracing him on the left. He winced at the whining hinges of the front door, but Seth didn't stir. And there on the front lawn, as a holy invitation, a patch of light was waiting for him. He and Roland walked slowly towards it. Tears filled Cleft's eyes as he thought—only for a moment—of all that he was leaving behind: the hallowed hemlocks and little roads of Dingmans Ferry; the people in their weathered skin, each wearing thin with time; the home he and Jane had made together. But with the entrance of that name, Jane, his thoughts shifted.

Jane was ahead of him, not behind. And his steps grew firmer as he realized that all he truly wanted, all he would *ever* want, was in front of him. He reached the patch of sunlight and then turned to smile at Roland, who nuzzled his face.

"Let's go home," Cleft said.

"You don't have to tell me twice," Roland said, bowing his head to the ground. Cleft followed his lead. And they were gone.

Seth woke to look out the front window only just in time to see the two bodies disappear. He threw off his blanket and ran out to the front yard in his socks. The patch of light seemed to wait for him. He bowed and disappeared.

***

When Seth found himself on top of the golden hill in the breeze, he saw Cleft and Roland fifty yards ahead, making their way to the well-trodden dirt road that led to the stone city.

"Wait! Cleft!" Seth called out.

Cleft turned and offered a knowing smile. It reminded Seth so much of his father.

"Read the book!" Cleft shouted back. "And keep seeking! You'll be alright!"

A lump formed in Seth's throat. This farewell was too similar to the one he'd faced at eighteen.

"But what if I have questions?!" Seth shouted back.

"You always will," Cleft replied, laughing to himself. "We always do. Just believe and keep seeking!"

And then Cleft surprised Seth for the last time. He called out to him with the very same words Seth had offered to his dying father.

"I love you, and I'll see you soon!"

Love seemed like such a potent word in the moment, stronger than everything in the world, maybe even the very thing that kept the world on its axis. That's why it had shocked Seth, to hear it so openly from this fatherly friend, whom he'd only really known for a matter of weeks. And yet he *knew*, deep in his bones, that it was the perfect word for the perfect moment—with its mystery, its ancient meaning, its mooring to both the past and the future. Tears ran down Seth's face, and he could only try to smile as he held up his hand. Cleft matched him for a long second and then shouted, "Seek, Seth! Seek, and you will find!" Then he turned to keep walking down the dirt road.

Seth could only stare from a distance. One day—maybe even soon—that would be *his* road. He and Narnia would be walking towards the city of white stone, with glory in their bones. But not yet.

35

ONE GOES ON, ONE CONTINUES

WITH EVERY STEP CLEFT and Roland took toward the city, they felt younger, as if their feet could lift time and weariness from their shoulders, letting it evaporate in the sunlight. Their bones seemed hollow, as if they were getting ready for flight.

One of the house-sized white bird-like creatures flew towards them, but there was no "whoo-poe" this time, no warning of "not yet." There was only the calming thunder of its wings. It landed some feet behind Cleft and Roland, and they tried not to stare. It felt as if they were being tracked by a gargantuan elephant. They could not make out a face, or even feet. The creature was so bright to them that it seemed cloaked in glowing white sheets.

Their pace quickened. With boyish vigor, Cleft and Roland began to run, laughing at themselves. Their muscles tickled as they stamped the ground and launched themselves forward, faster and faster—a boy and his dog. Cleft's hair was turning back to brown. Roland's face was golden, the white fur painted over by rich youth. All the while, the birdhouse floated behind them, silent as a swan.

Within a hundred yards of the city walls, Cleft noticed that the city seemed to be growing, in all directions. The closer he got, the taller its buildings became, the broader its walls, the deeper its depth. And he could now hear rushing water. In the moment, he thought of how *healthy* it sounded—not uncontrolled rapids rushing over rocks, but a warbling gladness, as if the water were speaking in birdsongs, singing a very old melody for anyone who would listen.

Then the solid stone gates, now towering above them, began to crack open. A sliver of silver-white light broke into the open, and at the base of the entryway were two figures. One was so bright that Cleft couldn't make out any of its features. It was like a standing star. But the other, just behind the first, was a girl. And Cleft's jaw dropped as he slowed his sprint. It was his Jane. Her smile was strong and certain, with the power to draw Cleft right out of himself. And yet, her face seemed to push Cleft's eyes toward the first figure. Cleft tried to look, shielding his eyes, but they hurt from trying to discern any features. A spark of hope ignited in his chest as he thought it might be his own father, Moses Warrington, who had passed from a heart attack when Cleft was in his thirties. But the spark faded as quickly as it came. Cleft had some visceral sense that this was not his father. It was someone . . . older, much older.

Sensing his faded spark of hope, Jane spoke. Her voice gently met the air with joyous confidence.

"He's here, too. I'll take you."

"Jane." It was all Cleft could get out before crying, but as he touched his own face to wipe away the first tear, something was different—his skin. It was softer and stronger. He was no longer the weary old pastor. He was a boy. He looked down at his arms and legs. His clothes were swimming on him. Jane laughed when she saw him notice, and the sound was so beautiful, like a sparrow song that dappled the ether with feathered light.

"And we'll get you some new clothes," Jane said, still smiling as she walked towards Cleft. They embraced, for a very long time. Cleft's face fell into her neck. He breathed in her scent of cinnamon and honey—a smell he remembered from their wedding day.

"Jane, my Jane. My Jane."

She cupped his face in her hands. "Not *just* your Jane anymore. Much better." She nodded behind her at the figure Cleft still couldn't see from its brightness. "You'll see him more clearly once you're inside."

And then the figure spoke only one word. It was a sound that penetrated Cleft to his pith, his heartwood, his marrow. It drew him back somehow beyond his childhood, beyond his earliest memories.

"Cleft."

The breath almost left him. He knelt down on one knee to catch himself as his heart raced. No one had *ever* said his name like that, like he knew every curve and contour of his experience, every wandering thought, every stuttered word, every hesitant movement. The tone reflected the love of an artist for his craft, for a masterpiece that had drifted through the halls of every museum on the face of the earth and had finally—with all its bumps and scratches—come back home. Cleft had no words to offer in response. He just stared and smiled.

And Jane laughed again.

"YCGB, my boy," the figure said. And Cleft could see him smiling. "But . . . you'll never want to anyway." Cleft's jaw dropped but nothing came out of his mouth. And then the figure pointed through the doors of the city and spoke in verse as Jane clung to Cleft's arm.

> There are things of light to work and keep,
> And castles where the holy sleep,
> And the river ever running wild,
> Where greatness bows before a child.

***

Back in the other world, Seth climbed the steps to Cleft's house—now emptied of everything but the memory of presence—and sat down on the couch. He was about to call Shannon to tell her what happened, but he noticed the leather journal resting on the arm of Cleft's recliner. A breeze had blown it open to the first few pages. There was a list of names—dozens of them. Could all these people be missing? At the very end of the list, a line divided the previous names from a handful of others. In parentheses, Cleft had written, "From voices or visions." The first name on the list was Marty Soccolowski.

Seth didn't know that Marty had been one of the few who had shown up to the first service at the white chapel. When Skotos had told them to talk with each other about what they wanted, Marty's answer was easy: rest. She had worked double shifts at the hospital in town for over a decade. Her husband had left her, and she needed a way to pay the mortgage on their little ranch house off of Park Road. They had no kids, so work was all she did.

At the chapel service, she talked to others about places she wanted to go—Fiji, Bermuda, St. Thomas, anywhere tropical. But these places were the veneer on top of her deeper longing just to stop, to sit and not have to rise right away, to let her aching joints settle and recover. Her rheumatoid arthritis was getting worse by the week, her knuckles so warm and swollen lately that she had trouble opening her hands. She'd done her best to conceal this at work, but it was getting harder. And her knees felt more and more like someone had slipped tiny shards of burning glass between the femur and tibia. It was a burning, often sharp pain after being on her feet for an hour.

Seth didn't know any of this, of course. But something told him to follow up with this woman first. He remembered Cleft's last words: "Just believe and keep seeking." He pulled the marble from his pocket again and held it up to the light coming through the front bay window.

"2,200 degrees," Seth said to himself. "Once a dripping liquid, now a solid sphere. All because of temperature."

He ruminated on the words, turning the marble in the light to follow the wisps of red, orange, and white. "Heat brings the shape; cold brings the carry." He stuffed the marble back in his pocket, closed the leather journal, and headed for the door.

Narnia followed him like a shadow. Seth looked behind him. "Ready to believe and keep seeking?"

"Don't think we have much of a choice," Narnia said.

"Well, there's always a choice."

"I'd say there's always a *choosing*."

"What's the difference?"

"The difference is who's in control."

Seth thought about the words as he looked for his keys. Then he remembered that Shannon had driven the car back home with Will and Livy. They'd have to come pick him up.

"Like right now," Narnia said. "Shannon's in control of the car. You don't have the choice of driving back home." Seth knew that if the cat had a human face, he'd be grinning.

"Yeah, yeah." Seth headed back inside and picked up the phone to call Shannon.

Narnia stayed on the front porch and looked out at the tree line and the rising sun.

"There's always a choosing."

36

WILL'S SECOND RIDDLE
AND PATRICK'S PAST

S ETH EXPLAINED THINGS TO the others the following day. He called them all over to his house—Lem, Bill, Travis, Gladice, and Jesse. They listened intently to all that Seth said, each of them brimming with questions that Seth seemed to feel even before they asked. Gladice was the first to voice a question, but she already knew the answer, and so did everyone else.

"Maybe he's coming back still. Couldn't he just be visiting that place, that . . . city?"

"The way he spoke to me," Seth said with a sigh of longing, "it was pretty clear that was farewell."

Gladice began to tear up. "Oh," she said softly. She covered her face as sobs shook her body like a brittle birdcage. Shannon went to the couch and put an arm around her. Gladice leaned into Shannon's chest.

"So, he left you that book?" Travis said, looking up at Seth from a recliner.

"Yeah. I guess so."

"Did he say anything else about it? Did you read it?"

"He did." Seth hesitated, trying to figure out how deep he should go. "And I didn't read the whole thing, Travis. It's as thick as *War and Peace*."

"What's *War and Peace*?"

Seth tempered his response. "A very big book."

"But I did read some of it. And I should probably fill everyone in. God knows I don't want to jump into this by myself. I don't know what to make of it, really. And it's downright creepy." He said the last word as he looked at Shannon, knowing how much she hated anything attached to that adjective.

"Maybe not with the kids here?" she said.

"I can play with them," Travis said. "Just fill me in later." Everyone seemed on board with the idea, so Travis bent down to Will and Livy's level. They were rolling marbles on the carpet.

"Hey, do you guys want to play hide and seek? Outside?"

Will needed no prodding. He jumped up and nodded. Livy kept her two fingers in her mouth and rose more hesitantly. Travis sensed her shyness.

"I bet you're a good hider, Livy."

Livy avoided eye contact, but hinted at a smile.

"Livy's really good because she's so small. She can hide *anywhere*," Will chirped.

"Just stay away from poison ivy, or holes in the ground."

"Perhaps I should go with them," Narnia said from beneath the wingback chair. Gladice and Jesse gawked at him, still very much unused to the idea of talking animals.

"Would you?" Shannon asked, as if talking to a friend. "That would be great. Livy tends to wander."

"Don't we all?" Narnia said as he shuffled towards the front door. And he sang quietly to himself.

All that is gold does not glitter
Not all those who wander are lost;
The old that is strong does not wither,
Deep roots are not reached by the frost.

Seth smiled. He had a cat that could quote Tolkien. Travis was counting with his eyes closed for all to hear as Seth told the others about the list of names in the book.

"There are dozens of them," he said. Shannon shuddered.

"So, not only are these people missing, but the memory of them has been wiped away from people who knew them?" Bill asked.

"Apparently," Seth said. "Which would make it pretty hard to find them—*if* we can find them."

"And there's a black door, you said?" Lem was addressing Jesse.

"That's what Cain went through," Jesse said.

"Then he might know somethin' we need to know," Lem said, turning and meandering towards the door.

"Well, Patrick might, too."

"That boy's the spittin' image of that Davidson kid who passed of cancer years back," Lem added.

"Davidson?" Jesse wasn't familiar with the name.

"Yeah. They had a farm off Park Road, for generations. But word was that their son Patrick got Leukemia and passed. And then they sold the farm and left. No one ever seen or heard from any of 'em since."

"Well," Jesse continued, "Patrick has stayed close to Skotos ever since the white chapel went up. I never see him anymore. He used to crash at my apartment all the time because he said his place wasn't much to look at. But . . . I've never seen his place."

"Well, we gotta find 'im," Lem said. He always had a way of flattening situations and pushing for action when people were still in the middle of processing.

"Do you think the people on the list are . . . you know?" Shannon said shyly, looking at Seth. She didn't want to finish the thought.

"I don't know. I certainly hope not, but I don't know what to think."

***

Travis was counting again. "One, two, three—and make sure you go easy on me!"

"We will! Come on, Livy" Will pulled Livy behind the trunk of a white oak tree on the side of the yard. Feeling an ounce of bravery, Livy shuffled over to the red maple tree ten feet away. She looked back to Will for approval, but Will was looking up into the canopy and mumbling."

"Will?" Livy whispered. He didn't respond. Travis was getting closer to the trees and could make out mumbling from behind the oak tree. An acorn fell from the heights and cracked him on the top of his head.

"Ah! Geez!" He rubbed his head and looked around to see if anyone saw. He could make out words coming from Will.

"Will, buddy, you can't talk if you don't want me to find you." He approached the oak tree and came within hearing of the words. His smile faded as he listened.

Threads that are open, where carving is king.
Roads for the blind, where sentences ring.
Sleepers. Sleepers.

"What, bud? What did you say?"

Will snapped his head to the side where a robin's song called him into the present.

"Gotta write it," Will said, running to the house.

"Hold on, little man! Write what? Oh—Livy, *great* hiding spot! I almost didn't see you!"

Livy beamed with a finger-sucking smile. Travis moved closer and held out his arm.

"Let's go inside real quick. You want me to carry you?"

Livy thought for a second, weighing Travis with her trust. Then she nodded and held her arm towards his neck. The sacred fingers could not be disturbed from their home in her mouth. Travis picked her up with one arm and jogged after Will, who was already pulling open the screen door.

"Daddy! Can I tell it . . . can I say it while you write it down? I don't know all the letters for the words."

"Tell me what?"

"The angel message."

"Angel message? Is Livy the angel? Did you guys come up with a new game? You're so creative!"

Will shook off the misplaced compliment. "No! The angel message—like the one before."

"What one before?"

"About the shadows."

The room grew somber like a doused candle.

"I'm getting paper and a crayon," Will said as he ran to the art supply bin in the living room. Seth looked at Shannon. She took a deep breath and shook her head.

"Here!" Will said with his paper. "I'll tell it, and you write it."

"Okay," Seth said, grabbing a book to slip under the paper and wishing for the first time since his exit that Cleft was there. "Go ahead."

Will delivered the riddle with seriousness, as if he were a soldier speaking in duty.

> Threads that are open, where carving is king.
> Roads for the blind, where sentences ring.

Everyone sat still and waited for Seth to respond. He was already running down a trail of thought but pulled himself back when he saw that Will was looking at him and waiting for validation.

"Great job, bud. Thank you for the message."

"It's a iddle."

"A what?"

"A iddle . . . like the first iddle. You told Mommy last time that what I wrote down on the paper was a 'clear iddle.'"

"Oh, oh—sorry. You're right. It is an iddle." Seth smiled and Shannon tried to hold in a laugh. Then Will and Livy ran into the kitchen to get a bowl of pretzels for a snack.

"Why didn't you correct him?" Travis asked with a grin. "Just curious."

"Because all the beauty and joy comes in the process, the story."

"What do you mean?"

"If Will and Livy learned language instantly, if they spoke now like you and I speak as adults, we'd be able to understand them right away. But we wouldn't see any journey, and we wouldn't remember what it was like when *we* tried to piece sentences together from the sounds of grownups. The history and the memory would be lost. And those are the most important things."

Everyone chewed on the words for several moments. Bill offered a contented "Hmm" in agreement.

"But that's not all he said," Travis added.

"What do you mean?"

"He said 'sleepers.'"

"Sleepers?"

"Yeah. Is that part of the riddle? He just said it twice."

"That somehow makes it creepier," Shannon said. "But I don't know the answer to this one like I did for the last one."

"Lemme take a shot, here. Used to be pretty good with riddles," Lem said. He scratched his cheek through his thick white beard.

"'Threads that are open' . . . so, thread is just fabric all the way through. But if it's open, then it's hollow, like a straw. 'Where carving is king.' Carving wood, or rock maybe. Then 'roads for the blind' are places where you walk, but you can't see well. 'Where sentences ring'—Oh! I got it!"

"Me too," Bill said.

"Tunnels," Lem said with pride. "It's tunnels."

"Tunnels," Seth repeated, almost bending the word into a question. "Tunnels and sleepers?"

The room was interrupted by a shaking boom. Will dropped his bowl of pretzels as he ran back in from the kitchen.

He was panicked, and Livy was already crying. The whole town of Dingmans Ferry knew that sound, ever since the bombing at Trinity Presbyterian. Everyone froze and looked at each other as the ringing settled into silence. Each person could taste dread in the air.

***

Patrick and Skotos emerged from behind a line of trees, waving away the smoke and peering into the crater they'd just created.

"Good. This is a fine start for the next one," Skotos said. Patrick nodded in approval. Lately, Patrick had been speaking very little. He acquiesced to every demand, focused on execution. For the first time in his life, he cared more about what he was doing than what he had. There was a darkness inside him that had been waiting for something to feed on, some light to devour. It was there for as long as he could remember. But it broke open and flooded his being the moment he'd decided to rid himself of his family.

His father and mother were, in his eyes, religious fanatics too far gone. They talked constantly of God's plan to heal him from his Leukemia, of God's "goodness" and "grace" and his hope for a "new body." The words sickened him as much as the cancer. They were bitter spices stewing in the atmosphere, plucked from a fantasy he knew was false. But in the last year of their lives, they turned to stranger beliefs—not just in the supernatural but in extra-terrestrials that would come for their salvation and give Patrick a new, incorruptible body. He had heard his father speaking on the phone to his uncle about something called "Heaven's Gate." And as Patrick's anemia grew, he saw there was no stopping his parents. They planned to sell the farm and move in with another family in Colorado, clear across the country. Patrick's brother, Lyle, was younger and too gullible to protest anything. Lyle also followed around his parents like a fly on a horse. He had no friends and a constant draw to his mother that Patrick found not just pitiable, but repulsive. Within a year, Patrick viewed all of them with disgust and foreignness. His heart and head encased themselves in glass, removing any possibility of meaningful interaction. As the moving day to Colorado approached, he had only one thought on his mind: how to rid himself of them.

He only had one idea, and it was a long shot. He asked his parents if they could all go to a lookout in the woods, so he could "see where God lived in the sky." His parents took the wording as a divine revelation that God might be calling their family to receive a special message for Heaven's Gate. His father and mother took turns carrying him through the woods while Lyle walked ahead of them. They were exhausted by the time they got to the lookout, but Patrick was well-rested, and a dark adrenaline surged through his veins like burning tar as he realized what he was about to do. He would have to wait until they were all on the edge, and he was behind them.

Patrick asked his mother, father, and brother to pray for his body as they looked up at the sky. They were so willing, ecstatic with the hope that blinded them to all evil. They held hands and began shouting out prayers. And that was his moment. It took great calculation and the awkward use of his body. He would have to throw himself at the three of them and then turn himself sideways in the air to make contact with all three bodies. But he had practiced in his bedroom and mastered the movement. The bulk of his weight struck the waistlines of his mother and father.

They had no chance. Within a second he heard their screams and saw their horrified faces as they plummeted eighty feet to a rocky bottom.

But his brother clung to a rock on the edge, yelling for help. Patrick crawled over to see him, how precariously he dangled.

"Help! Patrick! Take my hand!"

"No," Patrick said as he swallowed coldly. And that swallow seemed to house a saliva heavy with hubris and determination. *He had done it*, or nearly. The only thing that stood in the way was his annoying brother, the fly that always hung on the horse of his mother.

"But they won't give you your new body unless I pray," Lyle pleaded. Tears were running down his cheeks. Patrick looked at him with disgust.

"I never understood why you actually *believed*?"

Lyle was lost in confused anguish for the moment. What could Patrick mean? They were doing all of this for *him*.

"Go with your mom," Patrick said, as he stood and then ground his heel into Lyle's fingers. Patrick heard the scream, the pathetic yell for "Mommy." He also heard the sound of his brother's body hitting the stones at the bottom. He looked over the edge at the three bodies and felt only relief, not remorse. He would not have to worry anymore. And he'd be dead soon from this rotting Leukemia—gone from a world that seemed to do nothing but sicken him. He'd have to make his way down the precipice and cover the bodies with leaves, rocks, and sticks. But it was finished. Heaven's Gate was closed.

A week later, he went back with kerosene and matches to burn the bodies. What wasn't consumed by the fire was soon carried off by foxes, coyotes, and turkey vultures. The remnants of Patrick's family were now scattered over the landscape of

Dingmans Ferry. The town lived among their pieces without knowing it.

***

The odd miracle was that Patrick's body then began to recover. He'd planned on dying shortly after he carried out the murder of his family. He even sat in his room in the house, waiting, waiting to feel weaker, to fade and ossify like an autumn leaf. But the leukemia cells in his blood and bone marrow began to die out, even as he starved himself. He could feel it. And he eventually regained his appetite. He lived on his own in the house for some weeks before he realized he'd need more food. He had disconnected the phone in their house. But his body was getting strong enough now that he could walk for a few miles. He ended up in town just as he saw another boy and his mother moving into an apartment. He offered to help carry some things in hopes that they'd offer him a meal, which they did. And that began to be his new residence.

"What's your name?" the boy asked as he handed Patrick a small box to bring up the steps.

"Patrick," he said.

"Patrick what?"

"What do you mean?"

"What's your last name?"

Patrick froze as he realized he'd have to lose his last name.

"I can't say it," he admitted with feigned sincerity. "I have a problem saying vowels and my mom said our last name has a lot of them."

"Oh," said the boy. "That's okay. Patrick is fine. My name's Jesse. Hey, you wanna spend the night? My mom rented *Charlotte's Web*, and we got a VCR."

Patrick had never seen a movie. His parents had gotten rid of their television years ago because it was, in their words, "of the devil." He agreed with a sincere nod and saw the opportunity to be in the company of others who knew nothing about him. He could be a ghost here. By the time school rolled around, he was able to register as "Patrick Nunder," with the help of Jesse's mom. But he said and spelled his last name in secret and made sure his teachers only ever called his first name. He spent most nights with Jesse and his mom at their apartment. He told them his parents worked a lot. When suspicions rose, he would go into the woods and sleep there for a few nights before returning with a new set of excuses as to why his family was not around. He never mentioned to anyone that he had a brother.

37

THE TUNNELS

I T'S THE PRESSURE THAT purifies. For the marbles that Seth had carried around in his pocket, it wasn't just the intense heat that melted the quartz and liquified the glass. It was also the furnace pressure. And then, when each slug of melted glass was cut, pressure was applied by the cast-iron grooves to perfect their spherical shape. Marbles are products of pressing.

The same pressure plays its role in the earth's crust. Soil, sediment, and rock compress and push downward toward the earth's core. And it's this pressure that Skotos had been boring into, deep in the woods of Dingmans Ferry. For years, he had been tunneling, forcing engineers and excavators he could find to construct adits—entrances to his underground mines. Then he would use wealthy locals like Robert Gurssel to take equipment and bore spiral declines deeper into the soil and rock. He had found out the hard way that the tunnels would collapse without proper support: steel, concrete, and iron reinforcements. He began planning his tunnels by kidnapping local engineers and forcing them to work for weeks on end. When each tunnel reached a satisfactory depth and height, he'd let them go, swearing to take blood if they ever spoke. They never did. Skotos had the unparalleled ability to channel murder through his eyes. His was a darkness too deep to question.

And Patrick was perfect. He never questioned anything. He was machine-like, cold, and calculating, as Skotos was.

***

The two of them waved the smoke away and peered into the hole they'd created.

"Now *that's* what dynamite can do," Skotos said with a smile. Patrick matched him.

"We won't need this one yet, but I had to start planning it. The other tunnels are getting full."

"Full of what?"

"Bodies."

The word sunk into Patrick's bloodstream. He thought of the bodies of his family, how easily he'd disposed of them. A sickening greed rose inside him to see more, to look upon the ones that Skotos buried. It was something in the eyes of the dead that haunted him: their vacant stare, a final realization of the nothingness that consumed his insides. The faces of the dead seemed to portray what lived inside of them. He wanted to see them.

"You've . . . killed people?" Patrick asked, not in concern or surprise, but in a spirit of searching companionship. He had never had another person who knew what it was like to take life. The darkest part of himself opened its doorways.

"I have . . . but that's not these people."

Patrick was confused. "But, you said 'bodies' . . . so?"

"They're asleep. In a sort of coma. I put them there."

"Why? Why don't you just get rid of them?"

"That's a good question. And I'll answer it for you, because you're really the one I've been looking for."

A seed of pride sprouted shoots inside Patrick's chest and raised his shoulders. He had never known that feeling with his own parents. They had wasted their praise on Lyle and his immediate willingness to take them at their word. Patrick stood taller and focused on Skotos, happy to receive a lesson from the first person who actually seemed to *see* him.

"Killing destroys life, subtracts it, removes it from all *this*," Skotos said, waving his arms up at the canopy and the surrounding landscape. "But that's not the worst, not the darkest."

"It's not?" Patrick was hooked, like a hungry cat staring at cooked meat.

"No. It's not the removal of life that is darkest. It's the *withholding*. It's one thing to take life; it's another to carry it in your hands, to *wield* it, like a precious ore that someone else would give anything to have. I'm only interested in withholding . . . for as long as possible."

"Withholding . . . from other people, like, their family?"

"No, no. I mean, there's some sport in that, of course. But that's not the main end. I'm withholding from God."

Patrick was stunned in silence. Despite his cynicism and rejection of belief in God—a disbelief solidified by his encounter with Heaven's Gate—Patrick had the smallest sliver of space in his heart for the possibility that he was wrong. Skotos's words entered that space. They filled it like icy water.

"You thought God didn't exist?" Skotos said with a smirk. "That he was a fairy tale, a crutch for weak humans?"

"I . . . well I don't—"

"Ah. That thought is my work, too," Skotos said, grinning with pride. "So easy to convince you humans that what you can't see doesn't exist. Too easy." He began laughing to himself. A ball of fear began to grow inside Patrick's chest, but he was too fixated on this to let it overcome him.

"So, God does—"

"Yes, God exists. Deep down, you already knew that. It's not God's *existence* that you questioned or hated in your gullible parents and your puppy-dog brother. It was their *understanding* of him, their assumption of *knowing* him. The truth is, Patrick, God exists no matter what humans think of him. Nietzsche was dead wrong—now he's just dead though. And knows better."

"Nietzsche?"

"Friedrich Nietzsche—one of your philosophers, who could see the dark better than most. He wrote that humans had killed God and had nothing to replace him with."

"How could we kill God?"

"Well, he thought you could burn up *the idea* of God with your little Enlightenment toys, your rationality and discursive reasoning, your empirical wood blocks. You humans are such fools." He began laughing uncontrollably and then began coughing. He threw up black sludge on the dead leaves. Patrick stepped back in disgust.

"Eww! Are you, are you—"

"*Don't* ask me if I'm alright!" Skotos snapped, wiping his lips with his wrist. "The same sludge in me is in you. *No one* is alright." Patrick went silent and waited for Skotos to calm down.

"You can't kill God, precisely because of who God is. He's completely independent. He doesn't rely on your actions or

thoughts. Not mine, not yours, not Nietzsche's. But he does—"
Skotos started but found it almost impossible to articulate the
next sounds. His tongue wagged inside his mouth. His cheeks
felt numb as stone.

"He does . . . loub . . . lude—"

"Love?"

"DON'T SAY THAT WORD!" Skotos yelled so loud that
the trees shook and the earth shifted. "NEVER! NEVER SAY
IT!" Skotos was on his knees, pounding the soil with his fists,
lost in ancient animal rage. Patrick was, for the first time, legitimately terrified. And yet even now the terror allured him.
Here was a power he could, at last, respect. Here was someone
who knew what the world was really like, who felt his own rage
at words that had no meaning—words like "good," "right," and
this . . . "love."

"I won't say it again," Patrick said. Skotos looked up at him.
Blood was running down his cheeks from his eyes. Something
seemed to have exploded inside him.

"I won't say it. But I know what you mean now . . . about
withholding."

***

Cain had been sitting behind a maple tree about twenty feet
away. He had gone there to take a nap, but he awoke when
Patrick came tromping into the camp with Skotos. He had
heard all of their conversation. He looked down at his pants and
realized he had wet himself. When Skotos snapped at Patrick,
Cain lost control of his bladder. He touched his face and realized
he was crying. He might be a criminal on the run, but he was

in much more danger *here* than he would be on his own. He needed to find a way out. But how? Maybe he could go to Adams Creek for water and then sprint somewhere else. But there was nowhere to go except more woods. He couldn't go to the police. They'd just arrest him. He was trapped in the wild, with anywhere to go but nowhere to run.

And then it hit him: there was one place worth trying, a last resort. He had heard rumors of a white door in Childs Park, embedded in a giant boulder. He didn't know much about it. But if going through a black door had brought this much trouble on him, maybe a white door could do something different, something better. It was a long shot, but it was all he had. He could either make for the door, or hang around camp and wait for Skotos or Patrick to turn on him. He made his decision.

***

After Skotos wiped the blood from his cheeks and the black sludge from his lips, he was about to speak, but he and Patrick both snapped their heads toward the woods when they heard footsteps on the leaves. Cain walked over to the campsite and grabbed his water bottle, trying to look nonchalant.

"I'm gonna refill my water at the Creek. You guys need any?"

"Yeah, actually," Patrick said. "Here's mine. You can fill it up."

Skotos just shook his head.

"Alright. Be back in a while."

He walked towards Adams Creek without looking back but felt two sets of eyes burning into his back. When he was out of range of hearing, Skotos turned to Patrick.

"He's going to run."

"What?"

"Cain—he's going to run. And we can't have him speaking to anyone about our work." Skotos pulled up the black jeans by his left ankle and removed an eight-inch knife. "You know what to do."

Patrick looked at the shining metal of the blade. It tickled his nerve endings.

"But I thought you said we should be withholding. You want me to put him to sleep and bring him back here?"

"No. Not this time. Not everyone gets to be a sleeper. His time here is done. End him, and make sure no one sees you."

Patrick tried not to smile too broadly. It some quiet sense, he had itched for this since he had ended his family. He swallowed as dopamine flooded his brain. He took the knife from Skotos.

"This is your greatest test of loyalty and devotion, Patrick. Do this well, and I'll bring you all the way into my operations here. All the way."

Patrick nodded and disappeared into the woods.

***

About seventy-five yards away, on an old path that Skotos had made sure they stayed clear of, Martin Shoemaker was lying in the leaves. He wasn't drunk. And he wasn't sleeping. He had been *listening*. And he had heard everything.

"He's gonna kill my boy . . . my own flesh and blood."

He looked around him at his shoddy campsite, a place he often came to when he needed to sober up in solitude. He was searching for a weapon—anything he might use against a knife-wielding Patrick. He had nothing except his old bottle opener, a six-inch piece of metal with a pointed beak. That would have to do. He waited for a few minutes to make sure there was no more movement in Skotos's camp. Then he quietly stepped down a hillside before turning towards Adams Creek so that he could be parallel with Patrick. No one was going to touch his boy without going through him first.

38

THE UNLIKELIEST SACRIFICE

S ETH HAD BEEN THINKING about the tunnels ever since Will's second riddle came out. Tunnels . . . what in the world could that mean? He had little to go on except for Cleft's parting advice to look at the leather book he passed down, The Book of Cleft. Travis's offhand title seemed appropriate. It was all they had left of Cleft now. And Cleft had told him to read the book. Maybe there was something there.

He began pouring over the notes, sometimes scribbled with such frantic ecstasy that Seth could hardly read them. Beyond the list of names, there were scores of entries about the strangest sights—monstrous black bears with yellow eyes; ghostly horses overrunning school buildings and shops like white water over rocks; giant trees that stretched into the expanse of a black sky toward a pinhole of light. Seth planned to read all of them, word by word. But in the moment, he was searching for anything about tunnels.

A knock came on the door. Shannon and the kids were out running errands, so Seth jumped up from the couch to get the door. He wasn't expecting anyone. It was Jesse. He looked expectant and hopeful, like a stray cat who might wander into a safe haven.

"Jesse! Hey, come on in."

"Hey, Mr. Logan."

"Please, call me Seth. Mr. Logan sounds like an old man."

"Okay," Jesse said, clearly uncomfortable but willing to make the effort. ". . . Seth."

"I know it's awkward, but you'll get it. What's up? Everything okay?"

"Yeah. Yeah. Just . . . umm."

Seth let the silence stay until Jesse was comfortable.

"I guess I just . . . I used to talk with Cleft about the books we had read. And, I don't have anyone to talk to now. He was one of the few who figured out I read a lot. I thought . . . I don't know. I thought maybe we could talk books?"

Seth grinned ear-to-ear. "Are you kidding?! I'd *love* to. Cleft and I were starting to talk about books when he . . . well, when he went home."

"Home. Is that what we're calling it?"

"I don't know. But it seems like the best word. I could see it on his face—in his eyes."

"In that other place?"

"Yeah."

"Did he . . . did he seem, like, happy?"

"No. Much more than that. Much deeper. He wasn't just happy; he was . . ." Seth searched for the words. "Destined."

"Destined?"

"Yeah—like he was about to take a trip he'd been planning his whole life, and he had nothing behind him he could stay for. I don't know what was ahead of him, but he was moving towards it—actually, he was running."

"Running? I don't think I've ever seen him run."

"Oh, it was beautiful, Jesse. It was like every footstep toward the city took a year off his life. He grew younger as he ran. Roland, too. I swear he looked like a little kid before I couldn't see him anymore. And Roland must have been a puppy."

"That's awesome. . . . I miss the guy. Never told him how much his friendship meant to me, even for so short a time."

"Me either."

"But, I guess we'll get there, too."

"Yes. Yes, I believe we will. 'Dust thou art, to dust returnest,'" Seth started. And Jesse finished.

"'Was not spoken of the soul.'"

They both laughed in memory of their fatherly leader. Then their smiles faded.

"So, books," Seth said.

"Yeah—well, you're sure I'm not interrupting anything?"

"Actually, you are, but maybe you can help."

"What is it? Did you find something in 'The Book of Cleft'?"

"Well, yes. But not what I'm looking for, really. I'm trying to get a handle on this tunnel riddle from Will."

"Oh, yeah. I forgot about that."

"Last time he had a riddle, the answer was 'shadow,' which is a rough translation of Skotos's name. So, we had a suspicion that Skotos was about to act, and he did. But this time . . . tunnels?"

"Yeah, that is strange. So, you were looking in the book?"

"Yeah, but I haven't found anything."

"Hmm. Let me sit and think." They both moved to the living room.

"Jesse. Good to see you," Narnia said, from under Jesse's feet as he sat on the wingback chair.

"Oh, dude. Narnia. I'm sorry. Did I, like, sit on you?"

"I think you'd feel it if you did that."

"Right. But I didn't bump you or anything? I can move."

"No, no. Don't be silly. This is my favorite spot. It only makes sense that I share it."

"Okay. Well, maybe you can help us with this, too."

"I'll do all I can. . . . Seth, I'm just curious: What's the last thing Cleft has in the book?"

"It's just a question, after a bunch of thoughts about the people who went missing."

"What's his question?"

"It's just, 'Where are they?'"

"Hmm," Narnia said, but added nothing.

"Do you think that's a location?" Jesse said.

"The tunnels?" Seth said.

"Yeah."

"I guess it could be, but I don't see how that helps all that much. Is he thinking people disappeared into tunnels? And even if they did, where are we supposed to find them? There could be tunnels anywhere. There are *miles* of woods around here."

"Yeah, that's true. And people couldn't survive in tunnels for long anyway. They'd all be dead."

"Well," Narnia cut in. "Not necessarily."

"How do you mean?" said Seth.

"I mean, biblically speaking, there are two depictions of death. One is what we usually think of: the ending of life and the coming of judgment. So, that's death as an *ending*. But the other depicts death as *sleep*. How does that passage go? 'Awake thou that sleepest, and arise from the dead, and Christ shall give thee light.'"

"Ooh, that's Ephesians, right?" Jesse said.

Seth and Narnia were both pleasantly surprised. "You know your Bible, Jesse. Yes, it is. Ephesians 5:14. The idea is that someone can be spiritually sleeping, and that can be a kind of death. Awaking from that takes the power of God."

"Yeah—the power of the word. But that makes *so* much sense, doesn't it?" Jesse started. Seth and Narnia were happy to let him continue. "I mean, you have the word in Genesis 1 speaking life and creation, and then the same word in John 1 speaking new life, like a second creation. So, it makes sense."

"What, specifically, makes sense?" Seth asked, still trying to track. Narnia was obviously following but wanted to give Seth time to catch up.

"That there's just a word that wakes people up from the sleep of death: *awake*."

"Ah. I see what you're getting at. Yeah, that does make sense. How did I not see that before?"

"We see best in community," Narnia quipped.

"Hmph. I guess you're right."

"Still—" Seth said, coming back down from the realization. "Sleep as death, and tunnels? What do we do with that?"

"Hey, what was Will's riddle again?" Jesse asked.

"Let me grab it. I put a copy on an index card at the table." He went to grab it and came back in a moment. "Here it is," he said, beginning to read it out loud.

> Threads that are open, where carving is king.
> Roads for the blind, where sentences ring.
> Sleepers. Sleepers.

"He's putting them together, then!" Jesse said.

"What do you mean?" Seth said.

"The tunnels and the sleepers—the things we just talked about! I think the sleepers are in the tunnels."

"Okay. Okay," Seth started. "But even if that's true—and this is pretty wild, to even think that there could be dozens of people asleep in underground caverns—we don't know where the tunnels are."

A pounding came at the door, and they all jumped. Narnia shot behind the wall next to the front door, as a sentry. The pounding came louder. It was frantic, and they could hear heavy breathing. Seth went to the door with an eye on Jesse and carefully opened it. There, heaving for oxygen and dropping to his knees, was Martin Shoemaker, wielding nothing but an old bottle opener and a beet-red sweaty face. He reeked of cigarettes and alcohol.

"Help! You gotta help me, my boy!" He tried to say more but couldn't breathe. He collapsed on the front porch and passed out.

***

When Martin woke up, he was on Seth's couch. He'd only been out for fifteen minutes. As his eyes opened and he assessed his surroundings, he grabbed Seth's arm.

"Did you find him? Did you help him?"

"Easy, Martin. Tell me what's going on. And take your time."

"Skotos and that Patrick kid—I heard 'em talkin' in the woods. They're gonna kill my boy. I swear it. And you know they would, too. That Skotos, he's got a black heart."

"Yes he does," Seth said.

"Where's Cain? Where's my boy?"

"You haven't seen him?"

"Not since . . . his mother . . . it was an accident. But I think he thought he killed her."

Jesse and Seth looked at each other, confirming that the situation was growing darker by the second. Jesse had been an eyewitness to the demonic darkness that rose up in Cain, but he hadn't had the time to tell Seth yet.

"Killed her? What happened?" Seth said, and Jesse cut in, since Martin seemed to only half remember the whole situation—either because he wasn't there or because when it was reported to him, the alcohol was wiping out more of his brain cells.

"Let me tell you what I saw. Me and Cleft went to see him, after he was in the hospital. His mom was all choked up about how frail he was. She said he was like a little kid, afraid of everything. He wouldn't leave his room. So, we went back to talk to him, and he started to say something about a black door, and then his expression changed, like he'd just heard a voice. Cleft asked him about it, cause I think he knew it was Skotos's voice. And then . . . Cain's pupils—they went wide and black, like something else had just grown inside him and taken the controls of his body. That's when we knew we had to run. Cain grabbed a baseball bat and started chasing us, but he was weak. I think he tripped, but we didn't look back. So, I don't know. I just heard his mom try to block him. Maybe he hit her by accident?"

"That's what the cops thought," Martin said. "Tabitha had a split in her skull from that baseball bat. Had to rush her to the hospital, run all these tests and get her stitched up. There was some brain trauma, but the doctors thought she would be okay. When the cops asked if I wanted squads to go look for Cain, I told 'em no. I said I'd find him. I knew it was an accident. Cain would only run away if he really thought he killed her. So, I was lookin' ever since. That's when I found their campsite—way out in the middle of the woods between 739 and 209, south of Adams Creek. I got a campsite not far from that one where I go to sober up."

"So, Cain was there?" Seth asked.

"Yeah. He was there. And so was Skotos, and that Patrick kid. I ain't ever been smart, or strong, or brave. But my mother always said I had a dog's hearing. Even from about seventy-five yards out, I could pick up almost every word they said to each other. So, I just listened."

"What'd they say?" Jesse asked.

"How much you know about that Patrick kid? You good friends?"

"I've known him for years, so yeah. I guess I know him . . . but," Jesse paused.

"What is it?" Seth asked.

"Well, it's just that, now that I think about it, I don't really know him all that well. He doesn't talk much, never has. He followed me and Cain around, cause he said his family was never around. I never even met them. He just did everything we did, which means I guess I *don't* know him."

"Count yer blessings, then," Martin said, coughing. He reached for a cigarette from his pocket, but Seth shook his head.

"Not inside the house."

"Oh, sure. Sorry. Just helps me breathe a little. Anyway, count yer blessings. That boy—he's a killer."

"What are you talking about?" Jesse said with incredulity. "Patrick is quiet and . . . not very original, but he'd never hurt someone."

"No? How you know that?"

"I just—"

Martin cut him off. "I heard it from his own mouth when he was talkin' to Skotos. That boy murdered his family."

"What?!" Jesse said. "No way! Patrick? I've never even seen him throw a punch."

"I ain't said I know *how* he did it. But he said he did. And Skotos said he'd keep his secret. And then I figured it out. I ain't smart, but I got a memory."

"What do you mean? Figured it out?" Seth said.

"You 'member that Davidson family from years back, had the farm on Park Road?"

"Yeah, I've heard of them. People said they moved away when their son got sick . . . their son . . . *Patrick*." Seth felt sick to his stomach.

"They moved away alright, 'cause *he* moved 'em. I don't know where or how, but he got rid of 'em."

"And then what?" Jesse said. "He just . . . lived here on his own for years?"

"You ever seen his house or his family?" Martin pressed Jesse.

"Well, no. He basically lives at my place. We even have a bed for him. He says his parents aren't home much."

Martin scoffed. "Yeah, I'll say. They ain't never home. He made sure of that."

"That's . . . that's a pretty big leap. I don't know."

"Yeah, well, believe me, or don't. I know what I heard. And then Skotos sent that monster after my boy, said that Cain was a liability. That's when I saw Cain run off. But I don't know where he was goin' and I can't run much, not with these lungs."

"Not with the cigarettes that 'help you breathe,'" Seth said. Martin looked down with embarrassment.

"You gotta help me find him."

"Wait," Jesse said. "I might know where he went."

A spark of hope made Martin sit up straight, but then he grabbed his forehead and moaned. "Where?"

"Before I ditched Skotos—as soon as I saw him push Cain into that cement foundation, I told Patrick and Cain what I'd heard: that there was some white door in the woods that changed people. Patrick acted like he usually did, just staring off into space and listening. But Cain was asking me questions about it—where it was, who went through it. I told him all I heard from people was that the door was in Childs Park some-where. And the people who went through it . . . *changed* or something." Jesse looked at Seth, and they nodded with know-ing smiles.

"Changed how?" Martin asked, but then continued before Seth or Jesse could respond. "Well—that don't matter right now. You think he went there?"

"If he thinks the cops are out for him, then I don't know where else he would go, especially if Patrick really is tracking him. But how do you know Patrick is doing that?"

"Cause Skotos handed him a boot knife and told him to get rid of the body—that's how."

Seth and Jesse both swallowed and looked at each other. They knew what they had to do. They just sat for a moment on the edge of the decision.

"Alright. Here's what we're going to do," Seth started. "Martin, you feeling okay to walk?"

"Yeah. Yeah, I can walk."

"Good. Then I need you to walk to the police station and tell Tom Regent what you just told us. They'll want to see you in person for this."

"Ahh!" Martin grimaced. "That Tom hates me. Arrested me dam near ten times for nothin' but the bottle."

"It doesn't matter," Seth said. "He needs to know about this. You can tell him where to go: Childs Park. But tell him where Skotos and Patrick have been camping, too."

"Wutter you gonna do, then?"

"Me and Jesse will go the park and see if we can find Cain, and hope that we don't run into Patrick on the way."

"You gotta gun?" Martin asked.

"No. I don't. But if Patrick only has a knife, then me and Jesse can bring some heavy walking sticks I keep in the garage. With the two of us, that would be enough to disarm him."

"I'd hope so, but you don't know him as well as you think you do."

Seth and Jesse looked at each other. They knew Martin was right, but they didn't want to think about it in the moment.

"Alright. We got to move," Seth said. "You sure you're okay to walk, Martin?"

"Yeah, I'm good." He rolled himself forward off the couch and steadied himself before shuffling towards the front door. Then he turned back before opening the handle.

"You save my boy, you hear? Save 'im. I know I've been about the worst father in the world, and everyone in this tiny town knows it. God knows it. But I love my boy. Would give anything for 'im." At these words, a ball grew in his throat and he started to weep, even as he walked out of the house.

"Poor guy," Jesse said.

"Yeah. Well, he brought it on himself."

"I know, but that doesn't mean he isn't still a fly in a web."

"How do you mean?"

"I mean he's been stuck in something too big and nasty to see, for a long time. I've read about alcoholism. At a certain point, it becomes a disease."

Narnia had been silent until this point. "He *is* a fly in a web. But the sad thing with you humans is that you spin the webs that catch you."

They both let silence fill in the space around the words.

"Alright, we gotta go," Seth said. "Cain might be headed to Childs Park, but he doesn't know where the door is. We can head him off."

"What if he wants to go through it?"

"The door?"

"Yeah. I mean, *we* did."

Seth thought for a moment. "Cleft always said each person had to make his own choice. If he wants to, then he should. But we've got to make sure he even has the chance."

They grabbed the walking sticks from the garage and headed towards Childs Park in the red truck. Narnia sat between Jesse and Seth on the front seat.

"You think I'm doing the right thing, the smart thing?" Seth asked, looking down at Narnia.

"The right thing? Yes. The smart thing? Probably not. But courage has to supersede smarts sometimes."

Seth nodded. That was what he needed to hear.

***

Martin Shoemaker only got to Silver Lake before he turned back and looked in the direction of Childs Park. What was he doing, sending two boys into the woods with a killer? They needed him. And he needed, even once, to show his boy that he cared more for him than he did for the bottle. Too many times he'd shown the opposite. But if there was one time, one moment to challenge the paralyzing pattern of self-fulfillment, this was it. He turned and trotted towards Park Road, stopping every thirty feet or so to catch his breath. He reached for his cigarettes at the base of Park Road. He pulled them out, staring at the white and red Marlborough box. He threw them in the ditch and started climbing the ascent towards the park entrance. Seth and Jesse had no idea he was trailing them.

***

Martin's life had withered over the years.

At first a budding and passionate thinker—about everything from Carl Sandberg to Lenni Lenape history—he found himself drawn to colors, and he began developing as a landscape artist. The beauty of Dingmans Ferry gave him plenty to work with. His mind sprawled out over all he saw, soaking it in and letting it marinade in his soul until he could find the hues and palette to draw out his ponderings. Every work he did had a smokey aura to it, as if mist still hung in front of the image. His work was haunting, a blend of raw nature and dreamlike wonder.

He kept a gallery only for himself in the second story of a ghost barn deep in the woods, behind Trinity Presbyterian and Lake Kemadobi. He showed his paintings to only a few close friends, and one shy admirer (Tabitha). His best friend, Talee Munsee, was a descendent of the Lenni Lenape, who originally held the Delaware River region until the early eighteenth century, with the arrival of the Dutch and Andrew Dingman in 1735. The gristmills and sawmills that shot up just before and after his arrival, along Dingmans Creek, brought more settlers, and the Lenape were basically forced out in 1737 with "The Walking Purchase." Most of them left, but some families stayed and did what they could to adjust and then assimilate in subsequent generations. Talee Munsee was from one such family.

Talee had given the name këmpàkw (kem-bakh) to Martin in their early twenties. The name meant "leaf." When Martin asked him why he chose that word, Talee simply said, "Because you will keep growing." That was during what Martin would consider the golden era of his life. He was the young, struggling artist who married the love of his life before he even knew what life was about. He and Tabitha aimed to build a small ranch house and raise a family. In the meantime, he would work as a logger. It was tough labor, but it paid well enough, and he could use the weekends to keep painting.

But bit by bit, hope in that future began to dry out and crumble, like thin clay left out in the sun. Talee developed a rare form of cancer—neuroendocrine pancreatic cancer—which crippled him with stomach ulcers, blurred vision, and a rapid heart rate. He seemed to drop weight like beads of sweat, withering into a shell. He died in front of Martin, on his bed, just before his thirtieth birthday. The loss crushed Martin, ground his soul to a pulp. He swayed for weeks in constant drunkenness. Alcohol was the only thing that numbed his anguish. Even Tabitha felt powerless in the presence of such lingering absence. Talee was a special person: quiet, humble, quick to listen, and slow to speak—a set of qualities unmatched by anyone else in Dingmans Ferry, and maybe even the world. It was Talee who had constantly encouraged Martin in his art. He told him, "God made you a maker. So, keep making." And Martin listened. It was that simple.

The heavy drinking eventually lost Martin his job. By the time Tabitha was pregnant, she already knew that things were bad, that her home was no place for a child. But what else could she do? The trailer Martin had saved up to purchase would have to stand in for their dream ranch house. In fact, it would have to replace it. Because only a miracle would ever bring Martin Shoemaker back from the dark road he seemed bent on walking.

Martin stopped painting. He stopped working consistently, though he picked up odd jobs in construction or landscaping whenever he could. But he was a ghost for most of Cain's childhood. It was Cain's sudden change, after having gone through the black door—that slapped Martin in his soul. He picked his head up from the path he'd been staring at—a path of alcohol-soaked memory—and looked at his boy in the eyes. He had grown up. Cain had become a man. When did this happen?

He began reading through his old journals, which recounted some discussions he'd had with Talee about beauty and nature and spirituality. He even went so far as to revisit that ghost barn, which still housed his paintings, wrapped in black trash bags. Only some of them had been chewed through by mice. He stared at his paintings and walked back nearly two decades in time. And one of his paintings was a close-up of a red maple leaf. And that's when he remembered his name: këmpàkw. He was the one, his friend had said, who would "keep on growing."

Martin wept there, in the barn, and a fog seemed to lift from his soul. He saw clearly for the first time in years. He aimed to start turning a corner, no matter how hopeless it seemed, and no matter how many times he'd made identical promises in the past. He gathered some of his art supplies and made a list of other things he'd need to restart his landscape paintings. He walked into the trailer only to find Tabitha lying in a pile of broken glass on the floor, in a puddle of her own blood.

Now, several days after and several days sober, he was huffing his way up Park Road. At the gravel parking lot, he fished around for a fist-sized stone, in case he'd need it for defense. Then he walked north of the falls and into the woods, off the path. The timing was perfect.

***

Cain was standing in front of the white door, his jaw open, and his limbs shaking from weakness. He had been running for over two hours. And if this was his destination, he was now out of courage. What sort of door leaked light? And where could it go that would save him now? He might as well go to the police and turn himself in.

But . . . what if he didn't? He'd thrown his whole life away in a matter of weeks. What did he have to lose now? His mother dead, his father drunk and absent, his friends against him. He had no name for himself, and that had been the one hope of all his ventures. In pursuing a name, he had lost it. He had lost everything. He really did have nothing to lose now, and everything to gain by turning that handle. He reached out for it, and three things happened at the same time.

First, his body was drawn so deeply into the light that he fell forward, headlong into bright oblivion with a wide smile on his face.

Second, Patrick emerged from the other side of the boulder and dove towards him with the outstretched knife. It was aimed right at Cain's heart.

Third, Martin Shoemaker ran from the other side and leaped to intercept Patrick, with the stone in his right hand, and his other arm extended to block Patrick's knife.

In that one, tiny moment, there was salvation, justice, and sacrifice. Cain was blissfully unaware of the other two bodies and felt a peace he had never known as he fell through the threshold. Martin's right hand and the rock connected with Patrick's temple, knocking him unconscious. But Martin's left hand could not stop the knife blade in Patrick's grip from running into his own chest. After the collision, all three bodies were in the leaves: Martin moaning, Patrick silent, and Cain staring curiously into his father's eyes.

"Dad?"

"If I keep growin', then you keep growin'. Okay? You remember that."

"What? What are you . . . what happened?"

Cain looked down to see the blood soaking Martin's shirt and the knife handle protruding from his chest. He tried to shake himself out of his calmness.

"Dad! Dad! What happened?!"

"It's okay, son. It's okay."

Cain looked behind him at Patrick's body and his bloody temple. He pushed his body back in horror.

"Did he try to?!"

"Tried," Martin whispered. "Tried. But no one gets between me and my boy. Not now." He coughed up blood and started to lose consciousness.

"Dad! Dad! Wait! Hold on!"

"No time for that. You keep growin', okay? Keep growin'. Always. Love you."

"Dad! I'll get help! Just wait!" Cain pulled himself off the ground and rushed back to the gravel parking lot. Looking for help. Seth's red Ford Ranger pulled in at just that moment. He had stalled out on Silver Lake and had to get someone to jump the truck. That's why Martin Shoemaker had gotten there before them.

"Mr. Logan! Mr. Logan! Please, you gotta help! My dad! He got stabbed!"

It took Seth a second to recognize Cain, but Jesse was already out of the truck.

"Where is he?" Jesse asked.

"I'll take you! Come on!"

"Jesse, you go with him! I'm gonna run over to the house across the way and call 911! Go! I'll follow behind!"

But by the time Jesse and Cain returned, Martin was still and silent as the leaves underneath him. Jesse refused to give up hope. He heaved the body off the ground, being careful not to touch the handle of the knife in Martin's chest. They walked as briskly as they could back to the parking lot, where Jesse put the body down. Cain knelt over him, crying. He was whispering something as he hugged his dad's face.

"I see you now. I see you. I see you. Please don't go."

"Mr. Logan, we should go check the door. Patrick was there, too. And he looked like he was hurt pretty bad."

Seth nodded.

"Cain, we'll be right back. I can hear the sirens from the ambulance. They should be here any minute, okay?"

"Okay. Just . . . be careful," he sputtered through tears.

"We will be."

When Jesse and Seth got to the boulder, Patrick was still unconscious. Jesse checked his pulse.

"He's still alive, strong pulse. I can carry him back." Jesse went to lift him up but felt something crinkle in Patrick's back pocket. He pulled out a yellow sheet of tablet paper, marked with a roughshod map.

"What is that?" Seth asked. They both looked at the map and recognized certain roads: 739, Silver Lake, 209. But there were dotted lines leading to little doorway shapes. Each was marked "Adit" and then a number.

"What's an adit?" Seth said.

"Ah, I've heard that word before. Where did I hear it?" Jesse was searching his mind and all the pages of literature he'd read.

"Oh! An adit is an entrance, like a mine entrance."

"Or a tunnel entrance," Seth said.

They both looked at each other and got goosebumps.

"Jesse, this is it. This is what we needed."

"And look," Jesse said, pointing to a spot on the map right near Childs Park. "Adit 3 is probably right back there, a few hundred yards! We could—"

They both jumped and turned at the same instant. Patrick had woken up, assessed his situation without moving a muscle, and then bolted at the perfect moment, when both of their backs were turned. They ran after him, but that's when Jesse remembered the *one* thing he knew about Patrick, the only trait that set him apart in their group: Patrick was *fast*. He could outrun anyone, including the guys on the track team in high school. He and Cain used to tease him and call him Road Runner. After about thirty seconds of chase, Seth stopped and grabbed his kneecaps to catch his breath.

"Jesse . . . he's too fast. We gotta get back to Cain."

"But he'll get away!"

"We'll put the police on it. We got what we need from him for now."

Jesse rolled his eyes and watched the last remnants of Patrick's red shirt disappear on the other side of a thickly wooded hill in the distance. He turned and walked slowly back with Seth to the parking lot. The medics were zippering a black back over the body of Martin Shoemaker. Cain was sitting in the back of the ambulance weeping.

39

THE SLEEPERS

GLADICE SHOWED UP AT the parking lot to take Cain home. She was weeping and holding Cain's head on her shoulder. Tabitha was still wheelchair bound and at home. They were heading there next to break the news. Cain wept at the loss of his father, but this was mingled with the joy of learning his mother was still alive. He wasn't a murderer. He had a second chance. And he was bent on doing exactly what his father had told him to do.

Seth and Jesse decided to go home and come back to the park the next day with the rest of the gazers: Lem, Bill, Travis, Ethan—anyone willing was welcome. Seth was hoping that Shannon would be too creeped out and would happily stay at home with Will and Livy. He was right. But she was obviously shaken by the events of the last few days and felt very nervous about Seth taking the initiative in this. In the end, she let him decide.

"But walk away when it gets creepy!" she said. Seth laughed but promised. He asked Narnia to stay with them. But Narnia replied simply, "No can do. I'm *your* steward, not theirs. I go where you go." Seth didn't fight it.

They were also trying to figure out if they should ask Tom Regent to come, for backup. But they decided that would be overkill at this point, since it would let an outsider, a tweener, into their world unnecessarily. They could bring in Tom if they got any signs of Skotos or Patrick. Otherwise, he'd have to stay out for now.

***

It was 10:00 am when they all gathered at the bottom of Park Road. They had aimed to go to the gravel lot to park, but then they remembered it would be roped off with police tape as a crime scene for active investigation. They drove another mile up and decided to enter the park region from Myck Road. This was closer to the site of the alleged "Adit 3," so it worked out better for them anyway.

By 10:30, they were deep in the woods, looking for any sign of a cave or tunnel entrance. They had split up into groups. Travis, Lem, and Bill went in one cohort; Ethan, Seth, and Jesse in the other, with Narnia trailing behind, silent as a summer breeze. It was Ethan who found it. On the other side of a mound of dirt, surrounded by a ring of hemlocks. The excavator tire tracks were probably a few years old, but they were still visible. The six of them stood outside the entrance. A yawning black opening stood before them, and no one had the guts to enter first.

"Anyone bring a flashlight?" Seth asked. A bunch of groans suggested no one had.

"Brought a couple of 'em," said Bill. "Can't be too careful. I always carry a spare."

"That's my boy," Lem said with pride. "Let's do this. Remember: weapons at the ready."

"Grandpa, we don't have weapons. We've got sticks."

"*Anything* can be a weapon, young'n."

"Ugh. 'Young'n'? Who says that?"

Bill smacked Travis in the chest. "Come on, now. Show some respect."

"Alright. I'll go first," Travis said, taking one of the flashlights from his uncle's hand. Everyone else hesitated, so Narnia stepped up.

"Going to make a cat go before you, eh? What if I make up a rhyme to taunt you? Would that help? Let me see . . ."

> The cat walked off and did a dance,
> While the men all stood and peed their . . .

"Alright, alright," Ethan said. "Let's go."

One by one, they disappeared into the dark.

***

The tunnel was much broader and higher than they thought it would be. But after a hundred yards, it began shrinking. Eventually, it was about twelve feet high and eight feet wide—small enough to make Seth feel claustrophobic. He kept swallowing and trying not to pay too much attention to his breathing.

"Up here!" Travis yelled to the others. "The tunnel splits into three. Which way do we go?"

"I vote left," Ethan said.

"Is that based on intuition?" Narnia asked.

"No."

"Strategy?"

"No."

"Preference?"

"No."

"Then what's it based on?"

"My gut," Ethan said, rolling his eyes.

"Who votes that we all follow Ethan's stomach?" Some chuckles escaped from the group.

"I'm just teasing, Ethan. I'd go left, too."

"Oh, yeah? What's that based on?"

"Sight. It's bigger down that way."

They all went left. In a matter of minutes, the tunnel opened up into a broad cavern, at least thirty feet tall. Their flashlights shined on the ceiling above, and also onto dark bushels of hay and sticks lining the walls—from the floor to about ten feet up. Each bushel had something resting on top. And it only took all of them a moment to realize what they were looking at: human bodies.

***

"Sleepers," Seth said. Every hair on his spine stood on end. Ethan bent down and threw up on the cave floor.

"You alright, man?" Travis said, putting a hand on his back.

"Yeah. Yeah. Yeah." He bent down and threw up again.

"Guys, this is . . . so messed up. We gotta get outta here. Are these really corpses?" Travis said, backing up.

"No," Seth said with confidence. He felt he was exactly where he needed to be. He had *found* them, the ones Cleft had been looking for over decades. They were *here*. This is what Cleft meant by calling him the Seeker.

"No?" Travis said, still backing up.

"Corpses are dead. These people aren't dead. They're sleeping."

"How do you know that? They sure look dead?"

Seth walked over to a boy near the floor of the wall closest to them. He guessed the boy was around twelve.

"Seth, man, what are you doing?! Don't touch it!" Travis yelled.

"Pipe down," Lem said. "He's checkin' for a pulse."

Seth touched the boy's skin on his neck. It was still warm. And there, thudding with perfect regularity, was his pulse.

"He's alive. Normal pulse. He's just sleeping. They all are."

"Okay, so . . . WAKE UP!" Travis yelled. Everyone converged on him in an instant.

"Keep quiet! You, dote!" Lem said, putting his hand over Travis's mouth. Travis pushed his hand away.

"What? He said they were asleep. So, we wake 'em up."

"That yell was pretty loud, Travis. You see any of them rousing?" Seth asked. They all looked around the room at the bodies. No one had stirred. Each body, except for the rising and falling chest, was still as stone.

"Why can't they hear us?" Ethan said, still wiping his mouth from the throw-up.

"This is what I was afraid of," Seth said. "We got clues from Will's riddle about where to go, and we found out from him, too, that these people are sleeping. But we don't have any clue about how to wake them up."

Everyone looked around at the bodies. There were dozens of them—of all ages. Some children, some adults, a few senior citizens. Each was still and solemn, wrapped in a strong sleep.

"Maybe we shake 'em a bit? You know, just to wake them up," Travis said, reaching down to touch the arm of a man who could be his father's age.

"No, no. Don't touch them. I don't know what to do. I need to think," Seth said.

He pulled out The Book of Cleft and began looking through the pages again while Travis held the flashlight for him. After twenty minutes of paging through the whole book while the others looked at the sleepers one by one, he closed the book.

"There's nothing here, guys. I don't know what to do."

"Perhaps there's a word," Narnia said.

"A word?"

"Yes, to wake them."

"Why would there be a word, as if this is all some kind of magic trick?"

"Not magic, memory," Narnia replied.

"What do you mean?"

"I mean," Narnia started, "That if we all came into being *from* the word and live *through* the word, then maybe we need to be wakened *to* the word."

"Narnia, I can't do the theology thing right now. I don't know what word you have in mind."

"Oh, I don't have a word in mind. I was hoping you did."

"Nope. I don't."

"Hold on—Seth, what was that passage we looked at the other day? Ephesians 5?"

"Ephesians 5:14. Why?"

"How did it start?"

"Awake, O Sleeper?" Seth said. "Or something like that. But look, I just said it, and nothing happened. Everyone satisfied? Can we come up with a real plan now?"

"What about the Greek?"

"I don't know Greek," Seth said with irritation. "Nobody here knows—"

"*Egeire*," Bill said.

"What?" Seth asked, staring in wonder at Bill.

"*Egeire*. That's the imperative, the command."

"Okay, that's . . . impressive. I didn't know you could understand Greek. But it's still not doing anything."

"That's because *you* didn't say it," Bill said.

"What does it matter that I say it?" Seth asked, growing more irritable.

"Same reason that you got The Book of Cleft."

"Used to be mine," Lem piped in. "Did you know that?"

"No," Seth said. "No, I didn't. But if this is yours, then why did it go to Cleft?"

"The book can only go with what Cleft called 'The Seeker,' and every seeker was supposed to have a steward. But I ain't never got one. Neither did Bill. Cleft was lookin' for the next Seeker. Guess he thought it was you. That's why you got the book."

"So you really think if I say this Greek word, that's gonna do something?"

"No harm in tryin'," Lem said.

Seth shook his head and laughed. "You know what—fine. I'll say it."

He spread out his arms with mocking enthusiasm and looked up at the ceiling.

"*Egeire!*"

No one was prepared for what happened next.

40

THE AWAKENING

THE CAVERN SHOOK. SEDIMENT fell from above in drooping clouds. Everyone grabbed onto a wall for stability. But then the shaking subsided.

"Everyone okay?!" Seth shouted.

"Yeah, I think so," Ethan said. Everyone else nodded with wide eyes.

"We should get out before this thing collapses," Seth said. "Shannon told me to get away at the first sign of 'creepy.' That wasn't creepy, but it was threatening enough. We can do more thinking outside the cave."

"Wait—look," Travis said.

"Look at what?"

"This guy's body—it's . . . it's shrinking!"

Seth stepped over to Travis and watched with horror as the human body before them slowly condensed itself. But it wasn't just becoming smaller; it was changing form. The nose became hard and pointed. The arms thinned. The legs became skinny as twigs. The feet turned into pronged claws. And then, as if painted with watercolor, the skin turned dark and sprouted . . . feathers. The body before them was turning into a bird.

At the same moment, Ethan looked around and noticed that the other bodies were doing something similar. He also noticed a hole in the ceiling, about the size of a basketball hoop, letting in a ray of sunlight.

"This fella' too!" Lem shouted. An older gentleman, still dressed in a suit, was drifting inside his clothes. In a matter of moments, a black-capped chickadee nosed out of the neck hole in the suit.

"This one, too," Bill said, looking down at a woman, whose shoulders and back turned shale gray while her chest took on a burnt orange plumage. She had been wearing a white summer dress. But the pencil-thin legs of a sharp-shinned hawk now pressed on top of its folds like feet stepping on silken grass.

There were more. Harriers, ospreys, broad-winged and red-tailed hawks, kestrels, falcons, barn owls, crows, mourning doves, nighthawks, kingfishers, chipping-sparrows, warblers, meadowlarks, blackbirds, goldfinches, Whip-poor-wills, wood thrushes, cardinals, blue jays, and one very large bald eagle. It was a wildly diverse congregation of hollow-boned, heavenly-minded fliers. They were all making their calls so that the cavern was filled with the din of sounds locked inside chest cavities for God only knows how long. But then, slowly, all the sound tapered off into silence. Seth, Jesse, Ethan, Lem, Bill, and Travis felt as if they were standing on another planet. They were seeing too much to process, caught up in a whirlwind of impossibility. The silence sent their eyes spinning—looking at the birds and then at each other.

Then, as if on signal, the entire flock raised its wings and bolted for the circular opening at the top of the cave. The flurry of feathers and the whoosh of wings caught them all by surprise. And no one dared to stop them. With the last exit, by a yellow-throated warbler, they turned and stared at each other. No one spoke for what felt like minutes. It was Lem, eventually, who mumbled words in a whisper.

"They shall mount up with wings as eagles."

"Hmm," Bill said. "Isaiah."

Silence seemed the best response to the whole thing. Questions would only stain the wonder of the moment. So they stared at the light above, as feathers and hay drifted in the hallowed dark.

***

When they came out of the tunnel entrance, the sun assaulted their eyes. The wind was strong, like a great hand wiping its fingers through the canopy and clearing the world of debris. All was raw, clear, and wild. They hiked back to their cars without saying a word. They just stared in front of themselves, wondering where the birds had gone.

Seth opened The Book of Cleft as Narnia jumped into the truck bed and peered over his shoulder. The list of names at the front of the book began to alter. The ink from a selection of names faded back into the vanilla paper, disappearing like sounds in the wind. Seth drew the book closer to his face.

"The names! They're disappearing!" The group gathered around to look. But Narnia stayed where he was.

"Disappearing . . . or returning?"

"Returning where?" Seth asked, glancing over his shoulder.

"Back to where they were—or where they were going."

No one knew what to say to this. But they could all hear children's voices somewhere nearby. Down the road a hundred yards or so, two boys were chasing each other in the field, sprinting through the tall grass and holding out their hands to brush the surface of the big bluestem, throwing its red-gold crowns into the wind. One boy was wearing a beat-up red trucker's hat and was older than the other one. Something stirred in Seth's chest as he looked at the boy.

He heard Cleft's voice in his head, drawing it out of the well of memory.

> I first noticed it about fifteen years ago with a boy named William. He was a rough kid (fourteen years old at the time), bent on bullying anyone else who came near him. He always wore this red trucker's hat—beat up and dirty.

"Oh my God," Seth said.

"What?" Ethan asked. "You know him?"

"That's . . . that's William. That's the first person Cleft noticed had gone missing."

"You're sure?" Bill asked. "Lots of kids runnin' in open fields round here."

Seth walked over to the boy and stopped ten feet short.

"William?"

The boy looked at him—not with hostility or curiosity but with something else—contentment maybe.

"Yeah. Who are you?"

"My name's Seth," he said stepping closer.

"Are we not allowed to play here or something?"

"No, no. It's fine. I just . . . wanted to make sure you were okay."

"Why wouldn't I be?" William said, smirking.

"Hey, what's that?"

"What's what?"

"That yellow thing on the collar of your shirt."

William looked down and plucked it, holding it up to the light.

"Looks like a . . . yeah—it's a breast feather from a yellow-throated warbler. That's my favorite bird. You ever seen one?"

"Yes," was all Seth could say in the moment. "Yes, I have."

41

BIRD SEARCHING

S ETH GOT BACK HOME in a daze and recounted the whole story to Shannon, Will, and Livy. Will and Livy thought he might be making up the story, but they didn't care. That didn't affect their enthusiasm.

"So, your riddle brought us to the tunnel, Will."

"And set the birds free?" Will chirped.

"Yes, maybe. Maybe it did."

"Oh, Seth," Shannon said. "What have we gotten ourselves into?"

"I guess we're conservationists now."

"And detectives? Ugh, talk about creepy."

"It's not all that creepy," Narnia cut in. "If animals can talk, then it's not that far a stretch to see people turn into animals, and then find themselves again. It's all about the names, in the end."

"How do you mean?" Seth said.

"Well, Skotos seems to be *taking* names, with the promise of giving people what they really want. But he can't do that, really. Only God can truly give. If you find more of these Adits and sleepers, you're really handing people their names back."

"After a metamorphosis," Seth added.

"Yes, after their frame gets feathered and flies away, toward the light."

"And it all comes by a word. There's your theology again—from the word, through the word, to the word."

"Are you ready to talk about that at last?"

"Yes. Yes, I think I am. But I have some work to do first. Adit number 5 isn't far from where we are right now."

Seth stood and walked towards the door with a flashlight in his hand.

"Where are you going?" Shannon asked.

"Yeah, daddy. Where are you going? Can we come?" Will said.

Seth laughed to himself and looked up towards the sky through the bay window. The trees were waving like hands. The clouds drifted in serene silence. A cardinal was perched on the lower branches of the oak tree in the front yard. Seth took the marble from his right pocket. He smiled at it. For the first time, the marble actually sparked hope inside his chest. The world was a mess—a fire in a teardrop, with evil in the shadows and glory in the skies. But there was still clarity, still the confidence of the light that refracted through the marble, that refracted through the whole world.

"Seth—" Shannon said again, trying to call him out of his trance. "Where are you going?"

"To wake them up."

"I come too," Livy said around her two fingers.

"Sure. Why not? Let's make it a family affair." Seth said as they all stood up. He tucked The Book of Cleft under his arm and hugged Shannon with the other arm as Will and Livy clung to his legs. Narnia stood at the door waiting.

"Shall we?" he said.

"Mmm. We shall," Seth said. He opened the door and walked through the threshold.

"If I might say, you don't seem as tense lately, about your potential leaving."

"My exiting the world I love, with a steward at my side?"

"Yes. What changed?"

"My heart, I guess."

"Yeah? How so?"

"It was too big before. At least, it thought of itself as too big. I needed to shrink so that I could grow, to see my smallness and find my place in the sovereign wind."

"Sure you're not writing a book right now, as you speak?"

"It does sound that way, doesn't it?"

"Yes. That's a book I would read."

"Yes, well," Seth said as he held up The Book of Cleft in front of him. "I guess some books need writing, and others need reading. Maybe I'm doing both at the same time."

"I think we all are."

"Yes. Writing and reading."

"Are you ready to talk some theology now?"

"I am. Let's talk as we drive. We've got birds to beckon."

***

"Wait!" someone called from the driveway. It was Cain Shoemaker. He jogged over to the station wagon and leaned over to catch his breath.

"Heard you might be bird-searching," he said. Seth smiled, and so did Shannon. They weren't sure how much he knew, but it seemed clear that he knew more than they assumed.

"We are. Would you like to come along?"

"Was hoping you'd ask. And I think they were, too," he said, pointing down the driveway. There in Bill Watson's old truck bed sat a smiling company, each holding a flashlight. Lem, Travis, Ethan, and little Gladice. In the morning light, they were beaming, glazed with the sun and bent on the next grand task.

"We tag along?" Bill called out.

"Sounds good to me," Seth said.

Cain ran and jumped in the back of the pickup truck. The two cars turned out of the driveway and headed for the next miracle.

***

Many birds are sleeping—in the boughs and the branches, and in the dark places where no eye roams. Settled in their feathered frames, all flight trapped by trepidation.

Many birds are sleeping. Who will wake them?

About the Author

Pierce Taylor Hibbs (MAR, ThM Westminster Theological Seminary) is an award-winning Christian wordsmith and educator who builds things to bring readers closer to God. He's the author of over 20 books, including the Illumination Award-winning titles *Struck Down but Not Destroyed* (Bronze Medalist 2021), *The Book of Giving* (Gold Medalist 2022), *The Great Lie* (Bronze Medalist 2023), and *One with God* (Bronze Medalist 2024). This is his first novel.

He serves as Senior Writer and Communication Specialist at Westminster Theological Seminary. He and his wife, Christina, reside in Pennsylvania with their three kids.

Leave a Review!

One the biggest ways you can bless an author is simply by leaving a concise, honest review of the book on a site such as Amazon, GoodReads, or Barnes & Noble. It takes very little time, but it makes a big difference in helping other readers find the book and give it a chance. If you enjoyed this book, please consider leaving a brief, candid review. Thank you!

www.ingramcontent.com/pod-product-compliance
Lightning Source LLC
Chambersburg PA
CBHW061855310726
48972CB00004B/1031